WIZARD'S
FUNERAL

D1150114

BY KIM HUNTER

The Red Pavilions
Knight's Dawn
Wizard's Funeral
Scabbard's Song

WIZARD'S FUNERAL

Book Two of the Red Pavilions

Kim Hunter

orbit

www.orbitbooks.net

ORBIT

First published in Great Britain in 2002 by Orbit
This paperback edition published in 2013 by Orbit

Copyright © 2002 by Kim Hunter

The moral right of the author has been asserted.

A CIP catalogue record for this book
is available from the British Library.

ISBN 978-0-356-50311-0

Typeset in Revival 555 by Palimpsest Book Production Ltd,
Falkirk, Stirlingshire
Printed and bound in Great Britain by CPI Group (UK) Ltd, Croydon CR0 4YY

Papers used by Orbit are from well-managed forests
and other responsible sources.

MIX
Paper from
responsible sources
FSC® C104740

Orbit
An imprint of
Little, Brown Book Group
100 Victoria Embankment
London EC4Y 0DY

An Hachette UK Company
www.hachette.co.uk

www.orbitbooks.net

For Mark Lillie

Chapter One

Those who have not seen the dazzling towers, the obsidian turrets, the domes, the green-glass cupolas of Zamerkand, have surely missed the greater part of earth's splendour. The morning sun is quick to find high, golden porches bright enough to blind a traveller many leagues from the city. Polished lapis lazuli tiles bordering lofty battlements shine with a penetrating blueness. Silver gutters glint with points of light that might come from the divine weaponry of a warrior-deity. The city is a great geometrical flower opening to the morning, the light running and leaping from spire to column to belfry to campanile to flèche, like sacred fire racing from one heavenly petal-point to the next.

On the battlements stand the Imperial Guardsmen, their helmets flashing, their spearpoints glinting. Around the walls of the city, almost completing the circle but for a man-made tunnel of stone, there to protect the canal all the way down to the sea, stand the red-ochre pavilions of the mercenary army of Carthagans. Their weapons gleam with a duller light. Unlike those of the Imperial guardsmen, which are taken out only to polish before parades and drills, the Carthagan weapons are frequently used in anger. They are tarnished with constant employment: their surfaces scratched; their edges sharp, but wavy with honing; the flaws in their blades stained with the blackened blood of enemies.

Five miles long and five miles wide, the city stands in the South of Guthrum, rich and powerful, and ripe with wealth.

On one of the green turrets which looked out over the surrounding countryside stood a man who had slept very little during the long and ponderous night. He called himself Soldier and he was married to the queen's younger sister, Layana. Soldier saw the rider come from the West, from the Seven Peaks where the gods lived, and the wizards ruled. The rider looked exhausted, swaying in his saddle, his feet frequently slipping from the stirrups. Carthagans on their way to fetch early-morning water parted for him, allowing him a path, and the great wooden gates of the city, bold with brass and bronze, swung open as if this horseman had been expected for a very long time.

'Drissila?' called Soldier, not moving from the turret's balcony, 'is your mistress in the real world this morning?'

'I fear she is unhappy,' came the answer. 'The demons visited her during the night and are now within her.'

Soldier sighed deeply. He loved his wife with a deepness that is found only by a man who has lost a former love to dark fingers of death. She was his future, past and present. He would kill for her, he would die for her.

'Is Ofao tending to her needs?'

'Ofao and myself.'

'Thank you.'

The rider, now in the market square, almost fell from his horse onto the cobbles. Captain Kaff, of the Imperial Guard, was hurrying onto the scene. Others were scurrying forth, gathering their robes about them – officials of the court – keeping their hemlines clear of horse and donkey shit: Chancellor Humbold; Quidquod, Lord of the Royal Purse; Maldrake, Lord of the Locks; Qintara, Lady of the Ladders; Marshal Crushkite, Warlord of Guthrum. Even the ruler of Guthrum, Queen Vanda, had quit her boudoir to appear on the balcony of her tower on the Palace of Birds.

A raven landed near to Soldier's elbow as he surveyed this scene in the streets below.

'I'll wager a dozen the King Magus is dead,' said the raven. 'Pancakes, that is, fried in lovely hot corn oil.'

'You won't find a taker here,' replied Soldier.

'The King Magus is dead!' cried the rider in a ragged voice. 'Where is the wizard to take his place?'

'There you are,' said the raven. 'Pancakes for breakfast.'

'You didn't get a taker,' Soldier reminded him. 'Anyway, how did you know?'

'Oh, you know me. I fly here, I fly there. I talk with the wind.'

'But you've been outside my window all night.'

'Idiot, you've only got to look at the world this morning to see how it's changed. See how the sun shines brightly? Look how blue the mountains seem now, where once they were gloomy and oppressive. Listen to the sparkle in the cock's voice as he crows! The whole kingdom of the living and the dead has changed its aspect.'

And the bird was right. It had. Soldier had been too rapt in his own troubles to notice how much better this day appeared than yesterday, or the day before, or a thousand days before that.

The raven took to the air, settling some distance away on the pommel of a flagpole.

The rider in the square below was being questioned further now.

'Who inherits?' cried Humbold. 'Who is the new King Magus?'

'Why, I am instructed – instructed . . .' the rider was visibly wilting, but Captain Kaff shook him to keep him awake. 'Instructed to tell you that he is the son of a woman called Uthellen, of this city.'

'Of *this* city?' shouted the mob, now flowing from their shanties and hovels. Zamerkand might have had a shining coat, but it also had a rotten heart.

Humbold shouted, 'Who knows this Uthellen?'

There was a buzz and a rumble from the crowd.

Marshal Crushkite yelled, 'Someone must know her.'

Silence now fell upon the cobbled square.

'Anyone?' cried Captain Kaff.

The silence deepened.

Finally. 'I know her.'

All eyes looked up to where the voice had come from.

Kaff nodded his head slowly and grimaced. Humbold sighed. A trader called Spagg, seller of hanged men's hands, spat in the gutter.

It was Soldier who had spoken.

'You?' said Marshall Crushkite, who almost alone among the watchers was not an enemy of the man in the high tower. 'Is she in Zamerkand, Soldier? Where is she?'

'She used to reside in the sewers, along with her child, amongst the poor and destitute.'

There was a shuffling from the officials. The King Magus did not usually intervene in petty human affairs, being concerned with higher things, but he was invested with great power: enough to destroy any city, even whole countries. Only an innate sense of justness and rightness curbed the hand of the King Magus when it came to levelling those who had displeased him.

This, indeed, was a new King Magus. Would he have the same integrity as the last? Or would he settle a few scores, beginning his new reign with the slate wiped clean of any bitterness?

Queen Vanda spoke now, from the balcony of the Palace of Birds. 'Soldier, you know the order of things. There must always be the poor, the rich and varying degrees between. That he was raised amongst the wretched people of this city is the fault of social order, not of our government.'

Soldier did not necessarily agree with this point of view, but he saw that there was nothing to be served by arguing.

'The boy, when I last knew him, did not see himself as a victim of the state. There was no bitterness in his heart. But who knows the mind of a wizard?'

The queen sighed, her small, heart-shaped face pale with the effort of finding solutions. 'Can you find him?'

'I think so. He is outside the city, that I do know.'

'Then here is your task. You see your work before you. Chancellor, give Soldier all that he needs to form an expedition to find the new King Magus, so that he may be informed of his predecessor's death. He must take up his exalted post as quickly as possible.'

With that the queen left her balcony and swept into her chambers in a cloud of purple chiffons and silks.

Soldier was informed that he was to report to Captain Kaff within the hour.

He went to his wife's chambers, to see if she recognised him.

She did.

'You bastard,' she spat. 'Come to gloat over me in my madness, have you?'

She was hunched up in one corner of her great bed – a bed he seldom shared these days – the sheets knotted round her frail, diminutive form. His heart bled for her in her distress. Her face – normally animated and quite beautiful since the scars had gone – was screwed into a malevolent expression that filled him with disquiet. Soldier knew it was useless to argue with her. He simply bade her farewell.

'I must go away on the queen's business,' he said. 'I'll return as soon as I can.'

Ofao, also in the room, had to restrain his mistress as she leapt towards Soldier with her hands like claws, her nails ready to rake his face.

'Yes, go! You can't wait to get away from me, can you? Are you bedding my sister? Does the queen demand your body between her sheets? You must be laughing at me, the pair of you. The foolish Princess Layana, whose husband fucks the queen.'

'Your sister is as concerned for your welfare as I am,' said Soldier. 'There is nothing between us. In your heart you know that. I am going away to fetch the new King Magus and install him in his mountain palace. I will return as soon as possible.'

'Why come back?' she cried, savagely, struggling with Ofao's firm grip. 'Why bother to return?' Her face was a vicious mask. 'You know I hate you. Why would you want to come back to a wife who thinks you are dirt?'

He made the usual mistake of trying to reason with her, when rationality had already flown like escaping birds.

'You say that now, but when – when you are normal, you tell me you love me.'

She smiled, nastily. 'I only tell you that to unsettle you, to give you false confidence. *This* is my normal self. This is how I *really* feel. How could I love a man like you? You're a freak, a creature with blue eyes. No other creature — man, beast, bird — has blue eyes. And *who* are you? You do not know your name, you have no memory of your past, and you arrived here with nothing but a few scraps of armour. You can't possibly believe that I, a princess, could love a nobody . . .'

Soldier left the room quickly, before she could go on. Layana in her madness had the power to agitate him to the very roots of his soul. Seven times in the past year she had tried to murder him in the night. His scabbard, which sang out a warning when he was being attacked, was the only thing which had kept him alive. *Sintra* was the gold-thread name on his scabbard and it sheathed a sword named *Kutrama*, though he had arrived in this world with only the former, the latter having been lost somewhere on the way.

Soldier went now to his own chambers and dressed himself in light armour, not forgetting the warhammer he had wrested from an attacking Hannack. The last time he had seen Uthellen and her son they were hiding in a forest to the north. On his journey there Soldier might be attacked by Hannacks, or any other bands of brigands roaming the wastelands and countryside.

One thing he had discovered about himself was a deepseated rage which erupted during moments of battle, so that he was known as one of the most savage fighters this world had ever encountered. He was appalled by his own barbarity at such times. The overwhelming feeling of vicious hatred which surged through him was as frightening to him as it was to his enemies and watchers. He wondered where it came from, what had happened to him for it to be there in the first place.

'One of these days I shall find myself,' he thought, 'and I have no doubt I won't like who lies within.'

Armed, he went forth to Captain Kaff's quarters, where the Imperial Guardsman awaited him.

Kaff was one of Soldier's greatest enemies. Soldier had cut off one of the captain's hands in a duel. Now the captain fitted live creatures onto the stump that was his wrist. Today it was a sparrow-hawk. The effect was alarming. The raptor remained still on the silver-banded stump, with folded wings, unless Kaff reached forward, whereupon it spread its wings, flashed its talons, and raked the air with its hooked beak.

'There is a horse waiting for you at the gates,' Kaff explained. 'I have arranged that myself and a company of men will ride with you. You will need protection in open country. There are Hannacks about.'

'I'll go alone,' said Soldier.

Kaff stared at him, the hawk fluttering. 'You are a fool – as usual.'

Soldier ignored the insult. 'I'll take Spagg with me.'

There was a snorting sound from Kaff. 'A lot that idiot can do to help if you're attacked by wolves, or worse.'

'Nevertheless.'

A shrug from the other. 'Suit yourself.'

'And stay away from my wife.'

It was well known that Kaff was in love with Layana – had been even before the arrival of Soldier – and visited her often as a friend and advisor. In the old days Kaff had done nothing about his feelings of devotion for the princess because he had deemed himself unworthy. Then this nobody, this riff-raff from some war in an unknown place, had arrived and married her within a few short weeks. Kaff had been more than incensed. He was almost prepared to sacrifice the life of the new King Magus – wars, pestilence and famine come if they had to – if it meant that Soldier would die too.

Kaff said, stiffly, 'The Princess Layana has need of my services from time to time.'

'If you try to seduce her, I'll kill you. Captain of the Imperial Guard or not.'

Kaff smiled. 'You are assuming that this is possible, of course.'

'It'll be a great deal easier now I've taken one of your hands,' snapped Soldier.

The smile instantly evaporated and Kaff's lips curled.

'One of these days . . .' he muttered, gripping his sword-hilt.

'Just keep to your own bedroom, Kaff, and respect the rights of a husband.'

With that, Soldier left the captain's quarters and made his way to the market square.

A raven landed on Soldier's shoulder as he strode along.

'Well, well, still causing mayhem with the Guthrum army, are we?' said the raven. 'Still managing to volunteer for these suicidal missions? Got a death-wish, have we?'

'You can shut up, too,' muttered Soldier, worried that someone would hear him talking to a bird and think him mad.

'Oh, I *can* shut up – or I can chatter to my heart's content. I think that's up to me, isn't it? I'm entitled to my opinion of you, which is as low as it always has been. Soldier the hero? Soldier the moron. You could get killed out there, you know. Why didn't you take up the offer of an escort?'

'Where were you hiding?' muttered Soldier. 'Up the chimney?'

'Just outside the window, actually.'

'You want to be careful you don't finish up on the end of

Kaff's wrist one of these days. And as to the escort – I've more to fear from them than I have from a bunch of rogue dragons. There'd be a danger of waking up every morning with my throat cut. I prefer to go with just Spagg. He has his faults but at least he's scared stiff of me. Kaff has nothing but contempt for my skills as a warrior. He thinks he's better. What are you going to do? Will you trail along?'

If the raven could have wrinkled his beak in distaste, he would have done. 'With that stinking bag of dung, Spagg? Not on your life. Think I'll stay here and pick a few locks with my beak. There's no larders out in open country. I've got my stomach to think of, I have.'

The bird flew off.

At this time of day the market-place was thriving. In one corner of the square, vegetables. In another, meat. On the north-east corner, livestock – shuffling, snuffling, dropping today's wet turds onto yesterday's dried turds. The last corner was where frauds and gullible buyers met, along with eccentrics and those struck by lunar rays: fortune-tellers, physicians (as if anybody could cure anyone of anything!), gem-sellers, ivory-dealers, sellers of curios and carvings, and Spagg.

Spagg was a purveyor of dead men's hands. Not just men either, but women kill mostly for love and men mostly for money, and there is more money than love in the world. Once the murderers were hanged Spagg had a licence to cut off their hands and sell them as hands-of-glory: hands with magical properties, such as the power of invisibility. There were many unsatisfied customers, but Spagg always told them magic required belief and it was their lack of faith that was the cause of the failure, not the hands-of-glory themselves.

'What?' cried the short, hairy man as Soldier approached. Spagg saw the look in Soldier's eyes. 'Oh no,' he said. 'No, no, no. I went with you once before, but I ain't goin' again. I was lucky to get back with my skin and good eye intact. I ain't goin' to risk it a second time.'

'You haven't got any choice,' replied Soldier, firmly. 'Unless you'd rather explain your reluctance to the Queen's Torturer?'

Spagg picked up a rather blue hand with swollen knuckles and threw it down hard on the table.

'It's not fair,' he whined. 'I was just goin' to the temple, for the winter.'

'They won't have you this year. I told them you laughed at the gods when we were on our journeys. I told them you cursed the priests and swore at the deities.'

'That ain't true!'

'Yes, it is.'

'Well – you shouldn't be a tattle-tale, you snitch. I was under stress. Anyone would swear and curse with a bunch of bloodthirsty dwarves after 'em. I bet even the priests would let out a few oaths.'

Soldier shook his head sadly. 'You see, it's that kind of remark that gets you into trouble.'

Slowly and reluctantly, Spagg covered his stall and wheeled it from the market-place.

'I don't understand you,' he said to Soldier. 'You don't like me at all. Whyd'you want me with you, on these treks of yourn.'

'I find your company stimulating.'

'Liar.'

'Well, let's put it this way, there's not many people in Zamerkand I *would* want with me, so there's not much choice. I know you. I can judge your stamina, your courage – or lack of it – and every aspect of your character. Why would I take someone who is a mystery to me? I'd never know when to run and when to stand and fight.'

'But with me, you always have to run.'

'Exactly, I know where I stand – that is to say – run.'

'Funny beggar, ain't you,' grumbled Spagg. 'I'm splittin' my sides, I am.'

The barrow was locked in a stable.

'They'll all be rotten by the time I get back,' grumbled the hand-seller. 'They'll fall to bits.'

'You could pickle them.'

'Nah. There's one or two of 'em got leprosy, and I can't remember which. Puttin' *them* in vinegar only hastens the rot'.

The pair collected their horses outside the gates. They rode through the Carthagan red tents, Soldier collecting one or two greetings on the way. He was well thought of by the mercenaries. Not just because he was one of them, and a captain at that, but because also he was not a Guthrumite. The Carthagans were loyal to the country they protected, but they thought its citizens weak and pathetic. The Carthagans were short, dark and stocky, like small bulls. The Guthrumites were taller, pale and tended towards the lean. The Carthagans were soldiers from the womb. The Guthrumites had to be moulded into fighters like Captain Kaff – they had to be taught skills which came to their mercenaries naturally.

Soldier stood somewhere between these two types. What he had that neither of them possessed was an intrinsic fighting skill, learned in some other place. His moves could not be anticipated, because he was unorthodox. Somewhere he had learned to kill men without compassion, in ways that were new to this world.

Watching Soldier and Spagg leave, from a high position on the battlements of Zamerkand, was Captain Kaff.

Once the two men were out of sight, Kaff wasted no time. He changed from his uniform into a silk shirt, breeches and a flamboyant hat. He fitted a dove to his wrist and put a sprig of myrtle in his buttonhole. Then he hurried off towards the Palace of Wildflowers – the home of Princess Layana and her absent husband.

Forcing his way past the servants, he demanded audience with the princess.

They told him she was not in a fit state.

'She'll see me,' he said. 'She always sees me.'

'Not today. Not in her madness,' replied Drissila, firmly. 'In any case, my master will kill you when he returns.'

'*If* he returns,' muttered Kaff. 'All right, I'll be back tomorrow.'

'She might not be well by tomorrow.'

'Then the next day. I only want to talk with her. I want to make sure she's happy . . .'

'Of course she's not happy,' snapped Drissila. 'She's sick.'

'I mean, happy with *him*.'

The raven was a silent and unnoticed witness to all this. He flew out, over the walls, and caught Soldier up, landing on the rump of his mount.

The bird chanted in rhyme:

> 'Captain Kaff was there today,
> Captain Kaff won't go away,
> Husbands all, lock up your wives,
> Kaff is stalking through your hives.'

Soldier did not even look at the speaker.

'Humans don't live in hives, bees do.'

'Couldn't think of anything to rhyme with wives,' replied the raven, pecking at the horse's rump to make it trot rather than walk. The raven jogged up and down on the now bouncing rump. 'I thought it was pretty g-good myself.'

'So he *is* there?'

'I told you.'

Soldier was quiet for a long while, during which all that could be heard was the clopping of the horses' hooves.

'When I get back,' he said at last, 'I'll kill him.'

'That's what Drissila said. It didn't seem to impress him.'

'It will – I swear by the seven gods – it will.'

Chapter Two

Soldier and Spagg crossed an open country littered with trees and gallows decorated with hanged people. Here and there a tree fluttered with ribbons and rags, to denote sorrow for the departed. It was not a happy time for Guthrum, but, now that the old King Magus had died, perhaps they could return to a more civilised way of life.

Spagg looked enviously at the harvest of hands, but knew that if he cut them from the wrists of the dangling miscreants, they would probably rot before he got them to his stall. He noticed also, not without a queasy feeling of alarm, that many of the bodies had been scalped and their lower jaws had been cut away. The rooks and crows feasting on the softer parts were not responsible for that. Hannacks were.

There were no roads in Guthrum. Guthrumites were suspicious of such things. If you built a road, they said, the robber bands, be they Hannacks or others, knew exactly where to stand and wait. Merchants and the like preferred to vary their routes across country, using tracks occasionally, but making sure there were plenty to choose from. From time to time foreign engineers arrived in Guthrum, insisting that in such a wealthy kingdom roads should be built, eager that they should be allowed to put their skills to the test. But they usually ended up being stoned and their bodies returned to their home country.

Spagg came across a martyred priest, a young man with a sweet face, nailed upside down to a tree. The priest's inverted head was level with Spagg's own as the horse took him past. A skin-deep smile above a dark lock of hair which hung from the youth's brow caused Spagg to halt and stare at the boy. His gaze took him outwards, to the ends of the arms, along two branches. Slim, pale fingers drooped limp as lily petals from kissing-soft palms that had not seen rough work in their lives.

'What's he got to laugh at?' Spagg said. 'Look at them hands – beautiful hands – but ruined by spikes. I'd like to get the man what drove them nails through such a lovely set of hands.'

'Probably beast-people,' remarked Soldier. 'No doubt this boy thought he could convert them, and went forth with the Seven Gods in his heart, only to find that the beast-people worship more savage deities than any Zamerkand has to offer.'

The pair continued northwards.

From time to time Soldier had the uneasy feeling that they were being followed, but he could see no one behind him. There was a chance that he was being monitored by the queen, of course. Queen Vanda would not be above having a magician disguise himself as a creature of the wild to watch over their progress, but Soldier did not see the same bird or mammal twice and in the end he shrugged off his worries.

'If we go much further,' grumbled Spagg, 'we'll be in beast-people country.'

At the very moment he spoke, Soldier held up a hand. On the skyline was a mounted hunter, a naked man with a fox's head. A tribesman from the Fox-people. The russet head turned and saw them. The creature had a bow and a long knife stuck in a strip of hide around his waist. Soldier and Spagg were assessed, their considerable weapons noted, and then the fox-soldier rode below the crest. He was gone.

Spagg let out his breath. 'That's lucky.'

'Not necessarily,' said Soldier, a little worried himself. He had fought against the beast-people – fox-heads, wolf-heads, dog-heads – with the Carthagans. They were formidable: more intelligent than the Hannacks, whose stupidity hampered them in battle, and certainly just as savage. 'It may be he's gone for the main hunting party. We'd better move on quickly. Look, there's the tree line, over there . . .'

Within an hour they were inside the relative safety of dark woods.

The trees towered over them as they rode through the forest where Soldier had last seen Uthellen and her son. The child had been called a witch-boy in Zamerkand, but Soldier knew that the boy's father had been a wizard and his mother was an ordinary mortal. His only connection with a witch was the handprints burned on his ankles by the fingers of the sorceress who had acted as a midwife and delivered him into the world.

'I don't like this place,' muttered Spagg, looking up at the dark gloomy trees. 'I don't like it at all.' As he spoke the market-trader removed his hat and scratched his head.

Soldier stared. 'What's this? You've shaved your head.'

'Too right,' replied Spagg, replacing his battered broad-brimmed hat. 'If we meet any Hannacks, I'll keep my scalp. You on the other hand, with those fine, long, curly, black locks, will lose yours. I'll have fun, watchin' you get topped like a hard-boiled egg.'

Soldier knew that Hannacks, aside from being barbarous villains of the most savage kind, were born bald. They went through their lives being jealous of every hairy creature on the planet and would slice the top off an enemy's skull – or if that enemy was bearded, remove his mandible – and cover their baldness with the grisly wig. Not being over-fussy, Hannacks didn't even bother drying the scalp, or removing any loose bits of flesh. They had very little regard for niceties like that. Spagg had seen delighted Hannacks with blood running down their cheeks, parading in a lower jaw recently torn from some unfortunate bearded man.

'You seriously think that Hannacks will let you live, even though you haven't got any hair?'

Spagg shrugged. 'I dunno. It just seems a bit silly, temptin' them shiny-pated brigands with a fine head of hair.'

'You never had a fine head of hair. Your hair was a grey, greasy, plaited hank that hung down your back like the tail of a donkey.'

Soldier had halted his gelding. Ahead of them was a wide glade where no trees grew. The ground ahead looked treacherous. Spagg sat there on his jade, while Soldier on the better mount went forward, testing the marsh with a staff he had cut earlier. The pole indicated soft ground and the horse's hooves began to sink. He backed the gelding away from the edge, into the trees again.

This was strange. The last time Soldier had entered the wood, there had been no such bog in his path. It was as if the woodland were saying *thus far and no further*. The forest, or some magical element, had placed a barrier. Could it be that the wizard in the boy had emerged? Perhaps it was just Uthellen's son protecting them from harm? Or perhaps there was some malevolent presence hereabouts. There was an air of doom about the wide bog, which had nothing to do with the swarms of insects and dragonflies, nor the foul smell of marsh gas.

Soldier was happier facing mundane physical hazards – chasms, hostile warriors, monsters, storms – than he was with magic against him.

Spagg seemed to be unaware of any danger. He was picking crabs from a tree, singing softly, '*I am the ancient apple-queen . . .*'

'Shall we camp here?' said Soldier.

Spagg stopped singing. 'Why are you askin' me? You're the one who brought us here.'

'All right. We'll camp here.'

'Good. Give me time to fry these crab-apples. Ever had fried crabs? Dee-licious.'

Later, when the cook delivered on his promise, Soldier was inclined to believe him.

'That wasn't half bad. Fried in rabbit's fat? I must re-member.'

Spagg smirked. 'Not just a pretty fellah, me.'

As they bedded down on a mossy bank for the night, Soldier thought about splitting the dark hours between them, one standing guard while the other slept. He changed his mind when he saw that Spagg had collapsed on his blanket and had fallen instantly asleep. Soldier tried to remain awake, but it had been a long dusty trail, and eventually he too dropped into a deep and dreamful sleep. At some time during the night he was disturbed by the sound of singing, but he was too far gone to wake, which was a pity, because it was his scabbard warning him that enemies were approaching the camp and he was about to be attacked.

He awoke trussed with cords. In the morning's gloom he

could see small creatures, with large knotty ears on big heads, rifling through his saddle-bags. Spagg was also awake. The hand-seller was staring gloomily at the two dozen or so beings who now occupied the area of the camp.

'Goblins,' he muttered. 'Ugly bastards.'

The nearest goblin turned on him and spoke in a voice like sandpaper rubbing oakwood. 'You watch your tongue, baldy, or I'll cut it out.'

Spagg wisely took this creature's counsel to heart.

Soldier said, 'Forgive me, but what are you looking for? There's nothing of real value in those saddle-bags.'

A goblin in a red cap and green doublet came over to him. 'How do you know what's valuable to goblins and what's not?'

'Well, I don't — I only know what's of value to humans.'

'Then keep your rabbit-hole shut.'

'I just thought if I could be of any help. Was it you who placed the marsh there? A very clever trap.'

Redcap said, 'Yes, isn't it?' His mouth was the widest one Soldier had ever seen in his life. It seemed to stretch from ear to ear on that enormous head.

'Do you want to know what we're doing here?' asked Soldier.

'Not especially.'

'I'm looking for the witch-boy who used to live in the forest with his mother.'

Redcap shrugged. 'What about him?'

'He's the new King Magus.'

That stopped them. The searching was forgotten. They all froze in their current positions and stared at him.

'You're lying,' Redcap said, uncertainly. 'I can tell.'

'If you can tell, you'll know it's the truth.'

A female goblin had found the frying pan, still with the

remnants of last night's supper in it. Instead of licking the fat and pieces of crab-apple, she bit into the metal, covering half the pan with her mouth. Then she scraped her small, even teeth over the whole pan, leaving deep dents where she had brought her jaws together: the marks of her incisors. With her mouth full of rancid fat, she began to swallow, noisily.

'Stop that!' ordered another female goblin. 'Didn't you hear? The new King Magus.'

The goblin with the frying pan blinked, then tossed the cooking utensil over her shoulder.

Redcap said. 'It is true, then?'

'Yes,' replied Soldier. 'I have been ordered to escort the new King Magus back to Zamerkand.'

Soldier's bonds were cut away. So were Spagg's. A fire was lit for them. They sat around it warming themselves, for the morning ground had been damp and cold. A mist from the marsh had crept into the camp and now wound its way around the tree trunks.

'The boy,' explained Redcap, 'is no longer here. He's been taken by his mother to another place. A small country to the north-east. You may have heard of it. Bhantan?'

'No, can't say I have,' replied Soldier.

'Not surprised. You're a stranger here, aren't you? Can tell that by your blue eyes.'

Spagg said, 'I've heard of it. Ruled by twins – the Rose Prince and the White Prince.'

'That's the place,' said Redcap.

Soldier nodded at Spagg. 'I knew you'd be useful. You're not as ignorant as everyone says, are you?'

Once the goblins had been through everything the two men were carrying, they were allowed to proceed. A few things had gone missing, of course — a comb, a mirror, a ball of twine, some salt — but goblins are not interested in weaponry, food (or at least the kind that humans eat), except salt, of course, or money. Goblins are poor at making artefacts, and it is only manufactured objects which they take, plus the odd wool shirt or blanket, men's breeches being too long and thin for their stumpy legs, and men's boots being too small for their enormous feet.

The marsh was removed by the same method as it was placed there: magic. It was simply a matter of perception. Nothing had actually changed. The ground was in the same condition, but it now looked hard and unyielding to the travelling mortals The goblins had lifted the spell they had put on the place and now Spagg and Soldier saw it as it actually was.

'So,' said Soldier, as they rode through the trees once again, 'you know this place Bhantan? You've been there?'

'Everyone knows Bhantan,' replied Spagg, wearily, 'except you. A five-year-old child would have been just as useful to you as I am. Yes, I know of Bhantan. No, I've never been there.'

'Well, here's an opportunity for some experience.'

'I'd rather be at home, selling the hands of the hanged.'

This was ignored. 'Tell me what you know about it.'

'I've told you what I know. Ask your blasted raven. He seems to know everything.'

Soldier noticed the raven, perched on the back of Spagg's saddle.

'Know what?' the raven asked. 'Can't I leave you two for one minute but you get captured by goblins?'

'Bhantan,' said Soldier. 'Been there?'

'Been there, flown over it, dropped lime on the rooftops.'

'And?'

'Bhantan is a country ruled by twin princes, the Rose Prince and the White Prince. There's strict rituals to adhere to, even for the rulers, because it's that kind of place. Everything is ordered – too ordered. You can't scratch your nose, unless its the right time and place to scratch it, otherwise you get arrested and told to write an apology. If you can't write they stick you in front of a wall and shoot you full of arrows.'

'Is that true?' cried Soldier, alarmed. 'Are they that insistent on following their rules and regulations?'

'Absolutely,' interrupted Spagg. 'Discipline and prescription. Everything is prescribed and woe betide the man who doesn't know when to do what, and where.'

The raven continued. 'Two years ago one of the princes died – the Rose Prince. When that happens, as it eventually must unless they both drop dead the very same second, which is unlikely, you will admit . . .'

'Get on with it,' muttered Soldier.

'When that happens, the remaining prince goes into black robes and becomes the Black Prince. While they are both alive the Rose and the White Princes have to enter and leave the palace – and everywhere else – by their own particular doors, marked with the colours rose and white. With one of them dead, however, the Black Prince has to enter and leave by a third door, coloured dark blue. Don't ask me why *blue*, cause I don't know. It just is, all right?

'Recently, the Black Prince died. Over the last few years the court officials have been preparing the next set of twins down the family tree, and the set below them, to govern the country. All the rituals have been gone through a thousand times, for if the rulers can't get it right, why should the ordinary citizens? However, along came an epidemic of measles

– Bhantan has discovered to its horror that natural diseases apparently cock a snook at discipline, order and ritual – and wiped out both sets of twins. The epidemic took away a few sets below the next in line also, and now they've had to crown two urchins, having had to go so far down the family tree they ended up in the shanty town gutters.'

Soldier said, 'Serve 'em right, for being so rigid.'

'Thus,' said the raven, 'they have found that their system of government – one prince to rule at home, while the other goes to war – has crumbled beneath their feet. They suspect that the two new princes, identical twins, of course, dress in each others' robes and go through the wrong doors, just for fun. The shock! The horror! But how to discipline them, when no one really knows, except perhaps the mother who bore them, who is a simple soul and just sits and smiles through the barrage of questions, and asks if her interrogators want a cup of chocolate.

'Her sons have none of the manners of princes, nor the military training required of the White Prince, nor the administrative skills of a good Rose Prince, nor princely airs and graces, nor love of order. They are crafty, sly creatures, who hoard things unnecessarily against a time when they believe they will be in want again, as they once were. Individually they flout the rituals whenever they can, and each blames the other, for who can tell where the blame really lies?'

Soldier said, 'They sound like a tonic to me.'

'But no,' cried the raven, 'for the country is now in chaos! A square, walled city, with neat little houses all in rows, and one family to each house, and four courtyards, and four parks, and eight watchtowers, and sixteen flagpoles, and yet no one now quite knows where to be, and at what time, and who to meet and how to trade with them. The Weights and Measures

Department is in disarray, the Committee for Straight Streets has a wiggle in it, and the Council for Right-Handed Workers are all fingers and thumbs. Oh, monstrous twins, with no proper upbringing and a daft mother who sits and eats sweet-meats from dawn to dusk!'

Both Spagg and Soldier fell about laughing, as they stopped for a lunch of cold pasties washed down with water.

After a short lunch they continued, into wolf and bear country, where the occasional jaguar crossed their path. At least in this part of the world they had no need to fear Hannacks, for the bald-headed brigands were as much in fear of wild beasts as anyone else. However, they had to be ever watchful, and lit fires whenever they stopped. The raven left them after the third river they crossed, telling them he would be back, sometime.

Three days later they crested a ridge and found themselves looking down on a perfectly square city, neatly walled about. Symmetry was of the utmost importance in the architecture of that place below them, and even the goat tracks on the mountainsides around went in straight lines. The pair descended, Spagg a little more reluctantly than Soldier, since he had never learned to read and write properly, and if he were arrested he would have to rely on Soldier to get him out of trouble.

'I don't want to be no pincushion,' he muttered to Soldier, as they approached the gates. 'Don't you let 'em stick me with arrows.'

'I'll do my best,' replied Soldier.

'Halt!' yelled a guard on the walls. 'Tether your animals to the bar on the outside wall and then stand in the white circle and state your business!'

The pair did as they were told.

'We are here,' cried Soldier, from the middle of the marked area, 'in order to find one Uthellen, of Zamerkand, mother of a young boy.'

'Why do you want her?'

Soldier said, grimly, 'That's private.'

The guard disappeared. A little while later two gates opened with perfect precision on a device with chains and weights. Soldier and Spagg entered and were then questioned for three hours by a clerk, who wrote their answers down in an astonishingly slow hand. The quill scraping across the paper hardly seemed to be moving. When Soldier complained about how long the whole interrogation was taking, there was no comment, but his complaint was laboriously taken down in black ink on grey parchment. Soldier decided that if they were ever to finish the interview he would have to keep such frustrations to himself and economise on his answers. The whole charade took place in a huge cellar, the walls of which were lined with pigeonholes, each hole bearing a parchment similar to the one the clerk wrote on now.

Finally they were free to enter Bhantan's city, of the same name as the country, and seek Uthellen.

Being fatigued they went first to a hostelry, where they were given a towel and a bar of lye soap, a bowl of water each, and shown two beds in a room of twenty neat white beds.

'One at each end of the room,' ordered the servant, a young woman, 'on opposite sides.'

'To balance it up?' queried Soldier.

'Are you laughing at our customs?' said the servant, frowning. 'Because if you are . . .'

'I wouldn't dare.'

The Bhantan servant was still defensive. 'Tradition, protocol, etiquette, these are the things that order is formed on. Without order you have confusion. We Bhantans are never confused, because we know who we are and what to do, in any emergency. We are never in crisis.'

'That's not what we've heard,' said Spagg. 'What about these two new princes you've got?'

The servant blinked. 'Temporarily . . .'

'. . . you're in disarray?' finished Soldier.

The servant blinked again, refused to be drawn, and left them to the simple splendour of their temporary quarters. It was indeed a pleasant enough room, with low ceilings, thick, brown, exposed beams, a tiled floor, whitewashed walls, small windows. Above all it was clean – spotless in fact – not a speck of dust in the corners, not a cobweb, not a dead fly on any windowsill. And the beds were squared-down at the corners, the starched white sheets like drumskins, the pillows round and hard.

'Welcome to the Kingdom of the Clean,' muttered Spagg. 'Just one question – where do I spit?'

'Not if you value your life,' said Soldier, flinging himself, boots and all, onto his bed. 'You must learn to respect the culture of other societies.'

'Prissy missy!'

'Spagg, get up the other end of the room. Hurry on, it's quite a hike. I've claimed this end.'

'You would.' Spagg trailed all the way down the long hostel until he found his bed in the far distance.

Later, when they had eaten and rested, a male servant came to tell them that Uthellen awaited without.

Soldier hurried out to meet her.

'Uthellen,' he cried, taking both her hands in his, 'you still have the bloom of maidenhood upon your cheek!'

'Liar,' she said, with a wisp of smile.

In fact, she looked older than he would have guessed, with grey streaks to her hair and lines to her face, though she was still not more than thirty-five years of age. However, her complexion looked ruddy enough, not pale and wan as it used to be, and she seemed fuller of figure. In fact her maturity had brought with it a different kind of beauty: the type of loveliness that caused a man of experience to choke on regret. Soldier guessed those comely age-lines had been caused by care and worry for her bastard child, who had been in danger every minute of his life until now.

As he looked at her now, held her soft hands in his own, his heart was once more torn asunder. He loved his wife, it was true, but he had to tell himself that with strong conviction as he beheld this other woman. Uthellen was very dear to him. He had managed – the gods knew how – to keep himself from falling completely in love with Uthellen, who was as pure and lovely within as her outward looks promised. It was sheer force of will which kept them apart, not any natural feelings. If they had both followed their natural desires they would be infidels by now.

'And the boy?'

'He has been given a name, IxonnoxI.'

'A perfect palindrome,' sighed the Bhantanian servant in satisfaction as he was passing by. 'Such beautiful symmetry in the world of wizards.'

'And he is no longer a boy,' Uthellen continued, smiling. 'He is eighteen now. You'll meet him in a little while. Have you come to take us to Guthrum?'

'That's the idea. We'll need an escort though. Do you think the Bhantans will supply us with one?'

'I have no doubt of it.'

He noticed a wicker basket under her arm.

'What have you there?'

She smiled. 'Fruit. A traditional greeting gift to a friend. I bought them at the goblin market.'

'I'm glad you regard me as your friend.'

Spagg came down from the other end of the room.

'Food, eh? I'd rather it was the haunch of roasted pig, but fruit will do for now.'

The three of them sat down to eat.

There were quinces and sharp bullaces, bilberries, swarthy-looking mulberries, dewberries and sweet peaches, barberries, gooseberries and bright red cherries, medlars, plums and apples. They began eating, the juices running down their chins. Soldier could feel them doing him good, filling his veins with sunshine. Uthellen explained that no one gathered such luscious fruit as the goblins of Blackdown Wood.

'We just met a bunch o' goblins,' muttered Spagg. 'They was nothin' but villains and thieves.'

'There's goblins and goblins, just as there are different shades of mortals,' explained Uthellen.

'What a feast,' said Soldier, impressed by the variety. 'Is this all for the three of us? What about Ix — Ix . . .'

'IxonnoxI? He is out in the woods, beyond the city.'

Soldier looked up, alarmed. 'We'd better find him,' he cried, jumping up. 'I haven't yet told you why we're here. HoulluoH is dead. Your son has been chosen as the next King Magus. He may be in danger. What's he doing in the woods?'

'Practising wizardry. Oh, he *can't* have been chosen,' Uthellen said, distressed. 'He's not ready for anything like that yet. He's only just beginning to master his skills. He's not yet mature enough. He'll need to gather more wisdom. Surely there's another wizard, a much older and wiser one who takes precedence over my son?'

'HoulluoH proclaimed with his dying breath that the next King Magus would be the son of a woman called Uthellen. What's the matter, why are you crying? It's not just because he's young and inexperienced, is it? There's something else.'

Uthellen choked out the words. 'I shall lose him.'

'Lose him?' muttered Spagg, who hated women crying in front of him. 'You can't lose 'im. Everyone knows where the King Magus lives. In the Seven Peaks.'

She stared at him fiercely. 'Once he becomes King Magus he'll be lost to me. What does the most powerful wizard in the world want with a *mother*? He'll be out of my reach.' She broke down, sobbing again. 'He's only eighteen. I don't want him to go.'

The insensitive Spagg cried, 'Well, them wizards live more'n seven hundred years, don't they? He's got a bit to go yet. You'll have turned your own toes up long before he's due for the box.'

'She means go *away*,' Soldier said. 'Look, Spagg, you and I are going to have to fetch him from the wood. Now, before something happens to the boy. Come on, let's go. No grumbling. I'm not in the mood for it.'

'I'll come too,' said Uthellen, composing herself. 'I know where to look.'

Chapter Three

They found IxonnoxI in the wood, talking with fairies. Soldier was not fond of fairies. He seemed to be attractive to a particular kind of that race of creatures: fairies known as drots, who bit into flesh and lapped the blood of mortals with their rough little tongues. However, the wizard-boy dismissed his fairy friends and joined his mother, Soldier and Spagg.

'I know why you have come,' he said, nodding to Soldier. And to his mother, 'I'm sorry. I have been called.'

'It's not what I wanted.'

'I know mother, but it's my destiny.' He drew a deep breath. 'However, I'm not yet ready. HoullouH has died too soon. I must have more time to prepare myself. The funeral must take place before I can be installed as King Magus. that will give me a little more time to prepare myself, mentally, for the position I must occupy. First I must go to Zamerkand, where I was born, to meet with other magi. They will be journeying there, even as we speak. The inauguration must take place in the city of my birth, presided over by the Fraternity of Wizards.'

This was all news to Soldier.

'You know all this for a fact?'

IxonnoxI stared at Soldier with those penetrating eyes. 'I can guess what you are thinking. You're wondering about my powers now. Have I the gift of far-sight? Can I tell what others are thinking? Can I conjure legions of demons, jinn, genies or giants, to defend me? The answer is, no. I am almost as defenceless as the day I was born. I can do nothing more than a magician's tricks at this time: raise the dead, walk on air, bring on an eclipse. My great powers will come to me all at once, within the space of a second, at my inauguration. Until then I am as vulnerable as any of you.'

Soldier said, 'I'm alarmed to hear this. You're under my protection until we reach Zamerkand. I think the sooner we start out, the better. News will travel the land of the death of HoulluoH. There will be those out there seeking to take advantage of the situation before the inauguration. We must be on our way.'

'I agree.'

Soldier was amazed at how much the boy had changed in physical appearance since the last time he had seen him. Then IxonnoxI had been an awkward-looking – almost deformed – gangling, angular youth, all pointed elbows and sharp knees. Now he had a remarkable physique: muscular; finely-shaped; strong, straight bones. Soldier had been convinced he would grow up to be a hunched, wizened man, yet here he was, a tall and handsome creature with a body like a warrior. The transformation from duckling to swan was astonishing.

IxonnoxI saw him staring. 'It's only a matter of perception, Soldier,' he said, smiling gently. 'You see me as a lion where you once saw a baby ostrich, but I make myself appear as I wish. The youth needed to be disregarded and even pitied. The man needs to be feared. One body is as useful as another to me. I have no need for good looks, strong muscles, but they intimidate those mortals around me. Even you.'

Soldier acknowledged this to be true.

As they walked back to the square city, Spagg whispered to Soldier, 'We're made! A wizard – the King Magus, yet – is a friend of ours. We'll be rich, you and me. We'll have it coming out of our ears, eh? We'll crush our enemies like ripe plums underfoot.' He actually chortled out loud. 'Just you wait, Captain Kaff, eh? We'll have him deboned and baked in an oven – fed to that raven of yours. Chancellor Humbold? Why, we'll throw him into the sewers. I'll be chancellor instead. In fact, I'll be Lord of the Royal Purse and Keeper of the Towers, too.'

'You sure you wouldn't just settle for being queen?' said Soldier, sarcastically.

'Hadn't thought of that,' Spagg replied, rubbing his coarse hands together. 'I'll make you Warlord of Guthrum if you like.'

'Very generous of you.'

When they entered Bhantan, the city was having a crisis.

A courtier had kissed one of the twin princes on the cheek early that morning. Unknown to that prince, the courtier had red dye on his lips and had left a mark. It had now been proved that the twins swapped robes and left the palace each by the exit designated for the other. Protocol had been flouted. Culture had been smashed. Custom had been destroyed. The twin princes had been playing games with Bhantan's traditions! This was the most serious crime someone from Bhantan could commit. Its nobles were horrified, sickened to their stomachs. Its citizens reeled.

'A thousand years of perfect ritual has been thrown away,' cried the First Lord of the city, to a wailing populace. 'We have been betrayed by these two urchins in royal robes. Treacherous creatures, lower than lizards! I say they must be banished, sent out into the wilderness to live amongst the wolves and their kind. Away with them!'

The two princes, not more than fourteen years of age, stood on the steps of their palace and regarded the mob with contempt. The Rose Prince waved a hand at the speaker, as if wafting away his words. The White Prince stared at the First Lord with raised eyebrows.

'We are the rulers,' said the White Prince.

'We *set* the custom, as we may,' said the Rose Prince.

'Ours is the rule of law in the land,' they followed up in unison. 'Ours is to say who is banished and who is not.'

The mob were uncertain. Who to follow? The First Lord who knew all the rules? Or the princes, who were as they said, the legitimate rulers? It was all very confusing. Periwigged judges, prelates, courtiers, all stood behind the First Lord. Their choice had been made. A nurse and a mother stood behind the twins. They had no choice.

'It is our birthright,' cried the twins, in unison again, 'and we will see to it that our gardens are turned into parks for the use of the populace. We shall build a theatre, four-square in the poor quarter. We shall distribute coin amongst you, and bread and wine . . .'

That did it. There was a great roar of approval from the mob. The officialdom was not to be thwarted, however. Cavalry had come quietly up side-streets, their horses' hooves padded with blanket. They now surrounded the square and awaited the order to charge. The streets would run with blood if the mob did not disperse. Soldier and his friends were just entering the city gates as the people were making their way to their homes, grumbling and arguing. The twins had lost.

They had gone into the palace to pack their bags and steal as much as they could from the royal apartments, before being ejected through the city gates.

In his capacity as Captain of the Eagle Pavilion in the Carthagan Army, Soldier managed to obtain an audience with the First Lord. This great personage had other things to worry about, but he listened and eventually gave Soldier a cavalry troop to escort IxonnoxI across country, to the borders of Guthrum. Soldier thanked him on behalf of Queen Vanda, and preparations were made to leave the city.

The cavalry troop rode in a perfect square with IxonnoxI, his mother, and the Guthrumites with the supply wagons in the centre. It was all a bit too formal for Soldier, but he deferred to the cavalry lieutenant. These were not his troops to command, but those of a foreign power. Soldier would have preferred to send outriders to the flanking hills, and front and rear, but the lieutenant said such measures were unnecessary. He said he knew his own territory and there was nothing to fear, especially in this region.

They passed the two young princes, as they trudged through a valley dragging a sack of silver cups and plate along with them. The lieutenant did not know whether to salute or ignore the deposed rulers, and in the end he compromised with a curt nod. Uthellen asked if the travellers could join her in one of the wagons but the lieutenant refused, saying that he had orders not to assist the princes in their flight from Bhantan.

'I ought to confiscate that silver they're carrying,' said the lieutenant, who was not an unkind man, 'but I can't help feeling it's little compensation for what they've lost. If you've ruled a country, I suppose you're entitled to take something of it away with you.'

Uthellen said to Soldier, 'Well, I'm feeling sorry for them. They're just young boys after all, children brought up amongst the dregs of the city. You can't blame them. They might have grown up to be very wise and able rulers, if they'd been given time and training enough.'

'I agree,' said Soldier, 'but I think the lieutenant is right on this occasion. We can't afford to take any risks with your son's welfare. We must keep this journey as simple as possible. Taking the princes along with our party would complicate things and put two people with unknown intentions inside our circle, young as they are.'

'You can't think the princes would betray us?'

'I have no idea, and I don't believe we should experiment.'

Uthellen accepted this, though her kind heart suffered at the thought of those walkers, dragging their loot over desert and mountain, perhaps running short of water and supplies.

On the third day they were coming out of a mountain pass in their usual square formation when they were attacked by Hannacks. Soldier's magic scabbard sang out, but he could not see from which direction the danger was coming. In fact the so-called barbarians of Da-tichett had made kites out of human skin and flew down from the heights into the centre of the square. The Bhantan troops had been trained to fight forces bearing on them from the outside. They were utterly confused by having an enemy attacking them from within.

The Hannacks, their bodies gleaming with slippery oil, wielding war-clubs, long knives and sickles, cut into men and horses with no quarter given.

The Bhantan lieutenant was one of the first to die, with a sickle through his heart. He lost his scalp just a few moments later, to a warrior whom Soldier managed to dispatch before the severed pate had rested on the bald head for more than second. For a while it was just hewing and hacking. There was no finesse about the fighting skills of Hannacks. They killed anything on two legs, with as much energy and noise as possible. They wore the skins of former enemies as tattered cloaks. Their helmets were often made from the skulls of defeated foes. Their battle screams were horrifyingly loud because they themselves were almost deaf, having ears the size of cockle-shells.

Soldier fought desperately with his warhammer; cracking skulls, spiking heads and bodies. His scabbard saved him many times, from an attack from the rear or on his blind side. But eventually the Hannack reinforcements swept down from the hills on wild horses. These smashed through way through the remnants of the Bhantan cavalry, and carried off the wagons within the square. Some of the barbarians remained to kill the wounded and take hair and beards. Bhantan cavalry horses were gathered in. These would be sold to other tribes, since the Hannacks only rode hairy-ankled ponies of a stocky breed. Soldier seemed to be the only survivor. He was hemmed in by knives and clubs. Then his opponents lost interest in him, seeing their comrades gathering in the spoils. They left to pursue plunder in the shape of weapons and horses.

This primitive culture was unconcerned with their own dead: they left them on the battlefield as food for carrion.

Finally a Hannack on a horse came charging across the square. He swung a scapula-bone-club on a leather thong from his wrist. Soldier felt the blow strike his head as the war-club glanced from his temple and he fell into a black pit.

When he came to, Soldier found himself surrounded by wolves. The beasts were devouring the bodies of the dead. Instinctively they had stayed away from him, knowing he was still breathing. Why risk attacking live prey when there's meat a-plenty? They slunk away from him as he groggily found his feet. He staggered beyond the fighting area to where a stream was cutting through the turf. There he washed his wounds and drank his fill. After a long rest he felt he could at least go on. There was despair in his heart, however, for Uthellen and her son had been in one of the two wagons taken by the Hannacks.

'What am I going to tell the queen?' he cried.

'What indeed?'

He whirled round to find the raven sitting on the fork of a dead tree.

'You? Must you always plague me at times like this?'

'Plague you? I heard there was meat to be had and came as quickly as I could. I am a carrion bird, after all.'

'You heard?'

'Word travels on the wing.'

'Oh,' said Soldier, relieved. 'You don't mean they know of this in Zamerkand already – the people.'

The raven clicked his beak. 'You've been in a row, haven't you? You've been in a dust-up.'

'Dust-up is hardly the phrase.' Soldier sat on the bank of the stream with his head in his hands. 'I'm a disgrace to the red pavilions. I've lost the very person I was sent to guard.' He looked round, quickly. 'Spagg's gone too. Dead I expect.'

'That's no loss. Tell me something important.'

'Why wasn't I watching? Archers could have picked off those kite-men, if we had seen them coming from the skies.'

'Well, let's just sit here and feel sorry for ourselves, shall we?'

Soldier stared at the raven through narrowed eyes. 'I was betrayed,' he murmured. 'That's it!'

'Well, don't look at me. I haven't betrayed anyone since I

told my mother my older brother was a cuckoo and she threw him from the nest.'

'You were never a fledgling,' snapped Soldier, coming to his senses, 'you were an infant child, changed into a bird by a witch. What was her name? Clegnose. Unless you lied about that too.'

'No, no – just testing.'

'I'm in no mood. Oh, gods alive, what am I going to do? I can't attack the whole Hannack nation on my own. I'll have to go for help, which means admitting my failure. The queen will never let me go out after the boy again. She'll send that idiot Kaff.'

'You've got to go home, none the less. Hello, who's this?'

The bird was looking at the pass. Soldier turned and saw that the twins had caught up with him. He waited for them to come up alongside him.

'What's happened here?' said one twin. 'Had a row? Had a bit of dust-up?'

Soldier gritted his teeth. 'There's been a battle.'

'Oh,' the other twin said, nodding. 'And just you left alive? That's lucky. Or something else.'

'What do you mean, or something else?'

The raven whispered in Soldier's ear, 'He means cowardice.'

'I'm no coward,' he said, whirling on the twins. 'Look, I was struck on the head.'

Soldier began to gather some things together, as the two boys sat and watched him. Soldier found some goatskin water-bags which had luckily escaped punctures. He filled four of these up from the contents of others. Then he gave one to each of the twins and slung the other two over his own right shoulder.

'You'd better come along with me,' he told them. 'It'll be safer.'

'Where are you going?' asked one.

'Zamerkand.'

'That'll do,' said the other, 'but don't think we're sharing our treasure with you.'

'You can keep your treasure,' Soldier said, 'I've no desire for any of it. My wife is Princess Layana. I've wealth enough. All I require is my identity, which I'm sure you're not carrying in that sack.'

This answer mystified the boys and they shrugged at each other, before trailing on behind their new leader. The raven flew ahead. The boys watched it, puzzled by its obvious relationship with Soldier, then, as young people often do, lost their curiosity in familiarity.

Soldier soon found that the twins needed little looking after. They were both strong boys, physically. They were survivors. In the past it had been in a rat-infested ghetto, but they were just as able out in the wastelands beyond the Scalash River. Their year as princes had not softened them in the least degree.

On the trail, Soldier taught them the skills of staying alive in open country. He found that they learned fast. Soon they could set a snare as well as he could, disguising the human smell with dirt on the trap. They were willing to do their share of the work, fetching firewood, carrying water, skinning and gutting rabbits. He taught them to fish, to use a slingshot, to cut a staff and to make it into a spear. They loved it. They were natural born hunters, fishers and gatherers. They went out with empty bags and brought them back full of nuts, fruit, roots, fungi and occasionally a dead bird or mammal for the pot. Young people have no fear of failure. They throw themselves into learning new skills with all the enthusiasm and suppleness of youth. So long as they're enjoying what they're doing, there's no holding them back.

'My name is Guido,' said one.

'And I'm Sando,' said the other.

Soldier picked up a blackened twig from the cold ashes of the camp fire and marked the vest of the one who had spoken first.

'Guido,' he said, 'I need to know who I'm talking to. Promise me, the pair of you, that you won't exchange vests.'

They nodded. 'We won't,' they said in unison. 'We've learned our lesson.'

Sando said, 'Anyway, it wouldn't be any fun. We like you. Fooling those pompous old farts back in Bhantan, now *that* was fun. With you, it'd be like cheating.'

He believed they would refrain from fooling him. Soldier knew that they liked to be praised, for individual achievements. One would not enjoy the other receiving his acclaim. Perhaps that was where the officials of Bhantan had made their mistake? Maybe they only ever saw them as twins and never as individuals?

'What are you doing with these boys?' asked the raven. 'You can't trust them any further than you can throw a prince's palace. Mark my words, they'll turn on you, you know.'

'If they do, they do.'

'Oh, you're such a martyr.'

One day one of the twins, Sando it was, killed an antelope. He was, justifiably he thought, ecstatic. Guido was jealous, but managed to hide it fairly successfully. Soldier however was none too pleased, knowing that there was too much meat for the three of them. Much of it would go to waste, would rot and go to any carrion. Soldier was a great believer in not hunting for its own sake, but for food or clothing only. To kill more than one needed was an affront against nature.

However, on this occasion he said nothing to Sando. It was not a time to criticise. The boys were still very sensitive to his teaching. Sando would be devastated by such fault-finding, when in fact it had been Soldier's failure. Later, when it didn't matter, Soldier determined he would quietly give them a lesson on the glories of nature and the crime of waste.

They had just finished jointing the kill, when something the size of a large bear came plummeting down from the mountains.

'KERROWW!' cried the creature. 'SLAHGGUS. SLAHGGUS.'

The twins, pale and terrified, were on their feet in a second. What stood before them was a dragon. Had they been country boys they would have known it was a two-legged, red-bellied, green dragon, whose natural habitat was the barren wastes and mountains south of Falyum. It was a male of the species. That much was obvious.

The dragon's mouth opened and he repeated his words.

Soldier had not moved. He rested back on his elbows.

'Don't worry, boys,' he said. 'It's not dangerous. Give it a couple of cuts of meat. It'll go away once it's fed.'

Dubious, Guido slowly reached down and picked up a haunch, tossing it to the dragon. A wide mouth opened gratefully, catching the huge chunk of meat. Jaws full of thick, brown teeth closed. There was a crunching as they masticated the meat, bones splintering and going down with the rest in three or four huge swallows.

'SLAHGGUS!' growled the dragon, his strange eyes narrowing in delight.

'What's he saying?' asked Sando, still as rigid as a board.

'Food. He wants more food.'

Sando, this time, tossed the creature half a ribcage and

then they all watched it go the way of the haunch.

Now the dragon stood on claw-tip, high up on his hind legs. There was a crackling sound, like the shaking of old leather hides, and the dragon stretched his enormous wings. They could see the sunlight though them. The beast trotted over to Soldier and crooned over him for a few moments, seemed about to lick his face, then changed its mind and finally took a long ostrich-swift run along the dusty wasteland before taking to the skies. Its gigantic wingspan took it high up on a thermal, where it circled above, still crooning, before vanishing into the bright light of the heavens.

The twins began to thaw.

'What was that?' cried Guido.

'My offspring,' answered Soldier, laughing. 'It believes me to be its mother, since I was the first creature it saw when it hatched. Comes in useful to have a dragon around, sometimes.'

'I should say!' Sando cried.

The excited boys were full of questions. Soldier answered them as best he could, telling them that as a warrior in the red pavilions he had stolen the egg as one of his initiation tasks, thinking it to be an eagle's egg. The warm sun had done the rest.

Soldier did not feel too bad about the antelope now. Its meat had gone to a good belly. Soldier's dragon appeared from time to time and it was useful to have something to give it. A mother should look after her son, see to its wants. Of course the dragon could feed itself now – it was capable of hunting down and catching the greatest beasts in the world (except perhaps a blue-bellied, red-backed dragon, which was five times its size) but it still liked to think it was loved by its parent.

'Good thing it changed its mind about licking your cheek,' said the raven later, out of earshot of the youths. 'You wouldn't have any skin left on your face.'

This was true. A dragon's tongue was so rough it could take bark off the trunk of an oak. Soldier winced, knowing it. Yet, he realised, the dragon had guessed such a gesture would have harmed its mother, because it *had* changed its mind at the last minute. Was it an intelligent beast? Or had instinct taken over? So little was known about these shy creatures, the dragons of the world, no philosopher ever having studied them in depth. They flew in and stole cattle occasionally, and on the odd occasion, with a rogue, a person or two. But for the most part they lived in the uninhabited regions of the world, where philosophers rarely trod.

The day came when the turrets and towers of Zamerkand came into view. Their spearpoint tips flashed in the sun. Soldier heaved a great sigh. He was going to have to face the music now. He wasn't looking forward to it. Kaff would make the most of it. So would Humbold. There were many enemies in that sparkling city who would be pleased to see Soldier come to grief. Soldier hoped to have an audience with Queen Vanda and tell her his version before the vultures descended.

'Is that it?' cried Sando, coming up to his side and staring in wonder at the great city. 'It's a hundred times bigger than Bhantan.'

'A thousand times,' yelled Guido in excitement. 'We're going to have such a time there.'

A horseman had left the city gates, his mount kicking dust as he approached. Soldier saw that it was the hunter, the man who had been but a youth when Soldier had first woken on that hillside south of the Ancient Forest, by the Petrified Pools of Yan. Since that time the hunter had remained slim and lithe, had not filled out in the way that most men do on reaching maturity. Soldier accepted this fault without question. He owed the hunter his life, several times over.

The hunter had no hawk with him.

There was urgency in the horse's stride.

Clearly something was wrong.

Chapter Four

As always, the hunter's face was muffled by the indigo cottons in which he was invariably swathed. His voice – which Soldier had not heard for some years now – sounded strange. It was almost as if the speaker were trying to disguise the tone.

'Go,' said the hunter, breathlessly. 'Turn back. Run away from here. Word of your failure has flown ahead of you and reached the ears of the queen. She is very displeased.'

'I can't help that,' said Soldier, more irritated than afraid. 'Anyway, who brought word? We have been travelling as fast as possible. Who could have seen the action and beaten us back?'

'I don't know,' said the hunter, his restless piebald pawing the sand with its hooves, 'but I strongly urge you to flee.'

Soldier drew himself up with a sigh. 'I can't do that, I'm sorry. I have to face the consequences of my actions. I have failed, it's true. But I'm not going to run away from that failure.' He paused for a moment, before adding, 'Besides, I want to see my wife.'

The hunter clucked.

Once more Soldier was irritated. 'You find that funny? That I miss my wife?'

'I would have thought you would be pleased to find respite from that madwoman.'

Soldier took a furious step forward, then realised there were more important things to do than brawl.

'Never,' he said, in choked voice, 'speak of the Princess Layana in that manner again, or I'll have to take you to task.'

The hunter's eyes seemed to soften on hearing this threat, which again surprised Soldier.

'I mean it!' he said. 'No matter what I owe you.'

With that, Soldier turned away from the hunter and continued towards the city. The twins stayed for a moment, looking curiously at the hunter.

'Who are you?' said the hunter.

'We are the rulers of the Kingdom of Bhantan,' Guido said.

'Were,' Sando reminded his brother.

'Why are you with him?'

Sando glanced after Soldier. 'He looked after us,' he said. 'He is our friend.'

Soldier was now approaching the gates. The twins rushed to join him. The three were met by a squad of Imperial Guardsmen, led by Captain Kaff.

'You will accompany us,' said Kaff, a live rat locked onto his wrist stump with a silver amulet. 'Follow me.' There seemed to be little malice in Kaff's manner, nor really any triumph. More a simple satisfaction that at last the world had shown him to be right. This outlander who called himself Soldier was a useless human being, not to be trusted with important missions. Now everyone could see that such fools should be tossed into the sewers the moment they arrived in Zamerkand.

Chancellor Humbold gave Soldier a sickly smile as he entered the court and prostrated himself before the queen.

Queen Vanda was crimson with anger.

'Soldier, I am *so* disappointed.'

Disappointed? Humbold and Kaff exchanged glances of disbelief. They had expected something stronger to come from the queen's mouth. They expected her to be so enraged she would be close to losing her reason. They would have preferred to hear words like 'utter stupidity' followed by others such as 'dungeon' or 'immediate execution'.

'I most humbly beg Your Highness's forgiveness for my failure. We were attacked at the exit to a pass by Hannacks. There was a company of Bhantan cavalry with me, but they were slaughtered to a man. I alone survived the massacre. The King Magus designate was taken from me, along with his mother, and they are now captives of the Hannacks.'

'You alone survived?' spat Humbold. 'You *ran*, you mean. Cowardice is punishable by death, Your Highness. I suggest . . .'

'Be quiet, Humbold,' snapped the queen, seemingly more furious at this interruption than with Soldier. 'Did you run, Soldier?'

Soldier got to his feet, stiff with reserve.

'I was struck unconscious.'

'He was, he was,' piped up Guido at this point. 'We saw it all, didn't we, brother?'

'Yes,' cried Sando. 'We were standing on a ridge and we saw the whole thing. Soldier fought like a true hero. He was hit from behind by a cowardly Hannack.'

'QUIET,' roared Humbold. 'How dare you speak without being spoken to, in front of royalty.'

'We're royalty, too!' cried the twins in unison, rounding on him in annoyance. 'We're the rightful rulers of the Kingdom of Bhantan. You're just a court lackey! You're just a minion.

We're *princes*. We could have your head chopped off.'

The court let out a general gasp.

'We've been usurped,' continued Sando, speaking as if confidentially to the queen.

'It's all been a mistake,' Guido added, nodding hard.

Soldier explained, 'They played a trick on the city. They broke protocol. Apparently it's a heinous crime in Bhantan. They've been dethroned and banished. In fact they're just a couple of mischievous youngsters, full of youthful pranks. However, I'm sorry if this sounds immodest, but they tell the truth. I was attacked in great number and struck from behind. That's the simple truth of the matter.'

The whole court stared at the urchins. Marshal Crushkite, who had so far remained in the background, stepped forward.

'I don't know if these two boys are indeed princes, or whether they're gamins,' he huffed, 'but I don't see it makes a deal of difference, Your Highness. They've got eyes, is what counts. It doesn't matter who they are, they say they witnessed the attack.'

'But can we believe them?' said Humbold, silkily, still smarting under the insults from the boys. 'We've had no word from Bhantan that the White Prince and the Rose Prince have been deposed. These are probably two urchins Soldier found out in the desert. They suit his purpose very well . . .'

Captain Kaff, who was desperate to get in on the argument, was almost exploding with having to hold his tongue. He had no standing in a court full of nobles. He was a mere military man, with no title, and his warlord took precedence over him in such a gathering. Marshal Crushkite, however, was clearly on the side of Soldier, probably because Soldier was a military man too, and more probably because Crushkite hated Humbold.

The queen was looking confused. Her lips were tightening. A sure sign that she was about to make a nasty pronouncement. Suddenly the powerful if elderly and frail figure of Quidquod, Lord of the Royal Purse, spoke in that calm, considered way of his.

'It seems to me, Your Highness, that there are too many people here anxious to lay blame, and not enough of them coming forward with solutions to our problem. Our next King Magus is in the hands of the Hannacks. He is but a boy, and will not be invested with his great powers of wizardry until he is inaugurated. Thus we must expect him to be helpless in the hands of those barbarians of the north. We need to initiate a rescue. I propose that in order to redeem himself, Soldier takes a company of the Imperial Guard and wrests the King Magus from the grip of these savages.

'When Soldier returns – for I do believe he is the best person to lead this expedition – he shall be tried for his incompetence.'

Kaff could keep silent no longer. He spluttered, '*I* am the Captain of the Imperial Guard! Your Highness, I should lead any expedition.'

Again, Quidquod spoke quietly. 'Captain Kaff is a good soldier, but he is more used to drills and parades than warfare – especially guerrilla warfare. We need a man who can lead a raid. Soldier, *also* a captain, has fought many times – against the Hannacks, against the beast-people, against many of our enemies – and has proved himself a warrior of extraordinary prowess and . . .'

'And *savagery*,' broke in Humbold. 'He is a barbarian himself. Can we trust him on such an occasion? He would be more likely to see his priority as seeking revenge rather than rescuing the King Magus. Captain Kaff, on the other hand, is an officer whose loyalty is unquestioned.'

Soldier said, 'Someone betrayed us to the Hannacks.'

Humbold's eyes opened wide. 'Are you accusing Captain Kaff?'

Soldier realised he would be foolish to insist upon such a thing, with no proof to hand. In his mind he was sure that Kaff had had him followed northwards, and had alerted the Hannacks. They must have known that Soldier and IxonnoxI were going to emerge from the pass. Someone had betrayed the party to the barbarians and Soldier could think of no better choice than that of the Captain of the Imperial Guard.

'I'm saying *someone* did.'

'They shall *both* go,' said the queen, interrupting with one of her characteristic impulsive decisions. 'Soldier will command the expedition. It shall consist of a company of Imperial Guardsmen and a company of Soldier's warriors from the Eagle Pavilion of our friends and guardians, the Carthagan Army. That's my ruling. It stands.'

Both Kaff and Soldier let out an audible gasp. This was a recipe for disaster, but they dared not go against the queen's determined ruling. Her eyes were like flints at the moment. It would take very little to ignite her fury into chopping off a few heads.

She stood up, ready to leave the court. She shook her head at Soldier. '*Most* disappointed,' she repeated. 'My sister will be as displeased with you as I am, I'm sure. When – *if* – you return, Soldier, you will undergo Trial by Ordeal. You may make your choice now, if you wish. In fact, I insist upon it. Fire, water or single combat?'

'Fire, Your Highness.'

Her eyes opened a little. 'Not single combat? You are an exceptional fighter.'

'Single combat would involve a second person, a champion chosen by the court. This person might end up killed or injured through no fault of their own. The blame for the loss of the King Magus is all mine. Therefore I choose Ordeal by Fire.'

'So be it. In the meantime I shall see the ex-rulers of Bhantan in my quarters. Humbold, you will accord them all the status and privileges due to visiting royalty. I like to think that if ever *I* were deposed and seeking asylum in a foreign city . . .'

'Perish the thought, Your Highness,' murmured Humbold, his tongue between his teeth.

The ex-princes were looking up at him and smiling sweetly.

'Hhhhhummmmbold,' murmured Guido.

'Hummmmingboooooulder,' exaggerated Sando, in mellifluous tones, not to be outdone by his brother.

The chancellor gave them a look which would have killed twin bull elephants.

Kaff and Soldier left the court together. Kaff's rat was struggling, snapping at the air. The captain wrenched it from its socket and sent it scuttling away into the gardens. Then he turned on Soldier, shaking his empty socket at him.

'Why didn't you take Single Combat for your Trial by Ordeal? We could have fought again, legitimately. The court doesn't have the last say. The accused – you – has the right to influence who will be the opponent.'

'I know,' said Soldier. 'I have no grievance against you, so long as you stay away from my wife.'

'Yet you accuse me of betraying my country!' said Kaff, hotly. 'Oh, don't give me that look. You know you meant me. Let me tell you something, Soldier, which will save you a lot of grief. *I would never betray my country and my queen for the likes of you.* Do you understand me? You're not worth the loss of my honour.'

'If you say so.'

'I do say so.'

Soldier shrugged. 'This is neither here nor there, now. We've have been thrown together for this expedition. Let's not make any mistakes. I'm the leader. No successful expedition can have two leaders, so you'll obey me as if you were a corporal and I a marshal, is that clear?'

'Perfectly clear,' answered Kaff, his good hand on his sword-hilt. 'I've had my orders from the queen. You needn't remind me of them. Yours is the command, yours the responsibility if we fail. Yours be the glory if we are successful. I am merely one of the party.'

'There'll be no glory. I shall merely be correcting a mistake.'

Kaff nodded, not without satisfaction. 'That's true, of course. You're on a hiding to nothing. I'll pick out some good infantry from my guard. One hundred, eh?'

'No, not a full company. Fifty – all right-handed men.'

Kaff looked puzzled. 'But all my guardsmen fight right-handed.'

'Yes, but I want them to be *natural* right-handers. No left-handed men *taught* to fight right-handed. You understand? Oh, and a dozen expert bowmen, if you please, Captain Kaff, of either hand. I want cavalry – your best horsemen – on fast mounts.'

'As you wish. And how many Carthagans?'

'The same number.'

'Good.'

They parted, Soldier heading for the city gates and, eventually, the red pavilions camped outside the walls. Although he had not shown it in front of Kaff, he was feeling desperately low. If they went against the Hannacks with an army, which they could well do if they wished, they might as well send a rider ahead to warn the enemy. It would be a slow ponderous business, with as many bullock-carts of supplies as there were footsoldiers. On the other hand, a small force could move rapidly across country, with packhorses to supply them. They could strike swiftly and perhaps with surprise on their side. They could wrest the boy from the Hannacks before any execution could take place, whereas with a whole army on the march, signalling intent, the Hannacks would probably kill their hostages and take to the hills, where they would be impossible to winkle out.

Could it be done with such a small force though? A mere company or so of men? It had to be. There was nothing else for it. One or two men could not do the job. Ten thousand men would ensure the loss of the hostages. It had to be a hundred odd warriors, with swift horses.

Soldier went straight to his own pavilion, the Eagles.

'Lieutenant Velion,' he called to a woman officer, who was supervising some short-sword training in the arena outside the tent area. 'I want a volunteer to help me pick fifty warriors for a suicide mission.'

'I'm your man,' she grinned. 'Just let me dismiss this lot.'

She barked an order at the stocky men and taller lean women who were hacking away at wooden warriors inside the arena. They stopped hacking and trailed away to the river's edge to wash away the dust and sweat from their grimy bodies. Then Velion came to join Soldier, grasping him by his extended fist and gripping it in greeting.

'How is it?' she asked. 'Where are we going?'

They had known each other since they had both been mere foot-warriors in the same pavilion. Their friendship had developed from the time when Soldier had joined the pavilion as a desperate measure to get some status for himself in a land where he was unknown. Not only had he been a mystery to everyone else, with his unique blue eyes and lack of history, but also to himself. He had been a man searching for an identity still undiscovered, and Velion had taken him to her heart.

There was no romantic connection between the two of them. They were comrades-in-arms, as close as two men or women might be. In war they watched each other's backs. In times of peace they hunted together, indulged in sport, trained together. Soldier was, of course, a married man. Velion enjoyed sexual liaisons with both men and women: mostly the latter. They trusted each other to the hilts of their swords.

'Against the Hannacks,' explained Soldier. 'I fouled my line. I had the new King Magus in my charge and he was wrested from me. We've got to get him back. I'll understand if you don't want to come. It was my mistake. Men have already died because I wasn't vigilant enough.'

'As if none of us never makes a mistake. I'm with you.'

'Good. I want riders – fast riders. All natural left-handers. Oh, and a dozen archers. Those who can get thirty arrows in the air in a minute or under. And ten warriors from that region of Carthaga – What's it called? Jundra? – those ambidextrous fighters, that go into battle with two swords, one in each hand, and use them like shears.'

Velion nodded. 'Right. Now, these left-handers . . . ?'

Soldier explained what he wanted them for. She nodded, 'You never cease to amaze me with your ideas,' she said.

They called up the troops and went along the line with a sergeant-at-arms. Soldier paired them off with each other and told them to practice their sword-work on each other. He knew what he was looking for: a slight awkwardness in the use of arms. When he saw it he called the man or woman forth and asked one question.

'Are you naturally left-handed?'

If the answer was yes, which invariably it was, he sent that warrior aside, to Lieutenant Velion. Soldier knew that in most – if not all – armies, left-handers are taught to fight right-handed. For a soldier to fight successfully in formation a spear and sword needed to be worn and used on one side only, otherwise a warrior would tangle with his neighbour. However, if the whole contingent was left-handed, there was no reason why that group should not favour their left side for weaponry.

When they had enough warriors, Soldier told Velion to get them accustomed to using their weapons left-handed.

'Where are you going?' she asked.

'To see my wife,' Soldier said.

Layana, back in the Green Tower, heard Soldier ask Ofao quietly if his mistress was at home. He actually wanted to know if she was in her right mind.

'My mistress is well, master,' came back Ofao's voice. 'She awaits you in the White Room.'

A moment later Soldier's form was in the doorway, tall, lean, with tangled dark hair hanging to his shoulders.

'My husband!' she said, throwing herself into his arms.

He kissed her face a hundred times without stopping for breath. Then he hugged her so close it took the breath from her lungs.

'Oh – oh – I don't know what I would have done if you were ill,' he murmured into her ear. 'I need you so much at the moment.'

'Just at the moment?' she teased.

'For ever and aye,' he said, pushing her back so that he

could see her more clearly. 'Your hair smells so – what is it? Rosemary? Jasmine?'

She laughed. 'You never were very good with your scents and perfumes. It's musk oil.'

'Of course it is. How are you? You look fine. How beautiful you look these days. Has Kaff been sniffing around here? I ought to kill the dog. Did you send him away?'

'No, he's very good company – for me. I know you hate him, but he never tries anything, you know, and I find his conversation interesting and informative . . .'

Soldier raised his eyebrows. 'You do? I know a different Kaff.'

'The same. You just don't get the best out of him. You two do nothing but posture like fighting cocks and threaten each other. How can you see what is best in you both? He hates you too, of course, for which I censure him, for you are my beloved husband, and no man who draws a breath do I love more dearly, more devotedly, more passionately.'

He hugged her again. 'Oh, how I've missed you.'

'Show me then,' she said, loosening her belt.

When they had finished making love, Ofao was summoned with some smoky tea, which they drank slowly.

Soldier was lying on the couch with Layana nestled against him.

'I've lost the King Magus. I have to get him back.'

'I heard,' she said, tensing against the silken pillow. 'It will be very dangerous. Please take care and return to me. I – I wish I could come with you, but . . .'

But her madness would not allow it.

'I know. I know. Even if I manage the expedition successfully, the queen has ordered Ordeal by Fire.'

Now Layana sat bolt upright.

'What?'

'My punishment for losing the boy. It's only fair.'

'It's *monstrous*! My husband? Ordeal by Fire? I shall speak to my sister. I shall demand . . .'

'Nothing,' he interrupted her, soothingly. 'I have to do this.'

'That's ridiculous. How – how will you do it?'

'Grasp a red-hot iron. I could choose to walk on coals, but my eyes water whenever I think of it. My soles are so tender. I must have been a prince in my former life. Anything less than soft wool against them makes me grit my teeth. I shall grasp the poker with both hands, hold it for the requisite minute, then you shall apply the balm to my poor blistered skin and cool it with your tears.'

'I shall not weep for you,' Layana said, firmly. 'I'm not that kind of woman and you know it, but I shall be very angry with my sister. Oh, my dear, it will put your hands out of action for such a long time afterwards. Men who hate you will challenge you to duels, and I know you – you won't be able to refuse them.'

He snorted. 'Won't I? Just watch me. Do you take me for a fool? When I'm better, though,' his eyes narrowed, 'then I shall go and challenge *them*, and see who's the coward and who isn't.'

He stroked her hair while they both stared out of the window, at the going down of the sun in a crimson foam.

Chapter Five

Happily for Soldier, Layana stayed well until it was time for him to leave. Velion came for the captain at dawn, leading the left-handed Carthagans. Layana whispered in the lieutenant's ear, 'Look after my man for me — you know what he's like — impulsive, rash even at times, when it comes to his own safety.'

'Actually,' replied Velion, in the same low tones, 'he's surprising. His actions may seem spontaneous to the rest of us, but he thinks very quickly. But I shall watch his back for you. He's my good friend. I would do so anyway.'

'Thank you.'

The raven came back from a long flight and learned that Soldier was leading the expedition.

'What are you thinking of?' cried the raven, landing on the rump of Soldier's mount. 'Are you mad? The Hannacks are invincible in their own country. You'll be cut to pieces.'

'I made a mistake. I have to correct that.'

'I thought — listen — surely the queen was angry with you? Did she not put you aside in favour of Kaff? It doesn't make sense. Surely Kaff persuaded her that you were unfit for command? Didn't he put *himself* forward as the best commander of such a mission?'

The raven seemed amazed that the queen had retained Soldier.

'I know *you* don't think a lot of my prowess, raven, but there are others who do – the queen is among them, thank the gods.'

'Don't thank the gods yet,' cried the raven, flying away. 'You'll be able to do it in person soon, once the Hannacks kill you.'

Captain Kaff was at the gates with his contingent of the Imperial Guard. In his right wrist-socket was the claw of an eagle. Its tendons and sinews had been fused to his own, by a physician-magician, and so strongly was it now his own that he could wield a weapon: a dagger or a short sword. The talons were huge and vicious-looking, a weapon in themselves. Riding alongside Soldier, the Captain of the Imperial Guard confessed, 'I almost think you did me a favour when you cut off my hand – this claw is far superior.'

'I'm glad for you,' said Soldier, 'but you can't expect me to believe you hold no grudge against me.'

'Ah, as to that, there is more than one score to settle.'

'I thought as much. However, you will remember I am in command here. I will ask advice but will make my own decisions. I do not believe in committees. My word is law. Any refusal will be regarded as mutiny and the culprit will be hanged on the spot, private soldier or captain. Am I understood?'

'Perfectly,' replied Kaff, with composure, 'I would expect and demand the same, were I in command.'

Soldier nodded curtly. 'Thank the gods you are a military man and not a wet fish like that Humbold. I am sure if he were you we should be struggling all the way, with revenge as the only motive. Instead, we stand some chance of success on this mission. I thank you for that, at least.'

On the third day out they camped at noon just below a ridge. Soldier went up to the spine to view the country ahead and to meditate. His thoughts were on his eternal problem first: who was he and why was he in a strange land? He knew – or had the feeling – that there was at least one other from his home world also here. Perhaps there were more? Was that person also ignorant of their identity, as Soldier was? Had they also forgotten their origins? Was there a purpose to the two of them being here? Were they seeking each other out, or avoiding one another? So many questions, and very few answers.

Soldier was trying to make himself believe he did not care about his origins or his identity. He had made himself a life on this earth, and if there was another one, why, it could stew in its own juices. But such resolutions only worked part of the time. He was ashamed of the fact that he sometimes lied to Layana. His proclamation was that she was the only woman he loved: had ever loved. It was true that Soldier loved his wife with all his heart, but that other person, the one from the world he could not remember, had loved someone too.

She, this unknown woman, was lodged in a remote corner of his being, still a powerful presence. There was only a hazy image which accompanied this feeling: auburn hair sweeping away from a flawlessly pale brow; a slim figure striding along the banks of a burn; hazel-green eyes that bore into his own. But there were mists and shimmering waves of light that distorted these images, took them away from him just as he was on the point of recognising them.

And there was still more unidentified hate in his heart than was good for one man. Soldier had brought this hate, this rage, this bitterness with him from that other place. Sometimes it flowered, blood-red, when he was at his most passionate, in bed, in battle. Those who had seen him slaughter the Dog-man, Vau, knew of this vehemence, and were wary of it, not wishing to witness its blooming again. Some terrible wrong had been perpetrated on Soldier, in that other world, and there were those in this world who were paying for it. They were not innocent victims, but they were not guilty of the crime for which they were being punished. At such times Soldier's brain exploded into a red cloud of revenge, and when he came out of it he hardly remembered his own actions.

'Why can't I just be satisfied with this life,' he muttered to himself, grabbing a handful of soil and throwing it into the wind. 'I have a wife, a position, respect – all from nothing. I came here in rags and dented armour and now I am a captain, the husband of a princess, and famous throughout the region for my deeds. I'm the mother of a dragon, the adopted father of a wizard – the next King Magus no less – and most men envy me. Why can't I just be happy with that, and let all those other thoughts go? They may be false anyway. Perhaps I was born here, some quirk of nature with blue eyes.'

He could not convince himself either way, and so knew he was bound to continue in that same tense netherworld which he alone occupied.

Soldier tried to relax. He looked down on the scene below. It was a surprisingly fertile valley, extending into a plain, which lay beneath the far side of the escarpment. Not far away was a farmhouse. The farmer, a big man in the near distance, was at his plough. Two great farm horses followed his commands, as he turned a straight furrow. A thick, worn leather strap went over the right shoulder of the farmer and down under his left armpit, connecting him to his plough. In his left hand were the reins, in his right the plough handle. Soldier was impressed by the man's demeanour – his carriage and motion – and went down to speak. In some way he envied the man his peaceful occupation.

'Sir,' he said, 'you handle that implement with great skill.'

The farmer paused in his work. Clearly Soldier had broken into some sort of reverie. The farmer had been rapt in thought in his peaceful world on the frontiers of nature, where man's carving of the world's surface met the rawness of the wilderness. He lifted his hat and wiped his brow.

'Thank you,' he said. 'I have been at it from a boy. It would be more surprising if I lacked the talent.'

The rich, brown furrows of the ploughed fields stretched out ahead of the two men as they both contemplated the work. The earth had been neatly combed. One or two white chalk rocks stood blindingly in the sunlight. A few scattered flints lay over all, glinting where the nodule had been broken to expose the shining blackness. Birds were flocking in: gulls and rooks, mostly, looking for the food turned over by the ploughshare. In the far distance a fox was slinking around the edge, working his way towards a ditch down which he eventually glided like a red phantom, disappearing from sight once again.

'You seemed lost in thought,' said Soldier, 'when I came upon you?'

'I am a religious man,' replied the farmer, quietly. 'That is, I do not pray to the gods overmuch, but I listen to the voice of the natural world around me. I have my ear to the beating of its heart. I feel the spirit of the land mingling with my own spirit. It's a *good* feeling.'

'I can acknowledge that it would be hard to be here in these tranquil surroundings and not be a philosopher of some kind. What do you think of war and warriors? You see me? I am a commander. I take lives into battle and return sometimes empty-handed. Do you despise such men and women as me, who seek glory, rather than listening to the song of the earth?'

The farmer thought hard about this for a few moments.

'I don't *despise* you, for I don't know you, or what drives you to seek this glory. I can only say I have no interest in such things. It depends on which inner voice you've been taught to listen to. In all of us there is the voice which tells us to be satisfied with the world as it is, to borrow it for a time to grow our food. There is another voice which tells us to go adventuring, seek beyond the horizons, *change* the world, try to own it. If you follow the second voice you will no doubt run into conflict.'

'I am on my way to kill men, or be killed,' said Soldier. 'I saw you and envied you. I am jealous of the way in which you meld with the landscape, while I stand out like an awkward projection in my body armour and bristling with weapons. I wished I could be you.'

'I envy you for the things you will see,' replied the big farmer, 'and your experiences in new countries, in new climes, but you have a huge price to pay for those amazing encounters. I could not soak my soul in the blood of others to reach such things, however marvellous they be.'

The farmer took a skin of water from his plough handle and offered it to Soldier. Both men drank deeply. The farmer wiped his mouth with the back of his hand, before he made a confession.

'Once upon a time,' he said, 'I thought I could change the world. I sought to control things around me too. Listen: I was a young man, wandering the seashore, when I heard the waves moving the pebbles on the beach – hundreds and thousands of them – each with their own note, striking others with different notes, being of a variety of sizes and types of stone.

'I thought to myself, "Here is the chance to create a wonderful symphony of nature. I went to work. I spent a whole year arranging the pebbles behind a wall of sand, into types and size so that they would give out their notes in some sort of musical order. I wished to create a recognisable melody from their shuffling, a song or a tune which would impress other men with the music of sea and stone.'

Here the farmer sighed and looked to the horizon.

'Of course, I did not reckon with the wildness of my player. I had the instrument, all set up, ready to make the right sounds in the right places, but the ocean would not obey me. When I removed the barrier the waves came in at different heights, different strengths, and even changed their direction by the day, the hour, the minute. What resulted was the usual natural cacophony produced by the elements.'

Soldier was sympathetic. 'I'm sorry for that. I admire the power of your ideas, even if the execution proved impossible.'

'But I did not learn!' cried the farmer, throwing his arms into the air. 'I did the same thing again. I heard the dawn chorus one morning. How beautiful, I thought, but how much *better* it could be. This time I believed I *could* control things, since I was dealing with live creatures, and not the random effects created by storms and calms, the unpredictability of the weather. I chose to organise the birds into separate groups, tried to teach them proper melodies – the song thrushes here, the warblers there, the deep-throated geese and others behind – but alas, they grew bored, and after a very short time returned to the freeness of nature. They needed that to find their own flow, the joy, the individual creativity.

'Since then I have never interfered with the tunes of the earth. Would I make the wind sing to my lesser compositions? No, I am happy to accept what the world has to offer, take its largesse with thanks, and remain under its direction.'

The two men shook hands and Soldier went back to the ridge. When he looked down again, from its crest, the farmer was back at his plough. Soldier thought, 'How could such a man fail to be a poet, even if he never wrote a word on paper? A man who caressed the body of the world? A man locked to the earth as tight as any tree?'

The march continued towards Da-tichett, the home of the Hannacks. Da-tichett was separated from Falyum and Guthrum by two thick ranges of mountains, one a spur of the other. There were hidden passes to find and high saddles to cross. Guthrum had never ruled Da-tichett for very long. There had been periods in history when the Guthrum Empire had included the home of the Hannacks, but it was too remote, too wild and unruly to hold on to without a full occupying army. It could not be managed in the usual way, with governors and nominal troops, for the Hannacks were a bone-headed nation who thought with their muscles, not with their brains. They murdered each other without compunction, so there was not a lot of respect for authority, even though it was backed by the threat of force. They enjoyed force. They enjoyed pitting themselves against it – and were too unthinking to be afraid.

Hannacks themselves said that if you ever found a library in Da-tichett, the last Hannack would have already died.

The raven came to visit Soldier as he crossed the mountains.

'There's still time to turn back. Please reconsider. Your force is too small. You'll be chewed up by the barbarians. You're a fool, Soldier. Send Kaff in first. Let him take the brunt.'

'Go away,' muttered Soldier. 'Someone will hear you.'

'Oh, I give up.'

The raven took to the air.

The passes were not guarded. Hannacks were sure they would never be invaded again, since the last time they had been overrun they massacred the occupying garrisons to a soul, burned them and everything else the invaders had brought with them, and put the charred human remains on poles up on the summer snowline of the mountains.

These grisly objects were still on show now — charcoal figures of men and women stark against the white snow. They gaped with black mouths. They stared with black eyes. Their thin, crisp limbs snapped like twigs when touched. They moaned in the wind. Agents from a world of fire, they were silent reminders of the ghastly indifference Hannacks showed captives and their families.

The troops passed them as they went up and over into a country which was mostly bare of good farmland. It was easy to see, when looking at the sparse soil cover, why the Hannacks were raiders and lived by plundering their neighbours.

Soldier felt the fear drift through his column as they passed the blackened charcoal objects that had once been arms, legs, chest cages, skulls. It was a grim sight.

Hannacks were troglodytes. Their cave dwellings dotted the cliff faces which lay down below the heights. They had carved them out of sandstone and limestone. Whitewashed chimneys stuck out at all angles, from the cliff, or the plateau above. In front of the caves were the corrals where they kept their wild-looking ponies. Old fires, most of them spent, dotted the ground like burst black blisters. A filthy river ran through the countryside, full of effluence from the ponies and the people who lived there. Drinking water was collected in huge skins stretched over racks, making giant hide bowls. Even so, children were bathing in these bowls, swimming and splashing around, their excited squeals plain to hear from the heights above.

Soldier had a conference with his officers.

'What do you think?' he asked Velion. 'Where will they keep their prisoners?'

'In one of the big caves?' she said.

Kaff said, 'Did you see that hut without any windows, down by the second corral? My guess is that they're in there. Why have a hut without windows? You can't store grain or perishable goods in such a place: you need the free flow of air for that. Perhaps they have stock in there, but I doubt it – it's too low and awkward to keep anything but sheep or goats, and the Hannacks are not sheep farmers.'

Soldier pointed at Kaff, impressed. 'If they are in there, they're having to squat down low, because the ceiling is not more than a metre off the ground.'

'It's a way of demoralising your captives,' agreed Velion. 'Keep them crouched down in the dark.'

Kaff added, 'They'll be cramped. We can't expect them to run if we get them out. That means we can't sneak them out in the dark hours. We'll need the use of the horses.'

'We'll double up on the horses,' agreed Soldier. 'You're right. The best way would have been to try to creep down and let them out. That would have been quite risky, however. Hannacks are notoriously deaf, having those small ears, but their eyesight makes up for it. So here's the plan. Full-frontal attack. Hannacks, as you all know, are swift to retaliate to any threat. So we must be quick and clean.'

Velion nodded. Kaff nodded. All were agreed.

The two sets of cavalry were placed appropriately: the right-handers on the right, the left-handers on the left. Velion led her Carthagans, Kaff his Imperial Guardsmen. In the centre of the column was the Jundra detachment, mostly ambidextrous women, who used their swords like scissors. The idea was to sweep down, split the column down the middle and swallow the hut. Get the prisoners out, put them up behind the riders from Jundra, and ride back up the slopes to the high passes.

'I want the archers up here, ready to cover our retreat,' said Soldier. 'Each archer will stick sixty arrows in the sand in front of them, ready to pluck up and fire at will. Pick off the leaders or their horses, in that way they will fall in front of the riders behind and hamper them. Understood?'

The bowmen and bow-women nodded their heads, then set up their firing zone on a shelf above the slopes.

'Simple,' said Soldier. 'Let's go.'

He gave the command to charge. They flowed down the hillside. Almost immediately a horn sounded from somewhere and Hannacks ran out of the caves, or if already outside, dropped what they were doing. Instead of going for their ponies, as expected, they ran to defend their territory on foot. As the column approached the area, the air suddenly became alive with spears, thrown by the Hannacks.

Soldier could see the children in their makeshift swimming pools, watching the action with wide eyes. Hannack women, who did not fight, were gathering precious pots and running for the caves. The horsemen drove into the confused Hannacks, the flanks bristling with swords, the head of the column windmilling blades. There was no way in. Lefthanders, righthanders, both-handers — the horsemen were protected on all sides.

The invading force surrounded the low hut. Soldier leaped from his saddle, sprang to the door, which he found unlocked. Warning bells jangled in his ears. There was a strong smell of pigs coming from the hut. Indeed the squealing began the moment he opened the door. Hogs rushed out into the sunlight, running between the legs of the horses, causing panic. They tumbled on into the Hannacks, bowling some of them over. These were the lucky ones. Their comrades were being hacked down by the invading cavalry. Soldier saw Kaff reach out with his eagle's claw and tear a Hannack's face open to the bone. Velion was laying about her with her sword, cutting down on shoulder and neck. It was not all going one way. Some invaders' saddles were already empty, the horses being led away as prizes by Hannack women.

The swine ran through the slaughter, and back again, terrified and confused, squealing as if it were they who were being murdered.

'Oh, gods,' cried Soldier. 'A pigsty!'

Just when despair was settling on his soul, the raven landed on his shoulder and yelled into his ear.

'The totems! They're at the totems.'

Soldier looked up towards a mound at the far end of the troglodytes' village. Carved standing-stones – tall monoliths – stood in a circle. These had been hidden by the base of a ridge which ran out as a spur into the area in front of the caves.

Soldier remounted. 'Follow me,' he yelled over the hubbub. 'To the stones!'

He wheeled his horse and was followed by Kaff, then Velion,

as he led the column towards the standing-stones. Soldier could see the prisoners now, strapped to the bases of the totems. They were naked and looked wretched. It did not take a great deal of manoeuvring to ride through the stones and cut the cords. Uthellen was lifted up behind Velion. IxonnoxI went behind Kaff. And Spagg – Spagg? He found the nearest rider and leapt very agilely for a man of his age, up onto the rump of that warrior's horse.

'Away! Away!' cried Soldier, heading for the slopes which led to the high passes.

The Hannacks were on their ponies now, and in pursuit.

Soldier stayed at the rear. He and his riders kept turning and meeting the Hannacks head on, allowing the front of the column to climb to safety. Soldier's archers were effective now. They were picking off the leaders of the Hannacks, as instructed, whose bodies fell under the hooves of the ponies behind, sometimes causing the mounts to stumble and fall. The pass was reached. Those carrying the prisoners continued on, through the narrow rock walls, leaving other troops to block the way.

It was easily defended. Once they were all through the gap two or three warriors could defend it against thousands. Some of the archers came down from above and fired into the mass of furious Hannacks who were trying to force a passage. Bodies began to pile up on the ledge path, further blocking the efforts of the Hannacks to break through. The rest of the archers stayed high, raining arrows down on the mass of pursuers, until finally they gave up, retreated, fell back down the slopes.

Soldier knew his position was only temporarily tenable. The Hannacks would know of other ways around the heights and would be setting out to use them now. If the column stayed where it was they would be surrounded before nightfall and there would be no way out, no way back. The Guthrumites and Carthagans had to move soon.

Kaff said, 'Leave some of the archers behind, to keep the pass, while the rest of us escape.'

To the Captain of the Imperial Guard, his troops were expendable. The mission was all important, lives were secondary. Marshal Crushkite would have approved of such tactics. So would the queen. Even Jakanda, Warlord of the Carthagans, would have nodded in assent.

But Soldier could not leave men and women behind, to certain death.

'We leave now,' he said. 'All of us. We may have a running fight on our hands, but I think we have a chance.'

Kaff looked about to argue, but finally remained silent. Perhaps he remembered his promise that Soldier's command should be respected completely. Whatever the reason, he barked an order and his archers took to their mounts, as did the Carthagans moments later. The whole column then set off through the mountains. The Hannacks had not realised yet that the pass was undefended, but they would soon guess.

The column worked steadily through the mountain passes, aware that the Hannacks would not be far behind. Once they reached the border of Guthrum, they paused by a river, where they refreshed themselves, thirsty almost beyond reason. The prisoners were given clothes, the horses were rested, Soldier called his officers to his side.

'Do we run, or do we stand and fight?'

Kaff grunted. 'Yours is the decision.'

'The odds are about the same. If we stand and fight we'll be whittled down until we're overrun. If we flee, we'll be cut down from the rear, as the Hannacks overtake us. My own feelings are that I'd rather be on the move. There's something demoralising about defending a stationary site, something about the inevitability of being overwhelmed by a more numerous enemy. At least while one is moving the landscape changes, the odds lengthen, and one is *doing* something.'

'I agree,' said Kaff.

'And I,' replied Velion.

So began a running battle, almost to the gates of Zamerkand. Soldier's 'porcupine', as the column came to be known, moved across the landscape bristling with weapons on all sides. From within the ranks of the left and right-handers, and rear and front scissor-warriors, the archers fired out on the enemy as they attacked. Soldier lost more Imperial Guardsmen, more Carthagan warriors, on that desperate retreat across the wastelands. The gods only knew how many Hannacks went down, for they attacked regardless of the column's strength or position.

For every guardsman, every warrior, that was lost, Soldier felt responsible. It was he who had lost the new King Magus in the first place and so his was the blame for the deaths. However, finding Spagg alive was somewhat surprising for him. Seeds of suspicion entered Soldier's mind. Once they were back inside the gates of Zamerkand, Soldier decided to confront the hand-seller with his suspicions.

Chapter Six

'I've been thinking about the attack at the end of the pass, and the way the Hannacks were waiting for the Bhantan contingent and my party,' said Soldier to Kaff as they walked just inside the curtain wall of the city. 'I think they knew we were carrying the King Magus designate. I think they knew our movements and were ready to attack the moment we came out of that pass.'

Captain Kaff's head jerked backwards and his eyes narrowed to yellow-brown slits. 'Are you accusing me of being a traitor again?' he hissed.

Soldier frowned. 'No, not you – Spagg. I believe the hand-seller betrayed us to the Hannacks.'

Kaff cooled immediately. He shrugged. 'What would Spagg get out of it?'

'His brother, a man called Jugg, owns a farm up-country from Zamerkand, out of reach of the protection of the Carthagans. I understand it's often attacked by raiders, and he has to buy Amekni slaves from Uan Muhuggiag slave traders, to defend the place. Spagg might have struck a bargain with the Hannacks. If they agreed to leave his brother's farm alone, he would deliver the witchboy into their hands.'

But why? What would the Hannacks want with a witchboy, a youth destined to be the next King Magus? Not much of it made sense, and Soldier was determined to find out more.

'I'll have him arrested and tortured,' said Kaff, flexing his eagle-claw hand. 'We'll soon sizzle the truth out of him. Once we burn an eye out with a red-hot iron it's surprising how quickly the truth follows it. Very painful, losing an eye to a branding iron. If he doesn't confess quickly, we'll crush his testicles with stones. Why, I remember one old man we had. Wouldn't talk. Actually, he *couldn't* talk, I suppose, after we cut out his tongue and fed it to the lizards. We tried everything . . .'

Kaff was lost in some reverie of his own, staring into the middle distance, recalling fondly those tortures he had perpetrated of old.

'I'd like to interview him first, if you wouldn't mind.'

The Captain of the Imperial Guard shrugged his shoulders.

'Be my guest. Interview him. But I guarantee you won't get anywhere without the proper equipment.'

'Nevertheless.'

Spagg was sent for. He arrived in a grumpy mood.

'What's goin' on? I want to get back to my stall and start earnin' some money. I'm down to my last spinza. Hurry up, then. What is it?'

Soldier said, coldly, 'You'll be lucky if you ever see your stall again, hand-seller.'

'What?'

'You betrayed us,' fumed Soldier, convinced of Spagg's guilt now that he had him in his eye. The hand-seller's demeanour, everything about him screamed betrayal to Soldier. 'You set it up with the Hannacks – admit it. That ambush had inside knowledge behind it. Confess now, or later in the torture chamber.'

Kaff, sitting in the corner of the darkened guardroom, ran his talons along the bench, setting Spagg's teeth on edge with the scratching sound. Spagg stared at Kaff, then back at Soldier. He began to get scared now, knowing he was in serious trouble.

'You accusin' me of treachery?' he cried, trying to sound as indignant as possible. 'Is that what you're doin'?'

'Right first time,' murmured Kaff. 'Listen!'

Spagg went quiet and listened, but since he could hear nothing but the sound of carts rumbling by the windows, he said, 'What?'

'Can you hear the coals being piled on the braziers, down in the dungeons?' said Kaff, smiling. '*I* can. They're preparing for a long session down there. Not much sleep tonight, for the Lord of Thieftakers' minions, eh? They won't be pleased. They were looking forward to a night at the tavern, a few jugs of ale and a nice partridge pie.'

Spagg started sweating. He appealed to Soldier. 'Look, you an' me have bin through a lot together. I wouldn't ever betray you. Why was I tied to them standin'-stones? Answer me that. I was in the same fix as the boy and his mother. You can't do this. If he takes me down to the dungeon, he'll make me say I did it, but that won't be a confession, 'cause I didn't do it. People'll say anythin' if you give 'em enough pain. You get to a point where you'd rather die.'

This was true enough, and Soldier was reluctant to let Kaff have his way with Spagg, but betrayal was a heinous crime in his eyes. Cowardice in the face of the enemy; murder of one sort or another; theft of property; rape and pillage: all these things were lesser crimes, he felt, than that of betraying one's friends and comrades.

'You refuse to confess?' he said, not looking at Spagg.

'I didn't do it. I didn't. That's flat.'

'All right,' muttered Soldier to Kaff. 'You can have him.'

Spagg gripped the arms of the chair he was sitting in. His face went white with terror. He locked his legs around those of the chair, as if he could anchor himself to the spot.

'I ain't goin',' he yelled. 'I din't do no wrong. Help, ho, murder! Don't do it to me,' he broke down, sobbing. 'Once they get me down there I'll never come out again.'

'You should have thought of that before,' snapped Soldier, angry with himself as much as Spagg. 'It's too late.'

Guards were called in. They dragged Spagg, chair and all, to some stone steps leading down below the guardhouse. Kaff followed. Under the floor the city was wormholed with tunnels. One of these tunnels led to the torture chamber, where heavy-set men played with ugly iron toys. Soldier expected Spagg to tell the truth before they ever reached the torture chamber.

Spagg's desperate struggles, his fading screams, were pitiful to hear. Soldier winced and hoped that the hand-seller would see fit to confess quickly. He was convinced that Spagg was guilty. There could be no one else. The evidence – such as it was – all pointed to a member of the party. Soldier hadn't done it. Uthellen certainly wouldn't give up her son to Hannacks, herself along with him. That left the Bhantan guard, who had no interest in the matter. They had been massacred. It had to be Spagg. Probably he had signalled them with a mirror. There was no other way the Hannacks could have been on them so swiftly.

'It wasn't the hand-seller.'

The voice had come from the doorway to the guardhouse. Soldier was looking directly into the light. All he could see was a silhouette, but he knew the voice. It was that of IxonnoxI.

'What's that?'

'The hand-seller did not betray us.'

'Who then?'

'It was the raven.'

Soldier was stunned by this reply. Of course, the raven too had been following them on the wing. There was no way of knowing whether the bird was with them, or not, since it melded into the countryside, into the natural surroundings. It could have gone on high and signalled the Hannacks when the caravan was coming.

The raven? But why?

'It was promised freedom.'

Soldier had not even asked the question, except in his mind, but it had received a reply.

'What freedom? It already has freedom.'

'The boy inside wants to get out. My guess is that a wizard promised the raven he would change him back into a human again, if he betrayed me to the Hannacks. You realise you arrived just in time. They were going to kill us that night – all of us – Spagg included. They had been ordered to.'

'I thought you were to be ransomed.'

'No, I was to be murdered.'

Soldier said, 'That doesn't make sense.'

'It does when you realise that my father, OmmullummO, is still alive, somewhere, and wishes to kill me. He seeks to be the next King Magus. He feels he deserves to be. He's waited four hundred years for his brother HoulluoH to die, so that he can take over. For some reason he can't move freely through the world, but he does send his messengers. The bird was approached and eventually gave his assent to betray you.'

'Why not approach me – why didn't *I* get any messengers?'

'You are an unknown quantity. You're an outlander, an unfamiliar element. Better to work with known clay.'

'The Hannacks would have received a visitor? An envoy from this hidden wizard, your father?'

'Oh, yes. To them he would be a herald from one of their despicable deities. He probably appeared out of the night as a man of straw, or a wild beast walking on its hind legs, talking their language, whispering blood and death into their tiny ears . . .'

IxonnoxI was interrupted by a horrible screech from somewhere below the guardhouse.

'Gods and demons!' cried Soldier. 'Spagg.'

He moved quickly, grabbing a candle and leaping down the stone stairs, taking them in threes and fours. Once at the bottom he followed the passage, the candle flame wavering in the draught. Finally, he came to a chamber in which there were figures highlighted by bright fires. It was very hot in the chamber. Someone was at the bellows, causing the coals to flare and glow red. Another had on a thick mitten made of sackcloth, from which smoke was curling, even though the wearer had the iron by the cooler end. The smell of singed flesh was rank in the air.

'Stop!' cried Soldier. 'The man is innocent!'

The torturer, a small thickset man with pale-brown eyes, looked up. He was still holding the curled iron which glowed white at the tip. On his face was an expression which read, 'So what?'

Innocence, guilt, these were not the motives behind the

excellent work put in by most competent torturers. Getting a confession was what counted. A child playing kick-ball was not concerned about *how* the ball ended up in the goal, or whether the opposition was doing their level best to prevent that happening. It was the result which counted. So the subject was innocent. So what? All the more credit if one scored a goal.

'Release that man. Where's Captain Kaff? I thought he was down here too.'

'Gone to visit the palace,' said the torturer, still hovering over Spagg's face with the iron.

'Palace? Which palace?'

'The Palace of Wildflowers. The Princess Layana.'

Soldier looked wildly back down the tunnel. He had not yet been home himself.

'Does one of these lead to the Palace of Wildflowers?'

'Near enough,' sniggered the torturer. 'Now, Captain, if you'll excuse me. I've got work to do. I'm afraid only the officer who ordered the work can stop it. You'll have to find Captain Kaff first.'

Soldier drew his sword. 'I promise you, torturer, that if you do not release that man this instant, you'll be looking at your own intestines draped over your boots.'

The torturer saw he meant it. It grieved him sorely, but he used a rusty key to release Spagg from his manacles. Spagg had a dark hole in the centre of his forehead, not very deep, but it was still smoking. He immediately dunked his head in a nearby trough of water. Then he followed Soldier out of the torture chamber, not being able to resist a parthian shot over his shoulder at the torturer.

'When you're up for hangin', I'm goin' to ask to cut off your hands before they put the rope around your neck.'

'Next time you come in here . . .' the torturer tried a riposte, but Spagg blanked out the words with a loud and echoing fart, a sound he seemed to be able to produce at will.

The two men walked the passageway in silence. Spagg was near to exhaustion, mentally and physically. Soldier was thinking of the way Kaff had manoeuvred it so that it was he who called on Layana first, while her husband was left wanting. Would she see through that? Or would she think that her husband was tardy and put her second? A woman likes to be first with her man in all things. She likes to be thought of as best. Soldier had been outfoxed by a long campaigner in the stakes for Layana's good favour. Things were not looking good.

'I shouldn't have to compete for the affections of my own wife,' he agonised.

But what choice had he? He could not have let Spagg die under the torturer's irons.

When the two men were in daylight again, Soldier said, 'You should go home and rest.'

'I will, I will,' said Spagg, drained and strangely dampened. Soldier had expected the hand-seller to be furious with him, but there were no angry words. 'I gotta get some sleep. I'm so tired.'

Soldier went immediately to the Palace of Wildflowers. He was met at the door by Ofao, who took his breastplate, propping it up in the corner of the hallway. The slave from Amekni then produced a bowl of scented water for Soldier to wash his hands and face in; a comb and a brush for his hair; a clean singlet. He washed his feet in the remainder of the water and put on fresh sandals. By the time he was ready to see his wife, he was looking refreshed, but worried. Drissila gave him a disapproving look as he entered the room.

'Captain Kaff has been here,' she whispered. 'He came first.'

'I know,' muttered Soldier.

Layana was sitting on a sofa, looking towards the window. When she saw Soldier she jumped to her feet and threw her arms around his neck.

'You're alive and unwounded,' she said. 'How well you look, my husband. I have missed you so much.'

No recriminations. Relief flooded through him. He still felt guilty, though.

'I would have come sooner, my love, but a man was about to die – an innocent man – and I had to prevent it.'

She looked into his eyes. 'You don't have to explain to me.'

'But I do. I know Kaff was here before me.'

'Of course he was. You were the commander of the expedition. You had many more responsibilities than he did. Of course you had to settle your men, make reports, do all the things that a commander has to do before he can go home to his wife. I understand that. If you had run home to me without finishing your duties, I should have been ashamed of you. As it is, I'm bursting with pride. You come home victorious, a conqueror.'

'I have merely righted a mistake I myself made.'

'Everyone makes mistakes. I've known generals who committed troops to impossible battles and came home thousands of men short with nothing to show for it. I've known judges who've mistakenly executed innocents by the handful. Their statues stand in squares today. They are still revered. If you have great responsibility, you will make errors from time to time. It's how you deal with those mistakes which is important. The boy is here? And his mother?'

'I have them both, safe and sound.'

'There — there you have it. You lost them; but it was you who took the risk and found them again. Not someone else, correcting your mistakes. You. You did it.'

'I lost some good warriors. Some good men and women.'

'They were *warriors*. It's their work. You didn't sacrifice them, did you? You will see their wives and mothers, their husbands and families? You will offer your sincere condolences. There is no compunction to join the army. They had a job to do and they did it. We lose warriors out patrolling the borders every day. Hardly a thought is given to them. They would not blame you for their deaths.'

'No, I don't suppose they would — but I *feel* for them.'

'So you should. No one is saying you shouldn't.'

Soldier changed the subject.

'When did Kaff leave?'

'Just a few moments ago.'

She looked with smouldering eyes at the door, through which Kaff must have exited a short while before.

'I have nothing but contempt for a second-in-command who leaves his leader to tie up all the loose ends on his own, while he tried to steal a march on the man he should be assisting.'

Soldier could not help but feel elated. Poor Kaff. His scheme had backfired on him. He should have known that a princess, above all others, understood the nature and importance of duty.

Soldier spent an hour with his wife, then a messenger arrived to say he had an audience with the queen. Humbold was not in attendance. The chancellor was doing other things. Qintara, Lady of the Ladders, was there. And Maldrake, Lord of the Locks. Queen Vanda praised Soldier for the success of his expedition, but she had not the compassion of a loving wife, and told him he should not have lost the new King Magus in the first place.

'Go then,' she finished, with a more gentle tone, 'we are not displeased with you, Soldier. You will not be punished.'

'I don't have to undergo Ordeal by Fire?'

'No – but the next time, I shall have you burned alive, whole.'

Soldier was relieved. 'I understand.'

When he left the Palace of Birds it was night. Soldier decided to walk the cobbled streets, over to the palace of the queen's sister. Taking a short cut through an alley, he saw a rat in the moonlight.

Seeing a rat in an alley at night was not in itself an extraordinary thing. But this creature appeared to be ignoring the offal thrown out by a house-servant. It was sitting on its haunches, its red eyes gleaming as little points of light. Soldier passed the creature warily. Rats were as prone to fits of madness as humans. He did not want some crazed rodent leaping at his throat in the darkness.

Rats. In make-up they were very close to the human form, having the same number and type of bones, and who knew how nearly their minds were to human? Creatures of the midden they might be, but they were crafty survivors, with strong instincts that linked them to humans. It was said that in all worlds at all times humans were never more than two metres away from a rat. It therefore followed that a rat was never far from a human, no matter how much the two creatures hated each other.

Soldier was almost past the rat when it spoke to him.

'I come with a message from someone who has made your welfare his concern,' squeaked the rat.

Soldier reeled in shock. He quickly recovered himself. In

this world ravens talked. Rocks spoke. Why not rats, too? Soldier remembered what IxonnoxI had said. That his father had sent out messengers to those who might be useful to him. Was this a messenger from OmmullummO?

'What do you want?' he asked the bright-eyed rodent, as it sat on its hindquarters, staring at him. 'How many messengers are there?

'In answer to the first, I have some words for you. In answer to the second, why, how many rats and spiders are there?'

Rats and spiders? The sewers and tunnels below the city were infested with rats and spiders. Was OmmullummO somewhere in Zamerkand's sewers? If he was that close, he could surely move in at any time. IxonnoxI was in grave danger. Soldier had been in this world long enough to know that OmmullummO would have no compunction in killing his son, his child, having destroyed his own progeny many times over the centuries. It seemed that once a wizard had gone bad, there was no end to the atrocities he would commit in order to gain power.

'What are your words?' he asked the rat.

'My master wishes to know if you will stand with him once he is ready to emerge into the light once more.'

Emerge? Definitely the sewers.

'The man I stand with is the only man I trust – myself.'

'You wish me to tell my master you are against him? You must be either for or against. There is no middle ground.'

'Against then. Yes. Where is he, your master? I shall tell him myself.'

'No, no, you can't trick me like that,' squealed the rat, making off into the shadows. 'You've had your chance. You will suffer a terrible fate along with the rest of them, once my master is in control. Prepare to be quartered. Prepare to be crushed. Prepare to *die*.'

'Death is no great fear,' Soldier said, into the now empty shadows. 'We all have to face *that* at some time.'

Nevertheless, he was troubled. OmmullummO would be gathering supporters. There were always roughnecks and villains in any society who were ready to have their bullying legitimised. Once the thugs of society are unleashed, within the scope of the law, absolute terror is abroad. Murder is then no longer murder, but lawful killing. Innocents are swept into a furnace of violence, and mayhem rules.

The first rat must have reported very quickly, for OmmullummO sent another directly, to menace Soldier before he reached home.

'Prepare to meet the Prince of Terror!' squealed the rat.

Soldier was unimpressed. 'I *am* the Prince of Terror,' he replied, cutting the rat in two with his sword.

Layana was still temporarily sane, and he spent a blissful night with her. In the morning Soldier went to the market, to find Spagg. The hand-seller was back at his stall. Soldier had to admire his resilience. Spagg had stuck a semi-precious stone in the hole in his skull and was showing off in front of other stall-holders.

Something fluttered over the square and landed on a weather-vane, up amongst the rooftops. Soldier's mouth tightened. He strode over to Spagg. 'Have you got your slingshot in your pocket?' he enquired.

Spagg looked up. He was remarkably good with the shepherd's weapon, having proved so to Soldier once before.

'Always got it,' Spagg confirmed. 'Here.'

He produced the slingshot. Soldier bent down and picked up a piece of flint. He gave it to Spagg with the words, 'Kill that bird up there, on the weathervane.'

Spagg looked up, saw the target. 'The raven?' he said. 'You want me to kill the raven?'

'Just so,' replied Soldier, firmly.

Spagg whirled the slingshot round his head. The bird took off on seeing this activity, but Spagg had allowed for that. The stone whizzed through the air and struck the raven on the head, just at the end of his beak. It fell onto the tiles of the roof. It lay fluttering for a few moments in the breeze, then the body rolled down to the edge of the roof and dropped down into the square. Soldier went over to it and stamped on it, just to make sure.

'There,' he said. 'Damned traitor!'

A crushed red-and-black lump was stamped into the cobbles.

Spagg pursed his lips. 'You don't forgive easily, do you? What's the bird gone and done?'

'That which I accused you of.'

'Gave us away to the Hannacks, did he?' cried Spagg, now incensed. 'I'll 'ave a stomp on him too.'

Once the deed was done, Soldier felt some pity, even sympathy, for the creature.

'What an unhappy boy was in that bird. Yet, in truth, if he had still been human he would have grown to a man long since. It was only because he was trapped in the raven's form that he remained what he was, a street urchin.' Yet remorse swept over Soldier. 'Perhaps that was a little hasty. I should have waited, thought things over a little more. He deserved it, true, but I should have listened to explanations, excuses even.'

'It is a pity you didn't,' agreed Spagg, also feeling contrite. The raven had shared many adventures with them. 'I always say you act a bit too hasty for your own good, Soldier.'

'You're the one who killed him.'

'Yes, but you asked me to.'

'Do you always do as you're told?'

Spagg nodded, firmly. 'You're the captain. If you was to tell me to go and jump in a lake, I would. That's the trouble with you leader types. Once things goes a bit wrong, you start to blame your troops. Well, I ain't taking no blame on this one. *Get out your slingshot*, you says. *Kill that there raven*. Well, orders carried out, sir. Now you can take full responsibility for 'em. I'm just a common soldier, Soldier.'

Soldier was about to remonstrate with the hand-seller, when a bird landed on his shoulder.

'What's going on here?' asked the bird.

'Raven?' cried Soldier. 'That – that isn't you on the cobbles?'

'Her? No, she was a just a good friend.'

Chapter Seven

After a private audience with the queen, Uthellen took her son secretly from the city at night. Disguised as a crone, she left Zamerkand driving a cart in the back of which IxonnoxI was hidden. Her destination was the same forest where Soldier had taken them many years before. Queen Vanda had been entirely sympathetic to Uthellen's fears that the city was not the place to keep her son safe until his inauguration. Zamerkand, like any walled city of the time, was seething with spies, cut-throats and agents of foreign powers. There were too many people grasping at power in such times, and IxonnoxI was still very vulnerable. It would not be until he was installed in the Seven Peaks that he would have the full protection of the gods.

'The trouble with the gods is,' grumbled Uthellen to herself, 'they are amoral. It's all one to them whether the world is ruled by good, evil or a mixture of both . . .'

She drove the cart several miles from the city, before she and IxonnoxI took to their feet. Once in the forest, which most people did not visit due to the fact that a giant boar called Garnash roamed within its pale, she felt they could hide themselves from harm. The one she feared the most – IxonnoxI's father, OmmullummO – had great powers. However, he too would have to seek them out. He could not know their whereabouts except through his agents. The fewer animals, supernatural creatures, birds and, above all, people, that the pair came into contact with, the less chance OmmullummO had of finding them.

'Where is my father?' wondered IxonnoxI out loud, as they trudged along, over the meadowland towards the forest fence. 'If we only knew where he was!'

He had asked his mother the same question a thousand times, and a thousand times she had replied that she did not know, could not even guess. She had a *feeling* that OmmullummO was somewhere near or in Zamerkand, but that was just a nagging worry in the back of her mind. She didn't know whether to heed it or not, but certainly they needed to be cautious. If the old wizard were in Gwandoland, across the Cerulean Sea, or high up somewhere in the Unknown Region, she could afford to relax a little. But there was no way of knowing. Only when HoulluoH's funeral was over and IxonnoxI was installed could they drop their guard.

When they finally reached their forest home, a fairy glade in the middle of the woodland region which stretched a hundred miles in each direction, Uthellen thought of Soldier. They were fond thoughts. At one time she had been in love with Soldier – when they had shared this woodland place together – but that feeling had subsided. It had drifted away to be replaced by a less urgent and compelling feeling: a sense of fondness and love of a different kind.

She knew Soldier would be her dearest friend for the rest of her life. She knew that, had he not been married to the princess, he would have made love to her, and would have been just as happy in her arms as he was in the arms of another. It was an accident of fate that he had ended up in the bed of a princess. It pained Uthellen greatly — filled her with such agony sometimes that she could hardly bear to be herself — that she had betrayed him once. It had been in the market-square not long after she had met him, when he had begged her to marry him and save his life.

She had denied him. She had turned her back. Why? To protect her child of course. There had been a choice — actually there was *no* choice — between saving Soldier and protecting her weak and vulnerable child's life.

Still, Uthellen felt a sense of betrayal, a sense of turning away, which brought a pang to her heart as sharp as the point of an arrow.

How cruel destiny could be. If she had not been raped by a wizard, if her son's life had not been in grave danger, if she had been free, she could have gathered Soldier in her arms and loved him to the end of his days.

Blue eyes. His blue eyes had frightened her at first. No one — not man, not wizard, not fairy nor giant, had blue eyes on this earth. Where had he got them from? He believed, she knew, that he came from some other world — perhaps a place where everyone had blue eyes. If that were true, she knew of another from that world. She had not told Soldier this, but there was someone — she knew not whether man or woman — who now dwelt in Uan Muhuggiag.

A boatman had found this person on the uninhabited island of Stell, to the north of a string of islands of which Amekni, Begrom and Refe were three others. The blue eyes were all that were visible — according to the boatman's story — for the rest was swathed in calico, hiding form, sex and all else. Blue Eyes had claimed to be shipwrecked.

The boatman had taken the castaway to Gwandoland, the continent within which Uan Muhuggiag and Carthaga were bordered. Blue Eyes had then vanished into the interior of the former country. All this had not come to her directly from the boatman's lips, for he was found drowned not a week after the rescue. The boatman's story had been passed from his dying mouth into the ears of a lost wraith, who had turned up in a place of faery visited by her son.

IxonnoxI had listened to the wraith's tale, then asked that creature to forget all she had heard. When a witchboy told a creature like a wraith to *forget*, it was actually forgotten. Information had passed from one creature to another and a void replaced the knowledge in the messenger. The secret was now solely with IxonnoxI and his mother. Uthellen had been told by her son not to impart this alarming news to Soldier. She did not know the reason behind her son's request — he rarely gave her reasons for any of his decisions — but she respected a knowledge which had access to sources far deeper and greater than those available to any mortal.

'Mother, will you ever marry?'

The question had come from IxonnoxI while the pair of them gathered wood for their evening fire.

She stopped, disturbed, knowing her son was asking for a reason, not just idle curiosity.

'I don't know — why?'

'You must not wait for Soldier. He will never be yours.'

She was annoyed by the sure tone of her son's voice.

'No one can know for certain what the future will bring,' she replied, 'even a King Magus.'

IxonnoxI was not upset by the sharpness of her words.

'That's true. But even if Princess Layana were to die tomorrow, Soldier could not marry whom he chose. His path is set. His destiny preordained elsewhere. That is, until he reaches a point in his life when he will be free. The choice that he makes then will determine the fate of the world, and he will discover his identity. He will not be Soldier any more, but someone else, from another place.'

'I don't care if he is called Soldier, or any other name.'

'It's not just his name. He will be flooded with old memories. Memories of a childhood. Memories of his youth. Perhaps even memories of former loves. How do you know he does not love another woman on another earth? I have no knowledge of these things, Mother. A wizard is not subject to the same emotions as a mortal. But I see things, I witness what happens amongst you people, and I can gauge things. Soldier will have gone from us, once he gets his memory back, and another man will stand in his place, looking like him, speaking like him, but not *him*.'

A tear came to the eye of Uthellen.

'You are very cruel, son.'

'I don't know what that means. I try not to hurt you, though I don't understand what being hurt means. All I can be is myself. I am from your body, but I am not of your body. I am a wizard. I know the ways of the superworld, but the feelings of mortals are to me like the twitterings of birds to humans. We think we understand, but we do not. We can only guess. I have a desire to see you in a state of what you call happiness but I can't share that state.'

She knew he was telling the truth but it did nothing for her feelings of sadness and yearning. The man she loved could not love her back, would *never* love her back in the way she might want if he were free. Nor did her son love her, for he also could not.

She wept.

'I'm sorry, Mother,' said IxonnoxI, but he was not sorry. He could not be. He had merely said what she wanted to hear. His nurturing had taught him that his mother, and others, liked to receive sympathy.

She accepted the words, as a master accepts that his dog loves him, and was able to compose herself.

That night they had a fire going in the forest. Uthellen could enjoy activities with her son, even if she could not understand him. They were like two creatures sharing something which excited them both. She had always been a person who liked the outdoors better than indoors. Four walls made a prison to her, while she yearned for the wind, the sun, the night sky, even the rain in her hair, on her face. The smell of woodsmoke in the forest was better to her than the aroma of spikenard oil. Fresh air, a sudden burst of wildflowers on a bank, a clutch of brightly coloured fungi, soft star moss beneath her feet, the pungency of fermenting fruit – all these were as precious to her as her own health and vitality.

That night, the first night, she lay under the stars and composed songs, to sing herself to sleep. When the rustlings and calls of the forest would not allow sleep, she threaded the stars in her head, making a necklace of them. The networks of branches formed cobwebs through which she viewed the dusty moon. Fireflies played in the beams which fell like soft, yellow dust by her pillow of grass. She was as happy in those moments as any woman could be who has given birth to a special child, but in doing so has denied herself earthly pleasures.

Chancellor Humbold had been driven to distraction by the presence of the two princes from Bhantan. They ran rings round him. They heckled him in court. They whispered (in

his earshot) slanderous remarks about him and his adminis-
tration. Worst of all they stole things from his chambers.
Small items: a hat, some quill pens, a dragon's-tooth paper-
weight, a miniature portrait of himself in his chancellor's
robes painted by Minstrallus – the latter was considered quite
valuable. When Humbold complained to the queen, she
smiled indulgently and said, 'Oh, they're just young prank-
sters – you can't take them too seriously.'

But Humbold *did* take them seriously. When he ran into
them one day in a passageway he boxed their ears. In turn,
they kicked his shins and told him they would pay him back
at the first opportunity.

'One day we'll have our country back,' Guido said, 'and
you'll be sent as an envoy.'

'We'll ask for you specially,' said Sando, 'and the queen
won't be able to refuse us, or it'd be bad manners.'

'We'll stuff your bum with fresh rabbits' guts and have you
thrown into the wolf-pit,' Guido said.

'Or we'll pump your ears and nose full of icing sugar,' said
Sando, 'and stake you out amongst the royal skeps.'

'We haven't made up our minds yet,' Guido said.

'One or the other,' said Sando.

'Perhaps both,' finished Guido.

Humbold went away raging with fury. In his chambers he
calmed down once again. He had a great scheme, which was
already in motion. One day soon there would be no queen to
send him on errands. One day soon he would be King of
Zamerkand. The timing was not yet quite right, but the day
was not far off. Then those two squirts would have to watch
their heads. Humbold had already been in contact with
Bhantan. The princes, he had learned, had been banished for
ever. No one wanted to see them again in that small distant

land. They would not be missed. Their mother and nurse had already 'disappeared'. One good thing about the officials of Bhantan was that they never forgave anyone, especially their own kind who had fallen out of favour.

Layana had been out of the palace all day. Her sedan carriers, under the guidance of Corporal Tranganda, had taken her to see Butro-batan, the blacksmith. Cim, the blacksmith's son, now a stocky young man who stole the hearts of tavern maidens by the score, had brought her Wychhazel, a piebald horse which secretly belonged to the princess. Layana, when she was well, loved to hunt. It was not so much the killing of the game – though she saw no fault with that so long as it was to eat and not just for the sport – but being in the fresh air, being free. A princess is a prisoner for most of her life, simply because of who she is. Out in the fields and forests of southern Guthrum, she had the wind in her hair and the sun and rain on her face, and she felt unencumbered.

Corporal Tranganda and Butro-batan were taking huge risks by assisting Layana. If the queen found out that her sister was escaping Zamerkand, going out alone into the dangerous world outside the city, she would be very displeased. Queen Vanda still thought of Layana as her little sister who needed protecting. The queen herself would not go outside the city walls without a huge escort, and she did not expect her sister to, either. Layana was the only family she had left.

However, with her hawk Windwalker on her wrist, Layana frequently swathed herself in blue calico – sometimes wearing a light armour made by Butro-batan, as well – and went outside to see the world as it really was. It was on one of these trips that she had met Soldier – found him shocked and vulnerable on a hillside – and had brought him back to Zamerkand.

She spent the forenoon in her favourite hunting area, near the Petrified Pools of Yan, just west of the Ancient Forest. Right on the stroke of noon, however, there was a dead moon, an eclipse of the sun. It went dark within a few minutes and became very cold. Layana guessed that this phenomenon was to do with the death of HoulluoH.

'Come on, Wychhazel,' she said to her palfrey, 'it's time we were getting back to the palace and that husband of mine.'

Soldier knew nothing of these external adventures of his wife. In fact she had saved his life once or twice, by just being near him at the right time. He knew of the 'blue hunter', of course, but the rider's identity was still a mystery to him.

After waiting by the Petrified Pools of Yan, which were actually lakes of amber mined by the half-giants of Huccarra, she realised it was not going to grow gradually lighter as she expected. There was a glow coming from the blocked sun, but it was not bright enough to light the countryside back to Zamerkand. Layana usually found her way by the goat tracks, but they would be impossible to recognise in the dullness.

The Huccarran half-giants were not unfriendly beings. They were not *human* of course, but they weren't as vicious as faery folk, nor as belligerent as full-sized giants. Standing just nine feet tall, they looked as if they had been chiselled out of stone: squared muscles and thick strong bones made them appear as if they had been sculpted from gneiss. Their cropped hair did nothing to dispel this image, being sheared to within an inch of their heavy skulls and shaved around the neck and ears. Their hands were squarish and their fingers short and stubby.

Those fingers – the muscles of those hands – could crush a rock to powder. They were immensely strong. Their lives were spent mining minerals and precious stones, which they sold uncut to merchants and polishers for practically nothing. They chipped out amber from the petrified pools in chunks, but they also had access to blue john, chalcedony, sard, lapis lazuli, girasol, jasper, chrysoberyl, jacinth, bloodstone, moonstone and tourmaline. Their needs were simple. They lived in miners' shacks on the edge of the quarries they mined.

One or two exceptional half-giants were lazy and didn't like the idea of mining at all. One of these was Clokk the Sword-stealer, who made his living by gathering up weapons after battles, before the armies involved had time to gather their senses. These he would sell on, again for only a fraction of their real value, being as unbusinesslike as the rest of his clan. Clokk was not above entering private property and taking swords and daggers, nor requesting them from travellers he met in open country. The request was polite enough but there was of course a veiled threat behind it. In the gloom of the eclipse he came across Layana, stumbling around in the dimness as the edge of one of the amber pools.

'Give me crossbow, please,' asked the near-naked Clokk, standing foursquare in front of Wychhazel. 'Give me also dagger, thank you.'

Layana stared at the creature in the poor light, recognising his clan straight away. Over the other side of the amber lake fires had been lit to provide the Huccarrans with light to work by. There seemed to be tireless activity in that direction.

'I think I will not give you anything,' said Layana, realising she was being accosted by a highwaygiant, except there were no highways and this oaf was only halfway to being a giant. 'I think I will pass you by.'

'Me think me will break horse neck!' growled Clokk. 'Me think me break you neck also.'

'Me think me will let loose hawk,' snapped back Layana, 'so she can rip out your damn eyes.'

Clokk peered at the hawk on Layana's wrist. Then he gingerly touched his eyelids with his stubby fingers, as if wondering about such an attack on his person. Layana was no fool. She knew that even Huccarrans feared loss of sight: the most precious of things in a world full of brigands and bandits. One could do without a hand, or a foot, or even one's privates, but not without one's eyes.

'He not attack me eyes.'

'*She* will, believe me. I've trained her to go straight for the face and claw out those orbs with her talons. She can do it in a flash. You won't have time to put your hands up to protect yourself.'

Once again Clokk touched around his eyes. Then finally he stood aside to let her pass. Clokk asked her a question as she went by.

'How long sun go away for?'

Layana shook her head. 'How do I know?'

'What you do? You sleep outdoors? Many snakes. Many wolves. Many bears. You come stay with Clokk.'

He pointed. Layana stared. She could just about make out a lean-to shack, resting against the cliff face. It looked like a log-jam piled against a dam in a flood, but at least it was shelter. Clokk was right. There were many wild beasts abroad. Although Layana had been hunting here lots of times in the last few years, she had never been out overnight. It was unlikely she could make it back to Zamerkand in this half-light.

She was naturally suspicious of the offer, however.

'How do I know you won't murder and rob me, once I'm in your – your dwelling?'

'Never hurt man in house. Friend not let me.'

The friend Clokk spoke of, Layana knew, was his mate. Half-giants had no such things as wedding ceremonies. They mated for life, but it was a sort of unspoken agreement which was broken only by the death of one or the other of them. Female half-giants were indistinguishable from the males, having the same severe haircuts, the same rugged, chiselled build, and no breasts. They fed their young on wild corn mash mixed with goat's milk the moment they appeared in the world – had done for a million-odd years – and so evolution had got rid of mammaries. Only Huccarrans knew who amongst them were male and who female.

'I accept your offer,' said Layana.

'Maybe you make pay with one dagger?' suggested Clokk, hopefully. 'Sometimes this happen, yes?'

'Perhaps. We'll see.'

Clokk, towering over Wychhazel, whose wild eyes signalled her distrust of the stranger, took the reins and led the horse towards his hovel. Wychhazel allowed herself to be hitched to a broken dead tree near the entrance to the shack, while Layana dismounted. Clokk fetched a crudely-made box and indicated that Layana should put the hawk in it. She did so, knowing her main weapon would be negated. However, Clokk was as good as his word and simply led her into the shack.

Once inside he lit a lamp. There was no furniture in the place, only untreated, thick hides on the floor to cushion the occupants from the ground. Clokk hung the lamp above the square hearth which was in the middle of the room. Then from a black pot in the ashes of the fire, he ladled several spoonfuls of corn mash into two wooden bowls. He gave one of these to Layana and took the other himself. Layana thanked him and tasted the mash: there was honey in it. Its flavour was not too bad.

Halfway through eating, the hide which served as a door was flung aside, and the twin of Clokk entered.

'Hello, friend Mump,' said Clokk, warmly.

'Hello, friend Clokk,' came the reply.

They stared at each other with fond looks for a few moments. It was obvious to Layana that these two great lumps were enamoured of one another. Clokk's friend had obviously been working hard at mining amber from the petrified pools, for her fingernails looked dirty, cracked and chipped. There was a chisel in her belt and a hammer in her hand. Mump then turned to stare at Layana, before entering the shack completely and letting the door drop into place.

'Gone dark,' said Mump. 'No work in dark.'

'Me no work in light *or* dark!' cried Clokk, and the pair of them collapsed in laughter.

'You no work, ever!' shrieked a delighted Mump.

The laughter continued for quite a while, Mump having to lie down she was rocking backwards and forwards so much in merriment.

'You – you don't mind that Clokk never works?' asked Layana, once the noise had subsided.

'Feel sorry for Clokk, yes,' said Mump, putting a log amongst the cold ashes and staring at it as if she expected it to explode in flames. 'Poor Clokk never work.'

'You feel sorry for him? But his *choice* is not to work.'

'Yes, very sorry for that,' nodded Mump. 'Never mind, me work. Clokk big thief. He steal sword. Not easy for Clokk.'

Layana found it difficult to follow the logic of all this, but she acknowledged that she was in a foreign culture. Mump did not seem at all curious as to who Layana was or what she was doing there. She asked no questions except with regard to Layana's comfort. Had she had enough to eat? Did she feel cold at all? Which corner of the room would she like to sleep in? Then the general questions came thick and fast. How long would the eclipse last? Would bad weather follow? Didn't it seem as if it were getting colder, or was that just in the mind?

The eclipse looked well and truly set in. Layana went outside to settle her horse, unsaddling it and tethering it behind the south side of the shack to keep it out of the wind. There *was* a great wind coming. You could feel it. Layana wondered if the Kalloom was coming – the cold, dry wind which blew up from behind the Seven Peaks and brought madness and death with it. The Kalloom was not a seasonal wind. It came irregularly, out of nowhere, and devastated the landscape for a week or more, before dying again.

'Kalloom' meant 'breath of god' in the Oytledat language. The Oytledats lived on an island in the ocean beyond the coast behind the Seven Peaks. The great wind was circular in motion, sweeping over the land from the west, turning at the far coast before it reached the Isle of Stell, then back across the Cerulean Sea below the south coast, finally hitting the western isle of Oytledat. The Oytledats received the worst of the wind, which froze the island solid the moment it hit.

Sure enough, Layana only had just enough time to rig a shelter for Wychhazel, before the Kalloom crashed into the shack. Bits of rotten wood flew off the logs, some of them hitting her in the face. She protected herself with her arms and fought her way back through the icy blast to the door. She just managed to get inside before the heart of the wind struck the shack and rocked it on its retaining pegs. Mump and Clokk were squatting in one corner, looking terrified, while Windwalker was screeching, and clawing at her box.

Layana found the far corner of the shack, slipped between the stinking hides which layered the floor, and tried to block out the noise of the freezing wind which would take several lives.

Chapter Eight

Layana had left Soldier that day to his business, training the Eagles on the grounds beyond Zamerkand's city walls. But for a handful of raw recruits, newly arrived by boat from Carthaga, his warriors were mostly battle-hardened men and women. The recruits were assigned mentors from amongst the experienced warriors and it was up to those tutors to make sure the striplings and maidens were up to scratch when it came time to go to war. There were no concessions given to the newcomers as far as training went: they had to run as fast, jump as high and fall as light as their teachers.

'They don't look too bad,' Soldier said to his lieutenant, Velion.

'By Usk and Isman, they'd better not be. You know they go through a very rigorous selection process, back in Carthaga. A thousand may apply, a hundred may be chosen. They are then put through initial training there and then, on the Great Continent. By the time they reach us, they *ought* to be more than just "not bad".'

'Some were still pretty groggy from the sea voyage. I know many of them were seasick. Then they had that long, spooky boat trip through the canal tunnel up from the sea, with just candles to light the way. I expect at least some of them are regretting they ever joined the red pavilions in the first place.'

Velion shook her head. 'Not Carthagans.'

'Don't Carthagans have mothers? Comfortable homes? Brothers and sisters that they miss?'

'Every Carthagan leaves home at the age of seven, at the latest eight, and joins the community. They go to school together, eat together, sleep in dormitories. Their parents are only allowed to see them three times a year. On their birthdays, for an hour during the Festival of Coph, and during their one week's holiday in the seventh lunar month of Usk.'

Soldier shook his head, sadly. 'That's no home-life.'

'How would you know? You can't remember yours.'

'I have this *feeling* I had a happy upbringing. I see boys fishing in a stream, in my mind's eye. I see them running, swimming, climbing trees, and crawling back to a home at the end of a day, dog-tired and happy, to climb into a bed with white sheets.'

Velion snorted. 'That's just a daydream. It's not real. No child grows up like that. We all *think* we ought to have done, but reality is very different. And a bed with white sheets? Lucky if we got a straw mattress, full of horse fleas. That sounds like the life of a soft prince. Were you a prince in your other life, Soldier?'

At that moment the sun went out. Immediately afterwards, hail fell in stones the size of hen's eggs. They beat down upon the unprotected warriors and civilians. Those men and women with shields held them over their heads and such a clattering and clanging was set up by the hailstone storm it sounded like a religious festival. A nearby unprotected warrior was beaten down, first to his knees, then prone. Soldier, protected by Velion's shield, dragged the man under the small bronze cover.

The hailstorm went on for some time. The darkness did not abate, even when the balls of ice stopped falling.

Some time later, a runner carrying a blazing torch came through the city gates, looked about him, then continued in the direction of the Eagle Pavilion. Soldier recognised him. He was one of the servants at the Palace of Wildflowers.

'Master, master!' yelled the man, seeing Soldier. 'Come quickly.'

Soldier strode over to him. 'What is it?'

The servant stuck his own temple with his left fist, several times, before saying, 'It's our mistress, the princess. She hasn't come home.'

'Hasn't come home? Where did she go?'

'She went out this morning in the sedan chair, and she's usually back by mid-afternoon, but there's no sign of her.'

It was now the closing of the day.

The ground was littered with white balls of ice. People began slipping and sliding on them as they yelled at each other in the darkness. The sun was still obscured by the moon, just a rim of light around its edge. Warriors, quick-thinking creatures, had lit brands, but now the ice storm had stopped a strong wind had struck up, and blew the torches to pieces in their hands.

'Now the Kalloom!' cried the servant. 'My mistress caught in that foul wind.'

People around them had managed to get oil lamps with wind protection, and there was light.

Soldier pulled the servant roughly by his collar.

'Have you searched the city for your mistress? Have you any idea where she might be?'

'No – no, we haven't searched. Ofao said we need your permission to go out and scour the streets for the princess. Once it is known she is missing it will come to the ears of the queen. There will be much displeasure in the royal household. When it happened before the queen threatened to make the princess go and live in the Palace of Birds, where she could be watched by the queen's servants.'

'This isn't the first time it's occurred?'

'No – twice before.'

'Why wasn't I informed then?'

'You were not here, master – you were away.'

It was true. Soldier was not often in Zamerkand. The red pavilions were always out on campaign somewhere. And if they weren't, Soldier was on some special expedition for the queen.

'Who is with her?'

The servant said, 'Corporal Tranganda – he always accompanies my lady when she goes out into the city – and some guards, of course.'

Soldier was slightly relieved. Tranganda was a good man. Tough. Reliable. Not too afraid of authority.

'And the corporal is missing too?'

'Yes, master.'

'Get some search parties together *now!*' he said, striding towards the gates of the city. 'I want them in parties of six.'

By the time Soldier had got the search parties, they were no longer necessary. Corporal Tranganda arrived at the palace, having found his way by lamp light. He asked to speak to Soldier alone.

'Well, what is it?' cried Soldier, half out of his mind. 'Has your mistress been abducted? Why aren't you bleeding? Where are the wounds you received in trying to protect her?

Why are you not in some gutter, dying?'

The corporal held up his hands. 'My mistress – the Princess Layana – she – she is not in the city.'

Soldier was shocked. 'Not in Zamerkand?'

The corporal looked shame-faced. 'She often goes out on her horse alone, to hunt in the forest with her hawk.'

'Alone? And you let her?' shouted Soldier, finding it hard not to strike this man before him. 'You let her go out without an escort?'

'Sire,' said the corporal, with a glint of steel in his eye, 'the princess is her own woman.'

Soldier let this sink in. The corporal was right. If Layana had wanted to go out hunting alone, certainly no ranker in the palace guards would be able to stop her. He might report her, when they arrived back at the palace, but that would be a betrayal. Soldier hated treachery. The raven had betrayed him and when Soldier had asked why, the bird had replied, 'Because I am in feathers, and you are in skin.' Soldier was still hurt by the raven's deceit, but he did not keep his promise of killing him. He'd let him fly off after that, saying he did not want to see the bird again, even if his life proved to be as long as that of a pole-sitting sage.

'You're right of course,' he finally said to the grim-faced guardsman in front of him. 'You could not stop her. Nor should you. She has a mind and will of her own. What suggestions have you? Do you think she has been caught out by this darkness?'

'That's my thinking exactly,' said Corporal Tranganda. 'I have an idea that she is hunting down by the Ancient Forest. We should look for her in that region. In the meantime, sire, I suggest we speak with the servants, get them to hold their tongues. If this comes to the ears of the queen . . .'

'You're right of course.'

Ofao came into the room, wild-eyed. 'Captain Kaff,' he announced, his face pale with anxiety. 'Captain Kaff is here to see you, sire.'

The next second Kaff strode into the room. The Captain of the Imperial Guard looked about him. He was, like most people, carrying a lamp. There was a cut on his head, which bled onto his face. He peered into the corners of the room, shining his light as if seeking something.

'Captain,' said Soldier, composing himself, 'you are hurt.'

Kaff touched his wound, distractedly. 'The world has gone mad out there.' He peered around again.

'What are you looking for? Spiders?'

'The princess,' said Kaff, abruptly. 'I have reason to believe she has gone missing.'

'Have you indeed? And that is your business how?'

Kaff stared at Soldier as if he were a garden slug.

'The princess has always been at the top of my list of concerns.'

Soldier said, coldly, 'She has a husband who is quite able to allay those concerns. Do not intrude upon my ground, Captain. For your information, the princess is indisposed. She is unwell. I'm sure you know what that means, in a palace where the walls are padded with goosefeathers and there are bars upon the clerestories?'

'You're saying she's in her room? Insane?'

Ofao interrupted with, 'We do not use words like that when it comes to the princess . . .'

Kaff struck the nervous eunuch around the head with the talons of his claw-hand, drawing blood. Ofao reeled and was saved from falling only by the presence of Corporal Tranganda, who held him upright. Soldier's eyes narrowed at this breach of etiquette in his house. Kaff was not finished however. He hissed into Ofao's face.

'Never,' he said, 'presume to teach me – *anything*.'

'You obviously need to be taught something by someone,' snapped Soldier, 'you have the manners of a pig.'

Kaff took this calmly. He flexed the eagle's claw on his wrist.

'I have no time to argue with you, Soldier. I want to know where the princess is. What is Corporal Tranganda doing here, speaking with you, if she is not missing? The corporal always accompanies her outside the palace.'

Soldier had had enough. His straight right arm came out and his fist struck Kaff squarely on the jaw. The captain went down as if hit by an oncoming armoured horse at full gallop. Ofao and Tranganda were instructed to pick him up and carry him out into the street. Soldier and Tranganda were to go out alone, to search the area around the Ancient Forest and the Petrified Pools of Yan. Ofao was to lock the palace doors and gates behind them. If, when Captain Kaff came round again, he demanded entry to the palace, Ofao had Soldier's permission to threaten the good captain with a cauldron of boiling oil, should the Imperial Guardsman attempt to step over the threshold.

'I will not have that man snooping around my home,' growled Soldier, 'and if he's scalded to death because he's foolish enough to ignore the warnings, so be it. I'll take responsibility.'

Ofao, of course, hoped that nothing happened to Soldier in the meantime, or the responsibility would pass naturally to him.

Soldier and Tranganda rode out on swift horses. However, once out in the countryside, away from high walls and the artificial lights of the city, they found they had to slow to a walk. The wind screamed round them, threatening to blow them from their saddles, filling the air with broken tree branches, stones, and other debris. There was every possibility that the horses would lame themselves. As it was they were stumbling in the darkness every few minutes with a hoof in a rabbit hole or fox earth. Gradually the two men made their way south, following the glint of a narrow stream in the thin light from the blocked sun. Soon there was no sun, it being night, but the moon remained as dark as dried blood in the heavens. It was an eerie time, with winds picking up and screaming through them, then dying again and an unearthly still coming in their wake.

There were demons out there, in the darkness. They lurked amongst the ancient rocks and broken dead trees. And wild beasts, crazed by the eclipse. To keep them back Tranganda punctured his helmet with a dagger, several times, producing a bowl like a brazier. This he filled with combustible materials and set light to with his tinderbox. He stuck the upturned, blazing helmet on the tip of his spear, the butt of which he inserted in its leather socket on his saddle, holding the shaft with his left hand and the reins in his right. Thus they had the light of a torch to travel by. The flare in the high wind was not that bright, but its light frightened away demons and the fire kept away beasts.

By the time they reached the region around the Ancient Forest, the sun's grip on the moon was slipping. The moon was beginning to escape, sliding sideways, revealing light from her shy big brother to pour forth onto the planet beneath. It was in this light that they managed to pick up Layana's trail and track her to the shack of Clokk and Mump. They found a piebald palfrey in the corral at the back of the dwelling.

Tranganda told Soldier it was Layana's hunting horse.

'Is it, by the gods?' he said, surprised. 'I'm sure I've seen this mount before somewhere – or one very like it.'

He was too worried and had not the time to consider it further. Thinking Layana had been abducted, Soldier went immediately to the door of the shack and kicked it open, yelling, 'Layana, keep back – it's Soldier!'

He burst into the room, waving Xanandra, the sword forged for him by a weapon-maker of great repute.

Soldier had never seen half-giants before. There were two creatures in the corner of the room who looked to him as if they were made out of granite. They had broad faces and two rows of thick, even teeth in their wide mouths. He stepped forward warily, expecting them to rush him. Then he saw that they were cowering on the other side of the hearth, keeping the fire between themselves and the warrior. Their backs were hunched in a form of defence and their heads had almost disappeared down a cavity between their shoulders. Their arms were out and curved like crabs' claws in front of them.

This made them look to Soldier like neckless fiends about to pounce.

Soldier growled in the back of his throat. 'Bastards!' he snarled. 'Abductors!'

'A demon!' cried one of these fiends. 'Help, ho!'

'What have you done with my wife?' cried Soldier, looking wildly around the room and seeing no one else. 'Have you savages eaten her? Where are her precious bones? Where is she? Are those her clothes you're burning in that hearth? I'll slice the pair of you into rashers, the gods give me strength, and fry you on hot stones!'

Tranganda was now close behind Soldier. He whispered,

'These are miners. They're simple creatures, but they're not savages. You're scaring them to death, sire.'

'I'll burn this place down, if they don't tell me where my wife is!' cried the distraught Soldier. 'Why don't they answer?'

Two pairs of giant eyes swung to the far corner of the room. There was a hump under the floor. It began to move.

'Aggrrgghh,' yelled Soldier, 'they've buried her alive!'

Then, as his eyes got used to the gloom inside the shack, he realised the ground was covered with uncured animal skins. From beneath layers of these skins Layana emerged. She looked groggy from sleep. She blinked and stared around the room. Finally she focused on Soldier.

'Husband?' she said, a slow, lazy smile coming to her mouth. 'What – you wake me so early?'

Then, as her mind began to clear of the fog of dreams, she remembered where she was and what she was doing.

'Oh,' she continued. 'You've caught me at last.'

Soldier face was stern. 'Yes – at last.' He nodded, then his brow cleared before he added, 'Caught you at what?'

She emerged fully now, her clothes becoming visible. He saw that she was wearing indigo calico. The hunter? Of course, the palfrey outside. It belonged to the slim youth who had been the first person in this world Soldier had encountered. The same hunter who had rescued him on more than one occasion. His wife Layana was that hunter? It did not seem possible.

'Ah,' she smiled again as she witnessed the knowledge spreading through his mind. 'You *have* caught me. Well, never mind. I kept the secret for years. You've been very slow, Soldier, to catch up with someone who shares your bed most nights.'

'But why the secret?' asked Soldier at last, trying to take all this in with strangers in the room.

She shrugged. 'It began that way – and I enjoyed being the mysterious hunter, childish though it seems.'

'I don't know what to say – except that I owe you more than I thought I did.'

'Is one lover ever in debt to another?' she asked, softly.

There was a sharp cough from the doorway as Tranganda reminded them that there were other people present.

'Me not hurt her,' cried Clokk, as Soldier's eyes swept the room again. 'She eat, sleep, happy.'

He saw it was time to reassure the two owners of this property that he was not going to burn down their house, nor decapitate them in the process. This he did, learning as he did so that these were male and female half-giants, who mined the precious amber from the Petrified Pools of Yan. By the time everyone was comfortable again, the sun had fully emerged. It was time to get Layana back to Zamerkand, before her sister learned of her absence. Layana gave Clokk her dagger and crossbow, and thanked both half-giants for their hospitality. Clokk took the gifts eagerly and Mump was pleased to see him so happy.

On the way home Soldier told Layana that as he had known nothing of her activities as the blue hunter.

'We shall go on as before,' he said. 'Of course, when I see you outside the city walls on your piebald, I shall know it is you, but for you I shall pretend otherwise. How else can you enjoy the freedom you so obviously need.'

She thought this was best too, that they pretend this revelation had never come to pass. Soldier was merely another who shared her secret, as did Butro-batan and Corporal Tranganda. Layana needed this other life, to counteract all those hours she spent inside the Palace of Wildflowers, mad or sane.

* * *

In the meantime Ofao had ordered servants to carry Captain Kaff back to his quarters. They left him lying there on the front porch, prone, staring out at the dark sky with sightless eyes. When he came to, he remembered nothing of being struck. He recalled going to the Palace of Wildflowers, to remonstrate with Soldier, but the rest was a blank. All he knew was that his jaw ached. Had he fallen on his face for some reason? A fainting fit? He remembered being with Tranganda, Ofao and Soldier, but no matter how hard he thought about it, he could not bring back any mental picture of what had happened there. Why had they just dumped him here on his step?

He remembered one other thing.

'The princess!' he suddenly cried, sitting up.

Once again he set out for the Palace of Wildflowers. When he arrived there he found a quivering Ofao, who stuttered and stammered negative replies to his questions. Since Ofao would not open the palace to him, Kaff went back to the guardhouse and roused some of his men, saying they were to scour the city.

'The princess must be found,' he said.

Later a squad of men reported to him that the princess had been seen at the window of the Green Tower, looking down. Kaff went to see for himself. Yes, there she was, drifting behind the barred, high, narrow window in a liquefaction of silks and muslin. Her form then vanished into the interior of the room. Then another face appeared at the window. Grim. Hostile. It belonged to Soldier. The outlander stared down with hard, warning eyes at the captain in the street, then the shutters to the window were deliberately closed, locking out the world.

Kaff, the feelings in his breast in turmoil, made his way slowly back to his quarters near the west wall.

*   *   *

The raven arrived on the balcony outside Soldier's room and tapped on the window with his beak. Soldier heard the sound and eventually went to see what the raven wanted.

'I wish to have nothing to do with you,' said Soldier, coldly. 'I don't deal with traitors.'

'It wasn't my fault,' replied the raven. 'I was forced into it by unscrupulous people.'

'Liar! You wanted your old body back.'

'Wouldn't you, if you were me?'

Soldier said, 'I would never sell my friends for it.'

'Well,' the bird scratched at the sill with one of his claws, hanging his head. Then he said, 'Anyway, you killed my mate. We're even now. She was an innocent bystander, and you had Spagg kill her with his slingshot.'

'I doubt you knew the bird at all. I know you can't talk with other ravens. They shun you. They know you're not one of them, but a boy in bird's feathers.'

'What can I do?' said the raven, plaintively. 'Do you want me to go to Humbold and offer my services to him?'

'I don't care. You've forsaken your friends. You do what you like.'

'Well – I won't go to him,' the raven said, miserably. 'I don't like him.'

Soldier stared at the bird. He seemed very contrite. Soldier's heart was not of the material that hardened for ever. Where he saw remorse he was inclined to forgive. Of course, he could never *fully* trust the raven again. A treacherous act is not so easily forgotten. But he felt he ought to give the bird a second chance. After all, he had been Soldier's infrequent companion ever since Soldier had arrived in Guthrum. He was an irritating creature, this boy-bird, but useful, too. More than once he had picked locks or untied knots for

Soldier, when he had got himself into some tight corner or other. That counted for something.

'All right,' said Soldier, at last, 'we're friends once more. But don't ever betray me to another again. There'll be no more chances. A man must be able to trust. The only way to survive in such a world of chaos is to know who are friends and who are enemies.'

'Friend,' squawked the raven. 'I'm a friend.'

'See that you stay that way.'

At that moment there was a thumping on Soldier's door. He bade farewell to the raven and went to answer it. A herald stood there, breathless, holding out a note. It was from the queen. She wished to see Soldier immediately.

Soldier told Layana on his way through. The princess was worried.

'Do you think Vanda has found out about my escapades?'

'I don't know. The only way to know for sure is to go and see.'

'You don't have much choice, anyway.'

Soldier was met by a worried looking Chancellor Humbold, outside the court.

'Follow me,' said the courtier, sweeping on before, the hems of his various heavy robes polishing the floor as he went.

The queen smiled grimly at Soldier, but it was not about Layana, it was about him. Soldier, it seemed, had been invited to the King Magus's funeral – the procession and burial of HoulluoH, and the wake which came after. Everyone in the court was astonished. Especially the queen.

'I received the message this morning,' she said. 'It seems that HoulluoH himself requested your presence at the cere-monial burning of his remains. He informed his attendant creatures before he died. No one knows why. No one knew he had even heard of you. It's a very strange thing – very strange indeed.'

'Why *so* strange, Your Highness?' asked Soldier.

It was Chancellor Humbold, looking very disturbed, who replied for his queen.

'Because in all the records of our history, no mortal has ever been invited to – or witnessed – a wizard's funeral.'

'You,' added the queen, 'are the first!'

Chapter Nine

There was a vast platform of tightly packed moles moving across a wintry landscape. These blind creatures, dark velvets from the underworld (appropriate for a funeral in so many ways) carried the remains of the wizard on their backs. All that was left was a pile of bones and black hair. The long, lank wizard's locks flapped like some ghastly flag of the dead. The bones clattered together as the funeral raft rose and fell in a sea-like rhythm, rippling its way over the frosted turf.

The raft moved at the back of the night. Following behind were a thousand black horses yoked to the dawn. They pulled the morning at funeral pace across the plain, tethered as they were by long black ribbons to the edge of the next day. On the heads of the stallions were tall dark plumes, which stood unmoving in the wind. They wore cruppers and traces of black satin, collars of padded silk, and trappings of silver and jet. Their deepened eyes, dark as thunder, crackled with celestial sparks.

It was a magnificent sight, witnessed by only one mortal.

Funeral gifts had been tossed onto the raft by the mourners. There were multi-coloured fruits, few of which were familiar to a mortal. Seashells too, of such an exotic design they stunned the only human present with their beauty. Seeds, nuts, crispy carapace of beetle, blown eggshells, some natural, others clearly from a place other than Earth. There were painted wooden totems of chimeras, carved stone figures of imps. There were moon-moths in their hundred-thousands fluttering around the hearse with dusty wings, as attracted to a dead wizard's yellow bones as they would be to a lamp. There was white driftwood, looking more like bones than the bones, in twisted, tangled heaps, shaped by the sun, sand and the salt-bleach ocean which had torn it from its many foreign shores.

All that could be heard under the full, blood-red moon which filled half the sky was the blast of the cold wind and the chatter of demons. Over knoll and down dale went the murderously slow cortège, the air above a moving darkness fashioned of rooks and crows.

The snow-patched countryside around the raft was littered with demons, spirits, ghosts, ogres and giants of every shape and form.

There were low and magnificent monsters, too, of all varieties: the walking dead, blood-drinking creatures, dragons large and small, the Uldra who lived underground in cold places, Wendigo, Zaltys, Yakkus, Ohdows from the hot deserts of Gwandoland, and comparatively ordinary Knockers and Gremlins from the very gates of earth.

There were witches male and female.

But more numerous than any other set of creatures was the multitude of faery-folk present: Elves, Dwarfs, Pixies, Brownies, Trows (from the outer islands), Goblins, Hob-goblins, Leprechauns, Gnomes, Fenoderee, Cluricauns, Spriggans, Gwragedd Annwn, Coblynau, Bendith Y Mamau,

Tylwyth Teg, Leshy, the dreaded Drots which Soldier hated so much, the Unseelie Court and the Seelie Court.

And midst all these supernatural creatures was but one mortal, one man: Soldier, walking alongside the raft in a state of complete wonder. Half the world's bat-winged shapes flapped by his head, the running devil rushed past his shoulder, while the terrible, gaping ogre, idiot by accident of birth, stared and stared and stared.

Soldier hardly knew where he was. He felt the scene was being acted out around him, like an apparition. He appeared an observer inside someone else's dream, walking with strange and weird forms. Some sights chilled him, others made him want to laugh, even more filled his head with amazement. This funeral was no place for a human. Soldier could see what remained of the most powerful wizard in the world. The pile of bones and hair seemed to rise and fall, with a gentle rhythm, as if struggling to breathe some life into itself.

It was as if the wizard had died not just yesterday, but a thousand years before – yet even so tried to cling on to this life.

Even as they now walked, the hair suddenly combusted, burning with blue and green and orange flames which leapt up to lick feather of crow and rook. Then the bones caught fire. Soldier looked at this pyre, then around him at the amazing multitude of beings who marched with him on this seemingly interminable journey, to see if any were alarmed by this phenomenon. No one seemed perturbed, least of all the moles who carried this bonfire of dead wizard.

A demon, a fellow with cock-wattle eyelids hanging like flaps upon his cheeks, and horse-hair sprouting as a black fountain from the top of his head, seemed to notice Soldier for the first time. He shrugged his pointed shoulders, and screwed up his large, lumpy face with its complexion the colour of sulphur. Then he seemed to take offence at being stared at by a human.

'Why're you here?' growled the demon, his forked, red tongue flicking close to Soldier's face. 'You're mortal.'

'I was invited. In a way I'm not of this world either. I'm from another place entirely, I think.'

The demon seemed to lose interest.

Soldier said, 'The remains are burning.'

The demon glanced across the raft, which had moved three or four yards in twenty minutes.

'It happens. There'll be nothing left when we reach the mansion, but we'll make a show of it.'

'The mansion?'

'Up there.'

Soldier looked beyond the sea of extraordinary creatures to some cliffs. Halfway up the sheer face of these monstrous structures was a ledge with an imposing red-brick mansion perched on its edge. Soldier could not imagine how the building had got there. Perhaps those with wings had built it for their spiritual leader, HoulluoH, and now he wished to spend eternity within its walls? It was certainly a handsome residence, with round rooms on the corners, and bearing slated roofs. There were tall, spiral chimneys, sixteen he counted, and windows by the score. Strange weather vanes, perched on the tops of towers, spun like tops in the morning blast. Thick wooden doors, studded with square-headed nails, were open and ready to receive the resident ashes.

A leering devil dressed in priest's robes stood on the ledge outside the mansion, in front of the doorway.

Goblins were busy cramming the remains of the ashes into an urn, before the blast of the wind took them. It would not do, it seemed, to have a wizard's dust scattered far and wide.

'You see what I mean?' said the demon. 'Nothing left.'

Immediately behind Soldier the thousand horses had halted. The dawn stood at a standstill. Clouds were forming islands in the reddening sky. Winged fairies suddenly flew up to scatter the crows and rooks. Gossamer took the place of feathers. The backdrop of a waiting sunrise caught their colours.

Now the drumbeats! Now the trumps! Now the notes of flutes!

And now the eerie singing of blunt-headed snakes, whose horned-nose songs only ever came forth at funerals such as this.

'*O flown, the stars that were his eyes; flung, the nails that primped his feet. Now seeped, the semen from his loins, drained into the earth and seas. Gone the best of what was worst, gone the last of what was first. Gone the foulest nowhere wind. Ah, drained, those seas from vasty bladder. Ah, vanished, stems of nerve and neck. Torn, the hinge from jaw and joint. Ripped, the roots from teeth and tongue. O cropped, the magic flail that hung; gone those pocket-stones that rung . . .*'

And so it went on, dreadful forked tune, dreadful twisted words.

As the velvet raft reached the foot of the cliffs, a narrow, sloping chasm opened up. The moles flowed forward, down into the crack and so beneath the surface of the earth. The dawn-pulling horses were unhitched by boggarts and taken away, the black ribbons left hanging from the edge of the day, fluttering as sad shadows. The urn full of ashes was retrieved by winged fairies and carried aloft, up to the devil-priest in his black-and-silver garment and tall scarlet mitre. He took it with both hands, turned, and entered the mansion. Shells, fruit, eggs, driftwood, all disappeared with the moles below the ground.

One piece of fruit rolled from the pile and escaped being swallowed by the closing chasm.

'Moon-apple,' said Soldier's demon, answering his unasked question, 'from a jackfrost tree.'

A single fairy, a wily spriggan by the look of its long nose and ears, dashed forward and snatched up the moon-apple to munch.

'I *think* that's allowed,' muttered the demon, in a voice which told Soldier he was none too sure of the fact.

The snakes ceased their unhallowed strains.

All seemed to wait expectantly at the bottom of the cliff, looking upwards. Soldier did the same. Finally the demon-priest appeared, held up his hands, and the crowd around Soldier murmured. Up on the ledge the rock face opened to a square cave, the mansion rumbled backwards, into the mouth of this opening. Once it was securely inside, the cliff closed over the entrance and the mansion was locked inside. Not a seam or fissure marked the place. It was as if HoulluoH had never been.

Soldier was then amazed at how quickly the funeral procession dispersed. The fairies were gone in no time. The demons vanished into the earth at their feet, much like the funeral raft had done. The weird beasts and mythical monsters went next. The last to leave were the giants, out on the periphery, and they went towards the nearest mountains.

Day and night remained suspended in this awful place.

Soldier stood alone on the plain, the wind growing less intense by the minute. When it had died down, he trudged back towards Zamerkand and time began to move again. At the minute he was entering the gates of the city, it was once again nightfall, many hours having passed. Soldier went immediately to bed, intending to report to the queen the following morning. He fell into a sleep so deep it was almost death.

He was woken with a kiss along with fresh natural sunlight.

'Ah, you're well,' he said to Layana. 'How good life is sometimes.'

'Husband, you're famous. The first to attend a wizard's funeral. You must be very special. You are to me, of course, but now other people are beginning to think you are too!'

'Is it still winter?' he asked, looking towards the window.

'Only yesterday. Today it is summer.'

'That's good. It was obviously ordered for the funeral. Now that's all over, we can start our lives again. Is the new King Magus in his palace in the Seven Peaks yet?'

Layana said, 'I don't know. Look, here, this came to the door yesterday with a message that it was a present to you. It arrived just a few moments after you'd left for the funeral. I think you were supposed to wear it for the occasion.'

She held up a sealed glass casket so that he could inspect its contents. It was a robe of the finest, the sheerest silk, red in colour, but decorated with yellow phoenix birds. The instructions on the glass box said that the robe was to be handled with velvet gloves, the silk being so delicate it could not be touched with unclad fingers. There were some such gloves in a compartment on the box. Soldier put them on, opened the glass door, and gently removed the robe from within the casket.

'How beautiful!' breathed Layana, as the breeze lifted the robe and made it dance in Soldier's hands. 'How lucky you are.'

'But who sent it?' asked Soldier.

'Why, some foreign prince, no doubt. Or a magician friend of the queen . . .'

'Or a sorcerer, jealous of my place at the funeral. Remember the brigandine?'

Layana stared at the robe. 'I think this one could hardly have any fine poisoned hairs. Look how light and flimsy it is in the breeze.'

Soldier agreed. He draped the robe over a box-seat with a velvet lid, then had a bath, using the time to describe the wizard's funeral to his wife. She was filled with wonder and amazement at his telling, which made him feel quite special, since she was the native and he the foreigner. While he spoke she bathed his skin with soaps and oils, removing the dust of the plains, and making his skin tingle all over. Perfumed warm water cascaded from the mouths of mermaids, washing away the dirty water from the sunken marble tub, replacing it with clean.

Finally, he climbed from the tub, a fine figure, his skin glowing and smelling as sweet as any rose in spring. Layana put on the velvet gloves and held up the robe for him to step into. He turned his back to it, reached out with his arms to slip them into the mandarin sleeves, when suddenly something squawked and flew in through the window.

While Layana was still holding up the robe, a bird flew across the room and snatched it from her grasp with its beak.

'Hey!'

It was the raven. It took the garment to the window and flew through the bars. The delicate silk ripped as it was dragged through the ornate window guard. Then the raven opened its beak, letting the flimsy robe fall. The pair of humans at the window watched it float down, ever so slowly, to the ground beneath. It was like some colourful ghost escaping from the palace. Finally it settled on a trough down in the street. The stared to see it draped over the iron pump handle at one end.

Just then a half-naked man of the streets appeared around the corner. He spied the robe almost immediately. Looking furtively this way and that, he crossed to the pump handle and took the garment.

Soldier was about to yell down, but thought better of it, since it seemed ungenteel to shout from a palace window.

Both he and Layana watched as the beggar put on the robe.

The next moment the man was engulfed in flames. He screamed in pain, leaping into the near empty horse trough. Water splashed over him but still did not put out the fire, which burned with a supernatural intensity and colour. Finally the poor creature collapsed, lying in the dregs of the horse trough, his body still blazing.

By the time Soldier had run down the stairs of the Green Tower and out into the street, the fire was out. He found the charred remains of the beggar fouling the water of the trough. Ofao sent a servant to remove them and throw them on the rubbish heap at the back of the house. There was little else they could do for the victim of some fiendish plot to murder Soldier once again. Burial plots within the city were few and far between, and most bodies went on paper-reed boats to be floated down the covered canal to the Cerulean Sea, where the tides took them away.

The raven, for it was he who had saved Soldier, came to his shoulder as he walked back to the palace gates.

'That could have been you. Black bits of charcoal. You'd have made a nicer torch. You have more fat on you than that beggar. You'd have gone up like a priest's wax candle.'

Soldier acknowledged the raven. 'Thank you for saving my

life. I think you've wiped out the stain of your treachery now.'

'That was the idea – and to save you, of course.'

'I hope there's no irony in there.'

The bird fluttered its wings. 'Who can say? I'm just a boy with feathers. I never had no learnin', sire.'

'You know well enough. But, tell me, where did the robe come from?'

The raven shook its head, fixing Soldier with its beady eyes.

'I don't know. I swear. It's an old wizard's trick. When I saw the princess using gloves to hold the garment, I guessed.'

Soldier said, 'But it could have been precious silk.'

'I have no doubt it was, treated with some kind of flammable liquid, close to a gaseous state, which ignites when it touches the skin.'

'And you say you're an ignorant boy in feathers!'

The raven demurred. 'Well, one picks things up, here and there, over the years. I'm glad I was right, though. You might not have forgiven me if the robe had been a genuine gift. I took a chance.'

'You did well. I would rather lose the gift and err on the side of safety.'

The bird's tone became a little more serious. 'Listen, I have something to tell you. I haven't yet told you who made me the offer to betray you. It was a wizard, of course, but a bad one. This wizard bragged that terrible times were coming for good people, when his master entered the Queendom of Guthrum once again. I can only assume his master is an evil magus, intent on wresting power from the boy, IxonnoxI. What do you think?'

'I think OmmullummO is planning to return, if he is not already here. Uthellen seems to think he's near.'

'One more thing. Do you remember that round dungeon

we saw once, when we visited Uthellen and her son, down below? There's someone locked in there. I was down there, for another reason, and they spoke to me in my head. Not real words, you understand, just a notion. The prisoner asked me to let him out.'

Soldier stopped. 'I have a vague recollection – oh, yes, I do remember it. We were both intrigued by the size of the cell and who might have been incarcerated there. But I remember we thought that the occupant could not be alive, for there was no visible air supply, nor any hatch for food and water. Whoever had been sealed inside must have been dead for many years. Even the jailers thought so.'

'I'm just telling you what I feel.'

Soldier said, 'Who is he?'

'I don't know. It was just a notion, as I said. There was nothing definite there. I had the impression that he knew you. Perhaps it's someone from your old world? I have come to believe you are here for a reason. Could it be that the prisoner has sent for you to release him? I'm just casting ideas, here, sowing them as a poor farmer sows unknown seeds, scattering the ground with them, hoping they will grow into recognisable plants.'

This gave Soldier food for thought. He too believed there was a purpose behind his arrival in this world. Could it be he was here to find and release someone? His king perhaps? Or someone closer: a brother, a sister, a wife even? The gods forbid it – what of Layana if another wife emerged? Someone from a different life. There were those dreams he had, of a bride in blood-stained garland and bridal dress. No, surely not a bride. If that were so, how could he fall in love so deeply a second time? His heart would not permit it. Not a bride. But perhaps a dear friend, a very close friend, who called to him from across the tides of space and time, to come and assist him in his dire circumstances?

'Are you sure this prisoner is not just a tyrant? A despot who has deserved his incarceration? Some rogue wizard or other, from past centuries? My god,' a thought struck Soldier, 'perhaps OmmullummO? Perhaps the boy's father is locked in there?'

'You think a great wizard like OmmullummO would allow himself to be locked in a dungeon?'

Soldier thought about this. 'No – no, of course not. Unless he had been emasculated in some way, just for a short time, just long enough to get him into the cell?'

'In that case, we'd better leave well enough alone.'

Soldier shook his head, frustrated. 'Yet, if it *is* someone who needs my help . . .'

'You, my friend, are on the horns! I can't tell you which way to go. You must make the decision yourself.'

They left the subject there. Soldier knew he would ponder on it, long and hard, before deciding what to do. It was not something he could discuss with Layana. Any talk of his previous existence she saw as a threat to their happiness. Yet he felt that, even if he knew his true identity, and his old world was open to him again, he would choose to stay with her. Was love that flimsy? Could it be cast aside like an old shoe, simply because a better *life* lay elsewhere? Surely the call of this old world, which he knew from his deepest feelings had left him with ugly spiritual and emotional wounds, could not be stronger than his love for Layana? Guthrum was not perfect: far from it. But was any place perfect? Perfection did not exist. If it did there would be no need for religion, no need for good and evil, no need for life at all.

'You have many enemies, husband,' said Layana, when he

returned to his wife's side. 'You could have been burned alive. I think you should leave Zamerkand for a while, until the new King Magus is installed.'

'What about you?'

'I shall be all right. No one is trying to assassinate me. It seems you are a danger to someone quite powerful.'

'This might be another of Kaff's attempts to get rid of me, so that he can get you.'

Layana shook her head. 'No, I don't think so. He knows I would kill him now, if he harmed you. In the early days of our marriage he might have deluded himself, but not now. I don't even think this is Humbold's work. The snare was too subtle, too inventive. Even more so than the brigandine which nearly took you away from me.'

Soldier thought about it and finally agreed with his wife.

'But – I shall miss you so much,' he said, taking her in his arms. 'We seem to be forever apart.'

'It's the times. Once we have light and life in the queendom again, instead of darkness and death, we shall remain with each other.'

Soldier thought about IxonnoxI. 'The boy needs protection,' he said. 'I might go to his hiding place. I know where he'll be at this moment. He'll need a strong escort to the Seven Peaks.'

'I'm afraid, husband. You gave him a strong escort before, and look what happened. The queen wouldn't give you the commission this time, not where you've failed before.'

'I shan't do it for the queen. I shall do it privately.'

He left Layana to visit the queen and inform her of what happened at the wizard's funeral. Even Chancellor Humbold stayed in the court to listen. So did every courtier in the land: Frinstin, Keeper of the Towers; Maldrake, Lord of the Locks;

Derlish, Lady of the Sewers; Sebirtin, Keeper of the Chimneys; Quidquod — oh, many others — all in fact who were well enough to attend the relating of the tale. Soldier held them all spellbound with his powers of description. He knew how to tell a story and give it its best effect. (Captain Kaff, being on duty, could not be there and hated himself for it.) There were many sharp intakes of breath, much oohhing and ahhing, and exchanging of views in whispered voices. When he had finished, the queen thanked him for his services.

The Royal Scrivener had taken all down on parchment, writing furiously, sometimes glaring at Soldier when he went too fast, at other times so lost in the story himself he forgot to continue scribbling down the words, and had to race with rapid beating heart to catch up. Now the account was captured for all time. Later, when the monks copied the document in a more beautiful hand than the Royal Scrivener could produce, the initial letters would be illuminated, etched in colour, filled in gold and silver, and Soldier's words would be immortalised. The margins of the Book of Soldier's Story would be decorated with demons, monsters, fairies, giants, mythical beasts. There would be three volumes in all: one for the queen, one for the Great Library, and one to be locked away in a secret, fire-proof place in case the city was ever overrun and razed to the ground by barbarians. No one saw a need to give a copy to Soldier, since he held all its pages, all its words, in his head.

After the rendering, Soldier left the queen's palace to visit his companions and subordinates in the red pavilions.

Once again, it was not just Velion and the Eagle Pavilion who listened to the words, but half the army of Carthagans.

'What a tale,' said Velion, as they walked around the great

ochre tents to a feast afterwards. 'What a brilliant speaker you are.'

Soldier demurred. 'Oh, I don't know.'

'Yes, yes, you are. I've noticed that, when you speak to the warriors before a battle. You inspire them. You fill them with confidence in themselves. It's something I admire greatly in you.'

It wasn't hard to be a brilliant speaker amongst a people who loved the physical side of life and avoided learning like the plague.

'It's just a gift. I'm not responsible for it.'

'Nevertheless – ah, here we are . . .'

They had arrived at a great gathering of long, roughly-hewn tables, with benches either side. Thousands of warriors were already seated. They hammered the tabletops with their knife-butts when Soldier and Velion appeared, and a loud, grating 'Zzzzzzzuuuzzzzzzzz' noise filled the air. This was a sound of appreciation for their current hero, Soldier. He acknowledged the noise with a wide grin, lifting his arms into the air, which led to a roar of approval. Then he sat down at the head of his own pavilion's tables, his preened warriors looking like cockerels amongst a multitude of dowdy hens. He was *their* captain, this attender at the funeral of the most powerful creature in the world, and they were as proud as men and women could be.

'What's to eat?' said Soldier, looking at the repast. 'I'm suddenly famished.'

'First our traditional oatcakes,' murmured Velion, 'soaked in lard and fried to a turn.'

Suddenly, Soldier lost the edge off his appetite. 'How nice,' he said, without enthusiasm. 'No meat?'

'A little,' smiled Velion, knowing of her captain's distaste for fried oatcakes, 'but much later, when our bellies are full. That way you won't need to eat much of it. Meat's bad for you. It clogs the gut. Oatcakes, on the other hand, are full of the oily richness of well-used fat. You can *feel* them doing you good.'

He tried to feel it, but failed miserably.

Chapter Ten

Soldier spent many hours thinking about the conversation he had had with the raven. What of this prisoner in the round dungeon? Could it be someone from his own world? What if that person's mind had been so powerful as to reach out and pull Soldier from another earth to this one, in order that Soldier might free him or her? Perhaps the loss of memory, of identity, was a law of nature when crossing over? Once his work had been done here, and he returned to where he had come from, perhaps Soldier's memories would come flooding back?

'There are rumours that OmmullummO is in Gwandoland,' Layana said to him after a bout of her illness. 'Some say he will cross the sea soon and attempt to find IxonnoxI. It's also been said that OmmullummO has gathered together an army from the southern continent and is planning to land on the shores behind the Seven Peaks.'

IxonnoxI had still not emerged from hiding. Soldier had decided to respect Uthellen's desire for secrecy. He had not gone to their hideout in the forest, for fear of being followed. It was best the boy had time to become the man, before filling HoulluoH's sandals.

'Well, we could intercept him, with the red pavilions.'

'It's only a rumour. We don't know for sure.'

'The queen must have her spies out. Perhaps we should wait until there's more definite news.'

There was more than one source to support the rumour that the evil wizard was in Gwandoland. Sightings were being reported every day, by merchants and sailors and other travellers. Soldier was beginning to become convinced that OmmullummO had fled there during the reign of Queen Vanda's mother. It made sense. The southern continent, much of it unexplored, could hide a wizard more securely than the northern one. Of course even on this side of the ocean there was an Unknown Region, but if Soldier had been the one fleeing the wrath of the royal law he would have preferred a wide sea between himself and his pursuers. Oceans are often more effective barriers than either marshes or mountain ranges.

If OmmullummO was over the sea, then the creature in the dungeon was not him. Since he had begun to consider the matter Soldier had been having vivid dreams, of immolation and wrongful imprisonment, of a wretched creature in manacles begging for release. He woke, yelling incoherently, from these dreams. Someone was trying to reach him in his sleep-world, and though Soldier tried to ignore these subliminal entreaties to be set free, he found they played on his waking mind.

Soldier decided it was time to discover who the prisoner in the round dungeon was. If the occupant was someone who had sent for him, Soldier did not necessarily need to go back with that person. He was his own man. Any attempt to force him to return to his home world could be met with stiff resistance. There were plenty of places for Soldier to hide until the prisoner had left Guthrum and this earth. Soldier had made Guthrum his home, where he now had a wife, a post in the army of mercenaries, and where his heart now felt it belonged. He surely had no need to fear persuasion or threats. His position was very strong.

He went to see Queen Vanda and asked her permission to open the cell. She said she would think about it, if the key could be found, though she had a faint memory of her mother warning her never to set free 'the occupant of the oubliette'. Humbold advised that dungeons should be left well enough alone.

'Queens should not corrupt their minds by considering the dregs of our underground quods,' said Humbold. 'Queens are concerned with higher things, such as matters of state. One should leave convicts to the Lord of Thieftakers and his minions.'

Soldier went next to see the Lord of Thieftakers.

The jailers were called forth, from their subterranean world below the streets. No key could be found. Few of the jailers even knew the round dungeon existed. One or two vaguely recalled the cell described by Soldier as being in the deepest recesses of the maze of passageways and rooms which made up the world of the turnkeys.

The Lord of Thieftakers, never convinced that they should open the cell in the first place, told Soldier it would remain sealed.

'No one is in there, anyway,' said the lord. 'All we'll find is a stinking corpse.'

Soldier decided to act on his own initiative.

'Raven,' he said, 'I want you to go down there and pick the lock with that skilful beak of yours.'

'You're serious?'

'Why should I not be?'

The raven shrugged his feathered back. 'No reason, except you'll probably be hung, drawn and quartered if this goes wrong.'

Soldier went into deep thought. It was true that if he gave the order to open the dungeon and someone terrible emerged, he would be finished with Queen Vanda. Yet, if it was some harmless innocent? 'Then we have to let them out.'

The raven left Soldier standing in his favourite spot, on the balcony of the Green Tower, looking down at the activity of the market-place. Spagg was down there, selling his hanged men's hands. He seemed to be doing a brisk trade, considering the nature of his wares. Butro-batan was in one corner of the square, doing his farrier's work of shoeing horses. Soldier had yet to speak to this man about his wife's escapades. Butro-batan looked a strong, dependable type, but one could never tell from looks. Strangely enough, Corporal Tranganda was also there, sitting outside the tavern with some guardsmen, drinking ale.

At that moment a terrible storm hit the city. It swept in from the west, crashing into the castle and its walled town with such force that citizens were swept off their feet and thrown hither and thither. Thunderbolts destroyed houses. Lightning struck people in the street. The great plough horse being shoed by Butro-batan was blown over, onto its side. A heavy hay cart smashed into the base of the Green Tower.

People struggled, screaming in fear, out of the square. Soldier clung to the window bars overlooking the balcony, his feet clear of the floor. The wind was wrenching him from his anchor. Down below a woman was lifted up, the wind beneath her full skirts, and carried as high as the tower. Like a kite that has run out of breeze, she then plummeted to the ground, her skirts having blown inside out and no longer keeping her aloft.

Then the rain came, slamming into walls, towers, domes, and other architecture. It was a cold rain, very wet, with very little space between the drops. Within it, as Soldier was, it felt like a solid waterfall. Soldier managed to get his feet on the balcony rail, and from there he fought his way, inch by inch, back into the high room. There Ofao was attempting to close the shutters. He was astonished to see Soldier clambering in from the outside. He gripped Soldier by the arms, and pulled him inside.

'Quick, sire, close the windows and doors!'

Soldier helped the servant in his duties, until the room was secure. Layana came up a spiral staircase from below.

'What is it?' she cried. 'This isn't a natural storm.'

'I don't know,' replied Soldier. 'It came too suddenly. There was no build-up of clouds. The sky was clear the moment before it hurtled in out of nowhere.'

He peered through the twin-heart hole in the shutters, to see trees being uprooted, rooftops blowing apart, people being lifted off their feet and thrown violently about. There were more fireballs out there now, hurtling down from the sky. Drains were flooding in the deluge, pouring out into the streets. Canals were bursting their banks.

And still the heavens threw forth their debris.

As Soldier was peering through his spyhole, he saw something down in the streets which made his blood run cold. A man, an elderly man by his gait, was striding through the storm as if blessed by some protection no one else owned. The rain was streaming from his pale face, his hooked nose and lank hair, and soaking his flapping coat, but he remained unaffected by the wind. Where heavier souls were being whipped up and thrown rag-like away, he appeared immune to the force of the storm. There was great strength in his stride, great purpose. Soldier had the impression that here was a man exempt from ordinary trials: here was a man over whom the elements had no power whatsoever!

And behind this figure was a moving, black carpet of rats. They followed in his wake as if they were the hem of his dark cloak. These creatures too were not subject to the storm's fury. The squall went over them, around them, but not through them. When it was at its fiercest, a sudden blast, the front rats would grip the leggings of the man, and those behind would grip the tails of those in front, and so they would actually become a black bridal train, trailing out behind the man in the savage, destructive wind which had come from nowhere.

From nowhere!

Soldier remembered the funeral.

Such winds were associated with wizards.

Just before the tall figure left the square, he turned and stared up at the Green Tower, as if he knew he were being watched. Soldier was shocked to see the intensity of his eyes. Then a smile turned to a sneer on the man's features. He stared directly up at Soldier's spyhole and raised a bony fist in a kind of salute. Finally, the unshakeable form vanished into the driving rain which formed a blanket of shadows at the square's edge. He disappeared into the network of alleys and byways which ran in every direction from and to the centre of the town.

Clouds of soot now puffed from the inglenook fireplace.

Soldier could hear something struggling down the chimney. 'What?' cried Ofao. 'Ghouls? Gremlins?'

The servant rushed to the hearth and snatched up a poker, waiting where the soot fell in bundles to strike the intruder. What came out was neither ghoul nor gremlin, but a black bird made even blacker by the soot. It flapped its wings and shook its feathers, spitting out lumps of chimney ash in disgust. Soldier was just in time to stop Ofao braining the creature with the half-raised poker. The bird then coughed and spoke.

'OmmullummO!' spluttered the raven. 'It was he.'

'Who?' asked Soldier.

'The man in the round dungeon. It was he.'

There was silence in the room while this terrible news sank in. Then the princess let out a heartbroken moan.

Soldier cried in anguish, 'You set him free? I gave no order to open the dungeon.'

'Yes, yes,' cried the raven. 'You did. You said, "We have to let them out." Those were your very words, Soldier'.

'No, no. Those words were merely a continuation of my thoughts! I spoke out loud, but . . .' He groaned. 'Oh, what have you done? What have *I* done?'

'Woe is me!' cried Ofao, catching Soldier's infectious mood of despair.

'Woe is *all* of us,' said the raven, cleaning his beak with a claw. 'Or should that be *woes*?'

Once the initial shock was over, Layana was the first to collect herself. Her first thoughts were to protect her husband. In a more composed voice she told Soldier what he must do. 'You will need to flee the country. Go now, before my sister is aware of the damage that you've done. Why did you interfere in things you do not understand?'

The raven said, 'It's not much fun interfering in things you *do* understand. You can always predict the outcome.'

'Will you please, Husband, shut that bird up! I'm trying to think. IxonnoxI will need to be told as soon as possible.'

'I'll do that,' said Soldier, going towards the door. He turned at the portal. 'I'm sorry,' he said, to Layana.

'I know. Go quickly.'

He left, taking the stairs two at a time, until he was in the street. The storm was still raging, though not quite so fiercely as before, being merely the tail of what followed the wizard. Soldier fought his way through the wind to the stables, where he saddled a horse. Once that was done he was on his way. Riding across the outer bailey he saw that the gatehouse had been abandoned. Then he saw what had happened to the guards, whose empty skins were hanging from the spikes on the gate! Outside the city walls the red tents of the Carthagans were in chaos. Some had blown completely away, others had collapsed and were flapping in the wind, still more had ripped clear of their guy-lines and were in the process of scurrying across the sands like giant red crabs.

He noticed a harassed and busy Velion and called to her. 'A wizard is loose – OmmullummO. I have to warn the boy.'

She nodded and waved a hand to show she had heard.

It was night when he reached the outskirts of the forest. Looking up, he saw the silver stars fade and die in bunches, until there was nothing but blackness above, and an immense scarlet moon which filled the heavens with an ugly face. It threw its beams ferociously down at the earth, glaring intensely at Soldier riding beneath.

There was no beauty in the heavens anymore.

As he passed the forest fence Soldier was aware of a rider, behind him, coming up quickly from the south-west.

A Hannack? A beast-man? Yet his scabbard had not warned him with a song.

Nevertheless Soldier drew his sword, Xanandra, and held his horse. The figure in the saddle of the oncoming steed was barrel-chested and tall in the saddle. Finally Soldier recognised him. It was a man called Golgath, one of the Imperial Guard and the younger brother of Captain Kaff. Soldier kept his sword unsheathed, wondering if he was going to have to use it. Kaff had probably sent his brother to capture Soldier and drag him back to Zamerkand, so that the queen could deal with him.

'What do you want?' he growled at the man, as Golgath approached.

'What? A sword?' cried the other. 'No need for that, my friend.'

'I'm your friend?'

'Yes, don't you remember saving my life once? We were in battle against the Horse-people, one of whom was about to chop off my head with his battle-axe when you ran him through! I thanked you at the time and meant to follow it up, only I was posted overseas shortly afterwards. I've been in Carthaga ever since, in the post of ambassador.'

Now Soldier remembered, but in the heat of the battle, with helm and armour hiding identities, he had not realised the warrior he had saved was the brother of his mortal enemy. He was still very suspicious. How could he now go forth and find IxonnoxI if this man was with him? He could not afford to be compromised any further. IxonnoxI was not the only creature in danger. The whole world was falling around their ears.

'I can't afford to trust you,' said Soldier, speaking bluntly. 'You'll have to turn back.'

'But I know the hiding place of your friends now. It would be silly to send me away. If I were against you, I would do just that, and report back to my brother.'

This was true, of course.

'Do you love your brother?' asked Soldier.

'Of course – as a brother. But I owe him nothing. You saved my life. I owe you everything. If it were not for you I would be filling a hole in the earth.'

Golgath was a large man, a man born with the figure any warrior would envy for the purpose of their trade of fighting. If he were a true man he would be an invaluable companion. Soldier had been accompanied on all his quests by the wily Spagg, good with a throwing knife, but just as likely to run on being attacked. Soldier could do with someone to watch his back. But Kaff's brother? He wished he could speak with Layana at this moment and ask her advice. She would know both brothers.

Eventually he said, 'I think it's as you say. I have no option *but* to trust you. But let me tell you this. One hint of betrayal – one tiny hint – and I'll end your life there and then.'

Golgath smiled. 'You think you could?'

'I *know* I could.'

Soldier had spoken the words boldly and bravely, but both men knew that the outcome of any contest between them was not so sure. On his side Soldier had an unmitigated fury which, when unleashed, was more difficult to stop than a hurricane. He was also skilled in war. On the other hand, Golgath was a big man, versed in the use of weapons, a good horseman, a man bred to both single combat and battle. He was a 'hero', in the sense of the word that meant his stature was above ordinary men, his courage never at fault and his commitment total.

Soldier would have liked to think he might have the edge because of his keen mind. But Golgath, too, was an intelligent man. Soldier had heard that Kaff's younger brother had stopped the Carthagans from burning the library of an enemy city while it was being sacked. They said he looted it, taking away many books, but treating the stolen goods with great care, reading every single volume before the journey home was over. He claimed to be a poet (though all courtiers did that, while most of them couldn't complete a couplet without reaching for a rhymer's dictionary), was a learned astro-philosopher, a keen bridge-builder, and had been first in his class as a diviner of the outcome of battles.

Any fight between these two men would be a mighty duel, to be watched by god, man and beast.

Soldier found also, as they progressed into the forest, that his companion's manners were more refined than his brother's.

'You left Zamerkand later than me,' said Soldier, 'how was the queen?'

'Very angry with you. Had you been there you would have lost your head for certain. It's a good job you fled.'

'I didn't *flee*. I simply came in search of IxonnoxI.'

'As you say. Anyway, OmmullummO has already sent a pestilence to the city which was responsible for his incarceration. A green fungus is creeping through Zamerkand, rotting the wood and corroding the stone. It's amazing how quickly it's spreading. It literally flowed through building and along street, corrupting everything. Insects, mice and other pests have increased ten-fold. I suspect a plague will follow. It usually does.'

'You have seen this kind of thing before?'

'I have witnessed the displeasure of a wizard. HoulluoH

did not always hold Zamerkand in favour. You know we shan't be safe for long, don't you? OmmullummO will send legions of his creatures to hunt us down. We shall need to be on the move all the while.'

'I guessed as much.'

Eventually the pair came across the camp of Uthellen and the boy, in the glade known only to them and Soldier. Now Golgath also knew of the hideout, but this did not seem to perturb IxonnoxI, who had enough insight now to know who was friend and who was foe.

'Welcome, Soldier, Golgath,' said the boy. 'My mother will give you some food.'

Soldier found that IxonnoxI already knew that his father had usurped his throne.

'I see his footprints even now crossing the landscape to the Seven Peaks.'

Soldier said. 'Are you anywhere near ready?'

'Another year or so.'

'Another *year*?' cried Soldier. 'You gave me the impression you were close to being able to take your uncle's place as King Magus.'

The boy smiled. 'I am close. That is close, in the grand scheme of a wizard's life. My problem will now be to stay alive until my magic is mature enough for me to take on my father in battle. I will need your help then, Soldier. I will need you to lead my army.'

Soldier realised now that this was not to be single combat between two wizards, but a war. Such a war would rend the world apart.

'Is it necessary,' he asked, 'to drag humans into your struggle?'

'The Seven Peaks are in Guthrum only by chance,'

explained IxonnoxI. 'The King Magus rules far and wide, over the whole near, far and middle earth. You believe you come from another world, Soldier? Perhaps you do, but to cross from there to here, these worlds must be in close proximity. I believe that, if this is so, what happens on this earth will spill over into your earth, Soldier. If an evil rules this world for the next few centuries, it will affect the history of your birthworld. Perhaps you are the link between, the man sent from one place to another, in order to save both?'

Soldier felt very uncomfortable with this idea. He did not like the weight it put on his shoulders. He did not feel adequate for such a huge responsibility, for such an enormous task. The saviour not just of one world, but of two, or even more? He was just a small man, a man of limited talents, a man with as many petty faults, flaws, desires and troubles as any other. Why should he be the one with so great a burden? There were surely others more capable, more worthy? His confidence sank deep within him, refusing to be stirred.

Golgath was looking at him in awe, but Soldier said, 'I don't want to do this work. I'm not able to do these things. You have the wrong man.'

IxonnoxI refused to be drawn into an argument about it.

'There is no wrong or right man. There is only you.'

'But – but if I had been sent for a purpose, surely the plans would have been better laid. Why, I was nearly executed just for being here, yet Uthellen did nothing to save me. *You* did nothing. Surely, if this was ordained, I would have married Uthellen, so that I could watch you constantly as you grew up, guarded you, saw you into manhood, or wizardhood, or whatever you call it? Instead, I married a mad princess, a women assailed by demons of the head, whose marred beauty caused me to sate my bloodlust on her attacker. I am no saviour, no man of purity. You can see that.'

IxonnoxI nodded. 'You certainly have your faults, but one of them can't be helped, it's a human condition. To fall in love. I think you would have fallen for the Princess Layana even had she been the lowest peasant in the land. You are that kind of man. You follow your heart. But then if such a man as you followed his *head*, you would not fall in love at all – you would want to be the ruler of the world!'

Golgath said, 'He's right there, Soldier.'

'But I still don't want this work,' said Soldier.

'It will fall on you without the need to want,' replied IxonnoxI, and the subject was then at a close.

The raven came to Soldier as he was sitting alone, moodily contemplating a brown pool in the forest.

'Hey, ho? Why so glum? The world's falling apart – everything's rotting – bits dropping off everywhere – but that's no cause for a miserable countenance! Cheer up! Worse things happen on a cross-country flight!'

'Not to me, they don't,' muttered Soldier.

'So, now we're in the stew, eh? Letting the Grand Wizard of All Evil out of jail. Visiting pestilence and plague on the earth. Causing the deaths of thousands, perhaps millions. We're in *biiiig* trouble, aren't we?' cried the raven, far too cheerfully.

'I would prefer you to leave me alone,' said Soldier.

'Well, there's gratitude for you. I came to cheer you up, and get ordered away again! Oh, by the way, your wife's dead.'

'What?' cried Soldier in anguish, springing to his feet. 'My dear wife? Dead?'

'Not really,' cackled the raven. 'There! Don't you feel so much better now? You thought the princess was dead, but now I can assure you she's alive, even if she isn't all that well.

Isn't that a relief? Puts everything in perspective, doesn't it?'

Soldier cried, 'What do you mean, not all that well?'

'Did I say the princess?' said the raven, as cheerful as ever. 'I must have meant someone else.'

Soldier stood there in the gloaming in silence. He regarded the bird through narrowed eyes. 'One of these days,' he said, 'I swear.'

'Well, I can't stand here chatting all day, cheering you up like this. I must be off! There are birds to see, deeds to be done. Next time I come by I want you to be in a better frame of mind, then we can talk about more serious matters. Until then, try to watch your back. There'll be all sorts after skinning you. OmmullummO will send demon and devil against you. You must beware. You must be ready. Or run. Yes, perhaps that's the best thing to do. Run away. Well, I'll be off then.'

The raven opened his wings and flew into the shadows of the trees, leaving Soldier alone once more.

Soldier was fuming with the bird, but then he had to admit the feathered fiend spoke a lot of truth. He did only have two choices: to stand, or to flee. The second sounded the more sensible course at such a time, when enemies might come out of every rotten log. It was one thing to stand and fight in an open battle, where both sides were ranged against each other and there were no hidden forces. But this was going to be a guerrilla war for some time yet. OmmullummO wanted IxonnoxI dead and assassins were the best answer for that at the moment.

'Pack up,' he said, as he arrived back in camp just as that horrible moon appeared over the trees. 'We must be on the move.'

'What, now?' cried Golgath. 'At night?'

'Yes, now, while we know those howling beasts are wolves and not something far more sinister. Up, then. On your feet. Take only what you can carry. By dawn we must be somewhere else entirely.'

Chapter Eleven

Soldier took them out into flat marsh country in the Unknown Region. Like a hare being pursued by a fox, he felt his best defence was open ground, where he could see what was coming from any direction. Here he set up camp with IxonnoxI, Uthellen and Golgath. They made bivouacs from the tall reeds, simply gathering a bunch, trying it at the top and cutting out the inside reeds to form a hollow cone. Each had his own. For fare they set snares about the marshes for rabbits and fished in dank areas where pools had formed. Occasionally one of them managed to bring in a duck or heron, once even a swan.

In the meantime, IxonnoxI practised his art. He carried a stinking sack with him full of disgusting objects he had collected from various places: dried toadstools, dead birds and other creatures, slugs, snails, fetid toads, animal droppings of all kinds, the snot from the nostrils of larger creatures such as the cow or horse, feathers, frogspawn, the intestines of mice – all were among his loathsome collection. These he used, one way or another, to train himself. The two men complained of the stench coming from the sack, but IxonnoxI just shook his head and smiled.

He was still a callow youth with little experience in magic. It was amazing to Soldier that such a boy had been chosen as the King Magus, the most powerful wizard in the world, when he was clearly still a novice. He mentioned this to Golgath.

'Oh, well, it's the *timing* that's wrong here,' said that perfect courtier, who knew all things genteel and all things regal. Look on it as if a king had died and left his infant son to inherit the kingdom. The boy would have no inkling on how to proceed. He would need advisors, an uncle for regent, training – many things to help him. For the first few years he would be in great danger, from ambitious nobles and foreign enemies. But once he found his feet – and to survive he'd have to do that quickly – he would find he had the power to do almost anything.

'Many child kings and queens have learned artifice, have come into slyness and craftiness as a matter of necessity, and have been more secure rulers because of it. Adults who become monarchs have usually been cosseted until the time of their coronation – their king fathers or queen mothers protecting them until now – and then suddenly they find they have to make decisions, take responsibility, learn who to trust and who not to trust. It's much the same with wizards coming to power. This youth needs us to protect him. He needs a few years in isolation, in order to mature and grow into the mighty being he will one day become. OmmullummO will try to kill him before that happens.'

They watched the boy, as he taught himself his magic. The results were sometimes hilarious, sometimes bordering on the tragic.

One midnight hour they witnessed the art of raising the dead.

Since there were no human corpses out in the marshes at the back end of nowhere, IxonnoxI had to make do with dead animals. He found a wild horse that had become trapped in the mire and had died of exposure. The creature had been dead some ten days. It stank. It was riddled with small creatures, eating its eyes, gums and various soft-tissue organs. Its coat was manky and its mane and tail falling out.

Soldier and Golgath watched from a distance as IxonnoxI placed stones in a ring about this carcass, carved wooden idols on spiked sticks and plunged them into the bloated corpse. Putrid air hissed from the holes he made with the spikes, making the tattered hide, with ribs showing bare in places, deflate. Finally, all was ready. Night was the time for most magic, especially resurrection. Magic is susceptible to atmospheres. There is more *feel* to magic, which has a logic of its own, of course, but bends towards the preternatural. Philosophy was almost the opposite of magic, in that it required set rules and laws. Magic *drew* its rules and laws its surroundings, as dry paper draws moisture from the air.

The boy stood silhouetted by the blood moon. He was naked, burnished, gleaming in the dull light. Uthellen did not want to witness any of this: she had gone to bed early in her bivouac. Soldier wondered whether he should be in his: he shivered, not with the cold but with fearful anticipation. It seemed that all the world's darkness, from places hidden from the day, had gathered around the young wizard. Tendrils of night hung like black ribbons from the ether and trailed into the marshland grasses. Words came then, strange words, unpronounceable, unrepeatable only a second after they were spoken. They were full of a harsh consonants and ullulating vowels. Soldier and Golgath clamped their hands to their heads in pain, as the words entered their minds like searing irons, blinding their brains with the impact of unmeaning.

When they could see again, when the agony of those words had subsided, they let fall their hands.

The sight was horrific.

'It is!' cried IxonnoxI. 'It is!'

The corpse of the horse had risen to its feet. It shook its head as it tried to see through the eyeless sockets in its skull. Blind. It was blind and dumb, its orbs and tongue having been eaten by beetles. Bits were falling from its hide. Rotting intestines bulged from holes in its torso. Fluids dripped, flowed. Hair fell out.

The revived beast stumbled forwards, began trotting, cantering, and eventually broke into a gallop, charging round in ever-increasing circles, its mouth open as it whinnied deep from its hollow insides, distorted without the use of its tongue.

'Gods and demons preserve us!' cried Golgath, staggering backwards as the beast flew past him, wild and insane. 'May the earth swallow the beast quickly.'

Bits of mud and marsh grass were flying everywhere, from fore and hind hoof. Divots were catapulted at the moon. The creature thundered now, as it found its living form. Its feet hammered on the hollow peat, drumming out an unearthly rhythm. As Soldier struggled to get out of its way, it struck him with its shoulder, sending him flying into a bog. He sank immediately to his waist, yelling for help.

'I'm coming,' cried Golgath, ankle-deep in mire and fighting to keep his own feet. 'I'm coming.' His own feet were being sucked into the soft bog as he tried to reach Soldier while dodging the frantic dead horse as it careered around the marsh, unseeing, crashing into dwarf trees and smashing through reed beds. A tail flailed his face, stinging his eyes, as the runaway steed swept near to him, but Golgath kept his feet and managed to reach the sinking figure of Soldier.

'Your hand!' cried Soldier, the quickmud up to his shoulders. 'A strap or something!'

Golgath panicked and whipped out his sword, offering the blade for Soldier to grasp. Then he realised what he'd done.

'Sorry, sharp as a razor, I know.'

He whipped off his belt next and used the scabbard. Soldier grabbed it and Golgath dug in his heels. The big man managed to haul Soldier from the sucking mud, slowly but definitely. In the meantime the dead horse still flew around, narrowly missing both men in its chaotic motion. The steed then went straight for Uthellen's bivouac.

Soldier got to his knees and screamed, 'Uthellen! Wake up! Get out of there.'

Too late. The horse crashed through the reeds. Uthellen, naked as the moon, was kicked out of her bed. She rolled about but fortunately did not seem too hurt. She scrambled back to the shattered bivouac and retrieved a blanket to cover her modesty, finally remaining there, sitting up, looking startled and shocked.

The dead charger bore on, turning in a wide circle. There was a great oak on the edge of the marsh, with an old, thick trunk. The steed went crashing headfirst straight into a knurl of this old fellow, who stood his ground like any ancient, respectable oak should. The horse seemed to concertina all the way down its ribcage. Then it appeared to explode into bits of bones and hide, and scattered pieces of itself over the dyke on which the oak tree stood. Flaps of skin hung from branches. A hoof went spinning out into the night and ended with a splash in a natural ditch. The great eyeless head remained locked in the crotch of the oak, broken from the stem that had been its neck, divorced from the torso.

'It was!' cried a delighted IxonnoxI. 'It was!'

He seemed in no way alarmed at the havoc he had caused. The antics of his mad steed did not concern him. All he seemed interested in was the fact that he had managed to raise the dead. His mother had been injured. His friend and protector, Soldier, had almost drowned in mud. Yet there were no apologies, no remorse over a badly managed deed. Resurrection had taken place. The end justified the act.

'The youth of today,' muttered Golgath. 'They've got no sense of responsibility, have they? Selfish, right through to the core. I'm sure I was never like that, when I was his age. I remember respecting the rights of others, especially my elders and betters . . .'

He went on, in this vein, much as men do who have left their vibrant, devil-may-care attitudes back with their puberty.

Somehow they all managed to get to sleep that night. In the morning they had a visit from the raven.

'Things are happening out there,' said the raven. 'Good men are becoming villains and murderers, bad men are becoming unspeakable. Clean waters have been poisoned, the cattle are going stark staring mad. There is an evil unfolding in the land. It's killing the grasses with its foul odours, trees are rotting at the roots, birds are falling dead from the skies. The Snake-people have returned from their exile in the Empty Quarter. They're as nasty as they ever were, maybe worse.'

'And the good news?' asked Soldier.

'Nothing good. Something funny though.'

'Which is?'

'Several horses rose from the grave and went thundering about the countryside last night. It was mayhem. Some of the carcasses were so far gone they fell to bits during their first gallop.'

Soldier raised his eyebrows at this. 'That boy's magic is more powerful than he realises. These Snake-people – head of snake, body of man?'

'That's them. Eyes of demons, minds of devils. There's one over there, waiting to speak with you. He says he's an envoy, under a flag of truce. Don't believe him. Don't believe anything. Learn not to trust.'

Soldier looked in the direction indicated by the raven's flick of the head and saw a creature sitting on a horse, watching him, waiting patiently to be seen and called forward.

'You brought him here?'

'Yes, but he's alone. He trapped me in a rattan cage, using a delicious cat's liver for bait. Have you ever tasted raw cat's liver? No? It's to die for – and I nearly did. He said he needed to talk to you: that it was to your advantage. He said if I didn't take him to your hideout, he'd wring my neck and roast me over a slow, hot fire.'

'I suspect it was the second reason which prompted you to agree to meet his request.'

'You guessed right.'

'Advance,' Soldier called to the rider. He gripped his warhammer, aware that his singing scabbard had not felt it necessary to warn him of the approach of the stranger. 'Slowly.'

Close to, the monstrous reptilian-headed creature peered at Soldier. A forked tongue flicked incessantly from between two sharp, white fangs. Yellow-black eyes glared coldly down. The beast-warrior was armed with bow and heavy sword, sitting high in his saddle, his scaly face at variance with the suntanned skin of his arms, legs and chest. The near-naked warrior – only a ragged loincloth covering his nether parts –

was tattooed over most of his body. When he spoke the words came out like cold steam, partly through the mouth, partly through the slitted nostrils.

'Yshoo will gssive me the boy.'

It was not a question. The rider stated he was from OmmullummO and represented the wizard in these matters. He then went on to list the rewards for handing IxonnoxI over to the Snake-people. There were lands and castles, titles and deeds, villages, towns, mighty herds of cattle, lakes, even a mountain. Soldier remained unmoved. He told the Snake-warrior to leave before single combat took place on that shabby piece of turf.

'You have heard of Vau, the Dog-warrior? I am the man who slew him. They say it is a campfire tale now, amongst the beast-people.'

'Yshoo are he?'

'I am the slayer.'

The snake head nodded slowly, respect entering the eyes now.

'Perhapsssss they lie?'

'Why would they lie about a defeat? If Vau had killed me, and had boasted of the ease with which he destroyed me, you would have reason to doubt the story. As it is, it was I who killed one of their kind, efficiently, quickly, without any mercy. In fact, I hear they say that it was the coldest, most savage killing they had ever witnessed in their lives.'

'True it isss. That'sss what they ssssay.'

'Then you know it would not be an easy victory for you. Now go.'

The reptile-man glared at him once again, a cold calculation of his chances flickered through his eyes, weighing the odds of victory at single combat. Like many beast-people who had now come face to face with Soldier, he could not see how this human had earned his reputation as a warrior. To the reptile-headed horseman, this Soldier before him seemed as vulnerable as any other human. However, the fact remained: the dog-headed Vau had been a remarkable champion, and if this creature had defeated Vau, and others of equal stamp, then he had hidden qualities which it would be foolish to ignore.

Finally, the snake-head turned his horse and galloped off, westwards.

Soldier knew they had to move camp now. It would have been expedient to hide the boy on one of the smaller islands off the Guthrum shore-line: Oytledat to the west, or Stell, Amekni, Begrom or Refe to the east. These islands were almost all of what was left of the empire. They still paid tribute and owed allegience to Guthrum's monarch. Their citizens had been vassals of the Guthrum's queen for so long there was but a dim memory of former independence. The small-islanders were doing very well as part of the empire and for the moment any thought of freedom was lost in the feeling of well-being which sprang from having good trade routes with two continents and from their resident merchants and burghers, whose wealth filtered down to the poorest citizen.

However, to reach a port Soldier would have had to cross the country with his boy-wizard and that would enhance any current danger. It was best to stay in the Unknown Region, beyond the Scalash River, and lose the boy there in marsh or scrub woodland.

They found a crevice running between two high moors, full of stunted, bearded oaks. On either side the purple moors curved up to plateaus where they swept away, broken only by the occasional clutch of tors. There were small, stone dwellings in the far distance – the homes of boggarts, so Soldier was told – but boggarts never wandered more than a mile away from their crofts, so Soldier felt they were safe out of sight below the ridge which fell down to the crevice-shaped valley. There was clean water there, and some wildlife, and they were effectively screened by the beard-growths that hung from the branches of the oaks.

At night, under cover of near-darkness, Soldier and Golgath went up onto the moors to hunt. It was while out on one of these hunts that the raven came to them. They did not see it descend in the dimness of what poor light was to be had from the blood moon, the bird owning the midnight-coloured feathers of its kind, and drifting down soundlessly to its chosen perch. Golgath felt something land on his shoulder as his horse attempted to find its footing on rocky ground.

'Ahhhhh!' cried Golgath, frighted. He swiped at his shoulder with a gauntlet. The raven jumped the blow, landing back on his perch again.

'Don't do that,' he said, into Golgath's ear.

'Ahhhhh!' yelled Golgath again. 'I feel a demon's claw on my back! I hear its voice in my ear!'

'Demon?' cried Soldier, drawing his sword. 'Keep your head still, while I slice it in two.'

'Stop! Stop!' the raven shouted, flying out of harm's reach, 'it's me, you idiots. The raven. I bring another warning . . . too late, it's here, it's very, very near. Run away. Run! Run!'

At that moment Soldier's magic scabbard began her eerie song, which meant that an ambush was imminent.

Soldier turned his horse and said to Golgath, 'Ride! Quickly! Back the way we came.'

Golgath had now known Soldier long enough not to argue

with any instinctive decisions he made. He followed his friend's horse on his own.

When they were a good distance from the spot where the danger had been lurking, Soldier reined his mount. Golgath came up alongside him. The horses were heaving with the effort of the run and the two men, shaken and tired with concentrating on their path in the bad light, were feeling equally exhausted. This time the raven landed on Soldier's shoulder and he felt its familiar weight without shying.

'Raven. What's the hazard?'

'OmmullummO has sent a cockatrice to find you. It drags its ugly tail across the moor behind us in search of you. The creature leaves a trail of dead in its wake.'

'Dead?'

'Any living creature – except the weasel, of course – who sets eyes on a cockatrice, or smells its breath, or hears its hiss, dies in agony.'

Golgath was sceptical. 'You know it's coming? How do you know, if you haven't seen, heard or smelled it?'

'Because a weasel told me.'

That was fair enough.

'How do we kill this creature?' asked Soldier.

The raven replied, 'That's for you to decide. I tell you again, its breath withers all vegetation, the very sight of it is fatal, its hissing is lethal to living ears and the touch of its skin will shrivel a man to a hollow husk. If you stick a weapon into it – say a sword, or spear – the creature's deadly venom will travel from the cockatrice up the weapon and shrink the heart of the bearer to the point of death. I'll be very interested in seeing how you manage to kill this beast from hell.'

Soldier nodded. 'I'm sure you will be. I assume it doesn't know where our hideout is.'

'Not yet. But it has tracked you this far. When daylight comes it'll be on your trail again. It's only a matter of hours. You're all doomed.'

'Don't sound so happy about it,' said Soldier, through gritted teeth. 'Well, Golgath?' He turned to his companion. 'Any ideas?'

'The weapon,' said Golgath. 'It has to be a missile. An arrow. Or a thrown spear. Something of that sort.'

'Not necessarily a missile — a pit with spikes might work.'

'Ooooo,' the raven said. 'We're doing well, so far.'

'Be quiet, bird,' ordered Soldier. 'Now, what does this monster look like?'

The bird remained silent.

'All right, all right,' muttered Soldier, wearily, 'you can talk to me if you wish. Can I please know the physical nature of our enemy?'

'It's about two feet in length,' replied the raven, 'with the body of a cockerel and the tail of a snake. Its colour, including its wings, is yellow, and it has the eyes of a toad. Sometimes, so I'm told, it curls its horrible tail up over its back. It can split a rock with its glance. I've seen the devastation it leaves behind it. A strip of desert littered with debris. OmmullummO was said to have created this one from the egg of a cockerel, the egg being the root which grows a cockatrice. Cock's eggs, as you may guess, are pretty rare. If you kill his monster it's doubtful he'll manage to make another for a while. Not one of the same.'

The two men went back to discussing possible methods of killing the cockatrice before any of the party either saw, smelled, heard or touched the dreadful creature. It seemed impossible! How could one get near enough to such a monster without being killed? The raven waited patiently for the two men to finish their discussion, before telling them how it could be done.

'A weasel,' said the bird. 'You've forgotten what I've already told you just a short while ago. The weasel is the only living creature immune to the cockatrice's lethal charms. A weasel will attack the monster on sight. The same enmity exists between the weasel and the cockatrice as exists between a mongoose and a snake.'

'We have to trap a weasel,' said Soldier. 'Now, are we speaking generally of weasel-like creatures? Will a stoat do? Or a ferret?'

'I'm not certain, but I think they're considered of the same ilk,' replied the raven. 'What have you got to lose? If you can't catch a weasel, a stoat or ferret will have to do.'

'What shall we use as bait?'

Golgath suggested, 'Raven?'

'Very funny,' clucked the bird. 'Have you caught any rabbits lately? Or mice? Voles?'

It was dawn when they reached the oaks and they found Uthellen and the youth up and about.

'IxonnoxI,' cried Soldier, dismounting. 'Can you create anything yet? I mean, we've seen you raise the dead, but can you make a creature from nothing?'

'Not from *nothing*, no. What do you want?'

'A weasel, or a stoat, or even a ferret.'

The boy beamed with pleasure.

'I've got a weasel's corpse, here in my sack. A poor raggedy creature which I found hanging on a farmer's gibbet outside Bhantan. I collected several other carcasses from that gibbet. In fact,' he opened the sack and began rooting around, peering into his bag of treasures, And I've got moles and squirrels — and a dead young fox too! Would you like me to raise them all from the dead?'

The memory of raising the dead horse was still vivid in the minds of the two men, which caused Soldier to hestitate for a moment, but then he was mindful of the urgency of the thing.

'Just the weasel,' said Golgath.

'How soon,' asked Soldier, 'can the resurrection take place?'

IxonnoxI transformed the dead weasel into a live one within the hour. All the while the excited raven was telling everyone that he sensed the approach of the cockatrice, that if the wizard-boy was not quick they would all be cinders. He flapped around, landed, stamped around, and generally made himself a nuisance, until he was told by Soldier to stop hindering IxonnoxI or else.

'Or else what?' cried the belligerent raven. 'You want to fight me? In single combat? I'm a champion, I am. I've sent two crows, three jays and a dozen rooks to their grave. I'm the fastest thing on two wings. I could peck your eyes out before you could say "Jack Daw". You want to watch who you challenge, you do. I'm a veteran, I am.'

'How about you fight the cockatrice?' Golgath said, which had the desired effect of silencing the bird.

Finally, the weasel was alive and running. Running so fast around her flimsy cage she was in danger of breaking out. But her wicker prison held her. When they stared at her they could see holes in her coat, one ear was missing, and her hind kneebones were showing through her musty-smelling fur. Also, disconcertingly, her tail had gone, which made her rudderless and a little inclined to run sideways at times.

'Are you sure she's any good?' said Soldier, doubtfully. 'Will she get the job done?'

IxonnoxI was quite proud of his reincarnation.

'Of course. Good as any live weasel. I mean, a weasel that had not died in the first place. Now, one of us has to carry the cage, with her in it, to the cockatrice. I've also made this, for that brave person to wear . . .'

Uthellen stared at her son's invention. It was a mask, with eyeholes, such as brigands and robbers might wear. IxonnoxI had fashioned it out of reeds. However, stretched over the rather small eyeholes was a kind of filmy skin.

'You wear it like this,' explained the wizard-boy, putting on the mask and looking like some god of a primitive tribe.

Soldier tried it on next. His vision was slightly distorted. He could see shapes through the translucent eyes, shadowy forms, but nothing had a definite keen edge to it.

'What are these?' Soldier went to touch one of the eyes in the mask, but IxonnoxI yelled at him.

'Don't! They're delicate. They're fashioned from a weasel's eyes. Eyes I took from another of my corpses – one in a more advanced state of decay, it's true. But putrefaction apart, they'll protect the wearer from the glare of the cockatrice. If the weasel is the only creature which can look on the cocka- trice with impunity, then I believe we can use its eyes to peer through.'

'What's this crazed effect?' questioned Soldier, inspecting the membranes dubiously.

IxonnoxI said, proudly, 'I skinned the eyes and used spider's webs to stick the skins to the mask.'

Golgath shook his head in distrust. 'It doesn't sound very convincing to me. Surely it won't work – will it? I for one would not trust the skin from the rotting orbs of some dead weasel to keep me from being scorched to a cinder. Would you, Soldier?'

'I – well, truthfully – it seems a very fragile plan.'

'Do the weasels ever lose?' asked Golgath of the wizard-boy. 'Are they ever defeated?'

'Who knows?' IxonnoxI said, cheerfully. 'Do you know, raven?'

'If they were ever beaten, there'd be nothing left of them but ashes, so how *could* you know?'

'It all sounds rather risky to me,' Soldier complained.

IxonnoxI was serious now. 'What choice do we have?'

Both Soldier and Golgath admitted there was none.

Uthellen suddenly snatched the mask from her son's hands and said, 'I'll be the one.'

'One what?' said Soldier.

'I'll take the weasel out to kill the monster.'

Once the woman amongst them had volunteered to do the task, the two men immediately told her she couldn't, that it had to be one of them. Why? Because she was a woman and they were men. It was obvious why. Uthellen said it wasn't obvious at all, for she could do the task as well as any man. All it involved was carrying a cage and releasing the occupant. They protested. She protested. They protested harder. Eventually they drew lots. Soldier lost. They set to work on him.

They stuffed wax in his ears and plugged his nostrils with the same material. He could hear nothing, smell nothing. His ears hurt and his nose hurt. He told them there was too much wax and to remove some. They frowned and moved their mouths and he took this silent reply as a refusal. He was then handed the woven reed mask. Lastly he picked up the cage with the mad weasel still racing around in circles inside it, and walked off into the day. The others shouted their farewells, wished him good luck. These encouragements went unheard. Soldier felt very alone and isolated in his world of utter silence.

At noon he came across a swathe of deadness which ran across the landscape, a wide track of withered plants and hunched trees. The still bodies of animals and birds littered the scene. Even as he watched, an eagle dropped from the heavens and landed with a thump on the ground ahead. After falling to earth it never moved. Whatever had killed it — with sight, sound or odour — was behind a cluster of rocks ahead.

Soldier's heart was beating fast. He whipped the mask over his features. Immediately the world became a vague, misty place. He moved cautiously forwards, holding the caged weasel. The ragged weasel herself had now stopped hurtling clockwise round her prison and was up on her hind legs like a short pole, alert, breathing shallowly, expectant. Neck stretching, little head going from side to side, eyes staring keenly ahead, she *knew*. On the nape of her neck her hair was bristling. Her senses had warned her that her enemy was somewhere in the vicinity.

Soldier rounded a hill spur and immediately his flesh started to crawl. He could see a small, strange, winged creature just ahead, dragging a thick, loathsome tail behind it. On noticing Soldier the creature stopped, seemed to peer hard at him, then opened its foul beak. Whatever the sound was which came out, Soldier did not hear it. Whatever deadly vapours it was producing, Soldier did not smell them. Any hissing, any release of pungent gas, was wasted on the weasel-eyed Soldier.

Not on the resurrected weasel, though! She flung herself at the wall of her flimsy cage and burst through the wicker-work in a fury of excitement. Racing across the ground between her and the most deadly creature on earth, she hurtled straight into the face of her foe. Some kind of ancient hatred flared between these two protagonists. The reasons behind it had been long forgotten, but the enmity still simmered and boiled over whenever these two combatants met each other. On turf or sandy desert, on stony mountain or woody slope: they immediately rolled into a furious ball of biting, scratching fur and feather; teeth drawing blood, beak stabbing through muscled hide, spit and bits of body flying.

No human was meant to witness the battle of two such savage creatures. The attacks were swift and merciless, the injuries quick and horrible. Soldier was shocked to the core by the ferocity of the contest. Even through weasel's eyes it was a terrifying sight, an ordeal even, that he would gladly have forgone. It was not something which a human mind could absorb without horror welling up in the throat, without bile burning the belly. Better, he felt, to turn away from such a scene.

Yet he could not turn, could not cast his eyes down, for the terrible fight held his dread-seized brain in thrall.

Finally, out of that hurricane of fur and feather, the weasel emerged triumphant, licking her wounds with that small red tongue, satisfied that victory – once again – had gone against her eternal supernatural enemy. Soldier could see by her rolling gait, her swagger, that weasels were used to winning such encounters. There was such pride in her bearing, such arrogance in her tread. The weasel slipped away, into the rocks, and out onto the plain beyond, having been granted an extended life by a wizard-boy practising to become the King Magus.

With its throat torn out, the cocktrice lay in a pool of its own acid fluids, decomposing. Soldier had been told not to look on the corpse with the naked eye. Nor to remove the wax from his ears, for its after-life hiss was as deadly as ever.

He simply turned and left it, making his way back to where the others waited in the camp. When he reached them, he removed his ear and nose plugs. As he informed them of the victory, they chortled and let their relief be known to the world. They slapped him on the back and asked him to describe the fight.

'Never,' he said, meaning it. 'I never could.'

Chapter Twelve

In Zamerkand, events were moving at a pace. After OmmullummO had made his escape towards the Seven Peaks, Chancellor Humbold used the chaos in the land to his advantage. On the midnight hour two hired assassins entered the chambers of a sleeping Marshal Crushkite and stabbed him a dozen times in the heart. The murderers' rising and plunging daggers kept time with the strokes of the the clock. He was dead and gone before the striking of twelve. The murderers reported back to Humbold. He paid them and sent them on their way, over the Cerulean Sea. The captain of the ship which carried them had no knowledge of the murder, but Humbold had given him orders to throw the two men overboard, halfway to his destination. The captain believed they were street scum, responsible for crimes for which they could not be brought to justice under the law. He was happy to be their executioner, thinking he had right on his side.

Humbold then went to see Captain Kaff. 'Crushkite is dead,' he told the captain. 'Someone murdered him last night.'

Kaff sat up in bed, his bird claw gripping the sheets. 'Murdered? By whom?'

'No one knows, but I want you to take over command of the army. Assume a colonel's rank, first of all. Later we'll make you a general, once we have her . . . once we have the queen's approval.'

Kaff was surprised. 'I don't know. You mean we do *not* have the queen's approval for this appointment.'

'The queen,' said Humbold with narrowed eyes, 'is mad. Didn't you know?'

Kaff was silent for a while, then he said, 'Is this all legal? I merely ask out of curiosity.'

'In law,' said Humbold, sitting on the end of Kaff's bed, 'I can appoint whom I choose. I am the chancellor. But it's customary to seek the queen's agreement at some time. Purely protocol. Nothing to do with rules and regulations. That's all up to the chancellor. Me.'

'If you say so,' Kaff said, beginning to dress. 'I'll be with you shortly.' Ambition was a heady tonic, first thing in the morning. To find himself leaping from captain to a general's post before breakfast went straight to Kaff's head. Chancellor Humbold left him to pull on his socks in a thoughtful and rather jubilant mood. A colonel, shortly to be general, with a marshal's crest rising like a sun over the horizon, stood much more chance with an abandoned princess whose husband was out of the royal favour.

Humbold went straight to the Palace of Birds. 'Where is the queen?' he asked the boudoir slaves. 'Is she up yet?'

'Yes, up master, but still in the same mind.'

Good. Since the release of the wizard she had slid into insanity. And now she was still as mad as yesterday. Just so. He could commit her to a padded cell down below the streets. The Lord of Thieftakers was one of Humbold's men. So were most of the others. Only Frinstin, Keeper of the Towers, and

Quidquod, Lord of the Royal Purse, were his opponents.

Kaff arrived to join him now.

'I need some guards with me,' said Humbold, 'please fetch some. Two turnkeys are arriving from the Lord of Thieftakers to escort the queen to a safer place.'

'Safer place? What safer place? Why?'

'Have you no eyes? Have you no ears? There is a rogue wizard abroad. The queen will need protecting. In her madness she is vulnerable and liable to compromise the queendom. For her own safety's sake she needs to be in a secure place, with guards on the doors.'

Humbold's mouth was a thin line as he watched to see how Colonel Kaff would take this news.

Kaff was a little shaken, now that he realised what was happening. A coup was taking place. Humbold was removing the monarch to make way for himself. If the queen was mad then she needed to be protected from herself. Everyone knew of her malady, from the peasants up to the courtiers, but all Humbold had to do was say she had been jolted into a worse state of mind by the escape of the wizard who had cursed her with that madness. Humbold could keep her locked up, with his own guards on the door, all for her own good. There would be few who would brook him in this attempt. Frinstin and Quidquod only, perhaps.

'But – the queen. I mean, surely when she comes to herself . . . ?'

'When she comes to herself,' growled Humbold, 'she will only have the rats and spiders to talk with. Come on, get a hold of yourself, man. This is your chance to become powerful. Now, fetch some guards. I'll get the turnkeys. We'll put her away before her wailing wakens half the city.'

Kaff nodded. 'You're right. She does need looking after . . .'

He left and returned with some valued men. The queen hardly knew what was happening to her as a flour sack was put over her head and she was dragged forcibly from her boudoir. She scratched and kicked, screamed and cried out, but they took her quickly down the stairs, to a carriage in the courtyard, and thence to her cell. Servants tried to stop the turnkeys taking away their mistress, yelling, and fighting with them, but the guards ran them through and their bodies were bundled away.

Those servants and slaves who had witnessed the deaths of their colleagues realised a change in power was taking place. Most of them fell in with that immediately. Others ran away. Soon there was no opposition to the incarceration of the queen. Not from palace staff.

Quidquod was arrested in his quarters, not long afterwards. Frinstin, on his way to inspect one of his towers, was cut down by 'unknown assailants' in the street. His body was thrown into the canal. By mid-morning it was all over. Hardly a ripple had reached the public streets. At noon criers went out into the town and yelled the news from street corners. The queen was very ill. Chancellor Humbold had taken over as regent until such time as she was well enough to resume her throne. Marshal Crushkite was dead, killed, it was rumoured, by the escaping rogue wizard. The dangerous post of Warlord of Guthrum had been taken up by Colonel Kaff, shortly to be General Kaff.

When Jakanda, Warlord of the Carthagans, heard the news, he immediately broke protocol and entered the city.

Presenting himself to Humbold, he asked to see the queen.

'This is none of your business, Carthagan. This is our affair. Your duty stops at the gates.'

Jakanda heard what Humbold had to say, then put his own case forward.

'This is a monarchy. The throne is not passed on to commoners. The queen, if she is as sorely indisposed as you say she is, has a sister who can rule in her stead, until the queen recovers, or not.'

'Princess Layana?' said Kaff, standing by Humbold. 'Why, she is as mad as the queen herself. The whole royal family was cursed by OmmullummO. The Imperial Guard supports Chancellor Humbold in his generous offer to see over the kingdom. Neither the queen nor her sister have any children. There are no nephews or nieces. Cousins are so distant as to be worthless to the throne. Humbold it must be.'

Jakanda saw that it was useless to argue. He knew, if he wanted, he could storm the city. The Imperial Guard was no match for the Carthagan army. However, he asked again if he could see the queen, and this time he was taken down below the streets, to her cell. She flew at him savagely, trying to rake out his eyes with her nails. Jakanda had never seen the queen in this state: she had never received anyone when the illness was upon her. He had no idea that this was her normal self, for two or three days of any month.

'She does indeed appear very deranged,' he admitted to Kaff, who stood outside the cell. 'I had no idea she was so bad. I shall return to my army and we will continue as before, to guard the city as we have always done. Or await orders to go on campaign.' He looked towards the cell. 'The queen has my sympathy. I hope she finds her way out of her lunacy and can defeat the demons that plague her. I have heard they crawl into her orifices at certain times, then out again when they please. You seem to believe they are ready to inhabit her on a more permanent basis?'

'We think this is so,' said Kaff, trying to look sympathetic too. 'Who can tell with creatures of the night? They devour her brain and seem to have a taste for the royal mind. I doubt they will come out again until they have eaten it clear away.'

The warlord Jakanda left the warlord Kaff and returned to the red pavilions outside the city gates.

A court was convened to deal with the old man, Quidquod.

'You are accused,' said Humbold, now dressed in the robes of a regent and sitting on the throne, 'of embezzling the queen's fortune for your own use. How do you plead?'

'Not guilty of course,' thundered the old man, still capable of using his voice. 'You will all be damned! If not in this life, in the hereafter!'

He was of course found guilty and sentenced to hang at the chancellor's pleasure. Humbold did not get rid of him straight away. There was too much feeling amongst the populace at the moment. He had led the people gradually forwards by the nose. To start executing courtiers at this early stage he knew to be a mistake. However, the two ex-princes, Sando and Guido, were not even citizens of Guthrum, let alone nobles of its capital city. Humbold sentenced them to be hanged.

'Throw the bodies outside the walls of the city,' ordered Humbold, 'we don't want foreign carcasses littering our streets.'

'Are you sure about this?' whispered Kaff. 'What about Bhantan?'

'What about it?' asked Humbold, testily. 'They exiled them.'

'Yes, but that was *them*, not us. You can curse your own family, call them idiots and swine, but let anyone else do it and that's an entirely different matter. We need all the friends we can get at the moment. Even small city states like Bhantan. You never know, a change of government, anything can happen. They might be outraged, if not now, at some later date. I suggest we simply throw them in with Quidquod.'

'Good idea. They'll drive the old man crazy with their chattering. Hang them in fetters from the walls. I want them to suffer. Then send an emissary to Bhantan, saying we have put them under house arrest on suspicion of trying to start a revolt against the legitimate ruler of Zamerkand. Send a few gifts. A new treaty respecting Bhantan and renewing peace obligations, that sort of thing. That ought to do it.'

'Very wise,' whispered Kaff. 'A good decision.'

Thus Humbold came to the throne. Although there was no hanging of nobles, such was not the same for the common populace. Queen Vanda had been a fairly tolerant queen, as absolute rulers went. Humbold, however, was quite the reverse. Thieves were to be hanged without trial on the spot, so long as one member of the Imperial Guard was present to see justice done. Adulterers were to lose their middle two fingers of both hands, to be severed by the butcher whose premises were nearest the cuckolded person's house. Murderers were to be burned alive at the stake, a public execution for the entertainment of the masses.

'Well, that's a right kick in the teeth,' cried an infuriated Spagg, on hearing the latter ruling. 'Who's goin' to buy lucky hands if they're burned to a crisp? Charred and brittle? Dark as soot? Nobody, that's who. Humbold's robbed me of me livin'.'

He then had to go into hiding immediately, since the fourth command was that any persons found taking the chancellor's name in vain, abusing the same, showing disrespect for the new ruler of the land by word of mouth or by sign of fingers, would have his eyes picked out with winkle spikes and his liver drawn through his navel with a crochet hook. If he should then still be alive, he should witness the tying of four cob horses to his hands and feet, and experience being quartered.

Princess Layana was called to the court. She arrived, her chin held high and defiant. Her eyes cold with wrath.

'Am I to join my sister in her prison?' she asked. 'Or am I to be executed out of hand?'

'Neither,' replied Humbold in a bored voice. 'Right at this moment I don't want Soldier marching back here at the head of some foreign army, causing all sorts of mayhem, which I'm sure he will do if any harm comes to his wife. I'll deal with him later, but at the moment I'd rather he just simmered. I'm sending you on a ship over the Cerulean Sea. He'll doubtless follow you. In the meantime I can prepare myself in my own good time to deal with him.'

'Very clever, Humbold.'

'I think so.'

The new regent noticed an exchange of looks between Kaff and the princess.

'You can have her, Kaff, once we've dealt with him. Just go along with me for the time being. Be patient.'

Kaff nodded, his eyes averted from the princess.

'You scum,' she hissed at Kaff. 'I thought you were my friend.'

'I have never been your *friend*,' replied Kaff. 'I have always loved you.'

'Well, I could never love a coward and a traitor.'

'I'm no coward. As to being a traitor, your grandfather wrested this kingdom from another ruler, and there was not even a remote family relationship between them. Was that treachery? The powerful rule by right of might. That's how it is, that's how it's always been.'

'You vile, worthless man.'

She gave his face a stinging slap, which brought water to his eyes, and a numbed expression to his features. The shock of the blow from her flat hand went through him to the core. He realised in that moment what he had done. Any sliver of a chance he had ever had with Princess Layana was now gone. She didn't hate him. She loathed him. He could see the revulsion in her eyes as she stared at him. This hurt him worse than a stake being driven into his heart. He let out an involuntary choking sound and removed himself from her sight.

She was led from the court and taken to the canal dock. Humbold gave secret orders to his personal sorcerer that Layana should be taken to a prison called the City of the Sands. This monstrous place was controlled by a faerie race called the Piri. Those who were trapped there, either by accident or design, forgot who they were. Sometimes the city and its inhabitants lay petrified under the sands of the desert. Sometimes it emerged into the sunlight. When it was below the surface its captives turned to marble statues. When it rose into the sunlight and air again, they became people once more, to continue their eternal search for themselves. None could discover the name they sought amongst the other occupants of this pernicious city. Yet none could leave until they found it.

The Piri sometimes sold the prisoners of the City of the Sands to slave traders, when the price was right. It was a suitable place for a fallen princess.

By the time the news of Humbold's usurpation reached the ears of Soldier and his friends, Humbold had installed himself even further. He had begun the building of a new palace, to be called the Palace of Lions, a magnificent dwelling built in the park which Quidquod had given to the commonweal some twenty years previously. The park became his private garden and any citizens found wandering these previously public grounds were immediately beheaded. Statues of the queen and her supporters began to disappear from their plinths in and around Zamerkand and grand bronze figures of a stern but thoughtful Regent Humbold, sitting on a giant steed with powerful nostrils, took their places.

Previously the queen had had no symbols of royal power, but Humbold was shrewd enough to see that he had to endorse his position and make it stable. He had a jewelled sword fashioned by the famous goblin waylander, Culpernic, and stated that in future whomsover ruled Guthrum did it through the power of the Waylander's Sword. The blade, with its gem-encrusted scabbard, flashed like fire when it was drawn in the light. Humbold wore the weapon on state occasions and had it resting on a red velvet cushion at his feet on all others. Possession of the sword gave him the right of rulership over a faded empire.

Alone, without Golgath accompanying them, Soldier took Uthellen and IxonnoxI to a place of caves in the eastern mountains. Here there were only eagle's eyries and the nests of dragons. This was the home of the giant yellow dragon, as long as a warship, but mild and inoffensive if left to itself. The yellow dragons had been hunted almost to extinction by the Hannacks and now dwelt almost exclusively at the lower end of the long range of mountains, only the northern part of which bordered Falyum.

'I shall send some of the red pavilions to guard you,' he told the pair.

IxonnoxI shook his head. 'No, Soldier. It's best that few people know of our whereabouts. A few warriors won't stop my uncle. If he finds us he'll discover a way to kill me, whether I'm guarded or not. Keep my secret, that's all I ask.'

'It shall be.'

With that Soldier left them and returned to Golgath, who waited at a camp some two days' ride away.

Golgath and Soldier then headed towards Zamerkand. There were movements of beast-people around the country-side. They saw hunting parties and war parties of Wild Dog-warriors, Horse-people and Fox-people. Soldier never got used to seeing the horrible combination of an animal head on human shoulders. He could not help wondering whether they thought like a human or like a beast of the field, or even perhaps like a beast-person, a race apart whose mindset was unique to themselves.

The pair rode mostly at night, under a starless sky, making their way by the umber light of a hideous moon. Knots of snakes littered the paths. Giant spiders ran into and over bushes in that shimmery, light-footed way which caught the corner of the eye. Single rats formed king rats, twelve to a ring, which moved awkwardly across open ground with their tails linked, so that they made a protective circle of a dozen vicious mouths. The world was a frightening place where man, bird and beast jumped at shadows.

The raven arrived with the latest news.

'Humbold's in, Vanda's out.'

'What? Speak plainly,' cried Soldier.

'Chancellor's in, queenie's out.'

'So help me I'll strangle you, bird!'

'There's been a coup. What more? Queen Vanda's in a padded dungeon, along with Quidquod and the royal twins. Crushkite and Frinstin have been murdered. Humbold has assumed power and has glued his bum to the throne . . .'

The bird told them all that had happened since Soldier had left Zamerkand. 'And your wife . . .'

'Yes, yes, my wife?' cried Soldier, his heart sinking.

'She's been sent to Uan Muhaggiag. No one knows where. Banished. Exiled. Probably she's in some foreign jail – where I understand fungus infections are rife – rotting her little toes off.'

'You have a vile tongue, raven.'

'Just telling you the truth.'

Golgath said, 'What will you do, my friend?'

Soldier shook his head to clear it of the foul hatred that bubbled up from somewhere deep within himself.

'I – I must go overseas, of course. I must find my wife. Once I know she's safe, then I can go after Humbold.'

He rode in silence after that, letting the horse carry him forward, one hoof after another, rather than riding. He hung limp and uneasy in the saddle. The great bay was unused to this dead weight. It faltered occasionally, stumbling along in the half darkness. Once a bobbing-gnome sprang up from a hole in the ground and startled the reliable beast, making him rear. Soldier was thrown to the ground. He found his feet without a word and climbed back into the saddle. The gnome, vitriolic as all his clan, was spitting fire at both horse and rider. Soldier ignored the creature and continued on, still weighed by heavy thoughts.

When they reached Zamerkand, Soldier rode to see the Warlord of the Carthagans, his general.

'There's a price on your head,' said Jakanda. 'Despite my protests, you've been outlawed.'

'I guessed as much. But why are you supporting this despot? Surely your loyalty is to the queen?'

Jakanda shook his head. 'My loyalty is to my paymaster,

that is, whoever rules Guthrum. I cannot interfere in internal affairs. I run a mercenary army, Captain, you know that. It would not be right for me, a foreign general, to support one side or the other. No Carthagan general in the pay of Guthrum has ever entered Zamerkand at the head of his army, no matter what politics or shenanigans are going on behind the walls. I suggest you go back out into the wilderness, into the fast-nesses of the mountains, until there's some change in Zamerkand.'

'I might do that,' said Soldier. 'Or I might not.'

He left, disappointed. They got rid of the horses, passing on the mounts to Lieutenant Velion and the Eagle Pavilion. Then, disguised as ragged holy men, they entered the gates of Zamerkand. It was Soldier's intention to take a barge down the covered canal to the Cerulean Sea, there to take passage on a ship or boat heading for Gwandoland. However, on their way to the docks Soldier bumped into a solid figure.

'Watch where yer goin'!' growled the man, bending to pick a cabbage stalk from the gutter. 'You just about trod on my supper.'

Then, looking up, the fellow cried, 'Strewth! Soldier!'

Soldier clamped a hand over Spagg's mouth and threatened him with his fist.

'Quiet! You give me away and I'll break your neck. We're leaving Zamerkand tonight, and if I'm followed . . .'

Spagg grabbed Soldier's worn priest's habit, tearing it at the collar. 'Where you goin'? Take me with you. I can't stand this place. Since Humbold took over I've been starving. Look at me, eatin' stuff out of the gutter, and it's giving my gut what for, this muck. My belly feels as if it's full of ragworms and a covey of quails explodes from my arse every time I have a shit. Look,' he opened his mouth and stinking breath hit Soldier in the face, 'I've lost two more teeth. Just went loose on me. One fell out and I swallered the other in me sleep.

'Take me with you. You need a man-servant, you do. You can't even strap your own breastplate on without pinching your nipples. I'll cook for you,' Spagg made a sandpapery sound with his filthy fingers, as if kneading dough. 'I'll wash your soddin' clothes. I'll lick your rotten boots clean with me tongue and shine 'em up with the hair under me armpits. I'll nip the lice off your head with what teef I've got left, and pinch the fleas from your coat with me nails. I'll be the best man-servant you've ever laid eyes on – only get me out of this city.'

Golgath muttered, 'Who is this repulsive dwarf?'

'My old employer,' answered Soldier, 'before I became a citizen of this country. All right, Spagg. You can come. But any hint of disloyalty and Golgath here will hobble you with a spike through your ankles. Understand?'

'Understood,' replied Spagg, eagerly.

'I wouldn't waste a good spike on this repugnant gnome,' replied Golgath. 'I'll just crush his head under my boot.'

'Nice fellah, your friend,' Spagg said to Soldier, with a side-long glance at Golgath. 'Got a way with words, ain't he?'

The three men reached the docks and found a bargee willing to take them down to the coast – for five pieces of gold. Once they were on their way, surging with the current of the river which had been turned into a canal, Soldier relaxed. He lay back on bales of soft cotton and stared at the stonework which passed overhead. There were grilles every so often, through which he could see the night sky, but no stars. A world without stars felt strange to him. Stars were quite useless in them-selves of course, embedded as they were in the black cloak of the earth, but the sky seemed ghastly without them, empty and bland, as if someone had robbed a face of its features – nose, mouth, eyes, brows – leaving blank flesh.

When Golgath joined him, Soldier revealed his thoughts.

'The stars useless?' cried Golgath. 'Nothing could be further from the truth. I use the stars all the time.'

'You're a navigator?'

'No, an astromagician. The stars form magical patterns, which I use to predict the future.'

'I see. So now?'

Golgath threw his hands up. 'There is no future.'

Spagg now threw in his spinza's worth.

'I've always wanted to get my teeth into a star. They look so cool and crunchy, don't they? I bet they taste good – or did, when we had 'em. Food of the gods, eh? Inviting us to reach up and pluck 'em from their black branches. I've tried. Oh, I've tried. Some nights they look so close. But when you try they're always just out of reach. I've been to the tops of trees after 'em, an' towers, an' spires. But they're not so easy. You'd think when they got ripe they'd drop off, wouldn't you? But you try an' find a star on the ground. Hey, maybe they burst open, leave a kernel, like chestnuts? I didn't think of that. Yes, next time I'm out on a plain I'll look for star kernels to crack.'

Golgath shook his head in wonder and said to Soldier, 'You really think this fool can be of any use as a servant?'

Spagg frowned. 'Hey!'

'He's all right,' Soldier said. 'So long as you don't turn your back on him.'

'I resent that. I truly do. Me, who saved your life – oh, a dozen times.'

The barge slid on, down the internal workings of the long

snake which took it to the sea. All that could be heard was the occasional clonk of the bargee's pole, when he fended away a wall that got too close. Lamps swung, fore and aft, the yellow light travelling along the slick stonework of the canal's engineers. There were creatures on ledges, picked out by their glistening eyes: monitor lizards mostly, that fed on the ubiquitous rat. In the water itself, silver shapes glided by or under the bows. A contained world, a tunnel from the heart of a city to the open sea. Soldier wondered if his own wife had passed along this watery road not a few hours before him.

Sometimes he could swear he caught a whiff of her perfume.

Chapter Thirteen

When they emerged from the end of the tunnel, they came out into a basin filled with ships. It was morning. A great dull sun fought to penetrate the layer of clouds above. On the choppy ocean, outside the harbour, ships of all shapes and sizes were coming and going. There were the small, nippy boats with their squarish lugsails and their triangular lateen sails; there were ketch-rigged sailing barges and yawls. On a larger scale beautiful three-masted schooners, proud and puffed, were entering or leaving. Five-masted barques with laden decks and full holds cruised through the dancing sea with ease. Audacious brigantines cut across the bows of larger vessels, raising foul language from the masters. This was the busiest port in the known world.

'Quite a sight, isn't it?' said Golgath, to his two open-mouthed companions. 'Stuns you, when you see it for the first time.'

'No wonder the city is rich,' replied Soldier. 'I've never seen such evidence of trade.'

'Used to be twice as much.'

'Well, it don't do the poor much good, do it?' growled

Spagg, disenchantment following rapidly on the heels of enragement.

The three men walked around the harbour, bargaining with captains and masters for passage across the Cerulean Sea. Golgath was taken with a brig whose captain offered good passage, but eventually they came to an arrangement with the owner of a caravel, a smallish ship with a little more panache than the slightly larger brig. The caravel, called inexplicably the *Winged Goat-fish*, had more of a jaunty shape to its hull and had odd little sails in odd places. As he paced the deck he felt he had the right boards beneath his feet. He felt comfortable.

Spagg was already being sick over the side, even though the ship was still securely moored.

'I hate sailin',' he moaned.

'This is your first time,' argued Soldier.

'In real, yes, but I've often been on the high seas in me dreams, an' I'm nearly always as sick as a pig.'

Their cargo appeared to be walnuts, sackfuls of them. Even before they set sail they were cracking open those which had escaped their containers. Before they touched on the shores of Uan Muhuggiag they knew they would be heartily sick of them.

They set sail with an assisting tide at dawn the next day. Soon the land had dropped behind them and a silvery sea spread before them. All three men heaved a sigh of relief, knowing that they had been in danger from several points of the compass until they were actually on the water. The sea was running and Soldier felt exhilarated. If he had ever been on a ship before it had been completely obliterated from even his subconscious. He felt young and boyish, completely captivated by the feel of adventure, the smell of the salt in the wind, the rush of the foamy water beneath the vessel. There were still shore birds perched on the rails and spars, but they left the ship once it had reached a certain point. When Soldier looked back he could see only a dark grimace along the edge of the horizon. Then he blinked and the land was gone.

With water all around them they could have been on any world at any time. All threads, all ties with the land, had been severed. It was not a frightening experience. At that moment Soldier could have sailed the blue waters for ever and not cared a damn.

'Wonderful, isn't it?' he said to Golgath. 'Smell that air! So clean. So fresh. I know I shall sleep like a lamb tonight.'

'Someone doesn't like it,' replied Golgath, clinging to a stay with his right hand and pointing with his left. 'Spagg's just covered the sea with those mushrooms he ate for breakfast.'

Spagg was now lying on his back, in danger of being trodden on by the sailors who were at their tasks around him. He groaned, continually. Finally a burly sailor with a tarred pigtail picked him up bodily and carried him to a nest of ropes. There he was deposited, unceremoniously, where his legs were out of the way of mariners' feet.

'Thanks, mate,' he managed to groan, propping himself up against the base of a mast. 'Little bit gentler next time, eh?'

'Oh, I'll be gentle with you,' came the promise.

The turbaned figure in the loose nankeen shirt had the body of a hareem guard, but the voice was surprisingly feminine. All three men listening realised the sailor was a broad-faced, brawny female. The eyes behind the strong, thick nose, above the square chin, were sparkling. She looked covetously at Spagg, as he sat in a pathetic heap amongst the ropes, running her eyes up and down his shapeless body.

'A bit buttery, too much lard on you, but I like you,' she said, grinning. 'You and me could soon get those rolls of fat off, if we met in the forecastle a couple of times.'

'Marakeesh!' yelled the vessel's master. 'Get you back to your task, damn your lustful loins!'

'Yes, master,' she cried, moving but not taking her eyes from Spagg's crotch. 'Coming, sir.' She spoke confidentially to Soldier in an aside, nodding her head towards the ship's master. 'He was bitten by dogs and conceived by women!' Her voice was full of contempt.

She left Soldier puzzling over her remark.

A few moments later she was pulling on a sheet, her muscles rippling, her thick broad mouth chanting a shanty.

Golgath and Soldier were staring at Spagg. The little man looked revitalised. To their astonishment he turned a beaming face on them.

'I'm in!' he said. 'You poor sons-of-paupers will have to make do with salt-water dreams, as you sway in your hammocks and stare at the swinging lamp tonight. I've got my bed companion.'

Golgath said, 'Jinn and genies, Spagg, she'll swallow you whole!'

There was a nervous glance from Spagg, who then let out a hollow laugh. 'You're just jealous — both of you. I can see it in your faces. You're a pair of . . .' He never finished. His cheeks bulged and the next moment he was hanging over the rail emptying his belly into the ocean. Watching him, Soldier began to feel queasy himself. Soon, he too was ejecting the contents of his inmost of organs. Golgath moved away from the pair, upwind.

Just before sunset, when Soldier was feeling slightly less ill, there came a shout from one of the sailors.

'Dragon flying in on the port side!'

Everyone looked to port except Spagg, who was at the starboard rail and didn't know one side from the other anyway. Sure enough, a winged shape was descending in the crimson light. Like a large, plump bat, the dragon was a dark silhouette against the light sky.

'What's to do, Captain?' said Spagg, now with the others. 'Will he go for us?'

'Normally, they overfly ships,' replied the master, keeping a keen eye on the creature. 'They're not for landing on water and they get tired on the long flight over the sea. They've got no energy for attacking shipping, which would be a dangerous business for them, for if we damaged his wings he'd not make it across.'

Normally. But this one seemed to coming straight for the caravel. The master ordered the crew to stand by with harpoons. He hoped a show of force would deter the creature. But it seemed determined to go for the ship, not deviating in its course one single degree.

'Must be starved,' muttered the master, and in a louder voice, 'All right, stand by – when I give the order . . .'

The sailors hefted their harpoons shoulder-high like javelins.

'WAIT!' cried Soldier. 'Listen!'

A faint sound was coming from the dragon, as it descended on the craft, previously lost in the wind.

'Kerrowww. Kerrowww.'

'Don't kill it,' pleaded Soldier. 'It's my dragon. I mean, it's coming down because of me. I'm its – its master.'

'You own a dragon?' said Golgath, raising his eyebrows. 'I know of no one who owns a dragon. I'm impressed.'

The master was saying, 'I can't take the chance.'

'I implore you, Captain. Please. This creature is harmless if it's left to me to handle. I beg you. It's like a child to me.'

The master seemed dubious, but he refrained from giving order to kill the dragon, even as it approached the side of the ship, flying in low over the water. There was an awkward scrabbling for the rail with the dragon's claws. A last frantic flutter of the wings. Then the creature folded those wings against its body and shuffled around on the stern rail, getting a firmer purchase, before it began crooning again. The ship went lower in the water.

'KERROOOOW.'

Soldier went to it and spoke to it in a low voice. The sailors all craned their necks, trying to hear what he was saying, but actually Soldier was just making sounds, with no articulated words. He simply wanted the dragon to feel at ease. The dragon shuffled along the rail and then settled again. It was a blessing that the rail was strong and well-built in the shipyards of Uan Muhuggiag, for a two-legged, red-bellied, green dragon was about the size of a large bear, though its bone structure was not quite so heavy. Even so the rail creaked from time to time.

Finally, Soldier left the creature, which seemed quite content just to sit there and watch the ocean go by.

'What did it say?' asked Golgath, excitedly. 'Is it coming with us?'

'Who knows? I can't actually understand what it's saying. Anyway, they have very few words, male dragons of this species. It's only the females who can talk a lot. You ask Spagg. He's the expert. He's got all the answers regarding dragons.'

'Well, why does it like *you*?'

'I'm – I'm its mother.'

Golgath looked at Soldier through disapproving narrowed eyes: the disgust was clearly evident in his demeanour.

'I would never have thought you would be a victim to such infernal desires. Bestiality. With a *dragon*. It beggars belief. How grotesque . . .'

'No, no, not its real mother. And anyway, what you're suggesting is fatherhood, not motherhood.' Soldier shuddered at the image it threw up in his mind. 'No, I just happened to be there when it hatched. I was the first thing it saw, so it assumed I was its mother. Since then we've had a close but infrequent relationship.'

The master was perturbed, but agreed to leave the dragon alone. Such policy was always wisest in any case. When you messed with dragons you played with fiery breath. The sailors worked around the creature and soon got used to the plumb-bob shape that perched on the rail. They even started feeding the long-nosed, long-mouthed head with fish and scraps. One of them had the audacity to place his sailor's cap on the dragon's head, while he carried out an awkward task in the vicinity of the taffrail. The dragon drew the line. He dipped his head swiftly, once the sailor had turned away, and the cap was lost to the sea. No clown, Soldier's dragon.

One evening Soldier was standing with the dragon, when the master came up.

'Are we on a true course?' asked Soldier of the ship's captain.

Surprisingly, the master shrugged, looking up at the heavens.

'Who knows? There's no stars to navigate by.'

'What?'

The master smiled. 'Just fooling. Yes, I do usually use the stars, to assist me, but they're not absolutely essential. I know this voyage so well it's almost instinctive with me.'

Soldier was relieved. 'I'm glad to hear it. Don't you have *any* navigational aids then?'

'Oh, one or two. The shape of the waves, the colour of the sea, the rips, the swells, land birds, sea birds, wind direction, cloud banks, fish shoals . . .'

'All right,' said Soldier, grinning, 'I see the picture.'

The dragon, on seeing Soldier smile, made an unintelligible sound in the back of its throat.

'He's a strange beastie, your dragon,' said the master, nodding at the creature. 'I've only ever seen them from afar before now. Close to, they don't seem all that dangerous.'

The dragon opened its mouth to yawn and the master instantly changed his mind.

'What sharp teeth,' he murmured, drifting purposely now towards the bows now.

The stowaway blinked and then, with a rasping sound which woke the whole ship, proceeded to scratch himself under the chin.

In the event, the dragon's presence turned out to be fortuitous. Two sea monsters were encountered the very next day.

One was a harmless oddity which impressed the whole contingent of passengers, but did nothing in any hostile way. This was a creature the master called an aspidochelone, which looked exactly like a rocky, lichen-covered island. To unknowing eyes it *would* have been taken for land. It was only because the sailors knew it so well, they recognised it for what it was, a living, floating creature of enormous size. When the aspidochelone first drifted into that part of the ocean, sailors had made the mistake of mooring their boats in its generous coves, lighting fires on its back, and cooking the fish which nestled in its pools. The aspidochelone soon informed such invaders that they were not wanted and dived with them and their boats to an uncomfortable depth.

'She looks magnificent,' said Golgath. 'A stately leviathan basking in the gentle rays of the sun.'

'Lazy bitch, if you ask me,' snorted Spagg.

They passed by the great monster at noon, their bow wave caressing her insensitive shores. One giant eye opened to regard them. Spagg gave a start and a gasp, jumping back.

'What's she lookin' at me for?' he cried.

'If her eye is that large,' replied Golgath, 'her ears must be enormous too.'

'Bitch is a proper word, ain't it? It ain't an insult, is it?'

'Would you call your sailor friend a bitch?'

Spagg had been caught 'wrestling' with Marakeesh under the canvas of the jolly boat that very morning. Both of them had been naked, a sight (said the second mate who found them at it) not at all appealing to a lover of nature and natural creatures. Marakeesh had been flogged by the captain. Spagg, because he was a passenger, was warned that he and his friends would be dropped off at the nearest point of land, wherever it might turn out to be, if he attempted to corrupt one of the master's crew-women ever again.

'It weren't me,' he grumbled to Soldier and Golgath, 'it was *her*. She can't be satisfied, that one. Have you heard what she used to do for a livin' before she was a sailor? She . . .'

But they didn't want to hear. They weren't interested in anything but ensuring that Spagg behaved himself in future. Soldier had no desire to be cast away on an uninhabited island.

So, this first curiosity was left in the wake of the ship, and it closed its one open eye and continued to drift on the current.

The second monster was of a different kind entirely.

The day after the encouter with the living island there was a shout from the masthead.

'Ho! Black sails. Black sails a sea league to starboard.'

Even before the call was finished the ship became as a termite's nest threatened by an anteater. The crew began running every which way. The master appeared on the bridge almost instantly, still in his nightshirt and cap, and stared intently through a spyglass. Sailors were snatching cutlasses from a tray which had been rushed up from below. Others were arming themselves with wicked-looking hooks, fending pikes, and other longer weapons. The master snapped the spyglass shut.

'They're closing fast,' he said. 'Can't outrun 'em. We'll have to fight.'

Soldier stared at the distant ship. It was a sleek craft with many curves and points about it. It reminded Soldier of an exotic soldan's shoe, with its curled prow. He could see seafarers on her decks, bristling with metal weapons. The mainsail was large, square and as black as sin. The craft forged through the water, running before the wind, and would be on them in a very short while, unless something unforeseen happened.

'Who are they?' he asked the master.

'Amekni pirates,' was the answer.

'Can we bargain with them?'

'No. When they attack, they massacre every living creature on board, and then sink their victim ship. Simple as that. No mercy. They've never been known to take a prisoner yet. It's their way.'

'But that doesn't sound good sense to me. Money can be extorted from relatives and friends for hostages. Are you saying they don't take hostages – ever?'

'That's what I'm saying. They're ex-slaves. Embittered, full of hate. They prefer to satisfy their lust for blood and vengeance, rather than enrich themselves. Obviously the two come side by side, since they plunder the vessels before they sink 'em.'

During this explanation Soldier had been watching his dragon, closely. The dragon's eyes were keenly on the approaching craft. He clearly did not like the black sail with its fire-bird crest. When the pirate ship was close enough, the master of the *Winged Goat-fish* ordered a heavy catapult on the stern of the craft to fire on it. The sailors did so, but without effect, their rocks landing in the sea around the swiftly approaching vessel. They tried one tar-soaked ball of rope, which had been set alight, but this too sizzled in the ocean when it flew right over the bows of the foe.

The pirates were jubilant. They hung from the rigging of their craft and jeered like mad. They waved their weapons and informed the crew of the caravel that they were going to gut them like fish, cut off their appendages, prick the eyes from their heads, hang sailors by their tongues from the yardarm.

'We'll make you swallow turtle dung,' they shrieked. 'We'll boil you down for fat to grease our anchor chain.'

The sailors of the *Winged Goat-fish* waited in trepidation and fear for these berserk raiders to board their craft.

When the enemy was just three lengths from them, the dragon suddenly took to the air. He flew straight at the sail and attacked the fire-bird depicted thereon. To common knowledge there was no creature in the world resembling the fire-bird, which blazed with eternal flames and burned all that it came into contact with. But dragons, it seemed, did not like them, whether they were real or mythical.

Soldier's dragon ripped the sail to shreds within seconds. The pirates scrambled down from the rigging as their ship veered wildly and was broached by a lee wave. Sailors plunged into the sea, like maggots falling from a rotten piece of meat. The *Winged Goat-fish* sped past the stricken craft as it attempted to right itself. The sea was not stormy, but there was a heavy swell, and there were waves which could be bothersome to a ship suddenly thrown off tack.

Soldier's dragon did not return to the caravel. Instead he set off for the coast, which could be seen as a thin red line ahead.

As he flew off, the dragon let out a strange and penetrating cry. It could have been heard in far distant continents, it was so piercingly loud. Everyone put their hands over their ears, on both ships, and blinked away tears of pain. By that time the dragon was flying low over the water, shrinking to the size of a bumble bee within a very short time.

The pirate ship's steersman recovered his senses. He turned the craft into the waves, so that it righted itself. Within minutes the pirates had brought up another sail from the hold and were in the process of putting it on, when disaster struck them for a second time.

It was Soldier who noticed it first: as a chill wind seemed to riffle the surface of the water. A great dark patch appeared in the sea. Soldier brought the crew's attention to the phenomenon. Some looked up, mistakenly thinking what they saw was the shadow of a cloud. Others pinched at religious artefacts, small charms around their necks, believing a god was about to appear. The dark shape moved along, under the water, seeming to close on the pirate vessel. Small fish began arcing across the surface like silver rain, as they do when they're being chased by predators. Then the water bubbled, as if boiling from beneath. It was something the master thought he had seen before.

'Underwater volcano,' he said, firmly.

But what came up was not steam, nor showers of fiery coals, but a living creature. A great sea-serpent, perhaps called from the depths by the dragon's cry, surfaced in a hiss of spray and foam. It writhed there, unanchored for a few moments, seeking a purchase. Finally, it wound its coils around the black-sailed ship and began crushing it.

'Isman's lungi!' exclaimed a wide-eyed Spagg.

The whole crew of the *Winged Goat-fish* watched in horror as the pirate ship's timbers cracked and split under the pressure. Masts popped out of their blocks and crashed down on the decks. Planks buckled and flew out, some cracking apart and firing deadly splinters the size of daggers into the faces of the pirates. Whole men were squashed in the scaly coils of the giant sea serpent, which stank of weed and ooze a thousand years old. The squamous monster showed no mercy for its victims. Even as it dragged the wreck down with it to its home in an ocean trough, it sucked up the struggling bodies of drowning seafarers, swallowing them, leaving nothing but debris floating on the spot where the craft had been.

'Coph's corset!' whispered Spagg.

It was a shocking thing to have witnessed. True, the pirates had been out for blood. They would have slaughtered the whole crew, and the passengers. But still, the suddenness with which the dragon and the sea-serpent between them had dealt with a whole boatload of some sixty or seventy mariners was highly disturbing. It brought home the frailty of the human form. It was as if one had been smacked around the face by one's own mortality and then kicked in the backside by the grim reaper. Life was surely too precious a commodity to have it snuffed so completely, so callously, within so short a space of time?

The sailors all went about their duties in a kind of mechanical way, still dazed by what they had been forced to view.

The passengers busied themselves with staring at the distant shore, wondering what fate held for them in those red-stone hills, those sandy deserts of the hinterland.

Finally, the caravel was cruising into the harbour of Sisadas, the main port of Uan Muhuggiag. Here was a different scene indeed to the one on the other side of the ocean. Although there were many ships going in and out of the harbour, the shoreline itself was alive with activity. Here were open markets, full of colourful, exotic goods on display. There were hod-carriers with baskets full of fruit. Blankets covered with brilliant seashells lay between vendors of game birds with plumage that made pheasant cocks look like the beggars of the bird world. On the beach were poles bearing silver wolf-skin coats, red wolfskin leggings, black wolfskin hats. Over this way were caged pet bats for sale, young, frisky pet foxes, giant lizards on leashes, live scorpion neck charms with corked stings, live spider decorations that nested in the wearer's tangled hair.

Small bumboats bustled about on the water carrying textiles, carvings, bullwhips, knives, and many other goods out to sell to the passengers of the larger vessels in the harbour. In front of the markets there was shipbuilding all along the sea strand: large, potbellied boats called dhundis, not a metal nail in them, put together with pegs and caulked with vegetable oils. The peppery scent of juniper wood was in the air, and sandalwood, and cedarwood, and sweet fresh pine.

Soldier, Golgath and Spagg left the *Winged Goat-fish* and stepped on shore, now having to find their land legs. After being on board a ship that rolled and rocked with every motion of the sea, they found it difficult having nothing to counter-balance. Spagg fell over twice in the market-place, much to the amusement of the swathed people there. He picked himself up each time with great dignity and gave them choice mouthfuls of Guthrum, which, if they understood at all, they ignored. Spagg also had the disconcerting habit of inspecting everyone's hands, peering at them closely.

'Some nice specimens 'ere,' he confided to Soldier. 'Take a few of those back with me.'

'I thought you only sold hanged men's hands?'

'Well, you can see this lot are just cut-throats and villains, every one of 'em! Look, you can see it their faces. They'd have the skin off your cuticles if they thought they could get away with it. Nah, pick any one of them and I'll wager he's killed his grandmother for a stick of firewood.'

'How well-informed your judgements are, Spagg,' observed Golgath. 'Such objective opinions.'

'Well, you know,' replied Spagg, missing the irony, 'my mother brought me up to make decisions, not to sit on the fence.'

'Well-considered decisions.'

'Nat'rally.'

'What a wise woman she must have been.'

'None wiser.'

'I wish I had known her. Perhaps I would have been in time to prevent a disaster happening.'

Spagg frowned. 'What disaster?'

'The birth of her child.'

'Are you being sarcastic?'

'Me, Spagg?' cried Golgath, hand on heart. 'How could you accuse a fellow traveller of such a crime?'

'Well, just so's you're not.'

Soldier left them to it and went to look for accommodation for the three of them, before making enquiries as to the whereabouts of his wife.

Chapter Fourteen

They found a tavern with a spare room in the Kamala district. Actually, most of the rooms were empty, due to the fact that the public camel stables were situated just behind the tavern – the smell of dung was all-pervading and the flies were as big as hornets. It was not through shortage of money that they chose these accommodations, but Soldier wanted to remain as inconspicuous as possible while he was searching for Layana. There is one sure way of bringing attention to yourself in a new land and that is by spending lots of money.

Spagg, who often smelled worse than any camel, had the audacity to complain about the stink.

'What a pong!'

'I wouldn't be surprised,' said Golgath, 'if the camels are saying the same thing.'

'Meanin' what?'

Soldier was looking out of the window at the white rough-cast buildings which made up this end of the town. Beyond them lay a desert, who knew how wide, with tall mountains in the very far distance. Uan Muhuggiag was a vast country. There were deserts here, wide lakes, mountain ranges, occasional green valleys and verdant pastures, and a completely different sky. The blue of the heavens here was harder, sharper; the clouds whiter and with more shapely billows. Sometimes they looked small and smooth as white pebbles in a stream. At others they were tall, dark columns holding up the sky. As with the ochre red of the Carthagan pavilions, the colours on the ground were earthier, the hues not bright red, yellow, brown, blue or green, but more textured, as burnt sienna, amber, raw umber, aubergine, tawny and jade.

The scents and sounds here were different too. They had more depth to them. The smell of camel's dung, of unleavened bread baking in clay ovens, of a nearby carpenter's wood shavings, were more substantial than those that came from horse, metal oven and city carpenter's shop. The whooping throaty noise of a camel, the cry of the lampseller, the clanging of the goat's bell, had more timbre than in the land from which Soldier had come.

He loved the exotic feel to the place. He felt lighter, more vibrant, than he had done in Guthrum. Here his spirit was more at peace with itself.

'I'm going to the bazaar,' he told the other two. 'I want to go alone. What will you do?'

'I'm goin' to eat,' replied Spagg, with no hesitation.

'I'll stay and read,' Golgath said. 'I found a book of poetry in the cabinet by my bed. I shall study the arts.'

Soldier left them, going out into the dusty streets. There were no cobbles here, no flagstones. Earth was the matter underfoot. He made his way to the bazaar, where he found alleys lined with stalls dedicated to objects in gold, in silver, in ivory, fabrics, gems. One long alley for each material. He strolled down Gold Alley, along Silver Walk, through Ruby

Square. He found a long, narrow passageway in which only birds were sold: parrots, parakeets, songbirds, lovebirds. The vendors and buyers were dressed mostly in desert dwellers' robes: turbans, smocks, camelskin coats, hoods, face coverings which left just their eyes visible.

As he strolled through the suq, he made enquiries. His questions seemed to lead him to one man, the Soldan of Ophiria, a desert lord and king of the Cobalt Tribes. These were a people, he was told, who lived by raiding and pillaging others.

The soldan was a very powerful man, Ophiria being the vast desert region of Uan Muhuggiag, and his warriors were as merciless in battle as the Carthagans. In fact, both peoples had great respect for each other. Their only historical battle had ended in victory for neither side, with but two men standing amidst a sea of corpses. These two decided between them that someone must carry the news back to their respective homelands and agreed that they should walk in opposite directions. When they arrived in their separate regions, their peoples were so ashamed of them for leaving the battlefield alive, without a victory to celebrate, they were both banished. If they had fought, their peoples said, one man would have walked away the victor. Legend had it that the two survivors met up again and, with their wives, sailed off together to an unknown island, where they became kings and founded two new nations, one on the north side of the island, and one on the south. Sadly, they did not permit intermarriage between their two nations, and the result was that the two sets of peoples ended up fighting savage wars against each other for possession of the whole island. This was long after the original two warriors had died and the common bond between them no longer had influence.

It appeared, from his queries, that Soldier needed to speak with the Soldan of Ophiria, for this man had networks of spies throughout the length and breadth of Uan Muhuggiag, and would know where Layana had been taken.

When Soldier arrived back at the tavern, however, he found Golgath with a contingent of Carthagan warriors.

'Soldier,' said Golgath, 'you have to go home.'

'Why? We've only just arrived here. I have to find my wife.'

'These men,' Golgath indicated the small force of warriors, 'have come over the border from their own country. Queen Nufititi of Carthaga has received news that the Hannacks and the beast-people have joined forces to attack Guthrum. The pavilions there need reinforcements. We need to get back to help defend our homeland.'

Soldier wondered. Was it his homeland? He had made it so, by marrying Layana. It was his adopted country, there being no real memory of any other in his mind. He had dreams of course, but who was to say what was real and what was fantasy in that confused mind? Loyalty must be directed somewhere, and where better than the country who had adopted him, the country of his wife.

And what of Layana, while he was over there, hacking men to death? Would she be suffering, waiting for his rescue? He mentioned this to Golgath, saying there was a direct choice: either he joined with his brothers and sisters in arms, or he continued to seek his wife. Golgath was of the opinion that Layana would want Soldier to do his duty first, then sort out his personal life. The princess, Golgath said truthfully, was a resourceful woman in her own right. She might, by her own initiative, be planning or even executing an escape. Such a woman did not need to rely on a man, even if he was her husband, any more than a man would expect to rely on his wife to extricate him from the clutches of a captor. If Soldier were free to do so, she might wish him to come to her aid, but since he was called upon by his country to defend the land, then she would assume he would first settle the fate of the nation, then assist her.

'We leave immediately,' said Soldier. 'The sooner this business is over and I can return, the better.'

The two men went into the tavern to collect their belongings, before rejoining the Carthagans.

Spagg had refused, absolutely, to join them.

'I'm not goin' back over there, throwin' up every nautical mile, when I can be waiting here. I've got Marakeesh comin' to join me tonight.' He gave his two companions a black-toothed grin. 'She's going to knock on the shutter and I'm to let her in by the winder, save paying for a double room. We're going to drink some mead and get up to fruskie-friskie. A sea voyage followed by a bloody battle, then another sea voyage? You must be out of your heads. I'm staying and that's that.'

So they left him to his fruskie-friskie.

The black warships were waiting in the next bay, the harbour at Sisadas being too small to accommodate them. They boarded at midnight and the fleet was on its way within the hour. The sailing time was much swifter than on the caravel, these sleek vessels being designed for much greater speed. They had several banks of sail, a following wind, and sailors extremely experienced in the seaways. The voyage was uneventful. It was as though the gods knew there were more important issues at hand than displaying their own might and power through storms and monsters of the deep. They too were interested in the outcome of major wars between mortals, and agreed to suspend any show of petulance or bad temper which might normally come from the Seven Peaks.

The fleet hove to in a cove just off the Petrified Pools of Yan. The troops disembarked and marched across country, arriving at the gates of Zamerkand in quick time. Here the pavilions were already mustered for war. Soldier joined the Eagle Pavilion, taking over command from Lieutenant Velion. His warriors seemed pleased to see him.

Golgath went into the city. He was not of the Carthagan ranks and therefore could not fight alongside Soldier. He promised to see his friend again soon, but for the moment he had to fight with the Imperial Army, alongside the brother he loathed so much.

Soldier did not enter the gates, knowing that Humbold was dangerous within them. The situation was different now. The king of a country at war has new priorities, and for the moment Soldier was safe, so long as he did not flaunt himself in front of the man who hated him. If he paraded himself through Zamerkand's streets, however, he was asking to be assassinated. As it was, within his pavilion, surrounded by his warriors, he was virtually untouchable.

Soldier did have a visit from the new marshal of the Imperial Guthrum Army, Golgath's brother.

'Well,' said Marshall Kaff, throwing back the flap of Soldier's compartment in the vast tent which was the Eagle Pavilion, 'so your conscience got the better of you?'

Kaff entered with an escort of five officers, all with their hands on the hilts of their swords. Soldier recognised a lisping cavalry officer who had once tied him to a wagon wheel and flogged him. There were other old enemies there, too, amongst this unholy gathering. Soldier eyed them without favour, staring each one of them down in turn. Then he turned his attention to Kaff, who was examining his quarters with something close to a sneer on his face.

'I came back with your brother. The fate of our country is as important to us as it is to you and your kind.'

'Ah yes, my little brother. How is he?'

'Ask him yourself. He's joined the ranks of your own army.'

Kaff was truly splendid in his silver armour with its golden marshal's crest — a rampant bull — on the breastplate. Scarlet feathers dripped from his helmet and a magnificent sword was on his hip. Kid gauntlets hung from the teeth of a savage looking weasel. The head of this beast had replaced Kaff's missing right hand.

This man standing before Soldier was every inch the great warlord. Soldier was glad that Layana could not see him now, or she might have been swayed by the splendour of the uniform and the confidence of the man who wore it.

Soldier said, wryly, 'You seem to have done very well for yourself.'

Kaff had the goodness to redden under this remark.

'I have been expedient, it is true. You do not know the ways of our people as well as you think you do. Power goes to those who take it. I feel no shame. Queen Vanda's ancestors snatched power at a time of crisis, just as Humbold and I have done. They saw nothing wrong in doing so and neither do we. It's how we get our kings and queens. You think nepotism is better? Hereditary right? I think not.'

'If you say so,' replied Soldier. 'However, don't trust your new king and master too far. He'll destroy you, if he has to. He has sold his soul.'

'Tshaw!' Kaff exclaimed. 'Listen, there's a war to fight. We might all die in the coming battles, and there would be an end to our interest in the living world with all its faults and foibles. You and I might be lying together, brothers in arms, in a pool of blood at the end of each new day. It's possible we might be buried in the same common ground, locked in each other's cold embrace.'

'Perish the thought,' said Soldier, folding his arms.

'Indeed. So say I. But I'm merely trying to put things into perspective. Why worry about affairs of state, when the first thing is to survive a conflict.'

'A philosopher too?'

At that moment Kaff's younger brother entered Soldier's quarters. He paused on the threshold, seeing many of his former colleagues and his older brother standing there. Soldier could see Golgath was in a confrontational mood.

Golgath said, 'What do *you* want?'

'My dear brother,' said Kaff, bending to kiss Golgath on the cheek, 'I see you're as irascible as ever. You always were badtempered, even as a child. I still bear the scar on my scalp of the fire poker you hit me with in the nursery.'

Everyone naturally stared at Kaff's head, where no scar was visible because of the helmet.

'And I a bruised knee bone; which has not healed to this day!'

Everyone stared at Golgath's knees, hidden beneath his armour.

Soldier said pointedly to Kaff, 'Thank you for your visit, Marshal.'

'Ah. I must go. My orders are plain. But I would ask one favour before I leave. It's what I came here for.'

'Which is?'

Kaff took him aside and whispered confidentially. He seemed genuinely concerned.

'News of the Princess Layana.' There was a catch in his throat as he voiced his request. 'Please tell me if you have discovered her whereabouts and if she is well.'

Soldier was astonished. 'It is your master who has her captive.'

'But he will not tell me where, or who holds her, I swear,' replied Kaff earnestly. 'It is the one secret he will not divulge. I have sent spies out everywhere, in every direction, but still can find no trace of her whereabouts. I know you have been looking for her too. I implore you, tell me where she is, and I will do all in my power to have her released.'

'You would go against Humbold, at risk of your life?'

'Even that.'

Soldier believed him. It irked Soldier greatly that this man *genuinely* loved his wife, and had loved her long before Soldier had arrived in Guthrum. Had Kaff wanted her simply for her money or position, Soldier could have dealt with it. But having a man desperately in love with his wife made him feel very insecure. You could not blame a man for his feelings, however inappropriate they were. And there was always the possibility that danger to his marriage lurked in the background, when Layana had a safe haven to run to in times of stress. His fear was that if he should argue bitterly with Layana, over some little thing as husbands and wives are wont to do from time to time, she might decide that Kaff was better for her, and leave. The option was always there. Kaff did not look like marrying anyone else.

'I can't promise such a thing,' he told Kaff. 'My wife is my affair, not yours.'

Kaff stared at him for a long time, then spun on his heel and strode out of the tent. He was followed by the mincing cavalry officer and his cronies, who did not depart without tossing a sneer or two over their shoulders.

Not long after Kaff had gone, the bullroarers and the trumpets sounded. Drums began to beat the alert. An enemy was coming.

'I must get back to my men,' said Golgath. He locked forearms with Soldier. 'Good luck, my friend.'

'You too. Keep a good watch from those walls. Give us good support.'

'We will.'

Golgath left.

The red pavilions immediately struck camp. They were well-versed in the arts of war. Soldier led the warriors of the Eagle Pavilion to a ridge beyond the city walls, where they joined others. When the whole army of Carthagan mercenaries were lined up, ready for battle, he had the Wolf Pavilion on his left, and the Dragon Pavilion on his right. He trusted both commanders and men to stand firm. The whole army could be trusted to fight to the last man, if that was required to win.

In the evening light the barbarian hordes came across the darkening plain. They came in their hundred-thousands: beast-warriors of the Horse-people, the Dog-people, the Snake-people – many others. On their right were squadrons of Hannack horse, wearing human-skin cloaks and decorated with the jawbones of their enemies. There was also a motley group of odd tribesmen from the mountains and deserts of the north.

Here they came. Silent at first. Like shadows crossing the hinterland. A multitude they seemed. A sea of armed creatures, dragging with them battering rams, catapults and giant bows for shooting huge fire arrows over the walls into the city. There were not many heavy field weapons, however, for both beast-people and Hannacks were raiders and liked to travel into battle unladen. They were swift foot-warriors and light horsemen, quick into the fray, quick out of it.

Their numbers on this occasion were enough to strike fear

into the heart of the stoutest foe, however, as they poured across the plain.

The Carthagans stood, resolute and ready. This was what they were paid to do. To stand and fight. To defend Zamerkand against barbarian hordes. On the walls of the city Marshal Kaff's Imperial Army gathered, also ready with its defence. The Guthrumites would fight from within the city walls, ready to loose rainclouds of arrows on the enemy from the heights. Ready with the rocks and the boiling oil, should any of the foe fight their way through the Carthagan ranks to the stonework beneath.

The barbarians did not wait until morning, as had been expected. Unusually, quite out of character and against all military custom, they attacked in the twilight. Something had given them great confidence and they came pounding their shields in fury, in a great mass, swarming across the killing grounds, flinging themselves on the ranks of the red pavilions with tremendous force. They had a new leader, and they felt their time had come. It was their turn to rule the world, form dynasties, build empires, destroy neighbours. It was their turn to sack cities, enrich their nations, stamp their enemies into the dust.

And so it went.

Because the red pavilions were defending the city, they felt the need to protect the whole length of the front wall. This extended the line, especially on the flanks, where the ranks were not as tight. On top of this, the line was broken on the right by the unfortunate position of two of Guthrum's largest graveyards. The barbarians drove the Carthagan line left-of-centre further into these cemeteries, causing the red pavilion warriors to stumble and fall on the tombstones. The line buckled as the flank was turned by a single squadron of

Hannack horse-soldiers. A ragged hole opened in the defenders. The line extended even more, to close this gap, thus thinning the centre to the point where a Carthagan warrior's outstretched arm could not touch his companion's shoulder, and from that point onwards the defence was doomed.

The shock of the first wave of barbarians was held, but the second, the third, and the fourth were too much. They were too full of conviction, too sure of themselves. The cry 'OmmullummO!' was on their lips. The usurping King Magus had promised them victory and they believed him. A final clash, the multitudes of now screaming, shrieking warriors from the north throwing themselves at the ranks of the red pavilions, and they broke through. They poured into an ever-widening breach in the right flank of the defenders, and began to attack from the rear.

There was no rout, but there was a great slaughter. Souls ascending from the Carthagan dead cried 'Thank you,' for their release. The air was full of grateful spirits on their way skywards. Soldier could hear them, crying out, as they rose towards heaven.

The red pavilions fell back against the walls of the city. The excited Imperial Army above began prematurely to hurl rocks down, many of these missiles striking Carthagan warriors. Soldier and a group of his Eagle Pavilion were squeezed out to the left flank, then driven back towards some groves of trees, where they fought like tigers. It was no use. The day was lost. The whooping beast-people and their allies had defeated the Carthagan Army with astonishing swiftness, and were already celebrating by beating out the brains of those wounded foes who lay crippled or dying on the battle-field.

If darkness had not fallen, there would have been no escape. But night came rapidly on the heels of evening. There was no moon, and no one knew friend from foe. In the first hour of darkness, many of the enemy died at their own hands, comrade mistakenly killing comrade, the wanton slaughter having too much headway to stop. Meanwhile surviving handfuls of warriors from the red pavilions crept away, running, stumbling, falling, picking themselves up again, but heading with great urgency towards the ships. Where they could they carried with them their pavilion standards – Boar, Wolf, Hawk, Eagle – but to their eternal shame, some of these had been lost to the enemy. This loss was far greater to bear than that of a beloved commander or dear friend. A pavilion's standard was its soul, its spirit, and its capture was unbearable to its warriors.

However, there was no use remaining until the dawn. The war was lost. The unspeakable barbarians were at the gates. King Humbold and his citizens could not be saved by those outside the walls of the city.

For the third time in as many weeks, Soldier crossed the Cerulean Sea. The black warships were almost empty. They had crews, but there were no fleeing warriors to pack their decks. Most were lying dead on the battlefield outside Zamerkand. Many more had fled north, west and east, away from the shores. When Soldier looked back he could see the barbarian fires around Zamerkand, but he could not tell whether they had overrun the castle and its internal town.

He felt sorrowful, guilty and ashamed.

For the first time in many centuries, he and his companions had failed to contain the barbarian hordes. It shouldn't have happened. They had been heavily outnumbered, it was true, but they had been so before, many times, and had always been sure of eventual victory. This time the heart seemed to go out of the Carthagan Army. Perhaps it was that incessant chanting of a devil-wizard's name that ate away at their confidence? Or the fact that they were fighting as the light drained from the sky and the night prevailed over the day?

In the past they had rallied at such points, managed to find hard ground, to hold their position, to counterattack and eventually triumph. This time there had been no rallying calls, no shouts of 'To me, Carthagans! Strive and conquer!' There were just the sounds of desperate fighting, the moans of falling warriors, the expression of grateful souls being released from their body prisons, the sighs of the dying. They had been frantic in their efforts and urgent in their attempts. They had thrashed, flailed, fallen back, lost their discipline. Their stalwartness had fled them and they had found themselves forever on the back foot, not pushing forwards, losing ground, losing ground, losing ground . . .

Soldier put his face in his hands. This defeat dragged from the depths of his naked soul the shadow of a memory of another defeat, somewhere in his lost past. It was a bitter feeling, almost unbearable. The bile came to his mouth. He wanted to die. How could this happen again? Surely this was the reason why he had left his own world, his mind fleeing in another direction, to escape such shame? If only he had kept his head, called for warriors to stand ground, to hold the line. But he had not. Nor had anyone else. No officer, no sergeant-at-arms, had put forth such a cry. Soldier had seen their own warlord, Jakanda, fall in the third wave of the attack under the warhammer of a dog-warrior. No one had leapt into his position, called for rallying drum or trumpet, cried havoc on the foe.

The defeat had been too swift and merciless. Sprawling,

numerous tribes, such as the beast-people, with warriors who learned the art of war as a natural part of growing from child to adult, had untold fighters to call upon. They could absorb defeats. They soaked them up like a sponge and put forth still more hordes, without pausing to consider. The psychological aspect of defeat did not affect them. They were used to defeats. No shame was felt, only bitter determination to revenge themselves on their enemies. Gathering themselves together, the barbarian tribes paused only to build up their numbers again, before throwing themselves at their foe. They were relentless.

Carthagans, on the other hand, expected to win. Their army was hand-picked from disciplined, well-trained troops. It took a great deal of time and thought to produce such an army. Defeat was unthinkable, and therefore when it happened, the shock was devastating. Their minds were numbed by the thought. The impossible had happened, and they had great difficulty in living with it. In fact, some of them could not. On the battlefield, when the outcome had been clear, many officers and warriors had fallen on their swords. Others, those careful planners amongst them, had taken the poison they kept in their rings or lockets for the purpose.

It was pitiful. Here on the deck men and women were weeping. One or two threw themselves overboard, into the dark sea. No one tried to stop them. No one called for the ship to turn. They did not want to be saved. They sank beneath the dark waves, grateful that they did not have to face their families and friends in Carthaga. Their spirits, having been released by their masters, murmured heavenbound.

When the fleet arrived back in Carthaga, the people already knew. The conquest of their army had been foreseen by the temple prophets and there was great mourning in the towns and villages. The wailing of the living, more for the defeat than the loss of their loved ones, filled the air. They tore out their hair, rent their clothes, threw away their sandals and walked on cactus plants or hot rocks, in order to suffer. They needed physical pain to cauterise their mental and spirtual agony. Their humiliation was a terrible thing to witness. Soldier had never seen anything like it. Women covered themselves in ashes and ran mad-eyed through the streets, naked. Men struck themselves with clubs and whips, until they fell unconscious on the ground. Children lay prostrate on the earth, weeping and confused, wondering why the world had come to an end. They sacrificed dogs and doves, littered the streets with dead flowers, and shut up their houses to keep out the light.

It was dreadful. Soldier left for the border as soon as he was able, heading for Sisadas.

Chapter Fifteen

Here above the southern continent of Gwandoland, the stars were now visible. Soldier thought about this, as he trudged along the single dirt track which led to Uan Muhuggiag. It could mean that OmmullummO's power was localised. That he could only control the northern continent, and perhaps only the bottommost corner of that continent. Or it could be that the wizard had not bothered extending his magic to encompass Gwandoland, since perhaps he did not need to terrorise the nations across the water. To get to him, to remove him, they had to cross the sea and a landscape he controlled, and therefore he did not need to waste his time and energy.

The long, yellow-crusted track wound across rugged country. A wind was rising steadily, increasing in strength, swirling the dust. Hot air wafted from the east. Clearly a change in the weather was in progress but Soldier paid little attention. His heart was heavy. All he wanted to do now was find his wife. As to the fate of Zamerkand, that was in the lap of Humbold. His imperial forces might hold the city, or they might not. There would be traitors ready to open the gates to the enemy. On the other hand, it was not a city which could effectively be besieged. It had a covered canal to the sea, through which supplies could be brought. Unless the barbarians secured the other end of the canal, they could wait for ever for Zamerkand to capitulate.

Through the eddying sand Soldier could see a copse of trees ahead, throwing moonlit shadows over the dirt road. As he came nearer to the copse a rider entered the black bars of shadow from other side and rippled through them. He had what appeared to be an owl on his shoulder. They were heading directly for Soldier, on the same side of the road, though at a leisurely pace.

Soldier gripped his sword hilt, ready to draw if necessary. One did not trust strangers in open country at night. But the rider made no attempt to reach for a weapon. The horse was walking steadily, the rider's face to the front. He was swathed from head to toe in hunter's garb, the only opening a strip across his eyes, so that he could see where he was going. Soldier stepped to the right to allow the horse passage, since the rider did not seem inclined to deviate from his course.

The two passed each other without a word. At the last moment Soldier looked up to view the stranger's face in the moonlight. Then rider, steed and owl were past him, the hooves of the mount clumping on the hard-dirt road. Soldier walked on, the encounter etched in his mind, as the wind strength increased. Sand began blasting on his back. He hunched his shoulders and thought about looking for shelter. There was a group of rocks off to the right of the road. He decided it would be wise to shelter there until the storm had passed. By the time he reached the rocks visibility was down to a hundred yards.

Then he stopped, suddenly, a realisation hitting him. He whirled and stared back at the road. This action coincided with the stealthy movement of the rider, who was retracing his route. But the scene was indistinct, the shape blurred by darkness and sand. Soldier had difficulty in separating form from backdrop. Obviously the same revelation had struck the rider before it had filtered through Soldier's brain, for the horseman must have turned his mount long before the light had dawned on Soldier. The pair of them were now aware and the rider had returned, no doubt armed, hoping to surprise Soldier from the rear.

After this sighting all was lost in the whirlwind blast of a full-blown sandstorm, something Soldier had never experienced before. He found a crevice between two rocks, unfurled his cloak and made a makeshift tent to keep out the dust and grit. All the while he was there he wondered about the rider, swathed in cloth, and who might be under those wrappings of fabric. Twice during the early part of the night his scabbard warned him of a nearby foe, but nothing came of it, and as the darkness moved towards dawn the warnings ceased.

Several hours later, after the storm was over, Soldier left the clutch of rocks to look for the rider. There was nothing to be found. All trace, all tracks, had disappeared.

Soldier continued his journey and reached Sisadas two days later.

Finding the tavern he discovered that not only was Spagg still in residence, but Golgath was there, too. They seemed overjoyed to see him alive, thinking he had gone down with others in the battle. Soldier briefly recounted his escape to the sea and its crossing, then told of the sorrow and grief he found in Carthaga. Finally he brought his narration to an end as Spagg handed him a cup of wine. He quaffed it, gratefully, before turning his dark-ringed eyes on them again.

'My friends,' said Soldier, gripping their hands. 'What a terrible day.'

Spagg nodded, looking Soldier up and down. 'You've had a time of it, that's certain. Look at you. More dints an' dents in yer armour than in my old mum's saucepans. Clothes in rags an' tatters. Half the continent stuck to yer hair, the rest of it on yer face. You need a good barf in oils, you do. Some nice scented water. I would suggest a young lady to go with it, but I know you and your funny ways – savin' yourself for you wife, or whatever.'

Soldier shook his head. 'I've had a time of it, that's sure. But when it all comes down to it, I ran. I ran away. A warrior stays with his comrades and falls with his pavilion. Yet I ran.'

'The battle was over,' Golgath said, firmly. 'Do not reproach yourself. No good could come of remaining on the field to be hacked down by those barbarians. There was a retreat. Your leader had fallen, command had broken down, the day was lost.'

'Still, I ran.'

'Well, you need to rest now,' said Golgath. 'We're all heavy of heart. At least the city didn't fall. Kaff is holding it. It's under siege, of course, but the canal remains open. That's how I got out. My brother called me seven kinds of a coward, but I knew if you lived you'd make for here, and I decided I had to be here too.'

Soldier gripped his fist and looked away, full of emotion, so that the other two could not see his face.

Soldier was exhausted, but he wanted to talk. He lay down on a couch in the corner and let Spagg take off such pieces of his armour as were easily removed.

'I passed a stranger some nights ago, on the road from Carthaga.'

Golgath said, 'And?'

'I stared into his face, illuminated by the moonlight, as we passed each other. Further along the road I realised what I'd seen. Then a dry storm blew up, and blotted out every visible thing. I think the stranger came to the same revelation, a little before me – he was riding back when the sand obliterated all sight of him.'

Spagg was staring, open-mouthed. Golgath nodded.

'And what had you both seen?'

'He was a ghost,' said Spagg, 'an' he wanted to eat you.'

'No. Blue eyes. He had blue eyes.'

'I thought you was the only one in this world with blue eyes?' said Spagg. 'You sayin' this stranger's from the same place as where you've come from?'

'I don't know,' replied Soldier, wearily. 'If he is, I think we are enemies. It's just a feeling, but it's strong. Now I must sleep. I'm sorry, my friends, but I've been awake now for . . .'

He never finished the sentence. Spagg drew a blanket over him and put a finger to his own lips, but Golgath needed no warning to be quiet. The Guthrumite warrior left the room and went below, to drink, to ponder, to consider.

Hawk stooped on the raven. Black bird swooped away, going down to the troughs beneath. The wind was raising the tops of the waves and a white sea was running. It was dangerous down there, close to the surface where predatorial fish could leap out and snatch birds from the air. The raven had seen it happen, to gulls and fulmers. They vanished down the throats of sharks or barracuda in a flurry of feathers: one moment flying free, the next taken beneath the water to be eaten.

The hawk threw up out of his stoop and went high, keeping above the raven, but now less eager to fall on it.

'Ha! Worried you'll misjudge, with the water so close,' scoffed the raven. 'Didn't your master invest you with special powers, great courage, recklessness? You're no match for a bright raven.'

The raven knew that the hawk had been sent to kill him. OmmullummO had commanded the destruction of all ravens in the world, the complete annihilation of a species. Raptors of all kinds — eagles, falcons, hawks — had been given the task. This goshawk had followed the raven out to sea, at its own peril. Ravens, however, were survivors. There would be a slaughter but no massacre. They were wily birds, many of whom would avoid the destruction called for them.

In and out of the watery peaks flew the raven, keeping a wary eye on his pursuer above. Both birds were becoming tired. Already they had been mobbed by gulls when crossing the coast. Sea birds do not like land birds extending their territories. Such an unusual act unites them and they put their squabbles aside in order to mount a concerted attack on the invaders. The goshawk and the raven had been chased well out to sea before the gulls eventually gave up and returned to the beach.

Spume and spindrift flew into the face and feathers of the raven. Soaked, he was heavier than before, and struggled to keep his course. The hawk had fallen behind, but now caught up again, flying high above but just to the right of the raven. Small islands were now visible ahead. The raven would dearly have loved to have landed on one of them, caught his breath, gathered his strength, before the last push for Gwandoland. However, he overflew these patches of sand and rock, knowing that the hawk would fall on him as he tried to find a perch.

Finally, a larger piece of land came into view. It was the continent at last. The hawk came down now and tried to imitate harrier tactics, zipping across the wavetops and swerving into the raven's flight path. But this raptor had not the skill of his cousin the harrier. It needed the power gained from a high stoop, the impetus, to give it the impact needed. The hawk's deadly claw needed speed and weight behind it, to deliver the killing blow.

So the raptor climbed for one last attempt at a stoop to kill, the waves beneath regardless.

The raven watched out of the corner of his eye as the hawk got to halfway up its climb. Its efforts had become strained, its ascent slower and slower, until it seemed to had come to a stop, hanging there in the cobalt blue. Then the raptor's wings simply folded. It plummeted down, past the raven, into the sea. Exhausted, the hunting bird struggled in the water, flapping occasionally, the life going out of it. Then the inevitable happened: a mouth full of sharp teeth rose from beneath and ended its pains. A single grey feather was left floating on the surface.

'So much for you, you lump of claw and beak!'

The raven gratefully flew over the shoreline, again pursued by gulls for a while, then found a tree in which to roost.

'I've got a message from IxonnoxI,' said the raven. 'He wants you to know that he's in a safe place. He regrets the battle, but says once he's installed as King Magus, the wild tribes of the north will once again be contained. He can't promise no wars, of course, but he does expect to limit the extent of their destruction. Anything more?' The raven scratched his head with one of his claws, an athletic feat that had the three humans wide-eyed with admiration. 'Oh, yes, he's glad you escaped with your life and wishes you well in your quest.'

Soldier nodded. 'He trusts you with the knowledge of his whereabouts, does he?'

'Just because I've betrayed you once, doesn't mean I'm going to do it again.'

'No, but we realise you're capable of it.' There was some acid in Soldier's tone, as he added, 'He trusts you with the knowledge, but doesn't trust me.'

'I'm the messenger. I've *got* to know where to deliver the messages. Listen, you keep bringing up this business of my treachery, well, let me tell you, I risked my life to bring that message to you. OmmullummO sent a hawk after me – bloody-minded thing it was too, wanted to rip my guts out – and this is all the thanks I get?'

Spagg asked, 'What happened – to the hawk?'

'I saw it off. Dropped like a stone from the sky. Couldn't stand the pace. It's clogging the digestive tract of some shark by now. If anyone ever asks you which is the stronger bird, hawk or crow, you tell 'em that crows are wizards when it comes to stamina, and hawks are crap.'

'I thought you were a raven,' Spagg said, puzzled.

'I *am* a raven, but ravens are of the crow family,' explained the raven, eternally patient with ignorant humans. 'What the hawk lacks in stamina, I'm afraid you lack in intellect, my friend.'

'Hey!' cried Spagg.

The raven was thanked again for his message, fed, and sent on his way.

Soldier was still depressed about the battle, but he was coming to terms with the defeat. He felt selfish for worrying about his own concerns when his wife was imprisoned somewhere, perhaps suffering under the cruel hand of a despot.

It was time to do something. Golgath had arranged a meeting with the Soldan of Ophiria. Spagg remained at the tavern while Soldier and Golgath were taken by a guide to an oasis out in the desert. It was the first time Soldier had been on a dromedary.

'You have to roll with the animal,' explained Golgath, 'just as if you were on a boat.'

'I'm trying,' replied Soldier, not at all happy with his mount, 'but when he rolls right, I have a tendency to roll left. This floppy lump doesn't help. I keep slipping backwards.'

'You'll get used to it.'

Soldier's camel turned his head to look at this inept rider he had on his back, then purposely spat a great wadge of cud at the nearest hovel. It struck with great force, splattering on the door. The furious occupant of the dwelling came to the window, looked out, and gave Soldier a gesture which could not be mistaken, whatever the culture. Soldier felt inclined to return the signal in kind, but Golgath warned him against it.

'You'll end up in a brawl and we have work to do.'

It was a bright day as they approached the shimmering oasis. Then out of the palm trees came a great, golden monster, shining so brilliantly it hurt Soldier's eyes. It had a great long trunk through which it bellowed as it ran, full tilt at the approaching camels. The guide took off immediately, leaving his two charges at the mercy of the attacking elephant. They could do nothing, having little control over their beasts, and simply sat and waited for the inevitable.

The inevitable turned out to be better than they expected. The elephant came to a halt in front of them, still bellowing and stamping its feet. They could see now that it was made of brass, covered all over in strange symbols, and its eyes blazed with artificial wrath.

On its back was a wonderful brass howdah, truly a work of art, with lattice windows and four splendid flagpoles flying colourful pennants. Like the elephant itself, the howdah was polished to a brilliance which made the watchers squint. Close to, they could see that the metal 'hide' of the elephant was covered in small handleless doors, compartments no doubt, behind which were secret contents. The elephant's legs were fashioned from circular brass sheaths, which fitted into each much as did the sections of a retractable spyglass, so that the automaton could bend its legs when it walked or ran.

One of the windows of the howdah opened and a fat, smiling man emerged. Someone rushed up with a golden ladder and the man descended from the back of the brass elephant. The man saw Soldier and Golgath still staring at the elephant and he laughed.

'Marvellous toy, isn't it? Same-same from Xilliope, the city of brass out in the sands of the Ja-ja Desert. Everything in Xilliope is made of brass. They make small-small toys and big-big clockwork. Their smelters, their moulders, their beaters cannot be surpassed. They are same-same artists as the great creator of the world, the one great God who made all the men and all the beasts of the field, all the birds of the skies, all the fishes of all the nine outer seas and two inner seas.'

Golgath knew they were being tempted into an argument as to whether the world was created by one god or many. Had he allowed himself to be drawn he might have pointed out that constructing a world was far too much work for a single god. The idea that the world had been created at all was ludicrous for intelligent men, no matter how many gods were involved. Most rational philosophers decided that the world was just there and that gods had arrived on it first, inhabited the mountaintops, then made some people to fill the valleys and lower lands. If the world had been made by anyone at all, the greatest of these philosophers had announced, it had been coughed out by a giant mudfish.

'It is a beautiful beast,' said Soldier, running his hands over the brasswork and finding it burning-hot to the touch. 'You are indeed a fortunate man to own such a creature.'

The owner of the grand elephant beamed.

'Come, I am the Soldan of Ophiria. Please join me in my tent. There is hot-hot tea and biscuits.'

The soldan was dressed in green flowing silks, with a huge white turban on his head, pinned with a gem the size of Soldier's fist. He was barefooted but wore rings on his toes and torcs around his ankles. There was a diamond-encrusted dagger dangling from a golden belt. In the dimple of his chin he wore an emerald, which flashed green fire in all directions as he walked.

One of the soldan's arms was pure gold, with mechanical inner parts. Golgath had already told Soldier that the arm had been bitten off by a crocodile when the soldan was a child playing in the river which ran through his father's palace grounds. That same crocodile was now a pet, and inseparable from the soldan. It travelled everywhere with him, in a crystal tank hauled on a cart pulled by six beautiful dun oxen.

No one knew the relationship between the soldan and his pet. Some said he kept the creature in order to torture it, day and night. Others, that since it carried a part of the soldan himself it was due the same rights and privileges as the ruler of Ophiria. One thing was certain, the soldan never fed his enemies to his crocodile, as he did to his beloved dogs, and therefore it was surmised that there was something mystical in the association, some sort of interdependence of souls.

As the soldan walked to his tent, servants and slaves moved around him like anxious ants, soundlessly easing his passage from one spot to another – men with giant parasols; women unrolling carpets so that his jewelled feet did not have to touch the ground; children with mist-fine watersprays, puffing away with antelope bladders attached to pierced bamboo rods. The tent was huge – almost as large as one of the military pavilions of the Carthagan Army – and made of soft hide. It was dyed dark blue, and was decorated with tassels, and bells with pleasant jingling notes that justled in the breeze. There were awnings which stretched out twenty metres from the edge of the tent, under which were gathered many beautiful men and women, whose opulent garb suggested they were aristocrats of the soldan's court.

Just before they reached the trees Soldier witnessed a death.

There was man in the clutches of the soldan's bodyguards. These bodyguards blocked his mouth and nose with their hands. They held him there until his eyes bulged and his face began to turn blue. A look of terror was on the poor fellow's features. Then, shockingly, the prisoner's mouth was rammed against the opening to a hornets' hive. Of course, he was desperate for a breath and sucked in air, and with that air came a cloud of hornets. Soldier watched the man's eyes go wide with pain, as the hornets stung him in his throat and lungs. Thrown to the ground, moaning incoherently, it was not long before the poor creature suffocated and died, his internal parts having swollen monstrously.

'What did he do?' asked Soldier, horrified.

The soldan spat on the body and hissed, 'He saw my wife.'

'Just that?'

'My darling Moona Swan-neck was bathing. That devil made a suit of dogskin and crept up to the edge of the pool.

She thought him one of her same-same hounds. There his filthy lecherous eyes saw my dearest darling in her sweet-sweet nothings-on. This was one year ago. He knew he would die a horrible death, yet she is so beautiful men cannot resist throwing all caution to the winds to catch but a glimpse of her. Since then he has been tortured little-little every day, until now when in my mercy I have granted him escape from his pain.'

Golgath said, in a sincere voice, 'You are very kind, my lord.'

Hands went up in an expansive gesture. 'Of course I am, I am the soldan.'

'Precisely.'

They went into the tent and sat on carpets, any one of which could have purchased a small kingdom. In the shadows at the back of the tent was the dim shape of a long crystal tank, from which came the occasional splashing sound.

Having sipped tea, Soldier asked a boon of the soldan, saying his own dear wife was captive somewhere in Uan Muhuggiag and he required the soldan's help in finding her.

The soldan was enthusiastic. 'How much it is in the stars that you come to me with this request,' he said, excitedly, 'for *my* own sweet-sweet wife is also missing and captive of that brigand swine, Caliphat-the-Strong. He swooped on my palace in my absence and bore her away on a horse. That same-same night I tore my hair and swore he would die. You will help me get my own beloved back and I will help you find yours.'

Soldier thought about this for a few moments, knowing he had to answer quickly, and eventually agreed.

'I shall indeed try to help you wrest your wife from this robber, thief and abductor, Caliphat.'

'The-strong. Caliphat-the-Strong. There are many-many Caliphats in the desert. You must get the right one, or I shall have an ugly wife I will not know what to do with. If you steal the concubine of Caliphat-the-Fierce, I shall have to send her back, which will humiliate her and me also. If you take the courtesan of Caliphat-the-Red, I shall have to throw her to the crocodiles, which will hurt my sensitivity. If you steal the paramour of Caliphat-the-Crucifier, who is my brother, you will cause a family war and many people will be put to the sword. No, no. Caliphat-the-Strong has my Moona Swan-neck, the loveliest women in the whole world.'

Soldier glanced at Golgath, whose face bore the blessed, blank look of a holy man returned from a pilgrimage.

'Yes, Caliphat-the-Strong. I shall find your wife Moona — is there more than one Moona? A Moona Gazelle-neck, perhaps?'

The soldan looked shocked. 'No, of course not. There is only *my* Moona.'

'In which direction lies the territory of this Caliphat-the-Strong?'

'To the west.' The soldan peered hard into Soldier's face. 'Yes, I heard you had blue-blue eyes. How strange. How very strange. Yet only last week I heard of a man travelling east with those same-same eyes. Caravan owners met him on the road. He spoke with an odd-odd tongue. Do you know this man?'

'I know of him, but his identity is a mystery to me. I saw him myself. He wanted to kill me, I think.'

'Yes, I heard he is looking for one with your eyes, eyes like his own. Still, he has gone east and you go west. It is likely the twain of you will never meet again. His face, I am told, was hard-hard and cruel — not a face like mine or yours — but full of malevolence. Bitter thoughts have scarred his features. His heart, I am told, is full of hate.'

'Not like you and I, my lord.'

'No, we are *sweet-sweet* men. We do not bear rancour. We are as full of kindness as these same-same cups are of wine. See, through the open flap. It is time. Drink, drink, for that evening cloud, shaped like a hunter, has caught yon sultan's turret in a noose of light.'

The three men raised golden goblets to their lips and tasted wine that would have had a nightingale trilling for more.

'Those words of yours,' said Soldier, 'I seem to have heard such somewhere before. It sounded like poetry. I have some dim memory caught in the recesses of my mind.'

'I too,' murmured Golgath, with furrowed brow.

'And I, also,' said the soldan, astonished, 'and I *never* remember poetry.'

All three of them pondered on the majesty of these fine words. Three great sighs followed – none of them could remember where they first heard them or from whom. It was one of life's deep-deep mysteries, said the soldan, and no doubt one of them would wake in the middle hours and call out the poet's name, only to forget it again before morning climbed out of the bowl of night.

Again, they all stared at one another, in wonder.

Soldier woke just before dawn and found himself unable to sleep. He had been dreaming of Layana and was distressed on waking to find she was not there beside him. The others still being asleep, he went for a walk over the sand dunes. Just as the rays of the sun were striking the crest of a high dune, two demons came strolling arm in arm over the top, laughing about how one of them had recently possessed a human and caused that man to dash his brains out on a rock.

Soldier halted in his tracks. The demons came on, their eyes yellow slits in their long and ugly faces. In such circumstances a man would expect to be torn to pieces by two such creatures. They did not like their private perambulations interrupted by mortals.

But as they approached the expression of one of the demons changed, and with his arm still hooked in that of his companion, he said to Soldier as he passed, 'Didn't I see you at the wizard's funeral?'

'You did indeed,' replied Soldier in a very tight voice, conscious of his good luck. 'I believe we exchanged a few words.'

'I thought so. I never forget a shape.'

And with that the demons went on, still joking about the recent encounter which had ended in a suicide. Soldier walked on, wondering at his good fortune. Marvelling at the opening of the day.

Chapter Sixteen

Spagg declined to join the two intrepid adventurers on their quest to retrieve Moona Swan-neck.

'I've bin on an adventure with him before,' he said, pointing at Soldier with a fork loaded with mutton, 'an' not much of it was what you'd call a jolly outing.'

The fork went into his mouth and the lump of mutton vanished down his throat.

Soldier said, 'It would be well if you did stay here then, in case the raven returns with more messages from IxonnoxI. In the meantime . . .'

'In the meantime I'll be enjoying myself.'

They left Spagg carving himself some more slices of mutton. The hand-seller was growing fat and happy in this warm, lazy climate. Goods were much cheaper here than in Zamerkand, especially mutton and goat's meat, both of which Spagg loved. He couldn't get wheat bread, of course, but there were substitutes. Maize bread. Rice bread. And there was always some kind of fruit in season. Spagg's stomach would not go empty. Then there were the infrequent visits from his hefty paramour, who always rushed to see him immediately her ship hove into port. Spagg had stigmata. He had bragged to the other two – in a rash moment of weakness – that when he and Marakeesh made love she pushed her forefingers through the holes in his hands. To their utter disgust, Spagg told them that it made her more excited.

Soldier was beginning to get used to his dromedary. He had been trying to ride it like a horse, but now he allowed the animal its lolloping gait, its casual swagger, and he rolled with its movements. Both men were fully equipped for a journey through the desert. They took with them two extra camels, laden with supplies. They both carried astrolabes in case they became separated in one of the frequent dust storms which plagued the region. As with all deserts, water was the biggest problem. The soldan had given them a map of wells, but waterholes are but small specks on large open spaces and the pair prudently took several extra full goatskins, just in case.

Both men were swathed in cloth, such as the desert tribes wore, and at a distance would not be taken for foreigners to the land.

'My friend,' said Soldier, 'you didn't need to come with me on this quest. I should be searching for this woman alone.'

'You saved my life – I am indebted to you.'

'I'm glad of your company, please don't mistake my meaning, but I wonder how many times you need to repay me. A man might save many others on the battlefield, simply by being there, fighting alongside them. How long are you going to be indebted to me?'

'I shall tell you when I think I have repaid you in full. My life is worth more to me than you think. Besides, I am a man for adventure. My brother is the one with all the ambition.

Let him stick at home and stoke the watchfires on the walls of Zamerkand. I would rather seek the fabled city of Xilliope, from which such wonders as brass elephants come. Out here there are two-headed leopards. Out here are the winged lions. Out here the white rock-rose blooms and its fragrance is everywhere. Why would I want to go home to a testy wife and squawking brats, when I can be out here in the tranquil desert air, my mind mulling on odd poems?'

'You haven't got a wife, let alone children.'

'I might have, if I stayed home. A bored man will do anything to liven his day.'

Soldier had never been in a real desert before. Once they were on their way he was surprised at the amount of wildlife. There were snakes, lizards, scorpions, and a dozen different small mammals. Gazelle were not infrequent visitors to the eye and there was bird life in the form of ragged-looking buzzards, tiny birds that sought the beetles and spiders that emerged from under the rocks at night, and the occasional hawk.

The days were hot, with a fierce sun hammering down upon their heads. At night the temperatures dropped below freezing, turning the water in the goatskins to ice. The rapid change in temperatures caused the rocks to split apart with whipcrack sounds. Sometimes it was impossible to sleep with the clatter of stones that went on around them, with the bitter cold that dug into their bones, and the shuffling of animals.

One night they camped by a sweet-water well. In the distance were the dark, hunched shapes of a mountain range. They were weary and in need of rest. Some unusual clouds had formed in the sky and Soldier was afraid they were in for another storm.

'I always imagined deserts to be desolate places where

nothing was going on,' he complained to Golgath. 'How wrong I was about the lack of activity. How right about the solitude. I shouldn't be surprised to find a lost and lonely angel out here in these forsaken fields of grit.'

'I find it interesting. See how the horizons stretch in every direction. A man could feel the world was empty. Yet we know back there are sprawling cities, swarming with people as numerous as maggots. I find it refreshing to be alone in such a crowded world. What is an *angel*?'

Soldier looked surprised. 'You don't know? Perhaps that's something from my own world which hasn't crossed into this one? An angel is a very exotic creature. Some say they are the winged messengers of God, bringing not just words, but fire and death, to mortals. They are full of goodness and mercy.'

'They sound like it,' Golgath said, 'with their gifts of fire and death.'

'That's only for evil people. Angels are beautiful creatures, who stand on a knight's shoulder when he battles with his foes.'

'That should help,' snorted Golgath. 'A big fat ain-gel sitting on your back, weighing you down.'

'Angels are light and airy beings, more spirit than substance. I see you are determined to scoff and sneer,' Soldier said, stiffly. 'I don't know why.'

Golgath at last lit the campfire, after many attempts with a tinderbox, and stepped back to watch the flames in satisfaction. 'We could have done with your angel to start that, now couldn't we? It would have saved a lot of work. It's not the angels which I regard with contempt, but your idea of a single deity. It wouldn't work . . .' Golgath then went on to explain that the tasks of running the weather, making sure the seas did not overflow, filling the rivers, all that sort of thing, could not possibly be left to one single entity. There were far too many chores, far too many prayers going up, for one god to deal with. It was so obvious there had to be many gods to deal with multifarious earthly and heavenly problems. Surely Soldier could see that?

'Depends how much divine power the entity has.'

They continued to argue for an hour or two after the sun went down and the cold crept across the wasteland. Then they fell asleep, almost simultaneously. In the early hours of the morning there was a storm. They huddled with their animals under makeshift tents, keeping the dust and grit out of their lungs, until they felt the morning sun strike their coverings with a gentle but warming palm. Golgath went out first and his gasp brought Soldier directly on his heels.

'Look at that!' breathed the Guthrumite.

Soldier could not help but see it. A whole city, sparkling in the sunlight. Towers, turrets, spires, domes, just like Zamerkand. Actually, it was unlike Zamerkand in that it had no curtain wall. You could walk right into this city without being stopped at the gates by guards. It looked fresh and dewy, as if it had been covered by the sand many aeons past, when it was quite new, then uncovered in the night. Certainly it had emerged during the storm. No doubt this was a lost city which waxed and waned with the shifting sands of time and tide. Last night's storm had uncovered it. A storm tonight could cover it again, or simply leave the pinnacles of its tallest structures standing proud on the back of the world like the spines of a porcupine.

'There's movement in there,' said Golgath in an astonished voice. 'I can see figures in the streets, at the windows. That is no ordinary city. It's a magical place. A land of faerie. We should be gone from this spot as quickly as our camels will carry us.'

'Wait. Wait,' replied the entranced Soldier. 'This is all experience. Perhaps some good will come of it.'

'This is not some heavenly city full of your angels. Only *bad* can come of it. It doesn't look beautiful because it has a beautiful heart. It looks like that to draw foolish men inside. It's a lure, a bright feather and shiny spoon to attract a curious fish. Come, let us go. I can recognise a snare when I see it. Why do you think it appeared now, just as we were passing by? We would only regret pausing here.'

'No, no, I must go in. They may know something. You wait here, Golgath. If I don't return by midday, then fetch help.'

'Fetch help?' cried the frustrated Guthrumite warrior. 'Where from?'

'Anywhere,' said Soldier, unable to take his eyes off the glittering buildings. 'I'll be back in a short while.'

With that he ran towards the mysterious city. Golgath was tempted to run after him, clout him on the head and drag him back, but Soldier was a leaner, faster runner than Kaff's brother. It would have been futile. All he could do was watch helplessly as his friend ran into an obvious trap. Sometimes, thought Golgath, Soldier was as innocent and naïve as a baby. This was one of those times. It would be a second act of extreme foolishness to follow Soldier into that web of wonderful, tinctured architecture, so he had no choice but to wait here, outside, and hope that Soldier emerged unscathed before that bright clapper of a sun struck the vertical bell of noon.

Soldier entered the city, walking past sentinels on the outskirts.

'Remember!' warned the nearest sentinel.

'What? Remember what?'

'Not to forget.'

This made no sense to Soldier, nor did the words etched into the marble of an arch.

ENTER SOMEBODY, LEAVE NOBODY.

Soldier passed the first building, then the second, until he was in a central square, a kind of park where the trees were made of onyx and jasper, and the flowers of opal with malachite stems and leaves. It appeared that nature had petrified in this enchanted city, to allow its beauty to survive beneath the sands. There were birds like gewgaws, of olivine, agate and jade, which sang prettily from the branches, and clustered on the statues of jet, with chalcedony eyes that followed Soldier wherever he walked. There were beetles like emeralds that crawled on the flagstones, and butterflies with frangible wings, and coloured-glass dragonflies. Brittle fallen leaves crunched underfoot, shattering, splintering like porcelain beneath the leather sole of his sandal.

The square was full of people and Soldier attempted to speak to one of them.

'Sir . . .'

The man grasped his collar and stared into Soldier's face with vacant eyes.

'Who am I?' he cried. 'Tell me who I am.'

'I do not know,' answered Soldier, prising the man's fingers from his clothes.

'Help me find my name!'

'I cannot.'

The man left him, going on to someone else, asking them the same question, only to receive that question back in kind.

Thinking he had been unlucky to find a madman, Soldier

stopped a woman next, who stared at him with those same frightened and frightening eyes.

'Tell me who I am,' she said, 'and you may have my body. Look, I am attractive, am I not? See how my figure curves. Look at my red lips, my damask cheeks, my gently-swelling breast. I must know, or I shall go insane. Perhaps I am already. I have been here, oh, I can't tell how long. But I can't leave unless I find my name. How can I?'

There was sand in her hair, in her clothes, on her skin.

Soldier once more peeled away the fingers from his collar. He looked around him. All the citizens of this marvellous city were wandering around, as if in a daze. There was despair on their features, hammered there by misery. Soldier had entered this wonderful place expecting to be helped, only to find that it was full of citizens wanting *his* help. There was an air of doom about them. They said they were trapped, yet any one of them could have walked past the sentinels and out of the city, without looking back – couldn't they? Soldier tried this, retracing his steps, leaving the city behind. No one stopped him.

He could see Golgath waiting anxiously in the distance. The warrior waved to him. Soldier waved back, then to the consternation of his friend, re-entered the city. He still had not discovered the secret of this place and it intrigued him. It was a blessed puzzle.

'Please help me find my name?' pleaded another woman, pulling Soldier down to sit on a park bench beside her. 'I shall go mad.'

He did not tell her she already looked mad.

'How many people are there here?' he asked, looking round. 'Why don't they leave?'

'Hundreds, perhaps thousands, they cannot until they find their names.'

'Why not just walk out?'

'Impossible. They would never know themselves again.' She stared into his face. 'You're not like one of us, are you? How fortunate you are.'

She brushed a grey-streaked wisp of hair away from her face.

'It's been so long since someone looked at me without asking me the same question, over and over again.'

A small agate bird landed on the end of the bench and began chirruping. It seemed irritated by something, pecking with its tiny needle-sharp beak at the woman's arm. Its neb drew a bead of blood which hung there like a jewel. The woman gave the bird a hurt look and brushed it off the seat with her hand.

'A Piri,' she said. 'It's annoyed because we aren't milling around like the rest of them, doing what we're supposed to do. They own this city. It's their invention, this place of torture. You could set fire to it, if you are indeed free from its influence. Burn us all here. It would be a blessing, a great favour. Grant me such a boon . . .'

As she was talking another woman, strangely familiar, caught the corner of Soldier's eye, momentarily, and he turned to look. But the figure had gone behind some amethyst trees overhanging a glistening jacinth lake, on which glided two beautiful tourmaline swans. The sun shone with changing brilliance on this scene, light was lost amongst light, as it danced from one point to the next. Bright, glassy colours flashed and flickered, entrancing, but playing havoc with the eyes. Everywhere the effulgence from the gem-stones produced a dazzling and bewildering effect.

Soldier shook his confused head to clear it. His single brief glance at the woman, who had been just one amongst many

thronging the square and surrounding parks, had suggested
– what? Was this strange city playing tricks with him? Was
he indeed falling into a trap from which it might be impossible to extricate himself? What if he were to go looking for
this person? Perhaps she did not exist, in truth, and he might
spend eternity walking these streets, searching? It did not
follow that because his companion was trapped here without
a name, that the city did not have other forms of snares. It
might have a hundred different artifices to keep a free man
from walking out.

He took the woman's hand.

'I must go,' he said. 'I'm sorry I can't help you.'

She stared into his eyes. 'You are a good man.'

'I could,' he said, impulsively, 'carry you out of this forsaken
place and set you on the road for civilization.'

She shook her head, emphatically. 'Not without my name.'

'As you wish.'

Soldier took one last look around, at the press of hopeless
people in the square, then left by one of the long, narrow
alleyways.

On the way out he passed a surprised sentinel. He could
see now that the figure was a mechanical creature, made of
inanimate moving parts. Nevertheless, the sentry spoke to
him, 'You're leaving? Without your memory? Without your
name? I never heard of such a thing.'

Soldier smiled, grimly. 'I didn't know who I was *before* I
entered, so this terrible place of forgetfulness has no influence on me.'

'Lucky man.'

'Perhaps.'

It was a long walk across the sands. Finally, he was back
with his relieved friend and the camels.

'That was foolish. You might have been trapped in there,' Golgath said, after Soldier had recounted his experiences. 'Then I would have had to come in to find you.'

'Now *that* would have been foolish.'

They struck camp, still arguing, and went on their way westwards. During the afternoon, they looked back, and saw the tawny sands sweeping over the city. Gradually the desert climbed higher up the enticing turrets, now like the shining fingers of a disappearing hand, until the topmost pinnacles had sunk beyond trace. The lone and level sands stretched far away into the distance, with nothing to break their monotony. All that remained on the surface, like the tracks of small desert creatures, were the patterns left by the sighs of the prisoners.

They were crouched behind a sand dune. Down below them, in a shallow depression in the landscape, a long ribbon of laden camels stretched back to the horizon.

'A caravan,' Golgath said. 'Nothing to fear.'

'How do we know that? They might have guards. They might be hostile.'

'Oh, they'll have guards all right, but they won't be bothered about us. They're just as afraid of hostile tribes as we are – more so, since they have a great deal to lose. Look, they're stopping. I think they're camping for the night. We could go down and get a meal there. I think those merchants are Samanites – a gentle people, interested only in making money and becoming rich and fat.'

Down below the high dune the tents were being unfolded. Huge, black, sprawling affairs with a complexity of poles and guy ropes. Still, those raising them seem to be practised to the point of ease. Within a half-hour all the tents were up and there were fires going, pots boiling. People were calling on each other as neighbours in a new place do.

'Shall we make ourselves known to them?' asked Golgath.

Soldier was dubious. 'Is it safe?'

'Nothing's safe, my friend. You going into the city of forget-fulness wasn't safe. I can smell good cooking. I'm going down.'

'All right.'

The two men stood up and their camels, grumbling because they thought they were on the move again, also rose. Soldier led his two beasts down the slope of the dune, sinking to his ankles in the fine sand. He heard a shout go up and knew that they had been seen. Soon a young boy was racing towards them. Breathless, he arrived just behind his grin.

'My father asks that you take tea with him.'

Golgath said, 'Inform your father that we should be honoured. What is your family name?'

'My father is called Maalish and I am Bak-lan-Maalish.'

'Son-of-Maalish,' explained Golgath, in an aside to Soldier. Then to the boy, 'Where shall we wash our hands?'

'There is a bowl outside the tent, of course,' laughed Bak-lan-Maalish.

'Of course. We shall be with your father directly.'

The boy scooted off, half-a-dozen of his friends now with him, the girls squealing, the boys yelling.

The two men washed their hands in a copper bowl on a tripod, just outside the entrance to the great tent. Then they were shown inside by a veiled woman. Once within, the comfort was apparent. There were carpets everywhere. Not a speck of sand to be seen. For Soldier it was like being in a quilted house. Tapestries hung from the walls of the tent. Scented candles burned, lighting the dark interior. It was not exactly cool, especially with a fire going in a hearth of stones, but it was not like being under that cruel furnace of a sun. A young man sat in the corner playing soft music on a stringed instrument. Another, older, man was carrying brass trays with cups, from one recess to another. There seemed to be a hundred rooms in the tent, all hidden by discreet flaps.

'Welcome! Please sit down.'

The words had come from an unveiled woman sitting next to a middle-aged man. They were both handsome people, with broad faces and wide mouths full of good teeth. The man started to pour some tea into the cups from an exotic-looking pot, when he suddenly looked up.

'Oh – do you take sugar?'

'No, not me,' said Golgath.

Soldier, who had never drunk tea before, didn't know whether he did or not. He too declined. When he tasted the tea, it was very mild, and he was glad not to have it sweetened.

'My first taste of tea,' he said. 'It's very refreshing.'

The woman seemed astonished.

'You do not have tea where you come from?'

Golgath took it on himself to explain. 'There is tea in Zamerkand, but most people drink watered wine, or ale. Otherwise, they make do with water.'

'There's nothing wrong with water,' said the woman. 'My name is Petra, and this is my husband Yun Maalish. This is my caravan. I'm transporting sandalwood, silks, woven gold and silver and other goods to Sisadas.'

Soldier's scabbard suddenly sang out. He leapt to his feet and drew his sword. At the same time there appeared from out of the many folded recesses of the tent several armed men. They crowded around Soldier in a half-circle, threatening him with their weapons. Golgath remained seated, still sipping his tea.

'We are alone,' Golgath said to the woman. 'We have no interest in your caravan or the wealth it carries. It would be a gross insult to the gods if you were to cut down two innocent men while they were enjoying the hospitality of your tent.'

'Often,' she said, 'a band of brigands will send one or two of their number, pretending to be travellers, to our tents to spy on us before they attack, usually just at sunset.'

'I know. I know your ways and your fears and the tricks that are played against you. I have been here before, many times. My friend has not. He has a magic scabbard, which warns him of danger. That's what you heard. Naturally, he believed he was about to be cut down, which is why he leapt to his feet. I repeat, you have nothing to fear from us. We are two travellers alone, seeking a woman — the wife of the Soldan of Ophiria, Moona Swan-neck. Do you have any knowledge of her whereabouts? We would be most grateful. We can pay.'

Soldier, on hearing these words, sheathed his sword and sat down with his back to the armed men. At a signal from the woman they melted into the shadows of the dark tent. Yun turned to his wife and said, 'Are you sure?'

'I think they're telling the truth.'

'So long as you're sure.'

He went back to sipping his tea, which Soldier noticed had stained his fair beard brown. Then, to Soldier's astonishment, Yun took a short piece of tarred rope from within his garments and, putting it in his mouth, lit it from one of the candles. He sucked on this, drawing smoke into his lungs. Then he smiled and nodded at Soldier, having noticed his expression, before exhaling a cloud.

'Not tea, nor tobacco?'

'Tobacco?'

'This.' He held up the smouldering piece of rope. 'It's made out of a herb. It tastes good. Do you want to try?'

Soldier shuddered and shook his head. 'Not I.'

'I will,' said Golgath, taking the lighted weed. He drew a lungful of smoke and coughed. 'It's been a long time,' he explained.

Petra said, 'I have heard that Caliphat-the-Strong has Moona Swan-neck held captive in his desert fortress. Are you going to rescue her?'

'Yes,' replied Soldier, lifting his head. 'It is our quest.'

Yun said, 'What if she doesn't want to be rescued?'

Soldier looked shocked. 'Of course she will. She's the wife of the soldan.'

'Perhaps the soldan beats her? Perhaps she does not love the soldan? Perhaps she loves Caliphat? Perhaps she is now with child? Caliphat's child. Perhaps, perhaps, perhaps.'

Soldier did not know what to say.

'Will you force her to go with you?' asked Petra.

'No – yes – I don't know. You're confusing me. I think I shall hope she's angry at being abducted and willing to return.'

Yun said, 'One can always live in hope.'

A meal was then brought, consisting of goat's meat, camel's-milk yoghurt, green cucumber, cheese made from dog's milk, eggs, desert partridge and crisp, fried rock beetles. They ate their fill. Then came milk and honeycombs, and spiced hot apple juice. The front of the tent was opened for this feast and they watched the sun go down behind some distant dunes.

'Sunset,' said Golgath, tearing at a partridge leg. 'No raiders falling on you from out of the gloaming.'

'True. Perhaps tonight, while we sleep?' replied Yun.

'If they do,' Soldier said, 'we shall be fighting them alongside you, you can be sure of that.'

The cold night came in and the flaps came down. Soldier and Golgath were shown to separate compartments in the tent, in which there were blankets. Soldier felt good. He had eaten and drunk well, he was comfortably tired, and it was not long before he drifted into sleep.

Sometime later he felt someone slip beneath his blankets. He was horrified to feel a naked female form. Worse, it was not some single woman they had sent to him. It was Petra herself.

'Do not be alarmed,' she whispered in his ear. 'It is our custom. My husband expects it.'

He sat bolt upright, wondering why his scabbard hadn't warned him of this attack. He could feel Petra's soft breasts against his side. He was not unmovable. There were ominous stirrings in his loins. He needed to act quickly and decisively. 'I am not available. Please, if this must be done, go to my friend. I'm sure you'll find in him a willing partner. I have a wife.'

'Most men do, and I have preferred you. Would you insult me? Your hostess?'

'No, no,' he groaned. 'You are a beautiful woman. I wish with all my heart that I could, but I cannot. My wife – she is not as *understanding* as women like you. I am not good at keeping such secrets. We both believe in fidelity. She especially. I must stay faithful.'

'She will flay you?'

'To the bone.'

'Ah, a jealous one. I understand.'

Petra left him.

As she went out of the compartment, she asked, 'How do you help one spurned in love, in your land?'

'We comfort them with apples.'

She frowned and he realised she had got the wrong image.

'It's just a saying. We make an alcoholic beverage from the juice of apples. We get them drunk.'

'Ah!' She understood.

Shortly after she had gone, another naked form crept into his bed. Soldier groaned. 'Please, who is it this time?'

'Why me,' said the surprised voice of Yun. 'Who was it last time?'

Soldier was bolt upright again.

'What are you doing in my bed?'

Yun stroked Soldier's cheek. 'Why, isn't that obvious?' he asked, smiling.

'Please go, now.'

'You insult me.'

'I'm sorry.'

'In some quarters it is death to insult a man.'

'I'm very sorry. I'm married.'

'So am I.'

'But – I don't like men – not in that way.'

Yun clucked and shook his head gravely. 'Yes, I had heard there were such people, out in the civilised world. How bizarre. Well, I shall go to your friend. He's not so handsome, but perhaps he's not so picky.'

'No – no,' cried Soldier, alarmed. He was not so sure that husband and wife actually knew of each other's infidelities, despite what Petra had said. 'Why don't you stay with me for a while.'

'Ah, that's better.'

'I mean, just to talk.'

'Talk? We talked during tea. We talked about everything that I know there is to talk about. What else is there to say?'

'Well, we didn't touch on philosophy.'

'Bugger philosophy.'

'You won't stay then?' Soldier felt he had done all he could to prevent a scene. 'You might like to discuss the angel Ithuriel's Spear, the slightest touch of which exposes deceit. I think my wife has it locked in a closet somewhere and while I'm asleep she uses it on me . . .'

Yun yawned. 'Good night.'

He left. Soldier listened for a while. There was no following ruckus. Finally, he dropped off to sleep again, while the camels snuffled and snorted just on the other side of the tent wall.

IxonnoxI left his mother and went out into the desert alone. Wary of eagles and hawks, who might have been sent to spy on him, the boy wizard climbed a mountain and sat on a high ledge for seven hours. In those hours he contemplated the vast spaces within his mind, travelled through them, gathered strength from his own self. He garnered knowledge left him by his ancestors, wizards from different times, different worlds. He entered into the world of animals and selected the wiles and cunning of certain beasts, the trickery of man, the sureness of women, the vision of birds, the many and varied talents of snakes and lizards who were closer to the earth than any other creature.

He sought the secrecy of the stones, as he would look for the understanding of wood, the lightness of fire, the power of water, the cryptic nature of air.

He became closer to the nature of the mountain on which he was sitting, in an effort to discover the psyche of earth.

After seven hours he descended from the clouds.

Back at sea level, IxonnoxI went up to a boulder and without fear he plunged his fist into the centre of the large block of granite. It entered smoothly. He held it there for a few moments, then pulled it out as one might withdraw a sword from a pumpkin. It came as easily as if it had been buried in soft mud.

Now he was master of the rocks of the earth. He had control over them. Tomorrow he would climb a great oak and seek to understand it through its leaves, its great trunk, its networks of roots.

Gradually, slowly, all things would reveal themselves to him, if he should be graced with enough time to avoid a confrontation with the enemy, his sire, his father, rogue wizard and destroyer of Good.

Soldier woke to see a faery lift the edge of the tent, enter, and steal a drink from a bowl of milk standing by the centre pole.

'Hello,' Soldier said, to the squat figure.

The spriggan started, stared, and then grinned a grin with a mouth encircled by milk, the white froth clinging to his whiskers.

'Weren't you at the wizard's funeral?'

'I was indeed — I witnessed you stealing a moon-apple.'

'Ah well,' replied the goblin, 'you know us faery folk, always stealing something or other.'

'Won't that milk go off now?'

The goblin looked down into the bowl in his hands, knowing it would, simply because one of his kind had drunk from it.

'Yes, it's turning.'

'Might as well finish it off then.'

The goblin looked up again and smiled. 'Might as well.'
He drank the bowl dry and put it down by the pole.

'Night then.'

'Night.'

The goblin made his exit.

Chapter Seventeen

The last of the Drummonds was knighted by the king for his services in the war against the invader. He had been granted land rights all along the border and now commanded a sizeable army of villeins and vassals. Now that he was a powerful man, having the king's ear between his thumb and forefinger, other lesser knights came to his side. Some came because they thought they could further their ambitions. Others because they had nowhere else to go to. But the vast majority came because they knew of the knight Drummond's enmity towards the knight Valechor, and they too had scores to settle with this man, who was also powerful and commanded many other knights.

The king did not intervene in such squabbles. If one knight killed another, so be it, as long as the laws of chivalry were not blatantly broken, as long as the fight was moral and just. Men will hate men. Knights will find other knights who drive them to kill through ambition, jealousy, envy or revenge. All these were good reasons for one knight to destroy another. The king's family motto 'Love Well, Hate Well, Serve God, Fear no Man' was universal throughout the land.

Thus, all along the border, the families and clans knew that Drummond was back with vengeance in his heart. Valechor had slaughtered his family, a massacre out near Madman's Stones on the Black Moor, where Drummond blood had all but a drop drained into the peat ditches. This, for the murder of a bride, who had been herself a Drummond and had fled the clan to wed a hated enemy. Slain in her marriage dress of white. Left to stain the snows of the wood, her halo of flowers clutched in her pale fingers like a ring of hope, her eyes wide and wondering, the love in them faded to a dead rabbit's stare.

And this was the cousin! This surviving Drummond. This was the man who had led her into the woods, promising to take her to her lover and husband-to-be, the knight Valechor. Instead, leading her to her brothers, who waited with drawn swords, and slew their only sister for a traitor. They who had merely pulled each other's hair in the nursery when they were angry with their sibling now had murderous weapons to hand, and the unspeakable was done before it could be prevented.

Afterwards the blame was cast. Not the bride, nor the brothers and cousins who took her life, but the man who had bewitched a maiden with his beguiling talk of love. Valechor. Border-bastard. Land-stealer. Church-burner. Or if not him, his father. Or if not his father, his grandfather. All alike, that family. Drummonds had suffered over the centuries. It was true that in return they had fired stacks and barns, killed the odd villein, stolen horses and cattle, but *all* the border clans did that. It was a way of life, a way of death. But to draw a maiden forth, take her from her family not by force, but with silken words and reins of gold. Who could stomach that? Not a Drummond, that was sure. Drummonds looked to their own.

But now – *now* a Drummond held hands with the king as he walked through his palace gardens. Now a Drummond laughed at bad royal jokes and received the monarch's rough kiss on his cheek (and felt the queen's bejewelled toes wriggle between his thighs under the banqueting table). Now a Drummond slept with fine foreign ladies, the captive wives of barons and earls, instead of greasy kitchen wenches. Now a Drummond could take a fine beautiful princess for a bride, wed her, bed her, take her for his own. Drummonds had risen in the world. This Drummond, recently a knight, could command men not necessarily of his own family. Now a Drummond could lay in wait for a Valechor, in a wood, and fall on him with sword and fire, and not be charged by the law or rebuked by a higher authority. Now, now, *now* God and the angels stood legitimately with a Drummond.

'Stand on the oak boughs,' ordered the knight Drummond, 'they will be through here in an hour or less. Fall on them from the trees. Give them no chance to escape. No quarter. No mercy.' In an aside to his best knight, 'He had me whipped once, flayed in the market-place, now I shall tear the skin from his back and use it for my war banner.'

Thus it was done. Valechor, weary with a recent battle against coastal raiders, trudged with his knights and attendants along the narrow path through the wood. Screaming creatures fell out of the trees, dropping on those below. There was great confusion. Blood flowed, limbs were severed, screams of another kind rent the air. Valechor fought with fury, not knowing the name of his enemy or why he had been attacked in his homeland. He fought until all his knights lay dead around him and there was nothing to stay for. Still on his black steed, his foes having been unable to unhorse him, he rode back along the darkening track, towards a town which bore his name.

Drummond was incensed. He kicked at the bodies on the ground.

'These are not the corpses I wanted to see. These were merely in the way of the one I wanted. Now he has slipped out of my grasp. The next time it must be a full battle, armies on both side, and an agreement that no man leaves the field until either a Valechor or a Drummond holds the heart of the other in his fist.'

So it was stated, so it was agreed.

Drummond then saw to his own dead, and found to his utter horror and dismay his new bride, lying with the other corpses. A fiery warrior-princess, she had secretly donned armour to assist her husband in the destruction of his mortal enemy. A dagger, with Valechor's own crest on the pommel, protruded the eye-slit in her visor. Valechor's terrible crimes against the Drummonds had increased by one. He had slain Drummond's bride.

Drummond fell to the earth, his face in his hands, weeping for the loss of one he had truly loved. That dark-haired, dark-eyed girl from foreign shores had been snatched from him by that bastard son of a bastard father, Valechor.

In the early morning a flock of winged lions passed overhead. The caravanners panicked, thinking they might lose a camel or two, or even a child, but the lions were too intent on reaching somewhere – perhaps they were thirsty and heading for a distant lake – for there was no pause in the flapping of great tawny wings.

'Pass the maize bread.'

Golgath did as he was asked. Soldier stared at his friend. There was no sign of anxiety on his face. He looked pleasant and comfortable as he sat with their hosts around the fire, breaking their fast. Yun and Petra looked contented enough too. Soldier was puzzled. Had anything gone on? He had listened hard enough. Was he the only person here with a sense of probity? Perhaps in this world he was a prude, a prig, one to be looked upon and pitied, laughed at, sneered at.

'I had a dream last night,' he said loudly.

The others all stopped what they were doing and looked at him.

'I had a dream that – that the world had been turned on its head.'

They stared at him and chewed their bread thoughtfully.

'I had a dream that men and women did as they pleased. There was no right or wrong in matters of the heart. There was no such thing as romantic love. Only people enjoying the favours of people.'

Golgath raised his eyebrows then climbed to his feet.

'We ought to be getting on. I'll take the hobbles off the camels. You get our things.'

Yun and Petra threw sand on the fire and began to pack various cooking pots and utensils. The whole caravan was astir now, preparing to leave. Soon all was ready and it was time to part.

'Thank you for your hospitality.'

'Thank *you*, Soldier – and you too, Golgath – for your company. I hope you find your wife soon. A lost wife. That is tragic. And I hope Guthrum returns to sanity soon. I hear they have run out of space on the trees and are hanging people from the sky.'

It was a hyperbole, but it expressed the state of things. The two groups went their separate ways. Soldier and Golgath were going west, the caravan east. A hot morning sun began its laborious climb up the sky. They rode in silence. Soldier desperately wanted to ask his friend how he had spent the night, but the same modesty which had prevented him taking advantage of a willing woman also stopped him from enquiring about the night's activities. By noon the pair of them had pulled hoods over their heads and had gone into their own separate kingdoms beneath the folds of their clothes. By evening it was too late.

The raven made his own plans. His betrayal of Soldier had hurt him more deeply than he could have imagined. Coming as he did, from the gutter, the boy inside the bird had a different set of ethics to someone like Soldier. The boy had come from a dog-eat-dog childhood, where betrayals were common. You did what you had to do to survive. Every gutter-snipe understood that. Loyalty was a luxury reserved for the rich and powerful. The raven thought he could get over his fall from grace easily, explain it away to himself, justify it — but that was no longer possible.

Soldier saw things differently, and now that the raven was beginning to understand the outlander, it too was looking on such things as treachery in another way. He would never again contemplate betraying the knight. Soldier had saved his life by killing the snake. The raven would certainly have died if the cudgel had not struck the serpent and rendered it harmless.

Of course, the black bird saw the knight's shortcomings. Soldier was naïve, slightly unstable, certainly a fool at times. To go chasing all over the known world for a female when there were plenty to be had in Guthrum was mad. There was work to be done here, to overthrow the usurper. If Soldier did not see that, the raven did, and it had decided to do something about it. He sneaked down into the dungeons and found the queen's cell.

'Your majesty, I've come to set you free,' he whispered through the bars. 'I'm going to pick the lock with my beak.'

The twins, Sando and Guido, came clanking in their chains to the cell door.

'The queen's been moved,' said Sando. 'Along with the old man. There's just us in here now.'

The raven thought for a bit. 'What will you do if I let you out?'

Guido said, 'Spit in Humbold's eye.'

'Stamp on his foot!' cried Sando.

'That'll do a lot a good.'

'All right,' said Guido, 'how's this. Out in the woods are rebels who've escaped from Zamerkand. We'll persuade them to accompany us back to Bhantan, where we'll overthrow whoever's in power there now and then raise an army and come back here and kill Humbold.'

'Kill him dead,' said Sando.

'That sounds a bit better, but look, there's a whole horde of beast-people and Hannacks surrounding the city.'

Sando and Guido stared at the raven.

'We'll have to think a bit more,' Guido said.

'Maybe we can assassinate him, or something,' Sando said at last. 'I know a man who can make a dark assassin out of a dead baby.'

'Who'd suspect a baby,' said Guido.

'Dead babies are vicious. They've had their whole life stolen away from them.'

'Dead babies have got no conscience.'

'They'd stab him in the eye when he bends over the cot.'

'Bite him in the throat.'

'Creep into his bedchamber and drop poison in his mouth.'

'Push it up his nose.'

'Into his ears.'

'Other places.'

'Scuttle across the floor when the guards rush in.'

'Slide like a snail under the sofa.'

'Creep out of a high window.'

'Crawl along the gutter.'

'Be hidden in a gargoyle's gob when the wailing starts.'

'Laugh like a brook when the search parties run through the gardens below.'

'Get away before the bitterns boom in the marshes.'

'Before the bullfrogs bark.'

'Free as a bird.'

'Free as a *raven*.'

The raven in question gave the equivalent of a bird's sigh and shook his feathered head.

'I'm not sure it's such a good idea, letting you two out. Look, I suggest you escape down the canal to the sea. Stow away on a barge or something. Once there, go and see the Whin. Those half-giants won't fight for you – the Whin will only ever fight for themselves – but the invaders won't enter Whin territory. The Whin can be a formidable enemy if they think they're threatened at all. It's only their presence which has prevented the beast-warriors and Hannacks from securing the end of the canal. Both the beast-people and the Hannacks have felt the hammers of the Huccaran half-giants before now and they didn't like it.

'Anyway, once you're in Whin territory, seek out a bird-person living there . . .'

'A bird-person?' said Sando. 'One of the invaders?'

'No, not one of them. Her name is Kraaak. She's a Hawk-woman who's lived in the quarry for nearly thirty years. Bird-people and beast-people don't get on too well, so she'll be only too pleased to help you get to the woods where the remnants of the Carthagan and Guthrumite armies are hiding out. From there, you'll be able to get back to Bhantan. I think the original plan was a sound one. Get your own country back, then think about what you can do to improve the situation here.'

'Gotcha!' Guido cried. 'We'll do it!'

'There's a curfew, so don't get caught,' explained the raven. 'It's late and there'll be thieftakers in the streets.'

He picked the door lock with his talented beak, then the locks on the manacles which chained the twins to the walls of the dungeon. Leading the boys through a network of tunnels, he took them to a sewer. Once in the sewers the twins were able to find an outlet to the streets.

It was night. The pair of them scuttled through the dank, cobbled alleys of the city. There was evidence of Humbold's harsh rule all around them. There were cages hanging from arches with half-dead people and corpses in them. Bodies swung like pendulums in the midnight air from gibbets. Here and there, a staring head on a spike. The watch patrolled the streets in gangs of ten, cudgels in their hands.

At one point the royal pair had to enter a tower to escape the detection of thieftakers. They climbed to the top, curious to see what lay on the other side of the walls. They were amazed to see the number of watchfires burning outside the city. It seemed that half the world's barbaric creatures were out there. Guido complained that the air was ripe with the smell of uncured hide.

It's the tents, said Sando, they're made of animal skins that haven't been scraped. How clever you are, his brother replied. Yes, I am, aren't I, agreed Sando. But, argued Guido, the people stink just as badly as their tents, you'd think they'd wash, wouldn't you? Sando remarked, our mother always said, show a Hannack a bar of soap and he'll eat it in ten seconds flat. Our mother always said, show a beast-person a bowl of water and he'll float his boots in it, said Guido. She never said that – that doesn't make sense! Yes she did! I never heard her. You never listen. Clever buttocks! Yes, I am.

The twins left the tower and went back down to the streets. By sneaking through the shadows they eventually reached the wharves where the barges were moored.

Chapter Eighteen

It was a torpid day. The heat lay heavy on the edge of the lake, which seemed in truth to be a stagnant pond. There were no rivers running in and out of its waters. And there was very little rainfall in this region. It was as if the lake had spewed up from the underworld, a viscous, oozing flow of fluid as if from the belly of a wounded beast. The area smelled of dead weed and rotting fish. There was not even a breeze to turn the atmosphere over. Flies were everywhere and no birds to feed on them to keep their numbers down.

Soldier and Golgath stamped on resolutely. By late afternoon they were utterly weary, being only halfway round the lake.

Soldier said, 'Let's rest now and travel at night. It might be cooler in the dark hours.'

'It might be. We can but try.'

A fire was lit, not for the warmth, but to keep wild beasts away. Soldier found a feverfew herb growing nearby and threw some into the flames to try to drive away the flies and mosquitoes. It was a trick taught him by Spagg and it seemed to work. Golgath put some slowburning wood on the flames, which would smoulder all day with a red glow, and hopefully drive away any wild creature who came nosing round.

They did not bother to unravel their blankets. They simply lay on the shore and used their packs as pillows. Soon both were asleep. Instead of waking later, they slept until early dawn. In the grey light Soldier awoke and started up with a short cry. Around him and Golgath were bundles of stinking rags. Who had put them there? Was this a joke? Soldier scoured the hills behind with a keen eye. He could see nothing, no one. The landscape was empty of figures.

The fire was still smoking, sending up a spiral curl into the warming morning air.

'What's going on?' said Golgath, who had now woken. 'What's all this?'

'I don't know. I've just woken up myself.'

As they were speaking, one of the bundles of rags moved. Then another one. There were forms inside those heaps. One by one they stirred, sitting up. The nearest one stared directly at Soldier. His – or her – face was hideous: a mask of holes. Bits of flesh were hanging from the cheekbones, the lips had been eaten away, the eyes were two burning, feverish orbs in sunken pits. The creature spoke. The words were distorted by a speech impediment, caused no doubt by the fact that the mouth was ulcerated and, going by the rest of the person's face, there was probably something amiss with the tongue within.

'Thank you.'

'You're welcome,' said Soldier, 'but for what?'

'The fire. Wild animals. Leopards. They eat us.'

Golgath said, bluntly, 'I should have thought that a mercy. You're lepers, aren't you? Wouldn't you rather die a quick death?'

'No,' said another of the poor creatures, 'leprosy is a slow killer. We want to keep life as long as the next man or woman. To be torn apart by a beast, that is enough to frighten anyone. When the time comes, I shall throw myself from a high place. But not yet. Not yet.'

They explained to Soldier and Golgath that the two men were in the Land of the Lepers, the place to which all those suffering from the dread disease were banished.

'No one comes here,' said the speaker. 'We were surprised to see your fire.'

Soldier said, 'We are seeking the fortress of Caliphat-the-Strong.'

'Then your course is true. His land lies on the other side of the Lake of Langour.'

Soldier and Golgath naturally kept their distance from the rotting lepers. Some of them had dry leprosy, others wet leprosy. It was the latter who were the most contagious. Both sets left bits of their bodies where they had slept: the top of a finger here, the lobe of an ear there. They rose, helping each other to their feet, and trudged away, mindful of the fact that they should not approach two healthy men. Soldier felt great compassion for the lepers. His own problems seemed to shrink to insignificance beside theirs. They had to find food and good drinking water, remain out of reach of wild beasts, and lastly and most importantly, prevent themselves from falling into that deep pit of despair which awaits anyone with a terminal illness.

As they travelled around that side of the lake, Soldier and Golgath met with many more of the lepers. Considering their plight, they were a respectful group. Soldier thought they should feel great bitterness for their condition, and that there must have been blame in their hearts, for surely they were bewitched in some way. Some evil or jealous person had called for the demon diseases to enter their bodies, to turn them from normal healthy people into walking corpses. Yet for the most part they seemed to accept their fate, and at least not rail at the world in general. Perhaps they harboured a secret hatred for the person or persons whom they felt responsible for their condition, but Soldier and Golgath were not amongst those.

There was the odd exception. Once they were approached by a leper who seemed more than anxious to engage them, either physically or in conversation. Threatened with the sword, the creature went away, shouting unintelligible abuse, half-mad with melancholia and misery. It was a miracle to Soldier that the pair of them were not more resented. He expected at any moment to be stoned and subsequently robbed of his possessions. This did not happen. He was thankful.

On the third night they built their fire as usual. Both men had been bitten beyond patience by insects, which left huge, red lumps on their skin. Sandflies had attacked their ankles and legs, mosquitoes and other aerial pests had gone for the soft targets – the neck, face and backs of the hands – and some unidentifiable wingless creatures had crawled up into their tunics and left their groins and bellies a mass of bumps. Once they tried walking in the shallows of the lake, slimy as the water was, but merely succeeded in becoming walking homes for leeches. They then had to stop, build a fire, and burn the leeches off with a red-hot twig.

It was an unholy land, and it wasn't surprising to either of them that the lepers had been consigned to this foul region.

Soldier woke as the ashen dawn crept over his face.

Suddenly, he was alarmed to feel a sleeping form close to him, hugging his chest. A leper had come in the night and was sharing his blanket! Soldier leapt to his feet with a startled cry, wondering why the leper's skin felt so cold.

Once he was up, however, he could see that the figure who shared his bed was no leper. It was like no man Soldier had ever seen before. Completely in black, with a flimsy, shapeless garment wrapped around its form, a gruesome face framed by a black hood, the creature rose to its feet and dusted itself off. It was at least three feet taller than Soldier, but its features were so horrible that Soldier could not get his thoughts to dwell on the height of the figure. His horror was unbounded. It sent his mind reeling in a dozen different directions at once, and froze his heart.

'What?' said the figure in a voice that seemed to echo through invisible mountains, 'have you not seen Death before? Surely you have come across me in your dreams? Or your imagination?'

Death stared at Soldier with eyes that were deeper and blacker than caves in a ravaged cliff-face. His lips were chapped and twisted like the bark of an ancient tree. The skin on his face, if it could be termed such, was pitted and riddled with holes in and out of which parasites – perhaps worms or maggots – crawled.

'Never,' breathed Soldier, gripped with a fear and loathing that locked every muscle in his body. 'I – no, never.'

Death snorted.

'I am a warrior, not a poet. You should put the same question to the man over there. He has imagination in plenty.'

'Why do you look so when you speak to me?'

'I – I – anyone would. I never thought I'd be looking into the face of Death. Not yet anyway. And why do you sleep?'

Again that impatient snort. 'I have to rest, the same as anyone else. Even the Creator rested after His labours.'

Spittle from his mouth fell onto the ground beneath, from whence sprang yellowish-green, sickly-looking plants, which withered almost as soon they reached ankle-height. Soldier looked at Golgath, who seemed not to have woken. He lay still on the other side of the fire. Another fear came to assail Soldier's fast-beating heart.

'Did you come for him? Have you taken my friend?'

Death glanced across the fire and shook his head. 'No, no. I come for one in the fortress of Caliphat-the-Strong. But, now that I have seen you, I recall that I am to come for *you* at midnight in two days' time. It would save us both a lot of trouble if you would agree to come now. The journey here is tedious in the extreme. I'm always having to come to this region for the damned lepers, curse them, they die like crane-flies.'

'You-are-to-come-for-me?' moaned Soldier, in a hollow voice. 'Who is it that kills me?'

'No one *kills* you. Old age takes you. You have had your time, Mukara.' Death looked about him. 'It's a bleak and unwholesome place, Mukara of Oliphat, and I'm surprised to find a ruler of your standing wandering such a landscape with but a single retainer, when you are so near to your end. What possessed you to leave your sick bed?'

'Who?' cried Soldier. 'Who did you call me?'

'Why, that who you are, which is the Sultan Mukara.'

Soldier laughed, unable to keep the hysteria out of his voice.

'Oh, thank the gods, you are mistaken. I'm no sultan. My name is not Mukara. You have the wrong man.'

Death's eyes narrowed and he opened his mouth so wide Soldier could see unspeakable horrors within: naked figures of men and women struggling, writhing in knots; kingdoms that had been wholly overcome by pestilence and plague;

whole countries that had been devastated by war and famine. 'I never make mistakes,' he snarled.

'Do I look elderly? Do I seem sick?' cried Soldier, wildly.

Death stared hard at him, his mouth now tight. 'My eyes are ancient and misty with the passing time. Besides, things in the real world are never as they seem. You are as you are. Tell me, if you are not Mukara, then who are you?'

Soldier realised that he was in a catch situation. 'My name is Soldier.'

'That's a profession, not a name. What's your *name*.'

'I – I – don't know. I've forgotten.'

'Then how do you know you're not Mukara of Oliphat?' asked Death, reasonably.

'Because Mukara is of this world, and I am not. I come from another place.'

'Where?'

'I – I know not. Look, see my blue eyes?'

'No – but I've heard some birds and reptiles have blue eyes.'

'But not *men*.'

'I'm not interested in your blue eyes. I see only in black and white. I am *Death*. You don't know who you are, or where you come from. Are you mad? You cannot conveniently forget who you are, simply to avoid dying. And what a life you've had! Executions without number. Men who offended you by farting or blowing their nose at the wrong time. Women who refused to sleep with you and wept for mercy. Children who annoyed you with their crying. And not just in ones and twos! Slaughtering your subjects by the thousand when they complained about taxes. Marching whole regiments of soldiers over the cliffs to their deaths, simply to prove there was no limit to your power. You've kept me busy.'

'But . . .'

'We've talked enough. Time to go. Any last words? I can't stand dying screams, and banality is beyond the pale. Go on, say something original.'

Soldier remained in horrified silence.

Death sighed. 'Perhaps I can help. How about, "This malady clings to me like a doting mistress and fornicates with my heart . . ."'

'Wait!' cried Soldier, interrupting. 'You can't take me. Golgath there has not woken. With all this talking and shouting, he should have. Therefore I must be dreaming. I won't come with you. I'm going to roll into the embers of the fire in my sleep. The pain will wake me up. You, begone from my presence.'

Death folded his arms. 'You can't escape me, you know. I shall come for you, in two days' time, in Oliphat.'

'By then you'll have learned of your mistake.'

'That is your hope. Now I must leave. Goodbye – until we meet again.'

'One last thing,' Soldier said, vaguely recalling a nebulous shadow following the bones and hair of HoulluoH.

Death stared. 'Yes?'

'Didn't I see you at the wizard's funeral?'

Death pursed his lips and then shook his head. 'No, that was my brother, Oblivion.'

A burning pain woke Soldier abruptly. He yelled and sat up and rubbed the back of his hand. In his sleep he must have flung out his arm, putting his hand in the embers of the fire.

'What's the matter?' asked Golgath.

'My hand. It went into the fire during sleep.'

'You must sleep further away from the – curse the good Kist – wolves.'

Soldier saw that Golgath was looking around the camp. There were marks in the dust, paw prints. More than two-dozen giant wolves had been circling them during the night, drawing ever closer. It seemed that something had frightened them off, just as they were about to fall on the sleeping pair. Golgath looked up, expecting to see a winged lion in the vicinity. 'I wonder what chased them away?'

Soldier, still rubbing the back of his hand, jumped to his feet. 'We must be on our way. Come, let's strike camp. We're near to our destination now.'

Golgath nodded. 'You must put some butter on that burn. It's the best thing for it. And a dry bandage.'

'I know how to treat burns,' replied Soldier, irritably. 'But I don't know where to get butter from, out in the middle of nowhere.'

After grubbing some roots from the ground and chewing them for the moisture and food content, the pair continued their march.

At last they came to some high cliffs, where a narrow entrance cut vertically through the main face. This natural passageway was guarded by a score of well-armed men. They stopped the pair and asked them their business. Soldier informed the guards that they had come to join the army of Caliphat-the-Strong, that they were two seasoned warriors who were looking for a war.

'Seasoned, eh?' said the big, scarred leader of the guards. He suddenly swung a short sword at Soldier's neck. Soldier skipped aside, avoided the blow and kicked the man's legs away from him in the same movement. The big warrior landed on his back in the dust, much to the merriment of his comrades. 'Seasoned,' confirmed Soldier.

With nothing but his pride injured the leader dusted himself off and said the two could proceed through the long, winding pass between the cliffs with an escort of five men. This they did. The passageway, no wider than an arm's stretch on either side, snaked for a mile between two sheer rock faces. It was as if the cliffs had been sliced by some god with a blunt sword.

Finally, they came out at the other end to find a deep valley about two miles long and a mile wide, again surrounded by cliff walls. Around the valley the limestone had been carved into cave-houses with decorative entrances. These houses were remarkable works of creativity, boasting bas-relief pillars at their portals and elegant arches in which were carved beasts, birds, fish and other symbols of fertility. The higher ones, those halfway up the cliff face, were connected to others and the ground by simple sweeping bridges of stone, or stairs cut in the rock.

As Soldier passed by one of these cave-houses and looked inside, he could see they were simple enough within – one or two rooms carved out of the soft rock, meagrely furnished, often with a hearth in the centre – but their frontages were monuments to high art.

Goats and dogs wandered around the entrances, devouring any rubbish which might attract rats, and children ran squealing and shouting between these beasts.

In the middle of the valley stood a fort carved from solid, red sandstone, with towers that reached halfway up the cliffs and crenellated walls with lean, high arrowloops as the only source of natural light. Black-and-red banners flew from flag-poles on the towers. The entrance was a small semi-circular hole through which a man had to crawl. Soldier could see no other gateway or door into the place.

Indeed, when they reached the fort, their escort forced them down onto their hands and knees, and they scrambled through the low opening to find themselves in a courtyard beyond.

A warrior, clearly an officer, came to meet them.

'What's this?'

'New recruits,' replied one of the escort. The five men then left them with the officer of the watch.

'Where are you from?' they were asked.

Golgath said, 'I deserted from the Imperial Guthrum Army. He's from somewhere else . . .'

'I thought he was,' said the officer, interested, peering into Soldier's face. 'He has eyes the colour of sky. Are you from the sky, warrior? Do you come from a kingdom in the clouds?'

'Yes,' said Soldier. 'But I've also served as an officer in the red pavilions.'

'Carthagan Army, eh? Well, you have to *earn* a commission in the army of Caliphat-the-Strong.' He looked up. 'I've often wondered about men from the sky. I've argued in the barrack room, about sky-warriors. Some deny they exist, but here's proof at last.' He seemed very pleased with himself. Then he turned on Soldier again. 'Which cloud did you come from? Where are your wings?'

'They fall off. If you spend too long down here they drop from your shoulders like leaves from autumn trees.'

'Ah, I can see that. Yes, they would, wouldn't they? Probably turn brown and wither. What a shame. That really would have clinched it, to see your wings. Never mind. You've got the blue eyes.'

'May we see your ruler?' asked Soldier, becoming impatient with this fool.

'Oh, you don't need to do that. I say who can join and who can't. I'll assign you a barrack room . . .'

'But,' argued Soldier, 'we have news of the outside world. Surely the lord Caliphat would want to know what's going on out there?'

'You tell me and I'll tell him. Hey!' the officer yelled at a passing warrior. 'Here's one of them. Didn't I tell you they were real? Where there are flying lions, I said, there are flying men. Well, I've got my proof at last.'

The warrior shook his head and kept on walking.

'He's got *blue* eyes,' yelled the officer of the watch. 'Eyes the colour of the sky.'

A dismissive wave of the warrior's hand. He didn't even look back.

At that moment a voice came, from high above. The voice had musical tones, as if it had once belonged to a songbird. It was too lyrical and sweet to come from an inanimate instrument, but it seemed to have the same range of notes owned by a harp. All three men looked up. There Soldier beheld the most beautiful face he had ever seen. It was on the end of a long and elegant neck which curved gracefully into some lily-white shoulders with delicate collarbones. Dark ringlets, webbed with gold threads, framed the pale face, with its ruby bow lips and perfect nose. Two dark and fathomless eyes regarded the three men.

'Who is from the sky?'

For a moment the officer of the watch did not answer. It seemed he was caught up in an internal storm. When he did reply it was with a croaky voice, full of emotion.

'My lady, this man. He has eyes of lapis lazuli.'

'Indeed? May I speak with him? Bring him to my chambers.'

Once the face had gone from the window, the officer seemed to come out of a spell. He looked uncomfortable.

'I dare not disobey her,' he said, more to himself than the other two, 'she will denounce me. Yet, if he catches me visiting her, I could lose my head. Curse the woman.'

'That's not a chivalrous way to talk of a lady,' Soldier growled, still giddy with the beauty he had witnessed in the window. 'How can you talk of a lady in those tones.'

'Oh, you don't know,' replied the anguished officer. 'You don't know what she can do, simply by being who she is. Well, I'll have to take you up there now. Curse me and my big mouth. Why did I have to shout it? If *he* catches us . . .'

By *he* Soldier and Golgath guessed he was talking of his ruler.

They were first disarmed, and then they entered a tower within which was a spiral staircase. The arrowloops were few and far between, so it was a dim climb they took up to the woman's chambers, stumbling all the way, passing other passageways off on the journey up.

Soldier and Golgath had both, separately, guessed that the woman was Moona Swan-neck, and they could not believe their luck. They were going to make contact with the very woman they had come to rescue. Yet, there were troubling signs. Why was she so accessible? And why were there no locks on the doors? It did seem as if she was staying there voluntarily.

They were ushered into a room at the top. There was a fragrance in the air which went straight to Soldier's head. He felt as if he were drunk on wine. Then a form shimmered into the room, the liquefaction of her clothes announcing her coming by their rippling sounds. She stood slim and straight before them. Her hips, her breasts – her shape was divinity itself, and matched the beauty of her heart-formed face. Her hands had obviously been doves during some former incarnation. Her feet were small and neat, set in golden sandals, with shapely toes the nails of which were painted with scenes of landscapes and seascapes, over which fabulous creatures were caught in flight.

There were three men in the room, and every one of them wanted to enfold this wonderful example of splendid womanhood in their arms, possess her, protect her from all evil, kiss her sweet mouth, her cheeks, her brow. They wanted her to melt into them. They needed to hold her for ever, never let her touch stray to another mortal on the earth. They craved the sound of her voice whispering in their ears, the smell of the maddening perfume of her breath. They desired to make love to her with gentle caresses such as women had never known before.

'This is the sky-man? Yes, he has blue eyes, I can see. But how does that prove he is from the sky? He might be from the ocean. Or from some mountain lake.'

'I – yes – I think – my lady, you are right. Where is the proof? This man says he's from the sky, but he could be from anywhere. I am so gullible. I – am – I must yearn – I mean, I must *learn* not to believe everything I hear . . . I mean, where is my lord?'

The officer was trembling. Soldier could not tell whether this was because of the overwhelming loveliness before him, which indeed took away all breath, robbed a man of all other desires known – or whether it was the thought of being caught by his master which filled him with fear. Clearly the officer was so shaken he could hardly think straight, being in the presence of Moona Swan-neck, an earthly goddess, the closest

thing Soldier had ever seen to an angel. He found himself
speaking to her.

'You, surely, my lady, are from the sky?'

Her tinkling laugh filled him with great pleasure, making
him tingle right through to his very feet. He felt himself a
great wit. He turned and grinned stupidly at his two companions, who both stared at him with blank expressions.

'No, I'm not from the sky.'

'*What in thunder is going on?*'

All three men whirled to find a thick-set, black-bearded
man in chain-mail armour striding up behind them. His
armoured feet were actually making a good deal of noise on
the flagstones, but they had not heard the sounds.

The bearded man had been followed into the room by five
personal bodyguards.

'My lord!' cried the officer in a frightened voice. 'I was
ordered.'

'You were what? You mincing fool. Get back to your post.
Who are these gawking idiots?'

'Recruits,' stammered the officer, hurrying from Moona's
chambers, anxious to be out of sight and mind. 'Deserters.'

Caliphat-the-Strong, for it was obviously he, then turned
on the two men drooling over his concubine.

'What are you staring at?' he cried. 'You,' he rounded on
Moona Swan-neck, 'go and cover yourself.'

'I am covered,' she said in quiet dignity. 'You yourself chose
the clothes I am wearing this very morning.'

'That was when they were for my eyes. I can see your
breasts through that material.'

'It is diaphanous for the purpose.'

'Well, it's disgusting in company.'

With her chin tilted in defiance, Moona left the room,

leaving an ache behind her within the men.

'So, before you both die,' cried Caliphat, 'what have you got to say for yourselves? Are you married? Are you betrothed? What would your wives think, both of you lusting after another man's woman? She is mine, and mine alone. Any man who even . . .' Caliphat had gone red and swollen about the jowls at this point, the horror and passion aroused by the thought of another man lying with Moona being almost too much for him to bear. They could both see he was insanely jealous and that nothing was going to save them from the sword, even though all they had been doing was admiring beauty. Soldier said as much.

'I protest, my lord. I have a wife I love dearly. I admit the beauty of Moona Swan-neck is enough to stun a man on first seeing her, but that cannot be helped?'

Caliphat drew his sword. He looked a strong man. His features were thick and cruel, his lips swollen with arrogance. This was a merciless potentate, standing before them, who thought less than nothing of killing a fellow human being. He was an ugly man, not through any disfigurement, but because his looks told the story of overindulgence, of unchecked power, of a wicked and lustful life.

'Married, are you? Well, we'll make a widow of your whore.'

Soldier's expression suddenly changed. He felt the wrath filling his breast. In calling Layana a whore Caliphat had pronounced his own death sentence. The fury that rose from within Soldier, an ancient hatred and bitterness that appeared as bile in his mouth, could not be checked. Vau, the dog-man, had been the recipient of that rage, and one or two others, and now Caliphat-the-Strong was about to receive.

'You foul-mouthed bastard,' said Soldier.

The sword-stroke whistled over his left shoulder, as he

expertly ducked the blow that would have taken his head from his shoulders. In the same movement, Soldier snatched a stiletto dagger from Caliphat's belt and plunged it into the belly of the big man, the thin, steel blade piercing through the chain-link armour. Caliphat gasped, his eyes bulging. The movement had been so swift and precise that the bodyguards had still not reacted. They had been caught completely by surprise.

Caliphat staggered back, clutching his wound, the dagger still protruding from his stomach. His sword clattered to the floor. Golgath picked up the weapon and sliced through the shoulder of the nearest bodyguard, who was still staring at his master with puzzled eyes.

Soldier picked up an onyx ornament from a side table and smashed it into the face of a second bodyguard. The man fell at his feet. Now the other guards were alert. Not having time to draw their swords, two of them sprang forwards and grasped Soldier, trying to wrestle him to the ground. Golgath battled with the fifth man, who, being at the rear, had managed to arm himself. Caliphat was on his knees, still clutching his stomach and moaning, crying for Moona to come and help him. He wrenched the stiletto from his belly, it being caught in the mesh of his chain-link armour, and blood gushed forth from the wound.

'I'm bleeding to death!' he screamed.

The bodyguard whom Golgath had first struck staggered out through a doorway, onto the battlements. Soldier guessed he was going to summon assistance, but neither he nor Golgath could stop the man. However, Soldier managed to roll over so that he had only one man on top of him, and that man was hampered by his body armour. Soldier gripped the guard's throat in his strong fingers and strangled him, while the second guard beat him about the face and head with a mail-gloved fist.

Soldier's own blood ran into his eyes from the lacerations on his brow. He kicked the strangled man away and grasped the second guard about the knees, bringing him crashing to the floor. Soldier jumped up and brought his heel down on the unfortunate man's nose. There was a *crack* and the guard groaned, rolled over and lay still. Having dispatched these two – one dead, the other unconscious – Soldier went to help Golgath, but that able warrior had already run his victim through the thigh. The man was not dead, but incapacitated, concerned only with the open artery which was spouting like a red fountain from his loins.

Golgath then ran outside. The guard who had gone out there was pulling himself up onto the crenellations. He looked dazed and bewildered, and there was great pain in his eyes. The cloth of his brigandine had been forced into his wound by Golgath's deep, slashing stroke and he was trying to pull it gently from the slit. Golgath had no choice. The man would soon start yelling. Golgath drove his blade down beside the neck, between the collarbone and the ribcage, through the chest cavity, and into the man's heart. It was a well-practised stroke for the Guthrumite warrior, and the man died instantly. Golgath looked around, checking that no one had seen. There were warriors on other towers, on other battlements, but luckily none of them were looking his way. He quickly kicked the body flat and out of sight, then returned to the room where the fight had taken place.

He was just in time to see Soldier take Caliphat's head from his shoulders, in front of a terrified bodyguard still trying to staunch the blood flowing from his thigh.

Moona Swan-neck entered the room as the head bounced

across the floor and settled by a carved chest. She raised not a hair. Instead, she began to berate Soldier.

'What did you do that for?'

'He called my wife a whore.'

'Is that a reason to kill a man?'

Soldier was indignant. 'He was about to kill *me*.'

'And what's that in the scheme of things?' She seemed to be simmering with anger underneath. 'Why have you come here anyway?'

Soldier could not yet get over the fact that she was annoyed at Caliphat's death.

'He's such an ugly man. Vain and swollen with pride. It shows on his gross features. You surely didn't love him?'

Moona shook her head. 'What do you know of my mind? I have reasons beyond your measure. You have no idea. You come here to interfere. I see that now. My husband sent you. Did you ask *me* whether I wanted to return to Ophiria? No, you just went ahead and did what you wanted to do, without so much as consulting me.' She looked about her without no compassion in her face. 'Well, it's done now, we might as well go home.'

Golgath said, 'How do we get out of here?'

'There's a secret passage,' she replied, 'leading from behind the hearth in the Great Hall. I'll take you there in a moment, but I want to see to this man's wounds first.'

The distressed bodyguard was still trying to staunch the flow of his own blood and was becoming weaker by the moment. Moona went to a cabinet. It was full of vials and powder boxes. She took a small bottle and went to Golgath's victim. Within seconds of being treated, the wound visibly began to heal before their eyes. Soldier was astonished.

'How did you do that?'

'I am what they call in this country a "marabout",' she said.

'A witch,' explained Golgath.

She glared at him. 'Not a witch, exactly.'

He shrugged.

Once the young man was looking less pale, Moona said to him, 'Your ruler is dead. There is no point in revenge for the sake of such a man. He was a despot and tyrant. Will you, for my sake, keep your silence until these men and I are out of the valley? Otherwise, they will have to kill you before they leave. I don't want you to die. Will you do it? For my sake?'

He looked into her eyes and was lost. 'I will.'

'And if this one wakes up,' said Soldier, nudging the unconscious man with his foot, 'you will tell him that Moona Swanneck, the marabout, has put a curse on him and his family, and that they will all break out in boils and die a horrible death if he betrays us.'

'I will. I'll tell him,' said the young man, still staring into Moona's face. 'I won't let him betray you.'

Moona kissed the youth on the lips, softly, and then motioned with her head for Soldier and Golgath to follow her. Even before they had left the room, the wounded man was weeping, asking if Moona would ever return, or if he could follow her to Ophiria, once his wound was properly healed. She left him a bewitching smile, but no words of comfort.

The most beautiful woman in the world led her two rescuers down the spiral staircase, to a passageway which led to the Great Hall. The hall itself was decorated with stuffed men, some on the backs of stuffed horses, one even on an elephant. They stared out with glassy eyes from the prisons of their own bodies.

'The royal taxidemist was in constant work, I assume,' said

Golgath, looking around at the grisly, petrified objects. 'I would prefer carvings and statues, myself.'

'He liked to humiliate his enemies,' explained Moona. 'He cursed them every night to their faces, before retiring.'

Soldier said, 'The man was a monster.'

'He had his ways,' replied Moona, with some asperity in her tone, 'but he was never a hired assassin.'

Soldier took the insult without reply.

Before entering the secret tunnel, Moona found them all some indigo cloth, with which to disguise themselves as caravanners. Then with a lighted brand she led them down through the passageway, carved out of the rock. They came out of an empty cave-house at the other end and walked swiftly into the valley. Moona took them to a corral full of horses. She snapped orders at one of the stable boys who were grooming the beasts, and without questioning who she was he saddled three of the best mounts and led them out of the corral.

'I sometimes go riding,' she explained to the other two, as she swung herself into her saddle, 'and the boys know my voice.'

'You never tried to escape?' asked Soldier.

'I told you. I don't care where I am, so long as I am well treated and given everything I want. The soldan did that, but then so did Caliphat. All men have treated me like a princess. I *am* a princess, after all. It doesn't matter to me whose bed I share. I have the same contempt for one man as I have for another.'

Golgath said, 'You hold men in contempt?'

'Of course.'

Soldier said, 'You bite the hand that feeds you?'

'No, I give them use of my body. Look, I owe men nothing.

Everything they have given me has been paid for, between greasy, sweaty sheets. I could quite happily live my life without a man ever touching me again, but it seems they can't live with me without doing things to me. So, I let them, so long as they let me do as I wish, give me everything I need, and only bother me once or twice a month.'

Soldier was aghast. 'Have you never known love?'

'Never.'

Golgath said, 'But one day, you might meet a man and fall in love, and *want* him to take you to his bed.'

'That will never happen.'

They could not believe this.

'But what of beautiful young men? Do you not desire a youth's body? Does the shape and form of a hunter, with good looks, never move you?'

'Never. They have nothing to give. All they have is themselves.'

'All *you* have, is *yourself*.'

'Yes, but, everyone wants me,' she replied, logically.

Once they were out of the valley there was a choice of directions.

'The best way to go,' said Golgath, who knew the region better than anyone, 'is through a place called Oliphat.'

Chapter Nineteen

'I'm not going to do it. I'm not going through Oliphat.'

'Soldier, how can you put so much credence on a dream? Everyone dreams about death. It's all in your head. It doesn't mean anything.'

Soldier was not convinced. 'Why are there Dream Masters plying their trade in Guthrum this very minute? Certain skilled interpreters earn their living by explaining dreams. If dreams don't mean anything, those people would starve, and from what I remember Dream Masters go about in the very latest sedan chairs and own strings of thoroughbreds.'

'Charlatans!' confirmed Moona Swan-neck.

The raven arrived to add to the confusion.

'I've just escaped death,' were his opening words.

Soldier whirled, looking this way and that. 'Where? Where is he?'

'Up there,' answered the raven, nodding skywards. 'A harpy eagle. Huge creature. Came out of the sky like a thunderbolt and very nearly did for me. That OmmullummO is not playing fair. What chance do I stand against a harpy eagle? It's the largest raptor in the bird kingdom. I only survived by cunning and fortunate circumstances. I was flying under the branch of an old white tree at the time. The eagle's talons struck the branch. Took it clean off. That could have been my head.'

'You didn't actually *see* the figure of the Reaper then?'

'See what?' asked the black bird. He turned to Golgath. 'What's he on about?'

'He thinks Death will come for him in Oliphat. Look, Soldier, you said yourself that Death was after the sultan, not you. The sultan will be in Oliphat. If Death comes, then he's not going to take both of you, is he? He's just coming for the old man, who must be expecting him.'

'But,' argued Soldier, 'the timing's right.'

Golgath got annoyed. 'I can't understand you,' he said, stamping away. 'How can you be so cowardly? You're asking us to go a hundred miles out of our way, simply because you're frightened of a dark figure which could be a figment of your imagination. Soldier, I've seen you face fearful odds in battle and not bat an eyelid. I've seen you go up against fiends in single combat and relish the opportunity. Yet here you are, frightened of a little dream. I just don't understand you.'

The raven understood. 'Irrational fears are the worst. When it comes to facing physical danger, you can rely on men like Soldier. But add a touch of the supernatural . . .'

'All right, all right,' snapped Soldier. 'We'll go through Oliphat, but I'm going *straight* through. No staying the night, even if we're exhausted. I don't like doing it, but I will. Now, let's say no more about it. Raven, what news of Guthrum and the outside world?'

'Still besieged, but the Hannacks and beast-people are getting weary of waiting around. It's not what they're good at. Show them a pitched, bloody battle and they'll thank you for it, but they're not much good at kicking their heels. Those that remain are spending their days at dice or cards. Others go up to the walls and challenge Guthrumites to single combat. They've had a few takers. It's just as boring on the inside of the walls, and there's disease and corruption to contend with.'

'Any good fights?' asked Golgath, interested. 'Single combats, I mean.'

'Well, there was this one Hannack – Maggagerak I think they called him – who despatched a few heroes who dared venture forth from Guthrum to meet him on the plain outside. He kept tying their heels to his horse and dragging their headless bodies back and forth in front of the gates, calling for new victims. Nasty piece of work.'

Interested now, Soldier said, 'I'd like to have a go at him.'

'You're too late. Marshal Kaff got tired of his bragging and went out to meet him. Unknown to Maggagerak, Kaff had a live creature fitted to his right wrist – you know, the way he does? – it was hidden under a mitten, a velvet hood. In the heat of the battle, with their swords locked and their heads close together, Kaff let slip the hood and thrust a cobra's head into the face of his opponent. The snake bit Maggagerak on the bridge of the nose, the throat, the lips and cheeks, and it was all over within a few minutes. Maggagerak turned blue, shook violently for a short time, then let out his death rattle and died. Kaff walked away the victor.'

Soldier had a bad taste in his mouth. He turned to Golgath. 'Kaff – your big brother,' he said with some asperity.

'Well, he always was a crafty so-and-so.'

Moona Swan-neck said, 'I've heard wonderful things about Marshal Kaff. Wasn't he just a captain a little while ago? Now he's been promoted all the way to the top. He must be a great warrior.'

'Yes, well, people would think that,' replied Soldier. 'Any other news, raven?'

'Yes, Kaff took Maggagerak's body and crucified it on the battlements.'

'I mean *real* news,' snapped Soldier, testily.

'Oh, yes – the twins, Sando and Guido? They've been reinstated as rulers of Bhantan.'

Now this was something which really did interest Soldier.

'Humbold let them go?'

'No, I helped them escape. I picked the lock. They travelled north, gathered together an army of rebels, fairies, goblins, elves and other creatures of the field and forest, and went into Bhantan at the head of a strange army. They slaughtered the nobles who had exiled them and deposed the twins who had been put on the thrones in their place. They are now back where they came from, and send you their greetings, saying when the time comes for you to lead an army against the Hannacks and beast-people, Bhantan will join you in the fight.'

'Well, that's something,' said Soldier. 'Did they have to slaughter the nobles, though?'

'Things did get a little out of hand. They're not the most charming of youths. You should hear what they're saying about Humbold and what they intend to do to him when they get hold of him.'

'Perhaps they'll have time to grow more mature and wiser before that happens?' said Soldier, hopefully.

The bird stayed with them, all that day, feeding them snippets of news. The main thing was that IxonnoxI was safe, still out of the clutches of his father.

'Well, let's get to Oliphat,' muttered Soldier. 'I want that town behind me before dawn tomorrow.'

The two men rode on either side of Moona Swan-neck, each vying for her undivided attention. She answered questions they put to her, but rarely initiated a conversation. The men kept offering her things. A second coat? Was she too cold? Too hot? Were her feet chaffing on the stirrups? Perhaps Soldier's spare socks? Would she like Golgath's gloves to keep the harsh sun from her delicate skin? Soldier had a square of cloth which could be made into a protective hat. Golgath had a spare waterskin which would cool her brow. Perhaps, when she became too tired, she might like to ride up behind Soldier, holding on with her arms around his waist? No, no, protested Golgath, it should be *his* mount that the lady shared, for he was a single man. What difference did that make, said Soldier, for *she* was a married woman, and he wasn't asking to make love to her. He was simply offering her a ride. His horse was the strongest, so it made sense that she rode with him . . .

'This is sickening,' said the raven. 'I'm off.'

He flew away in clear disgust.

Moona said nothing, except to demur. She was perfectly all right, she said. There was no need to fuss over her. They weren't *fussing*, they replied. A lady was entitled to be as comfortable as possible. Would she like a sweetmeat from Golgath's saddlebag? No, of course not, it would make her thirsty. A twist of sherbet then, from Soldier's pocket? He had had it with him since Carthaga . . .

And so it went on.

They camped at noon for two hours.

'Who's going to the stream for water?' asked Soldier, unwilling to leave Moona alone with Golgath.

'I'll go,' said Moona.

'I'll come with you,' said Golgath. 'I could do with the walk.'

'In that case, you can get the water,' Moona said.

Soldier smiled and tossed him the water skins. 'Off you go.'

Golgath sat down. 'I've changed my mind. Actually my old war wound is playing up. My right foot – it's very sore. You go for the water, Soldier.'

'Moona? Will you come with me?'

'If you like.'

The pair set off, soon to be followed by Golgath. 'I've changed my mind,' he said, catching them up. 'I told you the walk would do me good.'

'It doesn't need three of us,' Moona argued. 'I'm going back.'

'I'll come with you.'

'Funnily enough, my foot is beginning to hurt again . . .'

They arrived in Oliphat to find the town in subdued mood. Their sultan was dying. The sackcloth and ashes were already being prepared and craftsmen were bringing on extra supplies of flails. Oliphatians mourned in a big way. They took death very seriously, especially the death of a potentate. They would don the sackcloth, smear themselves with the ashes, and whip themselves raw, once the old man kicked off his golden sandals and took Death by the hand. There would be ranting and wailing, genuflection and prostration, fasting, ringing of bells, clanging of gongs, beating of drums, rattling of sticks and bones. Not many of Oliphat's citizens were looking forward to the next few weeks, and when they saw who had arrived in their town they sent a deputation of their most senior male citizens, men of noble birth, merchants of great wealth, members of various councils.

'Moona Swan-neck,' they chorused. 'Your beauty is legendary throughout the known world. They say your face has spurred a thousand armies into battle. Your portrait hangs in the halls of kings of countries not yet discovered. In the deepest, darkest unexplored regions your name is whispered as a talisman. They say it is inscribed on the golden grail which men seek and never find. There are temples erected to your beauty. Lonely princes spend lifetimes beating a path to your door.

'Will you show yourself, reveal your great beauty, to our dying sultan? Perhaps the sight of your loveliness may revive him, bring him out of his illness, raise him from his deathbed. He is beloved of the people. We do not wish him to die.'

'We are in a great hurry,' she replied, with a blank expression, 'as you can see, my friends wish to be on the road leaving from the other side of the town.'

'We will see you rewarded with pearls, with sapphires, with ivory.'

'Oh, those? Pearls, sapphires and ivory?' murmured Moona.

'See,' cried Soldier. 'They do have a sultan that's dying. It wasn't just a dream. That much is true.'

'Oh, you probably heard it somewhere, on our travels,' replied Golgath, 'and it worked itself into a dream.'

'I don't think so. Remember your promise. We are not stopping.'

'Yet,' replied Moona, 'if I do not try to help this poor, dying man, I would be neglecting my duty.'

'To what?' cried Soldier. 'To whom?'

'To humankind,' she replied. 'To life!'

'You just want the gifts they're offering,' snapped Soldier. 'You're not interested in saving an old man's life.'

The hurt look that came to her face seemed to arrive so

smoothly, and without any herald, that Soldier was convinced she was faking when she said, 'How could you say such a thing? You do not know me. You *think* you know me, but you're very wrong. Look how these people beseech me. How can I refuse them when they implore me? I *will* go to the sultan. I *shall* do my best to revive him.'

'Oh, that's rich. That really is. How old is he? A hundred and eight? His penis is probably like a piece of string now. No doubt he's got as much passion in that husk of a body as a dead lizard. You think he's going to perk up just because he sees *you*.'

Golgath said, 'I don't think that's quite fair, Soldier. Moona just wants to try. Would you deny an old man?'

'Yes.'

But he was arguing in vain. They were led to Sultan Mukara's sick bed. Soldier saw by the sand-clock that it was still an hour to midnight. There was still time to attempt the revival and escape before Death arrived to collect his victim.

Moona was ushered into the royal presence.

'Where's the pearls?' she asked.

A citizen pointed to a casket by the door. 'There.'

Rheumy eyes regarded her form from the sick bed. The sultan was propped up on silk cushions, a frail, stick-like figure with yellow flesh hanging like pondweed from his bones. His face was sunken, his eyes lustreless, his hair dripping in coarse, matted clumps. There was a sickly smell about the room that turned the stomach. The stench of death was in the air.

At the sight of Moona Swan-neck, a light did indeed enter those gummed eyes. A feeble hand was raised an inch from the sheet. It was as if he were reaching for this earthly beauty. A rustle like the sound of rasping paper left the old man's lips. Then he seemed to collapse within himself again, destroying the excitement that had begun to ferment in his shrunken brain.

'Perhaps if I removed my clothes?' said Moona, without blinking. 'Perhaps then the sultan might find some lightness of being?'

Yes, chorused the citizens, that *certainly* might do it.

There was universal disappointment when they were all asked to leave the room.

Protests followed.

No, no, she was no dancer of the seven veils, there for the entertainment of the masses, she was a physician, trying to cure an old man. Soldier and Golgath, as her travelling companions, could stay as her protectors, but everyone else except the sultan would have to wait outside. They went, grumbling and glancing over their shoulders, hoping she would start before the door was shut. Once outside there was a mute, frantic battle between them to get the best positions for the doorway cracks and keyhole. Men might have been killed had they not been conscious of having to keep their silence. Certainly great wads of money exchanged hands, and daughters were promised in marriage. Land became a bargaining tool and old favours and debts were called in.

Standing at the end of the old man's bed, Moona Swanneck removed her clothes.

Two simultaneous groans reached her ears, coming not from the sultan, but from her two protectors.

The old man gargled. His eyes blazed. He sat up.

'Ga!' he said, reaching out with scrawny, arthritic fingers, like a child snatching at sweets. 'Gaaaaaaaaa!'

'It's working,' she said, calmly. 'I wonder how many caskets of jewels they're offering?'

At that moment a patch of darkness in the corner of the

bedchamber whirled like a wind and began to form into a shape. Before the eyes of the terrified watchers it developed into the rough contours of a man. Soldier recognised the shape straight away. Death stood there, dusting himself off.

His head lifted to regard the four people present. His horrible visage gave nothing away as he scanned the room. However, on seeing the naked Moona, Death pursed his lips. Finally, he nodded to Soldier, and said, 'Well, are you ready then? I told you I'd see you here. They never believe me. They think they can be in Iskanbul, when they're expected in Ud, but they always find themselves in Ud at the appointed hour, by freak wave, by runaway horse, by kite if it has to be, but they're always ready for the last journey.'

'You – you don't want me,' said Soldier, quickly. 'You want him – him in the bed.'

Death looked at the skeletal, shallow-breathing sultan, now sitting up in bed and trying to clutch at the nude Moona Swan-neck.

'Are you coming or not?'

'No,' replied Soldier, firmly.

'In that case, I'll just wait until midnight. You'll *have* to come then.'

They stood there until the sands in the glass ran out. At which point the sultan gave a strangled cry and fell across the bed stone dead. Death looked surprised. He stared at Soldier as if he expected him to do the same. When he didn't, Death reached down and gathered up the corpse in his arms, and shook it violently, until the soul fell out of its mouth. It struggled and squirmed, trying to crawl under the bed. He quickly gathered it up and stuffed it into the folds of his garment.

'I've never been wrong before.'

Soldier said, 'How do you know? You might have taken others, who didn't put up such a fight as me.'

'I don't think so.'

At that moment the door burst open and the senior citizens of Oliphat tumbled inside. They stared aghast at the dead man draped across his own bed.

'Our sultan is dead!' one wailed. 'Moona failed.'

'I didn't exactly *fail*,' replied Moona, trying to dress behind the wardrobe door. 'You should have seen him reach for me. It was a magnificent attempt. Unfortunately, the strength drained from his body. I think I ought to still get the pearls, sapphires and rubies.'

'Ivory,' said the head citizen. 'It was pearls, sapphires and ivory.'

'Thank you,' replied Moona. 'Yes.'

All the other citizens were staring at Death with horrified expressions on their faces.

Death, in turn, had singled one of them out for his special attention. 'You, the wheel-maker. I've got to come for you in three days' time. To save me a journey, why don't you come now? It'd be better for both of us.'

'Don't do it,' muttered Soldier in the man's ear. 'He does make mistakes.'

'Me?' cried the wheel-maker. 'But I'm fit and healthy. I'm only forty-eight years of age. I have a wife and family.'

'And a nephew, who kills you with a meat axe,' said Death. 'He's there, right behind you. Yes, the youth with the spots.'

The wheel-maker rounded on his nephew.

'You? Kill *me*! You ungrateful whelp! I took you in. I fed you when my brother died. I've been more than an uncle, I've been like a father to you.'

The youth looked sullen. 'You won't let me marry Drucilla.

You don't think I'm worthy of your daughter.'

'It's not a matter of *letting* you. You make it sound as if I'm the cruel parent keeping lovers apart. The truth is, Drucilla can't stand the sight of you. I'm not going to force my daughter to marry someone she doesn't love. I'm a good and thoughtful father. Go and find someone who likes you, then come to me for permission to marry.'

'I want Drucilla.'

'But she doesn't want *you*.'

Death said, 'All this is by-the-by. You can't interfere with Fate, even if you know about it beforehand. The fact is, *you're* going to die, and *you're* the one who kills him. Come to think of it, you might as well both come, because the nephew gets executed as a murderer . . .'

It was at this point that Soldier, Golgath and Moona Swan-neck crept from the room. On the way out Moona picked up the small casket which stood on a plinth by the door. She checked its contents and gave a satisfied nod. Within the half-hour they were on the road again, heading back towards the Cerulean Sea. Once out in the desert lands, the two men began to slip into their own routines. They rested in the afternoon, travelled on much of the evening, and settled down for the night around the striking of twelve. On the first night they were so tired they just about had enough energy to hobble the horses, then the three of them sank to the sands and slept where they fell.

The second night was different though. A fire was built to keep wild animals away and to counter the cold. Soldier laid his blanket on one side of the fire, Golgath on the other. They both watched each other, consumed by jealousy, to see where Moona put her bedding down. When she went at the top, to form a sort of open square, the two men could not go to sleep in case one or the other of them edged closer to her. Moona herself slept like a lamb.

The next morning the two men were tired and irritable with each other. One of them groomed Moona's horse, while the other watched suspiciously. The other made her break-fast, equally under observation from his fellow. When they rode together, each had his side: Soldier on the right, Golgath on the left. At one point they had both moved so close to Moona, in the middle, that she complained she felt like the meat in a sandwich.

'Get away from her, you fool,' said Soldier. 'Can't you give her some room?'

'Me?' yelled Golgath. 'What about you? You're almost in her pockets. Step back, I say. You're making an idiot of your-self.'

'I? I'm no idiot. If there's stupidity around it sits on the left.'

'On the right, you mean. You never could tell your army left from your navy right.'

'I know perfectly well which side is which.'

'You could have fooled me.'

'You're easy to fool.'

'Are you looking for a fight? Because, if you are, I'm the man to give it to you.'

'Are you though? Well, just step down off that horse.'

'Gentlemen! Gentlemen!' cried Moona Swan-neck. 'You're driving me to distraction. Just move away from my horse, both of you. That's right. Keep to your own sides. Upon my word! You're acting like boys of twelve. Men always seem to in the end.'

The pair moved away, still casting dark looks at each other across the rump of her palfrey. If one of them had a bow then, the other would be dead. Right at that moment they wished each other a million miles away, on some distant star. Moona rode on, seemingly ignorant of the growing hatred between the two men.

'I shall sleep in the rocks tonight,' announced Soldier that evening, while glaring hatred at his male travelling companion. 'Will you join me, Moona? You'll be much safer with me. There are men about who have no regard for the sanctity of womanhood.'

'Moona is staying here, with me,' snarled Golgath. 'If you want to go in the rocks, go there, and stay for all I care. In fact, why don't you leave altogether and search for that wife of yours. I'm sure she's missing you.'

Having said he was going to sleep elsewhere, Soldier did not feel he could change his mind. Inside he was boiling with anger and loathing for his former friend. He wondered now how he ever could have considered Golgath anything more than an enemy. After all Golgath was the brother of his most hated foe and adversary, Marshal Kaff.

Soldier took his blanket and settled down between two boulders. In the middle of the night though, while the stars were spiking the heavens, his bitter feelings had fermented to such a point he felt he had to do something about them. He had decided to kill Golgath while he slept. Soldier argued he would be doing the world a favour by ridding it of vermin such as that Guthrumite.

With dagger in hand, he sneaked round the boulders, only to come face-to-face with the man he was about to murder. Golgath was there, also with a knife, creeping towards the rocks. They stared at each other in the starlight, snarled, shouted oaths, then fell on one another. Their struggling in the dust woke Moona Swan-neck. She had enough sense to know that if these two men killed each other, she would be in grave danger of being lost in the desert, where dangerous beasts and nomadic robbers roamed at will.

'Stop!' she shrieked. 'Stop this at once, or I'll never speak to either of you again!'

It was the one threat which caused them to come to their senses and pull apart from one another.

'Bastard,' snarled one.

'Swine,' growled the other.

'Stop this fighting, this instant,' ordered Moona. 'What are you thinking of? You're supposed to be friends.'

'Friends? With that oaf?' cried Soldier. 'I'd rather be friendly with a crocodile.'

'I'll be a crocodile for you – I'll bite your stupid head off!'

'Why you – for a groat . . .'

'Here's a groat. Pick it up. Then do your worst,' said Golgath tossing a coin in the dust at Soldier's feet.

'Children, children,' pleaded Moona, who was used to men fighting to the death over her charms.

Soldier looked at her with narrowed eyes. 'You're frightened I'll hurt your lover, is that it?'

Golgath snarled, 'It's you she's been mooning over, with those big brown eyes of hers. I've seen the two of you, looking at each other. It's sickening.' He gripped his dagger. 'I've a good mind to . . .'

'Stop it, now!' yelled Moona. 'You – go and sleep in the rocks. You go and sleep over there. I'm going to stay by the fire where the snakes and spiders won't get me. You two will have to fare as best as you can out in the darkness. I don't want either of you, do you understand? I'm not interested in you, or you. I'd rather have a camel as a lover than one of you simpletons. Now, let's get some sleep.'

They stared at her, their mouths tight lines on their faces.

Soldier looked around him, into the darkness. 'You've got someone else, haven't you? There's a goat boy out there somewhere, isn't there? That's it. You want to get rid of us, so that you can meet your lover and engage with him. Well, I'm not moving from here all night.'

'And I'm not moving from here,' said Golgath, taking up a similar stance.

'Well, *I'm* going to bed,' Moona said, wearily. 'I really don't care if the pair of you die on your feet.'

The journey promised to be hell.

That is, until the youth with golden hair came by.

Chapter Twenty

The next few days and nights were the same. The two men were at each other's throats the whole while. It was a miracle that one of them was not wounded or killed by the other. It was only that in their blind fury they were not so accurate with their attempts. Had they remained cool and calm one of them would certainly have died. Perhaps both of them. They were so consumed by jealousy they were like two active volcanoes. Once or twice the scabbard's song saved Soldier from a pierced body. Moona acted as Golgath's warning device, preventing *him* from receiving a mortal wound. Moona Swan-neck was at her wits' end with both of them.

Fortunately this jealous feud was interrupted.

Halfway across the desert, they came across a golden-haired young man with a woman in tow. It was when they rode over a dune that they saw the youth kneeling, aiming a crossbow up into the sky. He loosed the bolt as they watched and a few moments later a winged lion plummeted to earth. It struck the sand with a heavy *whump* and lay there, limp, broken and very dead. The youth let out an exulted cheer, went and kicked the dead beast, before folding his bow and fitting it into a sheath which hung from his saddle.

The young man was not more than twenty. His muscles stood proud of his bronzed body, which owned the physique of a boxer. He was trim-hipped, strong-legged, and broad-shouldered, wearing only a pair of skin-tight pantaloons against the fierce desert sun. That he was some kind of athlete was only too obvious from the way he moved and held himself. His golden locks hung down to his shoulders in curls, framing very handsome features. Soldier had never seen a youth with such a pretty face, bearing such hard muscles.

But it was not the youth which held his attention.

It was the woman with him.

She was Princess Layana, his own dear wife.

'Layana?' called Soldier, excitedly, all thoughts of Moona instantly driven from his mind. 'I've found you!'

'Well, at last,' murmured Golgath, he too coming to his senses at the sight of someone from the outside world. 'Now perhaps we'll have some sanity around here.'

Soldier rode down the dune.

When he reached Layana, he leapt from his saddle and took her in his arms. But on looking into her vacant face, he knew that something was terribly wrong. It was obvious to him that she did not recognise him. She simply stared in bewilderment. She was dirty and dishevelled, her face smutted and her hair awry. The dress she was wearing was torn and her sandals scuffed. She looked like a woman fallen on bad times.

'Layana? Don't you know me?' he cried in anguish, holding her at arm's length. 'My own dear, sweet darling. You *must* know me.'

The youth was by his side now. The young man reached

out and prised him from Layana with strong fingers. Standing in front of her, as if to protect her, the golden-haired young man said, 'I'll thank you to keep your paws off my handmaiden, Blue-eyes.'

'Handmaiden? She is the Princess Layana, of Guthrum, and my own wife.' Soldier's mood changed. He drew his sword. 'Stand aside boy,' he growled, 'or I'll slice you into rashers.'

'That would be very wrong of you,' said the youth. 'You would regret such an action when I have done you no harm. I own this woman. I paid for her with good coin. Whatever she was before, she belongs to me, now. I purchased her from a slave caravan two days ago. I was told they had bought many people from a magical city, a people who could not remember their own names, and had a huge string of such vacant-eyed slaves. You should take better care of your wives. this one is now mine and I can do with her as I wish. You must have others?'

Incensed by this speech, Soldier raised his weapon.

'You will be sorry,' said golden-hair, standing there stiff and proud. 'You are in the wrong. I think you know it.'

Suddenly, Golgath was there, with them, and he restrained Soldier.

'Let me handle this,' he said.

Golgath turned to the young man.

'We are Soldier and Golgath, two officers from foreign armies. This woman here is Moona Swan-neck, wife of the Soldan of Ophiria. Who are you, sir?'

'I am Prince Paladan, of distant Xxiphar, in the south-east corner of Uan Muhuggiag. My father is the King of Xxiphar. I am travelling home. I will tell you, sir, what I told him. I purchased this drab with gold moidores from a slave caravan heading south. She is mine to use or abuse as I please. I have already had to beat her once, when she burnt my breakfast eggs, and I will do so again, whether or not she was the wife of that ruffian, or the daughter of the King of Kalamash himself. What she was before is of no consequence. What she is now is a slave.'

'*Drab*?' Soldier yelled. 'I'll give you *drab*. Beat her, would you? Beat my wife? I'll feed your head to the vultures, you snotty little hamster, with your golden pelt and buttery looks.'

Again, Golgath restrained the infuriated Soldier.

'The youth *is* within his rights, you know,' he told Soldier. 'She is a woman full-grown and has been rescued from the city in the sands and as such can be lawfully sold on the slave market. If she could tell us she had been taken against her will, it would be a different matter, but look at her. She doesn't know what time of day it is, let alone who you are.'

'Layana?' pleaded Soldier.

'You seem a nice man,' said Layana, speaking for the first time, 'but I know you not. Nor indeed, do I know myself. All I know is that I'm grateful for being taken from that terrible city, where no one knows their own name, and brought into the fresh air again. I was choked with sand when they dug me up. It's a wonder indeed to find myself alive and well. If it means serving for the rest of my days, it's better than being buried alive. Anything is better than being immured.'

'I was there myself,' groaned Soldier. 'Why didn't I see you?'

'There are many people there. Only very few of us were rescued. We are all very grateful and happy to be free.'

'Enough talking,' said the prince. 'Back to work, slattern. Fetch some water from the well. You must bathe my feet. Then you can skin the winged lion, and pluck its wings, after which we shall bed down for the night.'

Golgath had to drag Soldier away from the boy's camp and whisper in his ear, 'Not yet! Hold hard, Soldier. Let's delve a little deeper into the youth's ways and means. Better to take our time.'

Soldier stared back at the arrogant young man, who had now dismissed him without a second glance. It almost choked him to see Layana return with water and bathe Paladan's dirty feet, as if she doted on this young monster. To make matters worse, she was ordered to dry his feet on her hair, which she did without a murmur.

'I'll kill him!'

'Not yet.'

Soldier searched for other things he did not like about the youth and was happy to find several. Among them the prince's apparent disregard for the rules of hunting.

'He killed a winged lion,' said Soldier, 'simply to see it come crashing down out of the sky.'

'He has killed a winged lion for its coat,' said Golgath, 'which is perfectly legitimate.'

'He killed a winged lion,' breathed Moona, in quite different tones to those used by her male companions, 'and will give the coat to his lady.'

Soldier looked at Moona. So did Golgath. She was not looking at them though. She was staring at the golden-haired Prince Paladan with a faraway look in her eyes. She was rapt. Her big brown eyes followed his every movement and she sighed, deeply. Her little white teeth were biting her soft upper lip, gently, making her look very vulnerable, very desirable. Her thighs were pressed tightly together. Her right hand was clenched and her open left palm rested on her sternum. She seemed close to a state of grace within herself, coupled with something more carnal.

'How elegant he is,' she whispered, to herself. 'How lissome. How *strong* and manly.'

'Oh, you gods,' groaned Soldier, putting his face in his hands, 'she's infatuated now.'

'Which way are you going?' called the prince, to the trio. 'East or west?'

'North-west,' replied Golgath.

'Indeed? I am going that way myself. Perhaps you should join me, in case of brigands. I can protect you. I have food and water. You may share these — er — that lady, why does she stare so? Isn't she aware that it's bad manners to stare like that? Tell her to stop.'

'Moona, stop,' said Golgath.

She simpered and continued to stare.

'It's very disconcerting,' said Paladan. 'Is she weak in the head?'

'Not usually,' replied Soldier, 'but you may have noticed how beautiful she is? Perhaps you would care to trade her for your — your handmaiden? It's a fair exchange. This one has a very trim figure and nice soft hands, as well as a complexion a child would envy.'

'No — no thank you. I prefer my own slave. Yours looks simple. I don't want an idiot.'

'But her beauty?'

'Not so much,' answered the youth, with a yawn. 'I think I've seen better. She's got a certain charm, I grant you, but I think I'll keep my own to myself. If you think she's so beautiful, you keep her.'

Soldier was entirely frustrated. He had found his wife, and now he wanted to take her to safety so that he and Golgath could pursue their objective. They needed to assist IxonnoxI in claiming his rightful position from his father OmmullummO.

Instead, here they were, caught in a wrangle that seemed absurd and unnecessary.

By the time evening came around, Layana had skinned the lion and plucked its wings. She now spent the twilight hours working hard, scraping the great skin for her master. The feathers, precious enough in themselves, had been tied in bunches and hung from his embossed leather saddle. Paladan in turn was singing about being a famous hunter whom everyone admired and adored, for his looks and sweet nature as well as his prowess. Soldier was honing the edge of his sword on a rock and sending hateful glances through the sparks. Golgath stirred the fire and stared into the flames. Moona Swan-neck hummed a madrigal to herself.

It was more than Soldier's flesh-and-blood could stand, to see his own wife being worse used than a scullery girl. He ground his teeth and promised himself he would slit the youth's throat in the night.

However, Golgath anticipated Soldier's plans and kept a good eye on him. Whenever Soldier rose, Golgath did so too.

'If you try to kill him in his sleep,' warned Golgath, 'I'll wake him with a shout.'

'Why? Why are you protecting him?'

'Because I'm not sure what he's doing here and why he wants to keep company with us. Just be patient. I know it hurts you to see him with your wife . . .'

'With my wife?' groaned Soldier, in agony, turning to see that the pair of them were under the same blanket. 'I *must* kill him now.'

'No. No, you must not. Wait. It is best for all of us. You must think of me and Moona, as well as yourself. I don't think they're doing anything under that blanket – I believe it's just for warmth.'

'You don't *think*? Oh, my, what am I come to? Any other man would be dead by now. I would have torn their throats open with my teeth rather than see them treat my wife in such a fashion. And under the same blanket,' he moaned. 'I am a jealous man, Golgath. I cannot bear it.'

Yet, for some reason – a nagging suspicion in the back of his brain – Soldier did as Golgath said. He crawled back under his own blanket and tried to concentrate his mind on other matters. There was something amiss here, which he could not put his finger on. Why was such a youth travelling alone, across a dangerous desert, with gold moidores in his purse? It did not make sense. A prince. A popinjay. A young bird with bright feathers. There had to be some explanation which had not yet come to light. Golgath had smelt something too: an odour difficult to define. Perhaps the morning would throw a different light on the situation?

Soldier woke once, in the grey early hours, to see that Golgath was under the same blanket as Moona. Only he, Soldier, was alone with himself. This mad world had locked him out again. He felt an alien, a stranger, a thing out of place. Was this a nightmare of his own making? Or had he been sucked into a world which subjected him to excruciating torture for being an outsider? He woke Golgath.

'I told you, I'm jealous.'

'*You* are jealous man? We are both jealous men. I think the last few days has proved that. It's a wonder neither of us has the other's dagger in the heart, given the attempts each of us has made. I, for my part, am thoroughly ashamed of myself.'

'And I too,' said Soldier. 'I'm truly sorry. I don't know what came over me. After all, Moona is not *that* beautiful.'

'If only that were true. You know she is.'

Soldier sighed. 'Yes – yes, she is. You're right. I'm just trying to turn myself aside now. But, in the end, what is beauty? A surface thing. Shining lakes, virgin snows. But what lies underneath? A cunning, scheming heart? Or perhaps one as barren and as arid as a desert? Who knows? Moona is well enough, I suppose, but she does not have the spirit of my Layana.'

'No, but still – she is beautiful. A diamond has no real worth either – it is nothing but a piece of mineral rock after all – but men will kill and die for diamonds. You can't just dismiss something or someone because they are *only* beautiful. Do they need to be anything else? Beauty is itself.'

'I suppose.'

Soldier actually managed to get some sleep that night. The following morning they all rose and prepared for the trail. Prince Paladan rode first, with Layana trotting on foot behind, holding his mount's tail. Soldier came next, gritting his teeth in anguish at seeing his wife so treated. Then Moona, and finally Golgath. When they crested the rise in front of them a whole army lay in wait on the far side. They too were packed and ready for the journey. Warriors swathed in black rose to their feet and gave a loud concerted greeting to their prince, for it was his army who had been camped not more than a few hundred yards away.

Prince Paladan waved his hand in reply.

'Well, there you are,' muttered Golgath. 'The sinister feeling now has flesh on its bones. It's a good job you didn't kill him. We'd be finishing the journey tied by our ankles to the backs of fast horses, our heads bouncing off rocks and stones.'

Soldier said nothing. He was seething inside.

'He's going to die,' he murmured. 'He's going to die.'

'Not yet though!' warned his friend.

Later, Soldier managed to swallow his bile and ride up alongside the prince.

'So,' he said, 'you had a whole army at your disposal, Prince.'

'Ah, Prince now, is it? No more insults now, eh? Yes, I did. But I did not care to share it with you.'

You arrogant ape, thought Soldier, but he said, 'Well, you've certainly put me in my place.'

'I have, haven't I? This woman, I may let you have her when we reach the port of Sisadas, if you're more polite to me in future. You seem very desperate to get her back – why, I don't know. That is indeed a mystery. Being a mercenary officer you surely can get others as good. I have hundreds, thousands, like her, at home. Better in fact. She doesn't seem very well trained to me. I have a good seven hundred floor scrubbers who could see to my needs better. I also have six wives and three hundred concubines, so what need have I of an old woman?'

Old woman? This insufferable youth had a mouth as big as the Cerulean Gulf. Soldier longed to fill it with his fist, but he remained outwardly calm.

'That would be very noble of you.'

'Royal even,' said Paladan, with a sidelong glance. 'I am a *prince*, after all.'

'Yes, yes, of course. I'm deeply obliged to you, Prince.'

'Yes, well, I haven't promised *yet*. I may change my mind. I spent a lot of money on her, simply because my father wouldn't let me take any female servants with me.' The boy pouted. 'He said he wanted to make a man of me and that women just spoil me. Well, I went without one for at least three weeks, just to prove to him I could do it. Then, when the slave caravan passed, I thought, why not? So I purchased her.'

'You could have just taken her. You had an army.'

'It doesn't matter, does it? I have money too.'

A whim. To pay, or take, it was all the same to wealthy princes like this. Whatever was the least trouble to them. Whatever suited their moods.

'Yet you are mentioning the cost.'

The prince turned and gave Soldier a sweet smile. 'Ah, as to that, I might as well get my money back. If you want your wife I'll probably ask you to buy her from me, at a small profit to myself, of course. I've given her a certain amount of training, after all. She'll make at least a kitchen maid when I've finished with her, if not better. A few well-placed strokes of the cane might even raise her to the level of a chamber maid, though she seems extraordinarily stupid when it comes to beds. I asked her to warm my bed for me last night, expecting her to crawl under the blanket, yet the simpleton put some hot coals into a metal pan and put *them* inside, instead. Can you credit that? Of course the coals cooled later and I had to drag her in with me to keep the cold night from my bones.

'Women are so very warm, aren't they? Invaluable in that respect. They might not be good for much, but they do retain their body heat. Must be the fatty flesh they carry with them. If you touch a woman, which I have done on occasion, you'll find they have this soft, almost pudgy layer, which covers their bones. It's why they're so good at warming beds.'

'I see you have the wisdom born of curiosity, of science, like my friend riding behind us.'

'I like to think I can further the quest for knowledge.'

'You – you didn't take advantage of the fact that she is a

woman – to satisfy your carnal needs?'

Soldier's hand had crept surreptitiously to the hilt of his sword at this point.

The prince wrinkled his nose. 'Theg's thighs, look at her! She's filthy. She smells like a hog.' The prince shuddered. 'It's one thing to warm one's bed with a smelly wench, quite another to bury one's sword in her sheath. If we had the water to scrub her up a little – but then, she is an old hag. Look, I know what you're thinking. You believe that because I'm so beautiful I must have women all the time. You're wrong. I can be celibate, when the need arises. I know temple priests who are less able than I am to keep from females. Now, that insipid woman who travels with you is as clean as a mountain stream, but I have no desire to dip there either. She drools. Another simpleton, I'm afraid.'

'Oh, I quite agree. For an intelligent man like you, Prince Paladan, you need a woman with an equal mind.'

'Not equal. There I must disagree. A woman can never equal a man's mind. There's too many fripperies in there. Too much satin and lace. Too much embroidery. No, no. Not equal. But you can find women who are not stupid. I know. I've met one or two. They're few and far between, though. Not easy to find.'

Satisfied that his wife had not been violated, Soldier dropped back. As he passed Layana, he touched her hair. It drove agonies into his heart. She looked up, her dirty face a picture to him. It was all he could do not to dismount and cover that smudged and smutted visage with kisses. He wanted to fold her in his arms, tell her everything would be all right, make her happy. Yet, he knew she did not recognise him. The pain in his breast grew stronger on knowing this. How was he going to restore her mind to her? He couldn't even find his own? They were a matched pair now: a couple with no memory of who they were. There was some irony in that and he might have laughed, laconically, if he did not feel so miserable.

'Have a nice chat?' asked Golgath, coming up beside him.

'An informative one. I'm a little easier in my thinking.'

Moona said, eagerly, 'Did he speak of me?'

'Not a word.'

She pouted. 'He must have said *something*?'

'Oh yes, he called you a simpleton.'

Her face brightened. 'You see, I *am* on his mind.'

Both men looked at each other and raised their eyebrows.

Chapter Twenty-one

Soldier suffered Prince Paladan until they reached the outskirts of Sisadas, where the Soldan of Ophiria was still camped, awaiting news of his wife. Soldier and Golgath took Moona, who used her long elegant swan neck right until the last minute, twisted right round so that she could see Prince Paladan until they crested the high dune at the back of the oasis. Then she turned back and wept. The two men felt sorry for her. They knew how she was suffering, having gone through the same wretched feelings themselves. They knew it would pass, though. Soldier gave her a week or two to get over the golden-haired prince with the character of a horned toad and the soul of a slug.

Moona's husband, who had heard of her rescue, was waiting impatiently, sitting in the howdah of his brass elephant. When he saw her coming he pulled an organ stop and the elephant raised its trunk and trumpeted the soldan's joy. In turn, the trumpets of his troops heralded her coming with tuneless fanfares. The fat soldan made his elephant kneel and was there on the ground to receive his heavenly spouse. When she approached him, she knelt before him, which was wise of her since she would have stood a head taller than her husband in his flapping pantaloons, billowing shirt and wide golden sandals. She stared at his fat little toes, on the ends of his chubby feet, and burst into a new flood of tears.

'Ah, my love,' said the soldan, lifting her chin with his golden hand so that she could see his round face topped by an enormous turban, 'you have no need to cry-cry. You are safe now. You are here with me. Come, we shall go together to Xilliope on my marvellous elephant and find you a brass-brass camel to match it.'

Her head turned in his metal hand, looking back, and again she wept with great choking, heaving sobs.

'I want to go to Xxiphar.'

'No, no, my darling,' he smiled, indulgently. 'It's not pronounced like that. You say-say it like this – Xilliope.'

She turned with a mean look and growled at him. 'I want to go to Xxiphar, you fat baboon, not Xilliope.'

The soldan's expression shattered like glass. He stared down into her face. Something had happened to his darling to turn her into a less than heavenly creature. He looked up. The two warriors who had brought her back to him were standing just a little way off. They looked shifty, especially the one with the peculiar blue eyes. He never should have trusted them. Of course – a whole desert to cross – with the most beautiful woman in the world. They had found it impossible to resist her charms. They had violated his wife. She was not upset with her husband: how could she be? No, she must be overwrought, almost out of her mind, to have said such a thing to him. It was not her fault. It was theirs. They were to blame for this distressing condition of his wife.

They were smiling at him. Waiting, and smiling. It was more than he could bear. The soldan crossed the space between him and the two men in about five strides. He struck the one with the blue eyes, the one they called Soldier, with his ringed fist.

'That'll wipe the grin off your face!' he snarled.

Soldier looked utterly shocked and bemused. He recovered within a second and would have flattened the soldan, had not Golgath stepped between the two men, only to receive a blow himself from the soldan.

'What are you about?' cried Golgath, warding off another attempted strike by the infuriated soldan. 'Beware, my friend will cut you down, whether you be king of the world, or no.'

This warning sobered the soldan, who now took some steps back, towards his troops. He was still incensed, however.

'You violated my wife!' he shrieked.

Soldier was amazed. 'Did she say that?'

'No – but I can see how sad-sad she is.'

'That's because she's in love with the Prince of Xxiphar, you great oaf,' yelled Soldier. 'It's got nothing to do with us.'

All the wind went out of the soldan, and he seemed to deflate like a balloon losing air.

'Xxiphar? Oh, *Xxiphar*? That's what she – you mean Prince Paladan? That coxcomb? That curly headed small small popinjay who has a features like a six-year-old *girl*? She's in love with *him*?' The soldan's eyes narrowed. 'How did she meet him?'

'We ran into him in the desert,' replied Soldier, 'and she took one look and fell like a stone down a well. He *is* good-looking, and has the body of an athlete, but I think you'll find that she'll forget him in a week. It's just a young girl's infatuation.'

'Where is he?'

Golgath said, 'A mile or so distant, on the other side of

that hill. But he has a whole army with him. Seasoned troops. They wear black and call themselves The Immortals. They look more than a match for your troops.'

The soldan's nostrils dilated. He stared at the giant dune ahead, then turned away.

'Don't we get any thanks?' called Soldier.

'For what?' screeched the soldan back at him, waving his golden arm. 'For allowing my wife to consort with libertines? You won't get a brass-brass groat out of me. And you can find your own wife. I hope she falls in love with this Prince of Xxiphar, so you know what it feels like. I expect you couldn't keep your eyes off Moona either, the two of you. I expect she had to beg-beg you to keep your hands to yourselves. Go on, be off with you, before I have my troops disembowel you within her sight. Go, go.'

Soldier took a step forward, but Golgath said, 'Never mind, Soldier – we know where your wife is. Some people are never grateful. We'll have our revenge, one day. Men like him can't guard themselves against misery and misfortune.'

Golgath and Soldier now went back to where the prince was camped for the night. It was evening when they arrived. The air had a golden hue to it, as the sun was sinking behind tawny dunes. Prince Paladan was sitting outside his silk tent, with Layana in attendance, when the two men arrived back. As they approached him, however, something happened in the sky. The prince leapt to his feet and ran a few yards from his tent, before looking up again in a terrified manner.

'See,' cried Soldier, pointing. 'A male winged lion!'

The lion was now flying around the head of the prince. Its dark mane streamed out behind it. Its fur rippled in the wind that its flight was creating. On its face was a look of utter rage. Clearly it was filled with hatred for the prince. It now began to stoop, in the manner of a hawk, swiping at the prince's head with its claws. The prince weaved and ducked, yelling for assistance, begging someone to come to his aid. The great wings flapped, the lion rose and soared, then stooped again.

Golgath said, 'I know what it is — it's the mate of the winged lion he shot with the crossbow. He's come to exact revenge.'

Now the whole army had come out of their tents. They stood mute witness in the gloaming, watching the attack take place. No one moved to assist the prince. It was as if they were transfixed. One or two pointed, but most stared in awe at the spectacle.

'Help me!' shrieked the prince, lying flat on the ground with his hands on his head. 'Somebody help me!'

The irate lion swooped over his prone body and slashed, catching his hair, tearing out a clump of golden fuzz.

'Agghhhhh! My head. It bleeds!'

Still men stood there, as if mesmerised. No one really knew what to do. One or two archers fired arrows at the swerving, wheeling lion, only to miss hopelessly. This was not a crea-ture on a straight course, like the she-lion Paladan had shot with his crossbow. This was a maddened winged male lion with wings twice as powerful as his mate. Whirling about the sky, almost impossible to hit. In the time it took for an arrow to reach it, coupled with the speed of the lion, the creature was no longer a target. Arrows hit empty spaces. Even the best bowman in the land would only hit it by luck.

Just when it seemed the prince would die, Layana came out of her tent. In her hand was a bullwhip. Without a thought for her own safety she strode to the spot where the prince cowered on the ground. There she stood, magnificently heroic in the dying rays of the sun, and cracked the long whip at the lion when it stooped. Sharp sounds on either side of the lion's head, around its ears, caused it to veer away.

The creature looked confused. Three or four times it tried to dive on the woman who stood, legs apart, firm on the ground. Each time it came down she cracked an expert whip once, twice, thrice, about its head, not touching it, but causing it to swerve. It did not give up for some time, but eventually, as the light began to drain from the sky, the lion became frustrated, and finally it flew up towards the stars. They watched its silhouette cross the moon, wondering whether it would be back.

Soldier went immediately to his wife. 'That was wonderful,' he told her. 'You are so very brave.'

'Someone had to do something.'

'And you did it.' He took her in his arms and kissed her. Layana responded, but in a puzzled way. She was not sure she should be embracing this stranger who had just come into her life. The feeling of being held by two strong arms was nice, however, and she indulged herself. It created a warmness in her breast she had not felt for a very long time. His skin smelt pleasantly familiar to her, and this perplexed her a little. She allowed herself to enjoy it.

Prince Paladan climbed unsteadily to his feet, touching the raw spot on his head where his hair had been torn at the roots. He found blood, which alarmed him. 'That's enough of that,' he said, sharply, dusting himself off. 'Girl, get back to my tent. Fetch me some balm, some healing ointments. Can't you see I'm hurt, you selfish little trollop?'

'No,' growled Soldier, 'that's enough of *this* – this farce we are forced to witness every day. This is my wife. She does not remember it, but she is. We are leaving together – now.'

'You are not. You'll . . . AAAARRRRGGGGHHHH!'

Soldier had reached forward and had drawn the prince's own sword. He had plunged it into the royal foot, pinning it to the ground. The prince screamed like monkey on fire. Warriors from The Immortals began to move forward, to protect their prince, but Soldier had already clutched Layana by the arm and was striding out into the night with her. Golgath followed, ready to guard their retreat.

The prince continued to scream, but more coherently now, demanding the death of his attacker. His warriors pursued the three, who were now cresting the rise which led to the oasis beyond. They came streaming out of the tent area, running up the incline. It seemed as if Soldier, Layana and Golgath would be overtaken before they had got half a mile.

And that would have been the case, had not the soldan's army been on the other side of the rise, marching towards Prince Paladan's army.

After Soldier and Golgath had left, the soldan had sat and festered in his jealousy. Moona Swan-neck had continued to sob and demand she be allowed to woo Prince Paladan, in the sure knowledge that he was her soul mate. Finally, the fat soldan's simmering anger overflowed. Horns sounded, drums beat, and the army gathered on the plain behind the oasis. The troops were slightly bewildered. It was coming on to night and here they were about to embark on a military expedition. It did not make sense.

The soldan's senior officers strongly advised him against marching into battle at night. Things, they said, could become very confused in the darkness. Companies could often find themselves fighting companies from their own regiment. It was not unknown for an army to end up defeating itself. But the soldan was adamant. He could not wait until morning to kill that popinjay with the golden hair. The prince had bewitched his beloved Moona and would have to pay. He couldn't have a wife who wept for another man. It would not do. They would attack tonight and use the element of surprise.

Not send heralds and envoys? Not inform the enemy that they were at war? Surely, this was against all convention?

'We send no one, no warning – and we give no quarter – take no prisoners,' replied the determined soldan. 'I don't care if we slaughter them in their beds and they never know why. The prince will pay for having cuckolded me. I will tear his heart out through his mouth and hang it from my lance. Make love to my Moona?' The soldan choked on the words. 'I'll make him wish he had been born a pauper's son.'

'But he didn't touch me,' cried Moona, appalled at what she had unleashed, but also amazed at the power of her tears. 'He – he wouldn't even look at me. He said I was clean-scrubbed and shiny-skinned, and looked well enough, but he didn't want me . . .'

The soldan was doubly incensed at this. His wife, the most beautiful woman in the world, had been spurned by a snot-nosed prince who wasn't worth the muck stuck to the bottom of her sandals. If anyone deserved to die it was this arrogant boy.

'Sound the cymbals!' cried the soldan, drawing his scimitar as he was heaved up by many hands onto the saddle of his white charger, 'whirl the bullroarers! We march!'

They had not far to go. They met Soldier, Layana and Golgath coming down the great dune on their side. Immediately archers opened fire on those following the three escapees. Walking into a hail of arrows, the prince's men quickly deduced that they were under attack. Some turned and ran back down to the camp, with the cry to take up arms on their lips. Many of these died with arrows in their backs, or having been overrun by the forces of the soldan. They were chopped down within yards of their own troops. Torches had now been lit, in both armies, and two oceans of waving lights came together.

Soldier, Layana and Golgath watched from the top of the dune for a while, until the slaughter became sickening, the sweet smell of blood wafting up to them on their quiet hilltop. If they themselves had been in the fight it would have been a different matter, but they were onlookers, and not crazed by the fear and excitement that battle generates. From this point they stared down in horror at the carnage that was going on in the light of burning tents below, hearing the screams, seeing men – and women – being impaled on sharp objects, or having their heads removed with the swipe of a blade. It was all so ghastly when one was a peaceful bystander in the balmy air of a clear and pleasant evening.

'Let's go,' said Soldier, taking Layana's hand. 'We'll spend the night in Sisadas, then move on in the morning to Carthaga.'

Late that night, Soldier sat up with Layana and tried to explain what had happened to her. He told her who she was and what had occurred in the city to which she belonged. She took it all in, but confessed that she could not remember any of it.

'I like you,' she said. 'I can imagine I am in love with you, despite those strange eyes that seem to pierce through to my very soul. I must take things slowly, until I feel right again.'

One good thing, which Soldier did not mention to Layana in case it revived the demon within her, was that in her present state she no longer had bouts of insanity. Her madness had fled with her memory. It said to Soldier that it was indeed a curse, rather than an illness, which was responsible for that sporadic lunacy. While a sickness can be cured, when it came to maladies of the mind such doctoring was difficult. A curse, however, could be removed just like that, and the cure would be instant. It remained to find the one to take away the curse.

'You and I are the same now,' he said, with her arm around her shoulders, staring up at the bright stars. 'We have both lost our memories. I know who I have been since I became a Guthrumite, but I know not what or who I was before that time. You have recently lost your memory and are with me in the camp of forgetfulness. I feel this has brought us closer together.'

'I don't know. I *want* to feel close to you. I feel a certain security with you, but I am not wholly sure of you yet . . .'

'As you say, you must take your time, my darling, and move gently into the right state of mind, and heart.'

'Now, words like those can make me fall in love with you.'

Spagg was pleased to see them back. He had grown weary of his hefty lover: or she had wearied him. Spagg was ready to move on.

'I've 'ad a terrible time,' he told the other two. 'Flies, heat, dust. I 'spect you've been having a jolly one, trotting over the landscape, enjoyin' yourselves. Well, you can see by the state of this filthy room that things is awful here. Gettin' your laundry done in this place is like trying to find gold dust in a beggar's pocket. And the food's been disgustin' lately.'

'I had no idea,' murmured Golgath, 'that we were leaving you in such a hellhole.'

The next day Soldier, Layana, Spagg and Golgath set out towards Carthaga. On their arrival they found the population in a mood of strong determination. Having gone through the grief of losing their army to the Hannacks and beast-people they were ready to fight again. Men and women had been in training since Soldier left. It was a young army. There was no need to recruit new warriors, because almost every other male or female had been raised to the idea that they were warriors. It was the noblest profession in Carthaga, coming just before artists. Merchants and artisans came well behind. In the last row of respected professions stood physicians, magicians and entertainers.

However, Jakanda the old warlord was dead, killed in the battle for the gates of Zamerkand. A new leader was needed. The senators could not make up their minds who to appoint. Some were too young, some too old, many too inexperienced. They knew of Soldier and his exploits, as well as his deeds as an officer in the red pavilions. When they heard that Soldier was back in Carthaga, he was sent for. He stood before the senate and was asked to give an account of his experience as a fighter.

'I can only tell you half the tale,' he informed them, 'for the first half has been lost to my memory. I feel certain that I was a warrior then. I have been a warrior all my life.'

They told him that was what they wanted to hear and asked him if he would lead an expedition back to Guthrum.

'We must regain our self-respect,' said the senators, 'as a military nation. It is our livelihood. How can we expect other countries who employ our mercenaries to think highly of our fighting skills, while this defeat hangs heavy over our heads? We must destroy the army which besieges Zamerkand.'

'I accept,' replied Soldier. 'But why me?'

'I will tell you honestly,' replied the senior senator. 'If you fail, it will be because you are an outlander. It will not be the Carthagan army at fault. You alone will bear the blame.'

'And if I succeed?'

'It will be because of the warriors you lead into battle — the red pavilions — it will be because they are the best soldiers on this earth and because *any* leader, even a outlander, can win with such magnificent troops at his back.'

'So, the failure will be mine, the glory will be yours.'

'Exactly.'

They waited, sure in the knowledge that he would now refuse the commission.

'I accept,' he said, quietly, after a thoughtful pause. 'We must destroy Ommullummo's army and instate his son.'

Surprised, the senators nodded gravely. The senior senator handed him the marshal's baton. Soldier now commanded the red pavilions.

When he told Golgath, his friend was ecstatic.

'Now we can go back and destroy the Hannacks!'

'Or be destroyed,' replied the more sober Soldier, who had had time to reflect. 'Don't forget, they broke us once with OmmullummO behind them. Winning is all about what's in the head, as well as the heart. If they believe they're invincible, they very well might be.'

Layana offered no predictions on the outcome. In fact, she said very little. Her one comment on the matter was a demand.

'I should like to purchase some armour.'

'What?' said Soldier.

'I wish to fight too, alongside you three . . .'

'Don't include me, Yer Majesty,' cried Spagg. 'I ain't joinin' these two madcaps.'

Layana said, 'Well, I do wish to join.'

'I would rather you didn't,' said Soldier. 'You have no experience of war.'

'How do you know?'

'Well, I only know . . .'

'Just as you feel you have the warrior inside you, so I feel I could be useful on the battlefield.'

'You might be killed.'

'So might you.'

Any argument Soldier put up was swept aside. In the end he took her to an armourer, who fitted her out with Carthagan armour. As a woman, of course, she would not be alone in the Carthagan army. There were many in the ranks and amongst its officers. Soldier told her she was on his staff and would not be given a rank, or a pavilion to lead.

'You must accept the position of common warrior, just as I did when I first joined, and as all Carthagans do. You'll be with me at all times, so that we might look out for one another.'

'You won't shield me from the fighting?'

'There'll be enough of that to go round twice,' answered Soldier, grimly, 'you can be sure of that. If we survive it'll be more because of good fortune than anything else. The Hannacks and beast-people are well dug in. They won't be an easy enemy to defeat.'

'Anything else?'

'Yes, I've sent a message to Bhantan, asking the twins to attack the rear of the enemy army. I've promised them the head of Humbold as a gift, if we should win.'

'It's the least you can do.'

With that, Soldier went down to the harbour, to supervise the loading of the warships which would carry his army across the Cerulean Sea and to the shores of Guthrum once again. Just before the fleet was ready, some days later, the raven arrived.

'Look at you, with your marshal's baton. Don't get above yourself. Gad, you're a hard human to find these days.'

'Where did you try?'

'I've been over just about every yard of Uan Muhaggiag, ending up in Sisadas, before I came on to here.'

'What news?'

'The Hannacks and beast-people are expecting to be attacked. They've started to flock back to the siege from the hills. There's nothing like the scent of battle to get them out of their holes.'

'Do they know I'm leading the expeditionary force?'

The raven shook its black-feathered head. 'No. Even I didn't know. I heard it in Sisadas.'

'What news from there?'

'The Soldan of Ophiria defeated Prince Paladan. The prince's head stands on a stake by the great oasis. Nice-looking lad, eh?'

'What of Moona Swan-neck?'

'Died of a broken heart.'

Soldier was genuinely shocked. He had expected her to weep a little over Prince Paladan. But . . .

'She died?'

'Fell into a melancholy fever and wasted away in a week.'

'People don't die of lack of food in a week. Hermits fast for months before they die.'

'Something inside her – perhaps her own heart? – was gnawing on her spirit. It was her spirit which gave out, not her body. Anyway, she died. Her eyes were sunken and dim. Her body decayed from pining. I was told you could see the candle flame through her hand she was so thin. Then one morning her life simply faded away.

'The soldan is grief-stricken. He has her laid out in a crystal casket from which the air has been extracted so that she does not decay further. This casket is itself in a glass-walled tomb, by which he sits day and night. He himself is now lean and hungry-looking as a winter fox. There is a park being constructed quietly, around the pair, full of exotic trees, shrubs and flowers. He sends to all the four corners of the earth for apes, peacocks and leopards to populate the park.'

Soldier shook his head. 'I never would have guessed.'

'There, you don't know everything, do you?'

Chapter Twenty-two

The fleet of warships was ready to sail when the gift arrived for Soldier from an unknown source.

'A plant?' he said to Layana.

It was a potted bloom, a particularly exotic and marvellous flower, now in bud, but almost ready to open. One could see that once the petals unfurled, there would be a scarlet bloom unmatched by any other.

Layana, resplendent in her new lightweight armour, which she had requested in black, remarked, 'The pot itself looks a treasure.' It was gold and silver, inlaid with ebony and ivory. 'Look, there's an inscription.'

It read: *A Gift from the Gods, to Honour the Valour of Soldier, a Warrior whose Goodness is a Beacon to Us All.*

'Goodness? I wouldn't have thought I was particularly *good*,' remarked Soldier. 'I fight for my side, yes, but my motives are often quite selfish.'

'Well, someone thinks you're exemplary,' replied Layana, 'or they would not have sent this gift. I don't recognise the flower. Perhaps it really is from the fields of the gods?'

Soldier was secretly very pleased with the gift, or at least the sentiments behind it. Actually he was not one who appreciated flowers. He knew that in this world a rose with dew on it was regarded as as exciting and marvellous as the running leopard was to Soldier. While he would study the muscles and movement of the leopard with great awe, Guthrumites, Uan Muhuggiags and Carthagans would stare at a host of daffodils dancing in the breeze and experience the same sense of wonder. But a love of foliage was not in Soldier's nature, so without telling Layana, he sent the bloom in its precious pot to the Soldan of Ophiria, asking him to put it with all the other exotic plants around Moona's tomb.

The soldan was now going quite mad with grief. He pulled out his hair in clumps. He rent his clothes each time they were changed by his faithful servants. Finally he tore out his tongue with his own hands and would have plucked out his own eyes had he not been restrained.

When the flower arrived from Soldier, the soldan placed it at the head of the crystal casket. He was there when the bud opened – a huge, scarlet trumpet, its petals as large as a man's hands – and died of its poisonous perfume moments later. The plant was of a rare, deadly variety found only in deep jungles accessible to a few intrepid explorers. In its native habitat its noxious fumes killed any animal which ventured near it – and now it had killed the soldan. His people found him draped over his faded wife's casket. What incensed them more was the fact that thieves had found him first and stolen his golden arm.

The fleet sailed.

Halfway across the Cerulean Sea they were beset by storms. They battled through these, losing seven ships out of three hundred. When they came through the darkness, the white-flecked squalls and tearing winds, on the other side, there were still no stars. It was difficult to navigate without stars, but there were feelers-of-the-sea amongst the sailors, who could tell the position approximately by dipping their hands in the water and feeling the temperature. Eventually the fleet made a landfall on the mainland coast just southwest of the island of Stell. It was a wild, uninhabited stretch of sand, the coastline cluttered with giant driftwood, choked with drying weed and rotting shellfish.

They beached the boats and covered them as best they could with the white driftwood and weed.

Soldier then took his army on a forced march eastwards. On the march the raven arrived with news that Guido and Sando were camped just outside the Kermer Pass, and were ready to march southwards towards Zamerkand. Soldier sent word back of the approximate time it would take him and his troops to reach Zamerkand, so that the two armies could make a concerted attack, one from the east, one from the north.

Soldier's army arrived a mile distant from Zamerkand just as the shadows were growing to their longest. Trenches were dug, thorn fences were raised, guards were posted. Once all was secure he took time to ride ahead and survey the killing ground. As he approached the spires, the turrets, the towers and domes of Zamerkand, he felt a kind of fulfilment. He stood in the black bars of the tree shadows at the forest edge and gazed upon the old city walls. He was returning to his adopted home as marshal, head of the red pavilions which were now being raised behind him, within the secure encampment. He had arrived as a stranger, not so many years ago, in a strange world. Having a feeling for his own history, he joined an army – now he was leading it, supreme commander.

'That's my home,' murmured Layana. She came up beside. 'That's where I come from.'

He turned in the saddle. 'You recognise it?'

'I know it.'

She took his hand.

This is one of the first delights of falling in love. Touching the soft fingers and palm of one's beloved. There are one or two before it, many more wonderful mysteries to unfold after it, but holding hands for the first time is a magical moment, when two palms touch and two sets of fingers entwine.

Soldier was overcome. It had been so long since he had experienced such tenderness that he almost broke down. Now they were together again. The day rushed to a close, leaving the pair still touching fingers, while the impatient horses fretted and stroked the ground with their hooves, wondering what was going on.

That night the Hannacks and the beast-people celebrated the coming battle with hellish screams and the thunder of drums. Their fires were scattered all over the landscape around Zamerkand, on hill, in gulley. It seemed to Soldier and his troops that the foe had no fear, but all enemy armies appear thus to the opposition.

Soldier's army was ready before the break of dawn. With the first rays of the sun Carthagan archers loosed volleys of arrows which fell like hail upon the enemy camps. Every tenth arrow was a fire-arrow. Even before the day had much begun the tents and baggage of the enemy army were blazing. Hannacks and beast-people came pouring out of these areas of flame, like fleas abandoning a swimming bear's coat. Soldier's army was waiting for them, foot-warriors in three ranks forming a rigid semicircle around the north of the city.

His cavalry protected the flanks from stray groups of the enemy.

From the north-west came the smaller army led by Guido and Sando. The twins, still only fifteen years of age, were dressed in armour, one in white and one in rose. They rode black horses. They directed their troops from the same ridge on which Soldier, when working for Spagg, had found Jankin-the-giant's body hanging from a gallows. It was on this ridge that Soldier had chopped off Jankin's hands and put them in a sack, before being attacked by a rogue Hannack. His first. Now there were five thousand Hannacks, ascending the ridge from which the two princes commanded their small Bhantan army.

'No man runs, no man hides, no man gives quarter,' cried Sando.

He was the peace-prince, supposed to remain at home while his brother went to war. Yet he could not. The excitement of fighting drew him to his brother's side.

Guido drew his sword. 'For the ashes of HoulluoH and the birthright of IxonnoxI!' he cried.

One of his generals picked up the cry. 'For Sando and Guido! For the temples of your gods! For honour!'

Then the came the clash, as the first Hannacks smashed into the Bhantans, and the fighting was joined.

At the same time, Soldier's first line stood firm as the main brunt of the Hannacks and beast-people hit the Carthagan front. There was a shudder down the ranks of longspear-warriors. The line weaved, rippled, as it met the shock of thousands of screaming, half-naked warriors, the spears penetrating man and beast. The noise of hammers, swords and sickles striking metal shields was deafening. Once that first impact had been absorbed by the front rank, those Carthagans still alive and on two feet fell on their faces, and the second rank strode determinedly forward. Forward and forward, not hesitating to step on the backs of their prone comrades. They began to drive the enemy back. They were glint-eyed and steely-armed. As if they were one large machine, they drove resolutely, pressing the wild hordes backwards.

The Hannacks and beast-people found themselves on their back feet, retreating, ever retreating as the Carthagans gained ground. When the second line of the Carthagans was tired and depleted, they too gave way, this time to the third rank of warriors, fresh and ready behind them. In the meantime the first rank had reformed and marched immediately behind the third rank. Gradually the enemy was forced back and back, until they were pushed up against the walls of Zamerkand. There was nowhere to go from that point on. Soldier had rolled them up against the stonework, just as he had done another enemy in another place and time – up against a fortification they called Hadrian's Wall – though the memory of that old battle was locked in some dim recess of his mind.

Guthrumites on the battlements, and in the towers above, began to rain rocks and boiling oil down on their besiegers. Having been penned up in a diseased city now for a long time, they were more than eager to assist in the slaughter of those who had kept them there. The Hannacks and beast-people fought desperately. Some of them screamed, some of them barked, some of them howled, and some hissed as they died. They gave good account of themselves, there being few cowards amongst them, and the released souls of Carthagans could be heard thanking them.

Soldier and Layana fought side by side, each watching out for the other, neither knowing whether they would see the end of the day.

In the middle of the battle the skies went dark as a nebulous but misty form swept like a storm cloud over the land. This event struck fear into the hearts of the Carthagan army, since they knew that OmmullummO had sent his shadow to encourage his own army. Indeed, on seeing this sign the Hannacks and beast-people fought with more fierceness and determination. The battle was almost turned, until Layana, at great personal risk, rode up and down the lines of Carthagan warriors, calling for courage. 'Remember who you are!' she cried. 'Remember your ancestors and your comrades, crying to you from their graves to be avenged. Destroy this evil, now!'

It was more the sight of this brave woman warrior, flying up and down the lines on her palfrey, than any rhetoric or oratory that spurred the Carthagan warriors to a greater strength. Indeed, the words were often lost in the wind, but her fury and resolve were obvious to all. They reached down into themselves for more reserves of energy, redoubled their efforts, met the new onslaught with an unbroken wall of shields, swords, warhammers. After another hour's fighting the shadow left the skies, flew back towards the mountains, abandoning the invaders to their inevitable fate.

By noon the bodies were thick at the base of the city's curtain wall. Beast-people and Hannacks were beginning to flee in greater numbers, heading for Falyum and Da-tichett. There would be no official surrender. Hannacks had no idea how to do such a thing – they had no word for it and it never entered their education as a warrior race – and beast-people would rather swallow boiling tar than lay down their weapons. The fighting would go on until all those of the foe who were able had run away, and those who were wounded were deprived of their weapons. So it was only the coming of darkness that called an end to the battle.

'We've won,' said Layana. She removed her helmet in the light of the watchfires from the walls above. 'It's over.'

'For now,' agreed Soldier, catching the gleam of the gore splattered on the stones of the city. 'Another terrible slaughter.'

She turned her attention to him now.

'You have redeemed yourself, my husband.'

He had indeed. He said nothing, but even with the dead lying all around him, the sickening smell of blood in his nostrils, he could not help but feel elated. He had led an army into battle against a foe which had recently defeated that army. In truth, his was the inferior force, both in physical strength and, having been beaten once, also in spirit. Yet he had raised that spirit with quiet words and strong character. He had told his warriors, men and women, that this was their day. Then he had led them, from the front, straight at the ranks of their oldest enemies. It had been a simple strategy – almost no plan at all – of containing the foe and driving him back against an impassable barrier, and there cutting him down.

It had worked because his enemy were wild creatures, who loved to fight in the open, but who hated confined spaces. In such places they fought with a desperation which verged on hysteria, their first priority being to break out, rather than win a battle. It is the warrior with the cool head who wins the day, not the wild-eyed, slashing berserker. Soldier's warriors had kept cool heads. They had tightened the snare, then helped the enemy to choke himself. It was not an admirable way to win, but triumph usually comes to the clever, not to the vainglorious.

Soldier was satisfied with the outcome.

His troops were ecstatic. They could go back to Carthaga

in the wake of wonderful news. Even now there would be messengers running for the boats, crossing the Cerulean Sea, hoping to be the first to run through the streets of Carthaga with the news.

'Victory!'

'Revenge!'

'Victory!' again.

Joyous people would flood from their houses. The mood would be festive. Tables would be dragged out into the squares and parks. Wine would follow. Oxen would be roasted. Drums would beat, trumpets would blare. The whole of the continent of Gwandoland would know that the Carthagans were celebrating, and such spontaneous and wild celebrations meant only one thing. A victorious battle.

Soldier was satisfied.

'You are a hero!' cried Velion, throwing blood-stained arms around him.

'You triumph!' cried Golgath, locking hand with fist.

There were cheers from his tired warriors.

Soldier was satisfied. He made his way to the camp of Guido and Sando, to thank his allies. They too had played their part.

Chapter Twenty-three

The most joyous event to follow the battle was the recovery of the lost standards from the Wolf, the Crocodile and the Dragon Pavilions. The shame of losing them had been erased. They were now back in the hands of the Carthagans and some warriors actually wept when they were able to touch their pavilion's standard once again.

There was a meeting the following day, between the heads of two armies.

'Marshal Kaff.'

'Soldier.'

Kaff had come out with a contingent of his Imperial Guard. He stood before Soldier with a defiant look on his face, resplendent in silver and gold armour with the marshal's embossed emblem on his breastplate. There was a dove screwed into his stump.

Soldier was still in battle gear: plain breastplate, leathers, epaulettes and sandals. He had managed to wash, but not to bathe. Layana stood beside him, also still in her battle armour.

'Princess,' murmured Kaff, dipping his head. He then

reached out to take her hand to kiss it, without success. She glared at him.

'Who is this familiar person?' asked Layana, staring at Kaff. 'Why does he leer at me?'

Kaff looked shocked. Of course, he knew nothing of Layana's loss of memory. He stepped back and struggled to find some words, for clearly this woman considered him a stranger.

'He leers at everyone, my dear,' said Soldier, secretly amused. 'Pay him no heed.'

Kaff's face hardened. 'Clearly Princess Layana is either bewitched, or some accident has befallen her. She does not seem to know her friends. Perhaps she would allow me to escort her into Zamerkand? You, of course,' he added, addressing Soldier, 'as head of a foreign army, are not permitted through the gates, except by special edict from the ruler. No such edict has been issued and therefore you must remain outside the walls.'

'I have just saved your city,' hissed Soldier. 'And Princess Layana is not going into a place where she may very well join her sister in a dungeon.'

'I personally guarantee her safety.'

'You, Marshal, are in Humbold's pocket.'

Kaff went white with fury.

'I am my own man.'

Soldier said, 'Then bring the queen to me. If you do not, I shall come and get her.'

'You would not dare! In the whole history of Guthrum, the Carthagan army has never entered the gates of Zamerkand. It's unthinkable. No matter what our differences, you are still in our pay. We own you, as mercenaries, and there is an unwritten but undeniable code which states that a mercenary army never enters the city it is guarding. Especially it does not enter with the intent to interfere in local politics. It would be an invasion and we would have the right to resist by force any such hostile action. Do I make myself clear?'

Soldier raised his eyebrows. 'You would pit the Imperial Guard of Guthrum against the red pavilions of Cartharga? Are you mad?'

'We have kept out the beast-people and the Hannacks for the last several months. We can keep out the red pavilions. That's if you could get them to follow you. I don't think you understand what's at stake here. Cross that line, enter those gates at the head of your army, and you'll bring more shame on your troops than losing a battle to savage tribes. You would sink them for ever. They know that. They would never be able to go home again, to see their families. They'd be outcasts.'

'Is this true?' asked Soldier of Velion. 'Would you be outlawed?'

'Perhaps, yes,' she murmured, 'but these warriors would follow you into hell at the moment, without a thought for themselves. All you need to do is give the word.'

'Marshal Kaff,' said Soldier, gravely, 'if you do not surrender Humbold to us before the sun rises tomorrow, and release Queen Vanda into our hands, I shall have no alternative but to breach those walls. We are no savage tribe. We have engines of war. We have the power to smash our way in. We have engineers to build moles and ramps and effective battering rams. And when we do scale your walls, and break down your gates, as we undoubtedly will, I shall personally come looking for you and take pleasure in hanging you alongside Humbold.'

Kaff spun on his heel and marched away, followed by his friends and soldiers of the Imperial Guard.

Velion said, 'Will you really attack?'

'I don't know. I really don't know.'

'Whatever your decision, whatever the consequences of that decision, my husband,' said Layana, 'Guthrum cannot tolerate despots like Humbold. I hear he has made himself a jewelled sword, as a symbol of his right to kingship. If Humbold is making his own rules, you are entitled to do the same.'

Spagg, who had come up with the camp followers, had been about to go home. Now he stared at the gates of Zamerkand uncertainly, a sack over his shoulder. He turned to Soldier.

'If you're goin' to attack, there's not much use me goin' in there, eh? I mean, there'll be a slaughter, and if I go through them gates, I'll be the enemy, won't I?'

'We might not be able to distinguish between friend and foe. Wars are bloody and mistakes are made. However, if it does happen, I intend to forbid firing property and looting. If you lock your door and stay inside, then you should come through the conflict unharmed.'

Spagg nodded. He started off towards the gates.

Soldier called to him. 'Wait. What have you got in the sack?'

Spagg looked defensive. Soldier called him to his side.

'Open it.'

The hand-seller reluctantly rolled back the sack.

Layana said in surprise. 'The Soldan of Ophiria's golden arm!'

'Shame on you,' said Golgath, who had just arrived. 'Stealing from a dead man.'

'I didn't rob 'im. It was someone else. I robbed the robbers.'

'Did you kill them?' demanded Soldier.

'In a manner of speakin'.'

'They were targets for those throwing knives of yours?'

'You could say that. There was two of 'em. Right pair of cut-throats and purse snatchers, they was. Probably assassins to boot. World's a better place without 'em.' Then he added, with a touch of inspiration, 'Same as it would be without despots like Humbold.'

Soldier shook his head, wondering. 'If you're ever caught by Ophirians, don't come looking to me for assistance.'

'I shan't,' replied Spagg, shouldering his sack again. 'Anyway, I'm off to be rich. See you sometime, never I hope.'

He left. Golgath stayed. The Guthrumite had heard the news. He felt the need to argue Soldier out of any plans to invade the city.

'It's not worth it. We'll get rid of Humbold somehow ourselves.'

The following morning, at sunrise, they had Kaff's answer. The gates to the city usually opened at dawn. They remained shut. Shortly after dawn a message was thrown from the battlements of Zamerkand. It was not in the form of a written parchment or slate. It came down wrapped in bloody rags and bounced on the turf like a heavy ball. When the rags were unwrapped they revealed a severed head inside.

It bore the face of Queen Vanda.